THE LAST MASQUERADE

Translated from the Spanish by
Ernesto Mestre-Reed

THE LAST MASQUERADE

A Novel

Antonio Orlando Rodríguez

rayo *An Imprint of* HarperCollins*Publishers*

HarperCollins books may be purchased for educational, business, or sales promotional use. For information, please write: Special Markets Department, HarperCollins Publishers Inc., 10 East 53rd Street, New York, NY 10022.

Cover photo is a drawing by Leonetto Cappiello for Monnet Cognac © 2004 Artists' Rights Society (ARS), New York/ADAGP, Paris.

FIRST EDITION

Book design by Shubhani Sarkar

Printed on acid-free paper

Library of Congress Cataloging-in-Publication Data
Rodríguez, Antonio Orlando
   [Aprendices de brujo. English]
   The last masquerade : a novel / Antonio Orlando Rodríguez ; translated from the Spanish by Ernesto Mestre-Reed.
      p. cm.
   ISBN 0-06-058632-X
      I. Mestre-Reed, Ernesto.   II. Title.

PQ7390.R588A6713   2005
863'64—dc22   2004049186

05 06 07 08 09 DIX/RRD 10 9 8 7 6 5 4 3 2 1

To Sergio.

To Daina.

To Chely and Alberto.

Principal Characters

In Bogotá

Lucho Belalcázar Reyes, wealthy young man who, as a hobby, practices journalism.

Wenceslao Hoyos, his lover, law school graduate, a fanatic of boxers and of Eleonora Duse.

Esmeralda Gallego, painter and traveler, friend and confidant of the protagonists.

La Generala, señora of distinguished lineage, quasi-widow, mother of Lucho Belalcázar.

The Ugly Sisters, five, sisters to Lucho Belalcázar.

Melitón and Manolo Reyes, gentlemen, eminent *cachacos,* brothers to La Generala and uncles to Lucho Belalcázar.

Herminia de Hoyos, a worthy lady, devotee of Nuestra Señora del Campo, mother of Wenceslao Hoyos.

Dr. Hoyos, illustrious gentleman, rancher, father of Wenceslao.

Toña, old *negra* from Chocó, servant of the Belalcázar family and a reluctant medium.

Jasón, Cucuteño specimen, chauffer to Esmeralda Gallego.

Juan María Vengoechea, successful lawyer, friend and former classmate of Wenceslao Hoyos.

Alvarito Certaín, a little gentleman of old lineage.

Jorge Garay, a beautiful medical student.

Romero Villa, distinguished young man, law student.

Poncho Zárate, journalist of little economic means (or any other means), protégé of Wenceslao Hoyos.

The Belgian ambassador, accredited diplomat in Colombia, worldly man.

The Giant, subject of the Dutch Crown, lover of the Belgian ambassador.

Peñarredonda, prestigious surgeon.

Ana Bolena, society lady and well-known Bogotá writer.

The Asparagus, her niece.

Aníbal de Montemar, old lover of Esmeralda Gallego, living in Boston.

Mad Margarita, demented bag lady who lost her only son during the War of a Thousand Days.

Fray Rafael Almansa, pastor, Franciscan, chaplain of the little church of San Diego.

Lilibeth de Jesús, *mulata,* nun in the order of the Servants of the Resignation.

The Porter, nun in the order.

Florerito, spiteful singer.

In Barranquilla

Abraham Zacarías López-Penha, Jewish writer, author of the novel *The Shadow's Bride* and various collections of poetry.

Próspero Nacianceno, businessman, psychic and explorer of consciousness.

Sobeida, his wife, a bearded lady.

Melusina Jaramillo, equestrian.

Asmania, seamstress for the circus, a lady of few words.

Aboard the Fynlandia

Hort Ferk, captain of the ship, Swede.

Emilio De la Cruz, young man of high society, a dilettante and a fright to look at.

In Havana

Eleonora Duse, the one with the beautiful hands, Italian tragedienne.

Désirée Wertheimstein, her secretary, Austrian.

María Avogadro, demure maid, Italian.

Katherine Garnett, English aristocrat, friend of La Duse.

Fortune Gallo, Italian-American producer.

Guido Carreras, manager of Eleonora Duse's company.

Memo Benassi, leading man of Eleonora Duse's company.

Maria and Jone Morillo, sisters and actresses in Eleonora Duse's company.

Julio Antonio Mella, the Beauty, young Communist, president of the Federation of University Students.

Alfredo Zayas, president of Cuba.

María Jaén de Zayas, his wife, first lady.

Paco Pla, architecture student, blond, and a rower, also known as Señor Ears.

Bartolomé Valdivieso, *mulato* pharmacist, son of a Cuban senator, author of "To Eleonora the Sublime."

Agustín Miraflores, alias Scissors, negro, tailor at La Boston.

El Ecobio, cousin to Scissors and horse to Babalú Ayé, a criminal.

Gardenia Miraflores, sister of Scissors.

Ramoncito, nephew of Scissors.

Olavo Vázquez Garralaga, rich heir, versifier.

María Garralaga de Vázquez, his adored mother.

Graziella Gerbelasa, señorita and literary personality, author of *The Reliquary* and other books.

María Cay, Asian lady, ex-muse of the modernist poets, widow of General Lachambre.

Count Kostia, pseudonym of Aniceto Valdivia, diplomat and retired journalist.

Gloria Swanson, queen of Hollywood.

Esperanza Iris, Mexican *divette,* empress of the operetta.

Mimí Aguglia, Italian actress.

María Tubau, Spanish actress.

Josefina Ruiz del Castillo, Spanish actress.

Margarita Xirgu, Spanish actress.

Blanquita Becerra, soprano of Alhambra Theater.

María Cervantes, lady, pianist, and singer.

Misael Reyes, also known as The Unexpected One, uncle of Lucho Belalcázar.

Mei Feng, *Chino,* secretary or chambermaid to Misael Reyes; later, a corpse.

Atanasia, servant to Misael Reyes.

Fan Ya Ling, *Chino,* bewitching owner of El Crisantemo Dorado.

José Chiang, mulato *Chino.*

Jean Bonhaire, earlier, Rémond de Saint-Amand, shipwreck of the air.

García Benítez, Colombian consul in Havana.

Donato Cubas, inspector of the secret police.

Pompilio Ramos, assistant inspector.

Aquiles de la Osa, detective.

Ignacio Falero, detective.

Regla, *mulata* maid of the Inglaterra Hotel and Wenceslao's spy.

Pedrito Varela, in charge of selling series tickets at the Teatro Nacional.

Mrs. Carrie Chapman Catt, American lady, founder and president of the International Woman Suffrage Alliance.

Dulce María Loynaz, rich heiress and young poetess.

Flor and Carlos Manuel Loynaz, her younger siblings.

José María Chacón y Calvo, director of the Society of Conferences and founder of the Cuban Folklore Society.

Alejo Carpentier, new writer, editor-in-chief of the magazine *Social.*

Rubén Martínez Villena, young lawyer, writer, and revolutionary.

Rogelio and Armando Valdés, young medical students, descendants of the Trebijos.

Mina López-Salmón de Buffin, millionairess, philanthropist, organizer of the Ball of a Thousand and One Nights.

Habib Steffano, president of the National Academy of Damascus, former secretary to King Faisal I and advisor to the Ball of a Thousand and One Nights.

Adela, his wife, Scheherezade.

Aurelio Dalmau, costume designer.

Carlos Baliño, syndicate leader.

Alfredo López, another syndicate leader.

Pablo Álvarez de Cañas, social chronicler for *El País.*

Enrique Fontana, social chronicler for *Diario de la Marina.*

Francisco Ichaso, journalist for *Diario de la Marina.*

José Pérez Poldarás, theater critic for the same paper.

Genaro Corzo, theater critic for *El Heraldo.*

Enrique Uhthoff, journalist and author of the libretto for *The Girl Lupe.*

Ludonia La Rosa, *iyalocha.*

The countess of Buena Vista, Havana aristocrat.

Donna Ortensia, Countess Pears, former Duchess Mignano, and operatic singer.

Luis Vicentini, Chilean boxer, aspirant to world champion title.

A *gallego,* landowner, instrument of Satan.

From the World Hereafter

Anatilde de Bastos, seer and fortune-teller.

Rubí González, seamstress whore or whorish seamstress.

Rafael Uribe Uribe, general and liberal.

Arrigo Boito, poet and composer, old lover of La Duse.

In Memory

José María Vargas Vila, writer, aesthete, and polemicist.

Julián del Casal, modernist poet, author of *Snow* and other books.

Lenin, founder of the Soviet Union, embalmed Communist.

Sarah Bernhardt, *La Magnifique.*

Adelaide Ristori, ghost, dean of Italian actresses.

Clementina Cazzola, Carlotta Marchionni, Fanny Sadowski, and Celestina Paladini, ex-actresses, mocking spirits.

Matilde Serao, writer and ex-telegraphist, old friend of La Duse.

Gabriele D'Annunzio, poet, novelist, and playwright, La Duse's lover.

Martino Cafiero, Neapolitan journalist, seducer of the young La Duse.

Teobaldo Checchi, actor and later Italian consul in Buenos Aires, husband of La Duse.

Enrichetta, daughter of La Duse.

Thomas Alva Edison, inventor.

Rainer María Rilke, poet.

Isadora Duncan, ballerina.

Alessandro and Angelica, traveling actors, parents of La Duse.

The gentleman from Lisbon, messenger of voices.

THE LAST MASQUERADE

PART ONE

Everything
dragging with it tedium,
because I dreamt of other odysseys
and different exiles
and assorted escapes;
and a separate stillness:
never this plain succession of sun
rises and golden dawns
and moonscapes
(praised by the poets of
yesteryear).
Never this plain succession of
tiresome
refrains. Oh, what a catalog of
incompetence,
what an onslaught of stupidities.

León de Greiff

We are the delirious,
delirious from desire,
our tracks idle and mysterious,
and in our feverish hands a pyre:
the crimson scraps of a heart on fire.

Porfirio Barba Jacob

Look at me. Watch me closely. Don't be embarrassed. I am used to it. Make sure that I am woman made of flesh and blood. And if that is the case, please let me know, for sometimes I fear that I am nothing but a phantom, just another wandering soul.

There are many who believe that I love the theater. What a ridiculous notion! It is a serious blunder to believe that, a complete mistake. What I truly adore with all my heart is the arts. If I could have been a painter or a writer, or if I could have been blessed with a talent for music or dance, my story would have been different, much different. Theater was for me only a way with which to approach the arts. A means, not an end. And though some might think that I am putting on airs, I should make clear that I have had little interest in fame or recognition. My only hope has been to find a shelter in the arts, a haven that would make my life tolerable.

I

Wen has two idols, and a scrapbook dedicated to each one of them. He lives in pursuit of any photographs of his two favorite characters published in magazines and newspapers. And if in the waiting room of a doctor's office, or in the house of a friend, he finds a snapshot worthy of his collection, he rips it out without hesitation—sometimes surreptitiously, sometimes shamelessly—and puts it away in his jacket pocket, feeling not an ounce of guilt.

One of his idols is Luis Vicentini, the Chilean lightweight boxer who is poised to claim the crown from world champion Manny Leonard. Wen lives to extol the greatness of Vicentini's body, his smile, the way an upstart ringlet of black hair falls on his brow, of those mouthwatering biceps, and of those hairy and solid legs with perfectly round knees. I have always thought it peculiar that Wen would choose a lightweight as the object of his devotion. Had it been me, I would have been more inclined to choose a pugilist of greater heft, for I am an enthusiast of the flesh, but in any case . . . Wen follows the news of the Chilean's bouts closely, looking up the results in the sports pages of *El Tiempo* and throwing small parties to celebrate each victory, as he did when Vicentini knocked out Jimmy Carroll in Madison Square Garden.

As soon as he read the article that detailed the victory, he phoned Esmeralda Gallego, and together they decided to put together a *kermesse* that would take place in my apartment. Esmeralda thought that only twelve guests should attend the feast, one for each round of the fight, and Wen found the idea superb. In no time at all, they drew up a guest list and urgently sent off to the printer invitations that included Wen's favorite picture of Vicentini, one where he is shirtless, in his boxing shorts, staring at the camera and threatening his unseen rival with clenched fists.

The party was a great success, and in spite of a constant chilly drizzle, none of the guests failed to attend. All of us were dressed in black tie, as the invitation dictated. Esmeralda Gallego sported a gauzy white dress (more than substantially low cut), fishnet stockings, a striking blue turban, and to match this, a turquoise ring, the stone the size of a quail egg. The effect was tantalizing; but if you wanted to be bitchy, you could have well said that she looked like a badly wrapped tamale.

The scrapbook dedicated to the Chilean stud presided over the festivities. It was placed on a cedar console next to a vase of lilies, open to a page with a picture of Vicentini at the instant that the referee raised his arm in victory. Wen swears that this image makes him hyperventilate every time he sees it, for few things in this world are as enticing to him as the armpit hairs of his favorite boxer.

Esmeralda saw to it that Toña, *la negra* from Chocó who was my nursemaid, my *Chocoana,* received specific directions relating to the victuals, and, very much in keeping with Toña's style, she surprised us with an eclectic menu consisting of empanadas, picadillo wraps, pork soup with neck bones, House of Lords whiskey, and Pommery champagne. We all praised her bizarre combination and gorged like pigs.

During the first hour we gossiped about the theft of the monstrance at the church in Paipa; about General Pedro Nel Ospina's government and the inadequacy of his cabinet; about the magnificent and relatively cheap Packard with six cylinders and room for seven passengers, which was for sale at the shop in La Granja; about the precious silver tea set that Alvarito Certaín won in a charity raffle; about how, in Barranquilla, the latest craze was "ice cream dances," a cheap imitation of the tea dances of the grand hotels in the capital; about who was the greatest soprano in Colombia—Doña Matilde de Camacho or Señorita María Olarte Ordóñez; about the miracle French cream Chesebrough; about how underappreciated the new "queen" at the university was; and about how handsome—drop-dead handsome—Frank Appleby, the golf instructor at the country club, was and about whether or not certain rumors about his return to his native England were true. But the main topic of discussion was, of course, Vicentini.

Wen raised his glass, and, in a voice almost drowned with emotion, dedicated the first toast of the evening to the resounding and continued success of the boxer. He announced that the Tower of Iron had fallen defeated at the feet of the eminent gladiator, and went on with other such gushy exclamations, predicting that in the upcoming year of 1924, Luisito would become king of the lightweights. We all raised our drinks—some of us because we were truly touched, others out of mere courtesy—and we clinked glasses to the great success of the sportsman who was thousands of miles away from us, unaware of the fuss being made over his victory by eleven gentlemen and an eccentric painter. I doubted if poor Luisito had the slightest inkling of the existence of this city founded on a high plateau by a conquistador, who fancied himself an intellectual, in the name of Carlos V, of this place mobbed with politicians and priests, which even today, four centuries later, does not yet have a decent roadway to connect it to the rest of the country—of the tiny, chilly, gray Santa Fe de Bogotá. No, I suppose Luisito had no idea.

The party almost ended in disaster.

Near midnight, after almost five or six bottles of the bubbly Pommery had been uncorked, the House of Lords flowed abundantly, bottoms-up, and there was not a crumb left of the wraps or empanadas, Wen stood up, grabbed the scrapbook, and asked for silence, so that he could show the gathered guests his collection of memories of Vicentini. Immediately all conversations came to an end and he began his discourse.

Pointing at each image, my lover specified the date and place where it had been taken, and added any pertinent details about the important fights, along with glowing remarks about the Chilean's fierce demeanor, about his pointy nipples, which would make even the most serene observer lose his mind, and about the manly stance with which he faced the photojournalists at Madison Square Garden.

As can be expected, a few minutes into this and the guests grew restless. Although most of them stoically endured it, pressing their lips together so as not to make faces, some couldn't care less about Vicentini, so they soon returned to their interrupted dalliances and conversations.

Wen continued with renewed determination, raising his voice to counteract the mutterings and trying to hide his dismay over their lack of attention, but he couldn't avoid casting oblique glances toward the chatterers, hurling daggers at them with his eyes, hoping either to annihilate them or paralyze their tongues.

Devotedly, he showed us a snapshot where Vicentini appeared on a beach, enjoying the warm Florida sun, dressed in swimming trunks that highlighted all his goodies. (The blonde who accompanied him had been cut out of the picture and later sadistically burned in the chimney fire; naturally, Wen did not make the slightest reference to this incident.) And then, incapable of tolerating it one moment longer, Wen let out a rabid yell, slammed shut the scrapbook, and as if he were an avenging angel, threw himself on the guest who was nearest him, the unfortunate Juan María Vengoechea, whom he beat mercilessly over the head, while screaming: "Shut your traps, *cachacos!*"

Vengoechea went pale. He blinked as if he could not believe what had just happened and reached a hand into his pocket where—and this was no secret to anyone—ever since he had been assaulted by some creeps on Real Street, he always carried a tiny Colt pistol. Who knows what would have happened had Esmeralda Gallego not stood up from the chaise longue on which she was stretched out and dragged him to an adjacent room.

In the living room, there hung such a silence that you could carve it with a knife. The guests were uneasy and not certain whether to laugh out loud or to gather their things and scurry off. Then, unperturbed, Wen reopened his scrapbook and continued his interrupted paeans to the Chilean's perfect set of white teeth.

Without calling attention to myself, I slipped away toward the piano room where La Gallego held a cold compress on the brow of an ashen and still astonished Vengoechea.

"Please forgive him," I begged, holding his hand and looking in a dissembling manner at the frightening swelling near his right temple. "He is always throwing tantrums, and drinking makes it worse. Tomorrow he'll want to die and come running to you on his knees. You know how he is." I said this last bit with a knowing smile, alluding to the quasi-relationship between them years before, when they were both beginning their law studies at El Colegio Mayor de Nuestra Señora del Rosario.

"Don't be making excuses for him, Lucho," Esmeralda interrupted. "Our friend is cracked in the head. I wouldn't be surprised if he murdered someone for that man." And, lowering her voice, she added that she had yet to find what was so appealing about Vicentini. "This whole thing is ludicrous," she concluded with a sigh.

Ten minutes later, it was Wen who came into the room, circumspect and with shortened breath. He stood in front of his old classmate, looking straight at him, till suddenly he dropped to his knees and begged to be forgiven. From the doorway, half-hidden by the green damask drapes, the other guests looked in on the scene.

"I don't know what got into me, Juanma," Wen explained. "I lost my mind, I swear! But it wasn't me who did it, it was some perverse demon who possessed me!"

I looked at Esmeralda and she looked away so as not to burst out laughing. The whole scene seemed like a bad imitation of a Pola Negri film that we had seen some nights back at the Teatro Municipal. After letting Wen plead for a while, Vengoechea granted the longed-for pardon, and aggressor and victim embraced and were thunderously applauded by the rest of the gentlemen who now deemed it proper to burst into the room.

"My friends, everything is forgotten," Esmeralda Gallego said excitedly, and she ripped off her turban, mussed her short hair, and provocatively showed us her smooth nape, which unleashed another round of applause. "The time has come to shake your bones!"

She took Alvarito Certaín by the hand and ran out to the living room, we all followed her, skipping and squealing, overcome by a most unnatural euphoria. La Gallego put on a record on the gramophone, and right out came an infectious fox-trot. "Time to dance, little ones!" she said, and the incident, which could have ended up in a fight worthy of Vicentini and Jimmy Carroll, or in irreconcilable animosity, disappeared in a wild dancing session, in which pinches and kisses were exchanged, and which led some of the distinguished participants to pair off.

When we least expected it, Wen interrupted the music and demanded our complete attention to offer a new toast. I looked at him, raising an eyebrow to signal my disapproval, but he eased my apprehensions with a smile. "No, this time I don't want to toast Vicentini. Instead," he paused and some coughed nervously, "I want to toast someone who honors us with friendship and, I might as well say it, as a partner in crime." His gaze fell on La Gallego, who was sitting on that blond Romero Villa's lap, caressing the smooth-cheeked dandy's chin, playing with his gorgeous dimple. "Yes, my friends, I raise a glass to Esmeralda, the most radiant jewel in our society, one of the few marvelous women alive today!"

"The only marvelous woman in the world," Romero Villa added saucily.

"No," Wen responded, unable to contain himself, "there is another one, but it is not proper to mention her in these drunken festivities." And leaving a whiff of mystery in the air, he toasted La Gallego. "To the beautiful Esmeralda."

"To Esmeralda," we all repeated.

The dancing continued, this time to the beat of a slow ragtime, and I took a seat in a corner near Esmeralda and Wen. She was weeping quietly, and streaks of black mascara ran down her cheeks.

"What's wrong with the queen of the night?" I asked her. "The only one who dares demote the great boxer to second-class status?" Chivalrously, I kissed one of her hands, the one with the turquoise.

"I am very unhappy," she mumbled. "I am old, fat, and debauched." And she looked to Wen for comfort.

"Debauched, yes," he replied, without giving it thought. "And old, perhaps," he continued, more tentative. "But fat, no," he said forcefully. "You are Rubenesque. So dry up those tears," he demanded in a tone that offered no other alternative, "or you will end up genuinely dreadful." To cheer her up, he led her into the study and there they each secretly snorted a pinch of that white powder from the wings of fairies that was left over in the bottom of a small lacquered box.

At three in the morning, when all the guests had departed, all but Esmeralda and Jorge Garay, a most delicious medical student that Wen and I had our eye on, La Gallego decided that we should wake Toña and conduct a séance, an idea that Wen and the future doctor quickly embraced.

"Not at this hour," I complained. "Don't even think about it." But I couldn't stop them. They pushed me toward the servant's door and forced me to knock.

La negra awoke with a frown. At first she absolutely refused, especially because of the presence of Garay, who made her shy. Yet all it took for her to change her mind was for Esmeralda to pour her a shot of whiskey and coax her to down it in one gulp. We sat around the kitchen table, on which Toña set a glass of water. Wen lit two candles, and the five of us held hands.

I never doubted Toña's abilities as a medium. Before coming to work exclusively for me, while we still lived in my parents' house, she stood out among the other servants by her commitment to the Catholic rituals and by her devotion to the Holy Child. But one night, Esmeralda, fanatical about any type of occult experience, had the outlandish idea that we should invoke the dead, just as she had seen a famous medium in Rome do. Wen went along with her, and so did Vengoechea, and I, not wanting to seem a spoilsport, agreed to participate as well. We were four, but according to La Gallego, in order to summon the penitent souls, ideally there should be a fifth person. As we did not have a fifth one there, we convinced our servant to join the group. She gave in with great reluctance, for those things seemed to her things of the devil; and yet, to our astonishment, the spirits decided to show up. Esmeralda pointed out, elated, that none of the séance groups that she had seen in Europe had at their disposal a medium whose supernatural essence could so easily dislodge itself from its more fleshy matter.

"Toña is a magnificent telephone," she declared.

But despite our success on that first occasion, our "telephone" refused wholeheartedly to do it again, and then threatened to tell my mother that I was dabbling in witchcraft; this was the one other time that Wen and Esmeralda were able to wheedle her into joining them in their clairvoyant adventures, just for that one time and never again.

"Just to let you know, my little Lucho, I am doing it only for you," she whispered prudishly in my ear after we were all silent, ready to summon the beings from beyond. "I don't want anything to do with the dead, anyway; they can never decide when they want to visit and they drive me crazy with all their little horror stories."

"Sshhh!" Wen ordered.

With my left hand I was holding Toña's right and with my right I held Garay's left. Making the most out of the fact that we all had our eyes closed, I let my thumb suggestively caress the would-be doctor's knuckles. I imagined that Wen was doing the same thing on the other side.

Esmeralda began the invocation.

"Brothers and sisters from beyond the grave," she said in an ominous foreboding tone. "Invisible faculties, celestial souls, heed our call and bring forth your spirits, bring forth the wisdom from your world hereafter! Come, come you primal creatures, you fleshless bundles. We mortals call ye!" I am not quite sure if this plea was something that she had heard from another spiritualist or if she had made it up, for on each occasion it was a little bit different, but it always raised every hair on my body.

It seemed that the spirits were not much in demand that evening, for they came flocking into the kitchen. Toña immediately went into a trance and ceased to be herself, lending her tongue to the spirits (for a little while apiece).

First to speak was an Aztec who, before dying at the hands of the conquistadors, had suffered the unspeakable as he watched his wife and young daughters being raped by the invaders, and he cursed us in a rudimentary Spanish mixed with phrases of his own language. Fortunately, his disturbing appearance was brief and he gave way to a scientist who was deprived of his life in 1701 by henchmen under the command of the Hohenzollerns, rulers of Prussia. Wen, who during his stay in Hamburg had learned some broken German, spoke with the Teutonic spirit, updating him on many scientific breakthroughs that left him aghast.

Then my old nanny was struck by a violent fit. She shook and stuck out about a foot of her tongue, and we were about to put an end to the session, afraid that she would drop dead of a heart attack. But just like that, she regained her composure, and speaking in a voice that seemed at first angelic, but in which we could make out a flirtatious undertone, she introduced herself as Rubiela González. We all edged forward in our seats, for despite the six years that had passed, that name remained fresh in our minds. In her time, many pages were devoted to her in the daily papers, and she was a compulsory topic in the gatherings of the capital. Rubi, or Rubí—with the last syllable stressed, as she was known in the seamstress shop where she worked—was an attractive young woman of no particular distinction who was found dead one morning in the Córdoba barrio with twenty-eight stab wounds all over her body. When we asked her about the crime, she confirmed the explanations of the police as to why the murder would go unpunished. The guilty ones had been a band of women from that neighborhood who, jealous and afraid that the little dressmaker would strip them of their husbands and lovers, had conspired to finish her off like a bull in a ring, each with her own banderilla. It was our own Bogotá version of the vengeful murder of the tyrannical overlord in the playwright Lope de Vega's *Fuenteovejuna.*

And so the procession of disturbing apparitions continued: a Paraguayan priest who had been beheaded in a battle against the armies of the Triple Alliance; a *Chino* who could not understand one word we spoke (and come to think of it, he was probably Japanese or Vietnamese) and, to add one final surprise to the evening, General Rafael Uribe Uribe himself.

Hacked to death in October of 1914 on the west side of the Capitol as he was on his way to fulfill his duties as senator, this champion of liberal causes was most annoyed at the fact that the director of the Panóptico had allowed his assassins, Galarza and Carvajal, to come off as matinee idols in the movie that recreated the assassination, and not as the pair of gutless and soulless creatures that they were. The general's spirit had been in the theater on the night of the premiere, and he asked us to congratulate the producers, the Di Doménico brothers, on his part, and to tell them that aside from the aforementioned detail he thought it a splendid movie. His eyes even welled with tears during the last scene, his funeral, when the people of Bogotá gathered by the thousands to pay him their last respects. Esmeralda, who is a friend of Vicente Di Doménico, promised the caudillo to relay his message.

Afterwards, Uribe Uribe asked us if the conservatives were still in power. We told him that things were just as they had been since the days after his death, and with his characteristic matter-of-factness, as if to cap off his visit, he said: "Then I am sure that we are still without a working army, without fighting forces, without commerce, without industry, without a budget, without land divided proportionately among the people, and without a diplomatic corps, without, in fact, any of the qualities that make a country matter in the global sphere. Poor Colombia!" He blurted out a vulgarity upon departure, whereupon the table rose a few feet in the air and then came crashing down.

Frightened by the presence of so many voices arriving with memories of bloody and brutal deeds, I was about to step in and insist we put an end to the session, when an unusually warm breeze, blowing from who knows where, caused the candlelight to flutter, and a soothing peace descended upon us. Toña's features softened, and I daresay that her face looked suddenly beautiful.

"Good evening," the spirit said in a friendly voice that had a certain musical quality. She introduced herself as Anatilde de Bastos, fortune-teller and psychic. She was a Portuguese, who had moved as a child to Cadiz, on the Atlantic shores, and who had lived in that port town till the day of her death from influenza. On realizing how exhausted Toña was, she promised that her visit would be brief, and offered to answer one question from each of us. Garay was picked to begin.

The medical student, somewhat embarrassed, wanted to know what questions would be asked during his oral exams the following week. The fortune-teller revealed to him not only each topic that he would be tested on, but also took the time to suggest what each individual answer should be, if he wanted Dr. López, professor of anatomy, to award him the highest possible marks. Esmeralda let me down considerably, for when her turn came, she wasted all her curiosity on something as frivolous as the following season's hemlines. But our visitor was delighted with the subject and offered various details pertaining to it.

"And now you, my darling," de Bastos said, looking at me through the eyes of my servant. "What do you wish to know?" With a lump in my throat, I inquired how long would the one that I loved reciprocate my affections. "For as long as you live," she answered joyfully. "And it will be a long and adventurous life for both of you."

Wen, who was last, pulled a quick one that made us furious. He let Anatilde know that he would formulate his question in his mind, and in a clear-pitched burst of laughter, she accepted the challenge. Wen looked at her in silence, and after a long pause, the fortune-teller said, "What you already know, you don't have to ask."

And then Toña's head fell face-first on the table and she began to snore thunderously. We couldn't wake her, so we left her right there, covering her in a thick blanket and putting out the candles.

"It will soon be morning anyway," Esmeralda said. And to our dismay, since Wen and I were thinking of asking Garay to sleep over so that we could help him with his anatomy homework, she offered to drive him home. Sleepy-eyed, he had to accept.

I woke up at midday with a nasty hangover. Wen, perky and just out of the shower, already had a package wrapped in crepe, ready for our trustworthy Toña to deliver to Juan María Vengoechea as a sign of his remorse. Inside were a gorgeous silk tie of reversible fabric, a white rose, and a signed portrait of Vicentini.

"I can't believe that you are parting with that picture," I said to him as we got dressed for lunch at the country club, which was to be followed by a private golf lesson from Mister Appleby.

"I have another one," he said. "And the autograph is a fake. I did it myself."

"Can I ask you something?"

"Whatever you want, but whether I'll answer is a different story."

I told him that I was dying to know what he had asked Anatilde de Bastos. "Did it have to do by chance with Vicentini?"

"What you already know, you don't need to ask," he answered, trying to be mysterious.

Although, to be tactful, I had never made Wen tell me which one of his two idols he most admired, there were little details that betrayed him.

It was very telling, for example, that while Luisito's scrapbook had a leather cover, the other had a cover of silver and mother-of-pearl. And while anyone could pick up the Chilean's scrapbook and leaf through its pages and admire the pictures that showed him lifting weights at the gym, lovingly looked over by his manager Jorge Bersac, or signing autographs for children in Valparaíso, the other scrapbook was kept under lock and key in a secret drawer of Wen's writing desk, protected from curious glances and grubby hands. It was only brought out on special occasions, for close friends, and was usually perused by candlelight in a reverent and worshipful mood appropriate for her to whom it was dedicated: the greatest of the tragediennes. For there was little doubt that on March 26, 1923, after the death of the only actress who could compare to her, the divine Sarah Bernhardt, no one would argue that such a title did not belong to La Signora Eleonora Duse.

Matilde Serao used to make fun of my penchant for seclusion, of my obsession with solitude (which she thought excessive) and of the fear that strangers would arouse (and still do arouse) in me. She used to say that I was more real on the stage than in my day-to-day life, that I was more authentic, more believable, when portraying characters on stage than when I tried, in such a taxing and pitiable manner, to be myself.

As the years passed, I came to see that my friend had been right. The "role" of Eleonora Duse has not exactly been my most rewarding creation.

But I am not completely to blame. Let it be known that Eleonora is a boring character. Whoever made her up did so half-heartedly, did not endow her with the necessary vitality. I'll admit that in the prolonged drama of her life there have been some powerful scenes that demand a certain boldness in whoever portrays her; but these high-pitched moments are only that—isolated moments watered down by a predictable and monotonous plot.

With no flair, no warmth, Eleonora lacks the tragic aura of a Cleopatra, or the cunning of a Mirandolina, or the psychological complexities of a Nora or a Hedda. Always ill and querulous, fleeing from journalists, hiding in her books! She is one of those bland and shapeless roles that, if an actress is not careful, can ruin her entire career.

What kind of character is that, one who cannot express her feelings, who would rather suffer silently than risk a heated confrontation? Without making any excuses, let me just say that it is very difficult, quite a feat, to portray her in a passable manner.

I like myself better as the women of Sardou, of Ibsen, of Gorki. As the Princess Fedora, as Rebecca, as Basilisa. Strong, attractive, impressive women. Compared to them, who is the frail and evasive Eleonora? No one, or almost no one. Why waste time, then, fretting over her? You could actually say, if you took it far enough, that she doesn't exist, that she deserves attention only during those hours when she becomes someone else.

What was Victor Hugo thinking when he sent her that anagram of her name? Duse-Deus. As a lyrical tribute, it is clever, but how far from the truth!

2

My family happens to be if not the wealthiest in Bogotá (which, unfortunately, it is not) then at least one of the most distinguished, for the surname Belalcázar reaches back at least to the founding of the city, and Reyes is also quite old.

Another point of pride in the clan is that its members are more conservative than the caudillos that become presidents of the republic under the banner of the Conservative Party. This is neither a joke nor an exaggeration. I know from good sources how my family conspired with General Pedro León Acosta and other equally prestigious families against President Rafael Reyes and did everything imaginable to overthrow him. Although he was one of them, he had never been forgiven for how he had spinelessly handed out two ministry positions—for the Treasury and the Foreign Office—to the liberals. I would not at all be surprised if my family was involved in Reyes's assassination attempt in 1906, while he was going for an afternoon car ride with his daughter Sofía on the outskirts of the city. Both miraculously survived.

Political sentiment runs so strong in my tribe that newborns wear blue diapers so that they grow accustomed to the color of their party. And in our mansion in La Candelaria, where the cold and humidity seeped in through the stone walls, our father kept himself warm with blankets that had all been dyed blue.

My mother—a daughter, niece, and granddaughter of generals, the wife of a general, for all intents and purposes a *generala* herself—had to take charge of our household from very early on. She did it as befitted a woman of such temperament, holding on to the reins with a firm grip, on her left hand a lace glove, on her right an iron mitt. She was beautiful, though not in the conventional sense, but rather in the royal fashion with which she carried herself in her youth, which made her captivating. She was also a shrewd business-woman, and through lucrative investments and judicious manage-ment she oversaw a considerable growth in the Belalcázar estate—so that there was always enough, more than enough. Once, when against the advice of her counselors, she bought some lots near Chapinero, my uncles Melitón and Manolo chided her for throwing away the estate's money on dried-out strips of land that would never turn a profit. But some years later, when the intelligentsia from the city grew tired of the hustle and bustle of the capital and discovered that nearby haven of peace, they found it an ideal location for their coun-try homes, increasing the price of the property several times over.

A quasi-widow—for you could probably refer to her as such in her situation as wife to a much older man who, due to a brain fever, had been bedridden almost twenty years and spoke only nonsense—from her youth, she had made it her duty to be zealously vigilant about the future of her little ones. Especially her five daughters, whom she needed to provide with a substantial dowry, lest they all be doomed to forever fiddling with rosary beads in a convent. She would be the first to reluctantly admit that I, the eldest, the only son, hoarded the entire beauty quotient granted to her offspring by the Almighty. None of my sisters was blessed with my black eyes and thick eyelashes, or my rosy skin, or, much less, my gracefulness. Who says life is fair? One could say that on conceiving me, my parents put to use their finest in-gredients, and that with my sisters they made do with whatever was left at hand. Not at all pretty, with dark complexions, resembling more than anything those of the branch of the Belalcázar family in Antioquia, gaunt and graceless, all five of them are, however, happy and always joking and so innately charming that they are always at the head of the guest lists for countless balls and outings. But knowing that charm alone rarely gets a hen to the altar, La Generala has from the beginning done her utmost to put away a small fortune for each of them. She doesn't skimp when ordering gorgeous dresses from Mademoiselle Berthe Largentier, designer for the fashionable set; nor when buying glossy shoes in the latest style; nor when arranging for them to attend outings and soirées—all with the conviction that if you want to catch a good husband you have to spend a little, for only money begets money.

While it is true that the ugly sisters enjoy great popularity and have many gentlemen friends, as of today, only one of them, Teresa, is engaged to be married, and is preparing her trousseau with the aid of her sisters. For weeks, a young man had serenaded Lucrecia beneath her window, courting her, it seemed, with very serious intentions. And truth be told, she could not have done any better. But the fact that he had earned a degree in engineering in California, or that he had been one of the brains behind the construction of the thermoelectric plant in El Charquito, meant nothing. He was ruled out as a possibility by La Generala the moment she found out that this bird under Lucrecia's window came from a nest of liberals, so he was forced to take his songs elsewhere. Lucrecia mourned her suitor for months—hiding from La Generala, of course. And she lost so much weight that she was nothing but a bag of bones, but in the end she had to resign herself to never seeing him again. But I am sure that before long all five of them will don wedding dresses and that they will bestow me with many nephews, who, hopefully, will look like their uncle or their future husbands. For, after all, women much less attractive than they, their prospects made worse by meager dowries, have trapped husbands.

As for my future, La Generala envisioned it in luxuriant terms from the very beginning. In her mind, I would marry a young woman of noble birth, from the purest lineage in the country. No social climbers, for though they may be pretty, wealthy, and educated, who could know what impurities were mixed in the blood of their ancestors. No sir, my wife would be of more dependable stock, a cousin or the heiress of an upper-crust family.

As time passed and I grew older, La Generala realized that she would have to overcome a few obstacles before achieving her goal. To begin with, I refused to pursue a traditional manly military career, and to the shock of the entire family, decided that I would either enroll in the School of Philosophy and Letters, or not study at all. In the years following, La Generala began to find my attitude toward the fairer sex a little suspicious: I flattered the ladies but that was as far as it went, and I never boasted, as did my cousins, of my love affairs and conquests. She came to understand that getting me to the altar would be an arduous task, but one that she would no doubt see through to the end. She had in her arsenal a very powerful weapon: if I was to marry to her liking, I would immediately receive my entire inheritance in cash; on the other hand, if my bachelorhood continued, I had to be happy with the crumbs she handed out to me, day by day, barely enough to live on.

But La Generala had not counted on chance, and chance, for once on my side, dealt her a cruel blow when my godmother Bhetsabé Restrepo passed away and left me all of her assets.

The day I announced, in the middle of lunch, that I was moving into a *garçonnière,* the poor woman was dumbfounded. I thought it would be the death of her, the same as in 1903, when no one was quite sure how—whether by some magic trick or out of apathy on the part of President Marroquín (who was more worried about etiquette books than about his political future)—the territory of Panama disappeared from the map of the Republic of Colombia. That something like that could have happened to our country seemed to her unforgivable, and she still had not gotten over it. Not to exaggerate how serious she thought this was, but she was not going to let something similar happen in her own house. She could not see why anyone would want to flee the bounty of their family. Much less her son, whom, while he was still a bachelor and with strange tendencies, it was her duty to guide down the proper path!

I always wanted to live on my own, without anyone poking their nose in my business, or wanting to know where I was going and with whom, without being called Jewish because I missed Mass, or harassed about not courting Señorita Such-and-Such, or for coming home at three in the morning smelling of liquor. As soon as I found myself the proud owner of hundreds of shares of stock from Banco de Crédito Mercantil, and of almost a thousand acres of prime land in Tunja, I understood at once that no one could stop me from doing exactly as I pleased.

Of course, La Generala did not throw in the towel; she put on a fierce struggle to keep me and to make me live by the principles of a conservative Catholic household. Like a Knight Templar, she set off on her crusade and God save us all.

First, she tried to change my mind by way of reason, using whatever arguments she could think of. She talked so much that even the servants grew bored: about the dangers and difficulties of a life for a single man who was still unripe, barely twenty-nine years old, accustomed to being completely pampered; of the advantages of having a mother, five sisters, and a whole troop of servants at your call, ministering to your every material and spiritual need. What would I do, with no one to turn to, were I to wake up at night in the middle of an asthma attack? (I had an asthma attack once when I was seven, and it has never happened again.) Who would prepare for me my steamy beef consommé and tasty eggs and arepas in the mornings to dispel the effects of my alcohol-sopped bohemian nights? To convince me, she sought the aid of the ugly sisters, my uncles, and even our lawyers. But against all of her objections and rationalizations, I stood my ground and reassured her that my mind was made up.

One day, La Generala proposed a compromise. Instead of living by myself, and in so doing stir up the chatter and speculations of wicked tongues, why not go for a year to England? It was inconceivable, she argued, that someone who so loved literature had never set foot in the land of Shakespeare. Although she was willing to assume all costs and offered other tempting incentives, I rejected her generous offer. And then I let her fume, and from that moment on, thinking that she would be punishing me, she did not address another word to me. Taking her cue, I did the same to her. The standoff lasted a week, until, seeing that as I ignored her I was also looking through the classifieds for apartments and following up on the ones that sounded interesting, she decided that it was time to try another tack. She pretended to be gravely ill and filled the house with moans and medicine bottles. She went so far as to get one of my sisters to fetch the papal nuncio, who was a frequent visitor to our house, rousing him out of bed in the middle of the night to perform the last rites. Of course, her illness disappeared when she found out through the ugly sisters that I had already signed the lease on my bachelor pad. She finally admitted that, like it or not, she had been defeated, and she sent for Toña to get me.

"The lady wants to see you," Toña said, unable to hide her nervousness. She escorted me through the damp corridors lined with potted roses and geraniums, toward the front parlor.

My mother, as usual, had her hair in a tight bun and wore a pearly-gray knit dress and a wool scarf thrown over her shoulders. She was seated on the sofa, stitching my initials on a cushion, as if by coincidence. She was watched over by the austere portraits behind her of all the patriots in our family (husband, father, father-in-law, uncles, grandfathers, their outrageous mustaches and uniforms dripping with medals, all of the portraits framed in gold). I approached her and kissed her lovingly on the brow, but she did not flinch and continued, engrossed in her stitching. Toña made as if to leave.

"You stay right there," La Generala ordered in a dry voice and the Chocoana froze near the door, anxiously drying her hands with her apron. Without lifting her eyes, La Generala went on. She ordered me with a gesture of her chin to sit by her on the chair whose back was brocaded with golden threads and that had once belonged to a viceroy.

I sighed and obeyed her, expecting an ultimatum.

"So, you don't plan to marry your cousin Isabel," she said suddenly, with a certain trace of sarcasm, as if we were in the middle of a conversation.

"Mamá, you know that I consider Isabelita almost a sister, that to me she is . . ."

"Let's not beat around the bush, dear," she scorned. "Shall we? You were also not interested in pursuing, when you had the chance, General Ospina's niece. And you couldn't care less that all you have to do is say 'boo' and the Castillo Sisters will come running."

I took another deep breath, feeling annoyed and awkward, as she pinned her irate eyes on me. She was a cornered lioness who could not admit defeat and rabidly swiped the air with her paws. If I had not lived with her all my life, I think that at that moment I would have collapsed on the floor in panic; but those looks had ceased to intimidate me long ago, since the day when I had come into the fortune that would let me live comfortably within my own means.

"And you know what?" she continued, regaining her composure. "If that is what you truly want, go ahead. Go live in whatever dump you find, far from your loved ones. You must have your reasons, dark and bottled-up motives that I will choose to ignore. I am now afraid that you will never marry, and that the name of Belalcázar will vanish forever for lack of an heir."

"Well, there are our cousins in Antioquia," I said, trying to deflate her argument. "They could be in charge of that."

"I don't care about your cousins," she erupted. "They are third-rate Belalcázars, the products of unacceptable unions, and the farther away they are, the better. Let them stay in Antioquia with their mules and belt pouches." She paused and then added in a measured tone: "What I worry about is you. So I am willing to accept your plan on three conditions."

I almost burst out laughing. You had to give it to La Generala, she was impressive. A true titan. Without the slightest chance of recapturing all the ground she had lost, she kept coming at me out of pure honor.

"What are the conditions?"

"First, Toña goes with you."

I glanced at my old nanny, who agreed immediately, a frightened look on her face. Apparently, she had been asked beforehand. I found the idea convenient. Toña loved me, she worked like an animal, and she was neat and discreet. My mother thought that in saddling me with her, she would have a spy for her cause, a kind of black Mata Hari who would not miss a thing and would keep her informed of my every doing. But I was sure that once with me, free of my mother's grasp. Toña would be completely on my side, and far from betraying me, she would do anything to cover for me.

"I accept," I conceded. "Go on."

"The second condition is that you should be discreet and always, before you commit some imprudence, some atrocity, well . . . you can imagine what I mean, always to think of the dignity of this family. And, above all, to think of the future of your unmarried sisters, whose reputation and integrity cannot be tarnished by gossip from all the trash who envies us and wants to see our name dragged through the mud."

I accepted again, eager to hear the last condition, which was surely the most important.

"The third one is . . ." she stopped for a moment and regarded the oil portraits of her ancestors, as if asking them for strength to continue. She put away her stitching implements in the wicker basket and looked straight at me. "Third, and most important, I ask you that never, for whatever reason . . ." she stammered, unsure of what verb to use, "should you 'pair up' with a liberal." Her eyes reddened, and as if in harmony with one another, each let out a fat tear. "For whatever reason God has done this, since, as you know, sometimes His motives are mysterious and painful, I have a clear conscience. I know that in this house you had only the best influences. But I beg you, never get mixed up with one from the opposing party. You might as well put me in a grave and spit on it if you do. I could put up with anything but such a betrayal."

Unable to hold it in one more second, she burst into tears and hugged me, overcome by uncontrollable seizures. I have to admit that I was astonished. I could not believe what I had just heard. Defeated, La Generala accepted my special nature, so long as I practiced my specialty with someone of our political party.

"Toña, a glass of water," I screamed at my nanny, who hurried out to the kitchen.

"Do you promise me, Lucho? Do you give me your word?" the doña asked in between hiccups, her face pressed to my vest. "Will you swear to me? Never, never, never a liberal!"

"I swear," I said solemnly, and I wasn't lying. I was already obsessed with a certain Wenceslao Hoyos, a member of the Conservative Party, and my dream was to have him beside me for the longest time possible.

I had met him two weeks before at a concert at the Colón. He had just returned from his studies in Europe, and he told me that his family, like mine, was more conservative than the Spanish Crown itself. And he went on to explain that, after giving it much thought, he found that he saw only two substantial differences between the liberals and the conservatives. First, that the former drink in public and secretly go to Mass, while we take Communion in public and get drunk behind closed doors. And second, that they say: "Always with ours, whether they are right or not." And that we say: "Always against ours, whether they are right or not." If from first laying eyes on him I was attracted by his aloofness, by his flawless features, by that mix of innocence and mischief that glittered in his gray eyes, then these last comments made me fall hopelessly in love, and I made up my mind to make him mine, whatever the cost. Fortunately, it did not take much, for, as he later confessed to me, the idea to make me his lover had taken a hold of him as well. That same night, at the end of the concert, he fixed it up so that we would share a taxi, and as the car made its way through the dark narrow streets of La Candelaria, he began to flirt with me. "I wish I were cross-eyed, so that I could see you double," he said, and without further ado, threw his arms around me and kissed me so passionately I thought that he would bite my lips off. The following morning, when my sisters asked me about the swelling, the only thing that I could come up with was that I had pierced it with the sharp point of a compass.

My mother moved away from me and tried to regain her fierce demeanor. She took the handkerchief I offered her and, troubled by such a show of weakness, dried up all traces of her tears. Toña returned at that instant with a heavy silver platter and offered her a glass of water. Uncomfortable, my mother hardly wet her lips with the water and returned the glass to our servant, gesturing with a roll of her eyes that she should disappear.

"Oh, one more thing," she added confidently when we were alone again.

"But wasn't it just three conditions?" I protested, almost laughing at her.

"It is not a condition. It is a suggestion that I hope you listen to and follow without grumbling," she explained. "It will take little effort and when you do it, it will not only bring great joy to the woman who brought you into the world, but it will also do you good."

"All right, what is it?"

"Once a month, at least once a month, although twice would be much better, you will let yourself be seen at a gala function or a crowded ball, accompanied by some pretty young single señorita— any out of the many who stupidly would die to be seen with you, though you pay them not the slightest attention—and in the presence of all you should compliment them and pay gentlemanly attention to their whims. In this way, we shall counteract, as much as possible, the slander and ill-talk of this foul-mouthed town." With the look of a tyrant, she awaited my answer. "What do you say?"

"As you wish, Mother."

"You may go," she ordered sharply and with a soul-wrenching sigh ended the conversation. "You must have a thousand things to do and I still have not said my rosary."

"Your blessing, Mother dearest?"

"May God be with you and guide you," she said, dismissing me with a sign of the cross.

Fifteen days later, I left for my new house. Wen helped me arrange the furniture, some pieces bought to our liking from the fashionable shops, others chosen from what my godmother Bhetsabé had left me. Like a pair of lovebirds, we exquisitely decorated every little corner of the apartment. And to be honest, I pretty much let him have his way. He chose the Chippendale chairs upholstered in dark green silk, the Venetian mirror that we hung in the living room, the bureau inlaid with ivory, and the Gobelin tapestries and bronze statuettes that were scattered around the rooms. In the study we put two lacquer writing desks, one for him and one for me. Wen decided on a whim that it was imperative that we hang lace curtains and buy a piano, though neither of us could play a single note. When I told him that this proved what a snob he was, he took offense, explaining that he was not a snob, he was chic, and then treated me to a lengthy and footnoted dissertation on the difference between the two words. And so the piano soon arrived. I only stood my ground for one thing: I wanted a big couch with lots of soft cushions by the fireplace. He accepted, as long as I agreed to purchase a Bengal tiger's hide to throw over the carpet in the bedroom.

Toña listened to our conversations and sometimes couldn't help but laugh at some of Wen's absurdities. She too was happy to escape the prison of La Candelaria and to be free of the overbearing authority of its ill-tempered warden, and she showed it in small gestures of fondness and caring. At nights, she would prepare for us cheese and water sweetened with brown sugarloaf, and sometimes, while we were spread out on the couch as I read *Le Rouge et le noir* aloud to Wen, she would come over to us quietly and cover us with a wool blanket so we would not get cold.

I soon found that her consideration for Wen was disproportionate to the short time she'd known him, and such solicitude, I have to admit, made me insanely jealous. When pouring wine, the first glass that she filled was his. For dinner, we ate chicken or beef, according to the wishes of Señorito Wen. She prepared for him exquisite pastries that she had learned to bake from her grandmother in Santa Rita de Iro, and she went out of her way to fulfill his every wish. One morning, half joking and half serious, I reproached her for spoiling him so much.

"What are you talking about, my child?" she protested. "Don't be silly. If I spoil him it is because you love him. Stop loving him and see if I so much as look at him."

Although Wenceslao spends a good part of the day and almost every night with me, technically he still lives in his parents' mansion. It is not to our advantage to defy certain of the city's social circles, and moreover, I must keep my promise of discretion to La Generala.

Sometimes I go visit him in the impressive office that his father rented so that he could practice law. It is a few blocks from Santander Park, near my apartment. Two or three times a week, Wen heads for the office in a felt coat and hat, as if he had just stepped out of a fashion magazine, so that he can get together and chat with his friends and please his family, who dream of seeing him a senator in a few years. He has a typist at his services, whose main task is to make coffee and pour brandies. The rest of the time the good woman peruses all the papers and magazines and cuts out any article that mentions, even in passing, Vicentini or La Duse.

I like to go for walks, especially at midday, when the shop owners lower their metal grates and lock them with enormous bolts before they go out for lunch and to enjoy the siesta. In the park, near the statue of Santander, men play chess at tiny tables, shielded under the shade of ancient trees. Although I have never understood the game, I like to pass by and watch as the players move their pieces across the black and white squares.

At that hour, the streets are almost empty: most of the shoppers

ANTONIO ORLANDO RODRÍGUEZ

have vanished, the churches have closed their doors, and the worshippers have returned to their homes, and the public workers seek
refuge in the cafés, in the picnic areas, or in the restaurants where
lazily scribbled signs announce BREAKFAST STILL SERVED. The only people left on the sidewalks are the shoeshine boys determined to convince one of the few passersby how frighteningly dirty his shoes are,
the lottery vendors shouting about the fortune that awaits in one of
their tickets, and the obligatory beggars. Street traffic also quiets
down, and with it the brazen noise of the streetcar and automobile
horns and the two-note bells from the horse carriages. I sometimes
wonder if there is a noisier city than Bogotá in the entire world!

I go by Wen's and we have lunch at the Regina Hotel or any other
posh place. I tell him that he looks gorgeous, which he loves, and then
we talk endlessly about nothing. Toña grumbles that going to restaurants when you have plenty of delicious food at home is throwing
away money, but neither of us pays her the slightest attention.

As far as I know, attorney-at-law Wenceslao Hoyos has never been
in charge of a single case. I often ask myself how it was that he passed
all the rigorous exams at El Rosario when the subject does not pique
his curiousity at all. I think that the law only interests him if there is
some way of breaking it. Making money is not among his worries. He
doesn't even need to think about such things. As he is an only son, his
adoring parents, who see not the slightest flaw in him, each month
hand him more money than he can spend.

Given that I myself do not have many obligations per se, except to
scribble my biweekly literary column for *Mundo al Día,* which runs
under my penname Baal, or to read whatever interesting novel or collection of poetry I find in the bookstore, we do with time as we
please, whether it is to go shopping or to the movie theater, to attend
the bullfights at Luna Park or to brush up on our horseback-riding
skills, to sit and gossip the afternoon away at the Hotel Savoy or to
make appointments at the clinic of scientific massages for gentlemen
on Eighth Avenue between Seventeenth and Eighteenth Streets, or
anything else at all to spoil each other rotten.

In a word, we are young, we are beautiful, and we are elegant, both
of us distinguished and of superior quality. Fate has smiled upon us,

and as if that were not enough, we are as in love and devoted to each other as we were five years ago when we decided to share our lives.

Before meeting Wen, I was a man of few friends, a loner, a bit of a misanthrope who could spend hours and even whole days locked up in my room, with no other companion than my books. Not that I was a saint or anything, for ever since I was an adolescent I have been marked by an erotic nature more worthy of someone from the fever-ish coast than from the cold capital, due perhaps to my Andalusian an-cestors. At times, my blood would boil, but I would always find a way to simmer it down so that it would course again, cooled, through my veins. But I have to say, in choosing between some sexual adventure and, say, a book by Paul Bourget, literature always won out.

Aside from his impetuous nature, so unique and enthralling, Wen brought into my life a new awakening of the senses, a rabid desire to explore emotions and experiences unknown to me, an insatiable yearning to try everything before it was too late. And he provided me with a large circle of friends (where, as in the Lord's mansion, one can find whatever one needs) who without delay welcomed me into their hearts.

From them I found out that although it seems impossible and diffi-cult to believe, even in drowsy, traditional, moralistic Bogotá, as in any other city in the world, there are well-hidden secrets, a veiled life that the majority of citizens are not even aware exists. It is a noc-turnal underworld, small but with many different rooms, which only the initiated can gain access to. In one part of the city, there are pri-vate parties thrown in the luxurious suites of the Continental, the Plaza, and other hotels, where hashish and fine liquor are abundant and where the guests, members of the crème de la crème or the social-climbing rabble who have decided to take their place among us, show off their finest jewelry or whatever outfits they are wearing in Paris or London, and give free rein to their fantasies and stroke this or that palm seeking political favors. In some other part of the city, there are seedy dens of iniquity devoted only to pleasure, where it is ad-vised that you come without your precious jewels and that you get out of your car a few blocks before arriving, and where, for a handful of hours, the difference between social classes, as Herr Marx dreamed, is abolished, because what goes on has very little to do with class struggle and very much to do with the heightening of the senses: dandies and hoodlums, university folk and workers, the upper classes and the rubbish all mix together and partake of aguardiente, beer, and chicha, a potent maize drink. They dance, they smell and taste and solace themselves till dawn, keeping each other aroused with countless perversions.

In search of powerful emotions and fresh meat, Wen and I jumped back and forth between these two poles with great ease. One night we could be in the Belgian minister's opulent home near the Plaza de Independencia, dancing as guests of the minister and his lover, a Dutchman who flirts with anything in a pair of pants, and twenty-four hours later, with Juanma Vengoechea, Poncho Zárate, and Romero Villa, we could be lost in the alleyways of Las Cruces, looking for a bar known to be frequented by well-built working-class men, who were willing, as long as you offered them an aguardiente and a few coins, to offer up their bodies to all manner of groping.

From the very beginning, I was attracted to Wen because of his saint-demon nature. I had never before come across anyone in whom the spiritual and the carnal so indissolubly mixed. He would weep listening to one of Chopin's preludes, movingly recite the "Nocturno" of José Asunción Silva, or hover in front of a drawing by Mucha, which Esmeralda brought to us from one of her trips to France, relishing every line and streak of color; but later, he would drag me to Las Mercedes to watch, with the same delight, soccer matches between the teams A.B.C. and Bartolino. He scrutinized the robust, fierce, rather crude young men that made up the squads as if they were sculptures that had escaped from Michelangelo's studio. "Look at that forward's torso," he would say. "And don't miss out on those calves," and ipso facto, with a poke of the elbow to get my attention, he would call out almost out of breath: "Oh, don't miss that little blond one's ass, my love. What a tail! God bless him!" On such occasions, Wen behaves like a butcher: he chops up the athletes into chunks, saving from each of them the portions that, due to their magnificence, are worthy of appreciation, and throws out the parts that don't make the grade.

I was an excellent student. My teacher did not have to go to great pains, since I so swiftly learned my lessons. Esmeralda, his closest friend and confidante, has gone as far as to say that in our case, the student has surpassed his mentor. But I would never go as far as to agree with her.

To my surprise, after I moved into the *garçonnière,* Wen's mother and La Generala established a close friendship. They visited each other and exchanged recipes. They attended Mass together at the Church of San Diego, and sunk to their knees in front of the image of Nuestra Señora del Campo, whom Doña Herminia is much devoted to. This specific Virgin, while not being especially generous when it came to performing miracles, is, in a sense, a miracle of her own. It is said that in the middle of the seventeenth century, while the lapidary sculptor was carving the effigy, he abandoned the task because he considered the piece of sandstone he was working with to be too un-yielding. The block was placed over a stream to serve as a small bridge for the Franciscans who came to its secluded shores, and for the travelers and horse teams that passed through La Burburata on the way to Tunja; but it seems the Immaculate Virgin wanted to teach the unbelievers a lesson. One night, the father in charge of the monastery noticed how the stone glittered and gave off flashes of light, and on approaching the stream the following morning, he realized that the Mother of God had finished the sculpture herself, at which point the piece of sandstone immediately became an object of veneration for the astonished priests and their neighbors.

La Generala and Señora Hoyos also frequented the seamstress's shop Viuda Richard & Plata and privately bewailed the sorry state of their lives: one complained that she could not bear to see her husband day after day, bedridden and a stranger, incapable of looking after himself or recognizing his loved ones; the other one complained about having to live alone in the city for the greater part of the year, while her husband, now retired from politics, dedicated himself to breaking in wild colts and herding cattle (like a commoner) at the huge and flourishing ranch that they owned near Chiquinquirá. And if they came across other ladies that they knew, our mothers didn't pass up a chance to allude, in a playful manner, to those two incorrigible Don Juans of their two sons, such great friends, still single, still wom-anizing, who, in spite of all their chiding, had yet to settle down and prize them with grandchildren, but whose imminent plans with certain distinguished señoritas (whose names must be discreetly not revealed) would soon be known to all.

Sometimes, at night, when we were already in the bedroom at the *garçonnière,* in our pajamas and toasty under the comforter, Wen would jump out of bed; put on his felt slippers, and head for the study, from where he would return with the scrapbook dedicated to La Duse. Seated up against the headboard, he devotedly looked through the pages, going over each phase in the career of his adored actress and showing me pictures in which she was dressed up for the role of Mirandolina, in Goldoni's *La Locandiera,* or for the role of the Sicilian peasant Santuzza in *Cavalleria rusticana.*

"Let me see that," I interrupted him with sleepy eyes. "She sings opera as well?"

"Don't be such an animal," he answered, letting out a patient sigh. "Before it was put to music, *Cavalleria rusticana* was a play. An Italian poet named Giovanni Verga wrote it in 1883, expressly for her."

I couldn't resist, given such a fabulously phallic surname. "And does the writer do honor to his name?" I teased, as my hand found its way into his pajama pants and searched, groping in the dark, for the treasure. "Hello, *caro Signore Verga,*" I said then, in the voice of a puppet, egging Wen on. "Oh my, I see that you are cold and shrunken. I seem to remember that you are not always so *piccolino.* Perhaps you need some warming up, no?"

All this did not please Wen at all. He considered it disrespectful to his idol. Pretending to ignore my manipulations, he insisted on continuing to describe the costumes of the famous artist in the role of Santuzza: cream-colored blouse, a yellow-and-brown striped bodice printed with flowers, a white cotton neckerchief, and a flowery headscarf. . . . But on noticing that I was not paying any attention to La Duse's photograph, and, worse yet, that Signore Verga was beginning to respond to my repeated caresses, he cast my hand out of paradise, shut the scrapbook, and put it away under his pillow.

"You are incorrigible!" he said, turning his back to me. "Don't you dare, not with La Duse, or you'll get what's coming to you!"

God and I are old friends.

Sometimes we have long conversations. We sit alone in some dark room and talk about anything that comes to mind. I ask Him: "How much longer do you plan putting me to the test? Isn't it enough already? How much more do I have to endure?" And not that I am trying to come off as a victim, but whatever share of suffering was my due, I have already more than partaken of it. I have given sorrow all that I can give. "Enough," I say to Him. "No more." But He ignores my pleas and keeps me here, I am sure, to torment me, to remind me that it is He who decides when the curtain should rise and when it should fall.

At first, God intimidated me and I treated Him with an exaggerated reverence. Then, little by little, I overcame my fears. It's not that I don't respect Him at all, no, it's just that He no longer frightens me. Or not so much as before. As my confidence grew, I began taking Him down from the pedestal where my fear had placed Him. So now it is as if He were right in front of me, eye to eye.

I tell Him what I think of the world, of His choices, of how He treats people, of how unfair He is when handing out the dose of joy and grief that belongs to each of us. In the end, I tell Him whatever comes into my mind. I never ask for anything, because I imagine that He is sick of all the begging. I don't want any favors or special treatment, and perhaps that is why He enjoys my company now and again.

Recently, I have begun speaking to Him in a more familiar way. He, on the other hand, continues to address me formally. It is part of His strategy, I think. A trick, a way not to tighten, more than necessary, the knot that binds us, a way to keep a prudent distance. "You on your side, and Me here in the place where I belong." A cordial relationship, true, but one devoid of excessive familiarities.

It doesn't really bother me. He has to play out His part. For even God has a role to perform and, like it or not, He must fulfill it. If not, He would throw the universal drama off course. *Tutto é teatro.* But I can't imagine that He dislikes His character, for no one would turn down the role of the protagonist.

I don't argue the fact that God is very powerful; though about His omnipotence I have a few reservations. And what I really don't believe in, at the risk of being labeled sacrilegious, is His much-touted wisdom. I think that there is a great deal of exaggeration when it comes to that. You know how these things work, somebody says something, somebody else repeats it, and out of such trifles reputations are built. I don't mean to suggest that He is stupid or that He doesn't know how to do His job. He may be wise, and I don't mean to offend anyone, but so, also, is a tree, a beast, or a village idiot. In every creature there exists an element of wisdom inherited from nature that enables it to survive and flourish.

God is wise, but not quite as wise as He believes Himself to be or as those who catalog His achievements and mishaps would have you believe. He, too, makes mistakes, and serious ones at that, but He either covers them up well, or fixes them, or simply raises His chin and looks elsewhere not to have to face the consequences. For in the end, there are very few who dare criticize Him! Since He is stubborn, extremely stubborn, it is difficult for Him to admit when He is wrong, so He makes you believe that He is making you atone for some wrong, or that the consequence of His error is the price you must pay, not necessarily for happiness, which is a prize He rarely grants anyone, but for an infinitesimal portion of wellbeing.

These are not things that I say behind His back, illintentioned. We have talked about it face to face on more than one occasion. Or, to be more precise, I have talked about it in His presence, because I have never gotten Him to respond. He changes the subject, or pretends that He has fallen asleep.

Some adore Him, some doubt His existence, and of course there are many who simply use His popularity. As for me, I feel something resembling pity for Him. Just thinking about Him makes me infinitely sad. To have conceived the universe down to its most insignificant detail and to have built it on such a majestic and grand scale, only to have things turn out not quite as expected!

In the theater, everyone can't do everything. God was a good playwright, thinking up all the characters and the world in which they lived, even painting the scenery and sewing the costumes. But He was no good with the actors. Actors are the scourge of the earth. When they are not kept in line by the iron hand of a director, when they are allowed to improvise or to make changes or interpret characters as they see fit, they doom a production. The only language thespians understand is that of the slave master. God, poor thing, is a sorry director for the spectacle of life. In spite of all His shortcomings, He is too good, too permissive, too tolerant. I am not making this up: just take a look at the newspapers and see what is going on in the world. The puppets have rebelled, and after the mutiny they do as they please. A large part of humanity has betrayed its Maker. How else to explain so much pain, so much misery, hunger, hatred, the pleasure of destruction, the horrifying cruelty of war?

Someone else in His place might have unleashed His rage on humanity, would have annihilated His creation with one apocalyptic slap, to raise from the ruins a new set design and place in it less disobedient actors. But even for Him, that would be a grand effort, an awful task, so He pretends not to notice anything. What the eyes don't see, the heart needs not mourn. There should be a companion proverb that goes: what the ears don't hear, the mind needs not understand. Let the show go on, says a beleaguered God from the wings. Let the actors come and go from the stage as they see fit, let them recite their lines and interact howsoever they please. One more act and the farce will finally end. Curtains, curtains quickly, and applause, thunderous applause.

3

At first, it was hard for me to understand why Wen had admitted Poncho Zárate into his circle of close friends. Of all the other young men whom we knew, he was the only one who wasn't from a good family, or of great financial means. And you didn't have to be too observant to realize this: all you had to do is look at his run-down shoes, which he wore every day and which no amount of shoe polish or paint could spiff up, or take a good look at his umbrella, with its cheap handle and thick, rough cotton. If Poncho were a Colombian Rudolph Valentino, it would make sense, but aside from being scrawny, lackluster, and freckle-faced, he has a hooked nose with a wart the size of a lentil on it. He is not overly cultured, nor witty or talented in any other way.

Whenever we went to the movie theater or on some other outing, no one ever remembered to invite him. It was Wen who, with a suspicious generosity, always insisted on asking him along.

"Don't leave him out," he said. "After all, there is room in the car for six."

"That spot can go to Alvarito Certaín or to that hunk of a Dutchman from the Belgian legation," Juanma Vengoechea replied, not hiding his feelings about both the aforementioned.

Wen, however, continued his defense of Poncho.

"He's a very good person, a good soul, incapable of harming anyone."

"I know," Juanma Vengoechea answered, a heat rising in him, "but we are not discussing his canonization, only if he should come with us."

"Fine," Wen gave in, "if you want to invite Certaín or that giant, there's no problem, I'll stay here and that's the end of the argument."

Of course, in the end we would take Poncho Zárate along, who, to be blunt, did not seem like a bad person at all, just a boring one.

Esmeralda Gallego, usually an angel of kindness, could be awfully cruel to him. She couldn't really stand him. On one occasion, when we were at a benefit concert by the cellist Mister Kennedy in El Teatro Colón, she asked Zárate, as if making small talk, what toothpaste he used.

"Odol," said the poor wretch, flashing us a smile.

"Well, you should switch to Oloris," replied La Gallego coldly. "Your teeth are covered in plaque."

Anyone else would have responded in like fashion, putting her in her place, and Wen, I am sure, would have strangled her right there in our box, in front of hundreds of elegantly dressed and stupefied witnesses, but Poncho only smiled again, this time making sure that he didn't show his teeth and thanked her for her suggestion. I am sure that the following morning, on his way to the editorial offices, he stopped at the nearest drugstore looking for the new toothpaste.

Zárate is a journalist, not a very distinguished one, but a journalist nonetheless, at *La República.* In charge of international news, he is responsible for reading every newswire that arrives in the office and for choosing those that, in his opinion, merit publication among the ads for bubbly Limonela and Marconi's wireless services.

One day, as Wen and I ate our lunch at the *garçonnière,* a light went off in my head and I understood everything. I slammed my hand down on the table, and the spicy potato soup splashed everywhere.

"It's because of all of the information that he provides you with!" I screamed. "That's why you put up with Poncho Zárate, because he keeps you up to date on whatever arrives at the paper about the Chilean boxer and the Italian actress. Admit it!"

He looked at me as if I were mad, and continued eating, unperturbed.

"Admit it!" I insisted, slapping the table again, and this time Toña stuck her head in from the kitchen to see what was going on. "I promise that I won't tell a soul," I added.

He held the spoon halfway up to his mouth and his eyes shone wickedly.

"Of course, silly," he confessed. "Do you think that if it wasn't for that, I would put up with such a bore?"

The secret was out. Zárate, grateful for Wen's constant kindness toward him, provided Wen with many of the photographs and stories that, seated at his desk, my lover carefully pasted on the pages of his respective scrapbooks.

"Remember, you promised not to tell anyone," he said, after our dessert of custard. "Not even Esmeralda," he specified. "I don't want people to think that I am using him."

And so, during one of our country outings, it was Zárate who let us in on the news that changed our lives.

We decided to go on a picnic with a group of friends, and all went to La Sabana station to grab a train to Mosquera. The journey transpired almost without incident, as we chatted about the new opium den that Wen and I had recently visited, fixed up with every oriental comfort and luxury; and about the pair of lovers who, after having their picture taken near Tequendama's Leap, committed joint suicide by throwing themselves over the waterfall. Esmeralda said that she had never liked that place, for though it was inarguably beautiful, a sinister air hung over it. To prove it, she reminded us that in 1913, some time after the premiere of the film *Tequendama's Daughter,* which was produced by Francisco Di Doménico, its leading actress, a young woman whose last name was Peralta, had lost her life under tragic circumstances. Our chat then zeroed in on *Like the Dead,* the new film by the Di Doménicos, which consisted of a prologue, six parts, and an epilogue, and featured members of the most exclusive families in the capital. Poncho Zárate tried to figure out from La Gallego if it was true that the screenwriter Antonio Alvarez Lleras, author of the novel upon which the film was based, had squabbled with the Di Doménicos about the casting. According to rumors that Poncho had heard, about the leading man there was little argument, it would be the dashing Rafael Burgos; but as far as the leading lady was concerned, things were more complicated. While the writer thought that the role should go to Matilde Palau or Isabel Van Walden, Vicente

Di Doménico was not so sure, and on two or three occasions had mentioned the possibility of offering the part to La Gallego, convinced that although she lacked experience and was, obviously, no longer that young, her spirit and distinction could contribute much to the success of the picture. Esmeralda only smiled enigmatically, and as much as he tried, our journalist could not get her to comment one way or another. At that moment, a whistle from the locomotive warned us that the train was approaching its destination.

At the rustic station in Mosquera, a carriage pulled by two horses awaited us. It would take us to El Algarrobo, the ranch owned by the Vengoecheas. Our plan though was to lunch not at the house but in the pastures near the river, so there we headed, carrying all our food and supplies.

Esmeralda Gallego looked, why deny it, splendid. She had chosen a rather bucolic outfit for the occasion. She wore a light blue skirt and a see-through white muslin blouse decorated with ribbons. The *ensemble* was rounded off with coffee-colored shoes, flesh-colored linen stockings from Scotland, and an Italian straw hat. In her right hand she held a delicate Chinese parasol, and hanging from her left arm there was a basket containing a smoked ham that she bought at El Escudo Catalán. Poncho Zárate had put himself in charge of two baskets: one with bread, white and yellow cheese, and preserved fruits, and the other with biscuits and confits made by Toña for the occasion. And I was in charge of a box with two bottles of wine and twelve bottles of Pilsner. We followed Vengoechea, who was walking arm in arm with the Dutchman, to the chosen site, and Wen, wielding his camera as if he were a professional photographer, took pictures of the group and the scenery.

"I didn't think to bring the portable gramophone," I said.

"It's better this way," Esmeralda responded. "We will listen to Mother Nature's music."

The place chosen by Juanma, under the shade of a leafy willow, was ideal. We spread on the grass a linen tablecloth that perfectly complemented La Gallego's skirt, and made ourselves comfortable. It seemed that the walk had made us hungry, for we devoured the food in no time. The Dutchman said that our cheeses couldn't compare to those from Volendam, his native town, but it didn't stop him from using his powerful jaw muscles, which Vengoechea stared at droolingly, to finish all of them off.

Once our bellies were full, we stretched out in the sun like six lizards, doing nothing and talking of the earthquakes that had been recorded a week before in Nariño. Then, suddenly, Juanma invited the minister's lover to go with him to see the ancient fossils on some rocks a half an hour's walk from there, and he asked in an expressionless voice if anyone else wanted to accompany them on their paleontological expedition. All of us quickly declined his offer (the previous night he had warned us that he would shoot with his Colt pistol anyone that showed the slightest interest in those prehistoric trace remains), so we watched him go, a beatific smile on his face, almost levitating, as he anchored himself to one of the colossal European's arms.

"Can you imagine that great hulk," Wen mused, tickling my ear with a blade of grass, "wearing just a fig leaf and a pair of clogs!"

Esmeralda made a face as if she were envisioning it to the last detail, and asked: "What size clogs, do you suppose?"

"I would guess extra extra large," I said.

Poncho Zárate let out a deep sigh as his only comment.

An agreeable breeze passed through the willow's foliage. A flock of cranes flew above us and landed on the river to cool off and drink from the current. Unaware of our presence, the birds screeched, flapped their wings, and searched for insects by digging in between the river stones with their long beaks. I thought of how delicious they would be if Toña got to roast them. And without saying a word, I stood up, took the camera, and photographed the lovely scene.

"Has anyone heard anything about Alano C. Dunn?" Esmeralda inquired in a weary voice.

"Who is he?" Wen asked.

"A Jamaican," I answered.

"Oh," he added disdainfully, turning over so that the sun wouldn't burn his face. "And why is he of interest?"

Zárate offered an explanatory summary. A group of dangerous criminals had been let out of their dungeon with the intent of having them repair a wall in the gardens of the Panóptico. As if mocking the guards, Dunn, one of the more bloodthirsty of the criminals, had inexplicably disappeared in the plain light of day. It was thought that the fugitive had leaped over the wall like a panther, landing right on Sixth Avenue and disappearing into the crowd of passersby.

"It's a big story," Esmeralda assured us. "The police are still looking for him, but to no avail."

"If I was the police," Wen said, "and they put me in charge of such a mission, I would go crazy." He took out from who knows where a little jar of cream, opened it, and smeared his nose to prevent it from peeling. "To me, all black people look the same. The same thing with Asians." He thought about this for a moment and then continued. "I wonder if we all look the same to them?"

I thought of how it would be very difficult to confuse the Dutchman with Poncho Zárate, but I chose not to share my thoughts.

La Gallego suggested that perhaps there was some black magic involved in Dunn's escape. She had heard that those who practiced voodoo were capable of unimaginable feats, like chewing glass without the gums bleeding, for example, or sticking pins under their nails, or breathing underwater.

"The papers just publish that in order to sell more copies," Poncho complained, "news of fugitives and of stabbings on the Paseo Bolívar. They have even forbidden me to publish certain things about the escape. . . ." Suddenly, he brought his hand to his mouth, horrified. "Wenceslao! What's wrong with me? How can I have forgotten to tell you?"

Wen covered his face with a corner of the tablecloth.

"No! No, it can't be," Wen uttered. "Vicentini was whipped again?"

But that wasn't it, Zárate assured him, no, and I let out a sigh of relief. Luisito's defeat by decision after ten rounds to the Yankee Johnny Shugrue had almost caused a nervous breakdown in his Colombian devotee. Esmeralda had to cancel a tea at which she was to introduce us to Pedro Nel Gómez, the watercolorist from Antioquia, whose works were being exhibited at the Santa Fe bookstore, and go immediately to the bedside of her despondent friend.

"This has nothing to do with boxing," the journalist said. "This is about La Duse."

Wen gulped, waiting.

"Three days ago, she arrived in New York. It had been eighteen years since her last visit to the city, and she received an extravagant welcome, with marching bands, a police parade, and everything. The first thing she did when she set foot in the United States, as is her custom, was to publish an ad in the *New York Times* letting journalists know that she would not grant interviews and begging them to respect her silence. She opens in a week, in a black-tie premiere of Ibsen's *Lady of the Sea* at the Metropolitan Opera House."

My lover was frozen. Not one muscle in his face, usually so expressive, moved while Poncho Zárate finished his report.

"She will also be in Boston, Baltimore, Philadelphia, and Washington. The tour will end in the last days of December in Chicago. Isn't it fantastic?"

"Yes," Wen whispered, dazed. "It is."

"When she performed in London and Vienna some months ago, it was rumored that an impresario had wanted to sign her up to tour Gringolandia," Poncho recalled. "But no one thought it was possible. . . ."

"It was said that those productions were going to be her swan song, her farewell to the stage," Wen said in a measured voice. "But like a true phoenix, La Signora has risen from her ashes one more time."

"We'll see how it goes for her," the journalist offered, "those *tournées* are always so exhausting and you know how delicate her health is."

"How old is that woman?" Esmeralda blurted out, fanning herself with her hat. "Once, when I was passing through Milan, someone who fancied me invited me to see an opening of I don't remember what play by D'Annunzio. One where she was missing an arm."

"*La Gioconda*," Wen said.

"Yes, that one. But I was feeling so exhausted, I couldn't bother to go. Afterwards, I heard that it had been a complete fiasco. She must be very old. I thought that she had retired a long time ago."

"Bernhardt performed till she was eighty," I pointed out. "They couldn't get her off the stage even after they cut off her leg! She was so audacious that, lame as she was, she took on the role of *The Lady of the Camellias*. Compared to her, La Duse is a baby."

"She is sixty-six years old," her number one fan interjected. "She has never lied about her age. Never hidden her flaws with makeup. Never even dyed her hair. She is not an actress, she is a goddess."

After a while, the explorers returned. Vengoechea was still floating on air, and by the expression on his face and the way he hummed softly to himself, we assumed that they had found not just fossils but the entire skeleton of a mammoth. The Dutchman sat by Esmeralda, presented her with a bunch of daisies that he had picked on the way, and started to search all the baskets for more food. Amazingly, he found some crackers that had survived our onslaught.

Juanma remained standing, fluttering from here to there in ecstasy, till he glanced at his watch and realized that it was time to put an end to the picnic.

"If we want to get on the four o'clock," he said, gathering up the blanket, "we have to leave for the station now."

And then, a splendid black bull unexpectedly appeared a short distance from us. We had no idea where the beast had come from, or if it had just appeared out of thin air, as if by magic. It had pointy horns and a small white mark in the shape of a cross on its snout.

"*Olé,*" Vengoechea shouted out and joyfully planted himself in front of the animal, waving the blanket. Whatever happened between him and the giant Dutchman on their excursion we were not quite sure, but it was rather clear that our friend was drunk, and not necessarily from drinking too much. Wen, Zárate, and I tried to stop him from making the young bull angry, but he shoved us away.

"Charge, my little bull, charge," he squealed euphorically, wrapping himself in the blanket.

Fortunately, the animal was content just to look at him out of the corner of its eye as it continued grazing disinterestedly.

"I say *olé,* damn it," Juanma screamed, working himself into a frenzy. "You fucking *maricón* bull! You lump! Why are you ignoring me?"

It was then that Esmeralda Gallego lost her patience. She handed back the daisies to the Dutchman, leapt on the frustrated matador, and took away the blanket. Then she herself stepped in front of the bull and, defiantly fixing her eyes on him, adopted a pose that would have been the envy of any bullfighter. What happened then was fantastic: as if an invisible hand had stuffed some very hot chili peppers up its ass, the beast let out a frightening bellow, lowered its brow, and charged wildly at us.

We all ran for protection behind the willow, all but La Gallego, who began a series of passes worthy of the praise and cheer of the crowds at the bullring in La Magdalena.

In her hands, the blankets flowed as gracefully as a red bullfighting cape. As we watched, astounded, Esmeralda performed all kinds of dangerous passes, teasing the bull's horns with iron mettle. Each time, we would howl and close our eyes, sure that this time the bull would maul her, but she would find a way to have it rush by her like a runaway train, barely grazing her with its haunches. There was no doubt about it. She was possessed: some spirit, perhaps a matador who could not stand to be away from the ring, had snuck into her body and taken over her actions.

"Olé," the Dutchman murmured, at first meekly, but then at the top of his lungs, and with growing enthusiasm, the rest of us began to cheer on Esmeralda's feats with a chorus of *olé*s. It was a tremendous display of the art, even more daring than before, executed with arrogance and scorn. If it had been a ring, her performance would have earned her both of the bull's ears as well as its tail. I had not seen anything so extraordinary, when it came to bullfighting, since 1908, when my uncles Melitón and Manolo had taken me to see La Sorianita, the Spanish woman who fought a bull on a bicycle. Majestic and very erect, her weight resting on one hip, her turns slow and precise, La Gallego forced the bull to run from here to there till, frothing at the mouth and exhausted, it fell at her feet.

"Good boy," Esmeralda said, caressing its snout with the tip of her shoe. Then she took a long breath, folded the blanket, and giving not the slightest significance to what had just happened, asked us if we were going to help at all with the cleaning up.

Still speechless, we placed bottles, plates, and glasses in the baskets and headed for El Algorrobo, where there was a car ready to take us to the station. It was a shame that I did not think to take pictures of the event.

Our train car was full of passengers on the way back. Without discussing it, we decided not to mention the bullfight. The Dutchman, seated next to La Gallego, spoke of dikes and windmills for the entire ride. Zárate napped, and Juanma Vengoechea, Wen, and I looked out silently at the pastures that paraded, one after the other, past the train's windows. The melancholy and subtle landscape of these grasslands always causes me to become a bit anxious.

When we finally arrived at the apartment, Wen grabbed me by the shoulders. I thought that he was going to talk about our bullfighter, but no.

"Sit down," he said, very serious.

"What?"

"I have made up my mind and you can't say no."

"Huh? What are you talking about?"

"We're going to New York. You and I. To see her, to see La Duse."

"Oh, you scared me," I said, letting out a long breath. "That's not a problem. Of course, if you want, we'll go."

He was euphoric and forced me to dance with him from room to room.

"We're going to New York!" he sang. "We're going to New York!" After a few turns we landed on the bed. "It's our last chance to see her perform," he said, on top of me. "We shouldn't miss it for the world. And . . ." His eyes shone. "I've been thinking, if we put our minds to it, perhaps we can achieve what no one else has: an interview with her."

"Don't you hate journalists? Haven't you told me that they are worse than the plague?"

"If Baal and Wenceslao Hoyos put their measureless charms to work, she won't be able to resist," he answered elatedly. "You'll ask the questions and I'll write down the answers. Imagine. Newspapers and magazines from all over the world will publish it." He brought his lips to mine and kissed me over and over. "Tomorrow I will book a spot on the first ship that sails."

"Tomorrow is Sunday," I said sarcastically, "and in case you've forgotten, you have agreed to accompany your mother and grandfather to five o'clock Mass."

"Then I'll do it Monday, early as I can."

"Fine," I said, trying to calm him down, not imagining in the slightest that the following day, at dawn, an earthquake would rock Bogotá, and along with the shanties of the poor and the coffered ceilings of churches, Wen's plans would come crashing down.

There are exceptions, but in general, actors are animals. Who would know better than I, who from childhood have put up with their braying and roaring without once getting used to it? Though I'll say this; they are shameless but hardy. In the end, that is the one quality that a performer needs, the ability to hang on, to withstand all the blows and swings of fortune, to survive, even when exhausted. I learned it from my parents. I knew it from the day I was born. Now, if you add to that a little bit of beauty and a little bit of luck, perhaps you can make a career of it.

We have a reputation for being dimwitted, crude, and stupid. And it is not, fair to say, a reputation that we don't deserve. We are a band of mediocre simulators, clowns who ape others, trying in vain to copy their gestures, their manner of speaking, the way they react to things. Only through great effort and a lot of pain and suffering do we actors ever manage to ennoble ourselves, to transcend that first stage and become true creators, or even aspire to that state.

I try to explain it to other actors. I struggle to make them understand, but there are few who do. I tell them: "Imagine that above your head there is a ring of iron, and a huge, powerful magnet pulls you upwards, trying to trap you, to distance you from the truth. It is against this force that you must resist and keep your feet on the ground." To float is to lie. If you float, you will never find the gift, the gift is in the roots, not in the branches.

I ask them also to forget about the public, not to be distracted by their stares, and never, never to aim to please them. The public should be respected but not feared. We don't work for them. Yes, they pay, but only to be witnesses to our endeavors. I beg my actors not to offer the audience the whole loaf of bread; just a bun is sufficient. Even a few crumbs are enough to remind one of the smell of bread when it comes out of the oven, to savor it, to feel its texture. *Less is more. The essence and not the appearance of the thing.*

Sometimes I think that none of them understands me, that they do as I say reluctantly, only to please me, and it makes me angry. Other times I am overcome with a great sadness. Should I just give in? Oh, if I didn't need them, if I could perform, in my own manner, all the roles in a play: men, women, young and old. If they weren't so indispensable!

I could act without saying a single word, as I proved when I tried my luck in the moving pictures; I could even act with my eyes wrapped in a bandage, forfeiting the magnificent power of a glance. What I could not do is give up my hands. The hands speak, sing, cry, and the fingers are their tongues. Remember what Rilke wrote about Rodin's hands? "Hands whose fingers seem to scream out of the five mouths of an infernal Cerberus. Hands that walk, sleep, hands that give rise to their desires, feelings, whims."

I met Rilke in Venice, one or two summers before the war. Years before, he had dedicated a work to me, titled *The White Princess*, in the hope that I would stage it. For three weeks we saw each other daily, sometimes alone, sometimes with Prince Thurn und Taxis who was also in town. We talked about art, about poetry, about love, about death. It had been two years since I had been on stage, and he wanted very much for me to resume my career. He told me about his play and I asked him to have it translated into Italian. But he didn't do it. I think that since it was a work from his youth it no longer interested him. I don't remember him saying anything about my hands. Perhaps he didn't find them beautiful. Even then, they were already the hands of an older woman. Rilke knew how to be discreet. Whatever he thought about my hands, he kept it to himself. He was a devoted and attentive friend. I never saw him again. It would have been lovely to stage *The White Princess*. I wonder what became of Rilke? Or of Maeterlinck? I was able to perform one of his works, *Monna Vanna*, but not very successfully. Perhaps no one understood, or maybe it wasn't much of anything in the first place. What was I talking about? Oh yes, the language of the hands. I digress.

In the hands there lies, if not the whole secret, at least a good part of it. Wherever they go, the eyes follow them. With them you can lead an audience anywhere. The word, the living word, the lived word, when authentic, is a sword; the movement of the hands is another sort of weapon, more subtle, more powerful.

Acting . . . What is it? When I was thirty, I thought I knew. But not now. No longer. I don't know. I have never known. That question has kept me awake many a night, but now I try not to think about it. What I do know, and I think very well, is what acting is not. It is not faking it. It is not imitation. It is not making those who watch you laugh or cry. It is not showing off like a trained animal so that they may see your gorgeous figure, your flowing robes, or hear your beautiful and compelling voice.

Sometimes I think that the craft of acting should be thought of as a liquid. To become water. Wine. Quicksilver. To adapt yourself to the shape of the vessel that holds you, to empty yourself inside the character, fill it up completely, take it over. The character is a cavity you have to spill yourself into. You stop being who you are to inhabit the character.

It is anguish trying to put this into words, trying to explain it to others. Some things are difficult to teach. The emotions, for instance, sorrow, joy. "Signora Duse, prego, teach me how to be afraid." "Teach me how to hate." "Adesso! Subito!" No, no, it is absurd. It can't be done that way. So I say it to them again and again: "Lend your bodies, all your senses, your ideas, your energies, to the character. Feed her with your disappointment and your joys, those that you carry with you and those that you remember from other times. It is the only way to approach the truth, the only way that you will see the light, at first far away, and then closer and closer, until finally you're able to make progress toward it, stumbling, falling, getting up again."

I am not saying that the work of the actor is all about the emotions, that everything can be reduced to feelings. I think that it is also essential to use the intellect. Perhaps that is why Conrad was so horrified by the theater and called it a place of sacrilege. Because of the lack of intellect displayed on the stage.

It was years before I understood why I was so unfulfilled. At first, I thought that my deepest desire was to be a great actress. When they assured me that I had succeeded, I knew that it was not what I had wanted. It was nothing. Actresses explicate their characters. They put on their costumes and smear on their faces. They are parrots who repeat, sometimes skillfully, sometimes not, the words of the playwright. What I wanted, in truth, was to be an artist. More like a painter, or a composer, or a poet than an interpreter.

Pretentious? Perhaps.

Ambitious? No doubt.

"Y ou don't feel like coming?" he whispered. I responded with a grunt and disappeared under the blankets.

On the anniversary of his grandmother's death, Wen always went with Doña Herminia to the first Mass at the Church of San Diego. His mother never forgot the date and always insisted on taking his grandfather with them, a man who just a few years before was an energetic, domineering individual, whose favorite pastime was giving orders, but who recently had degenerated into a decrepit old man who merited not as much as a glance from the rest of the family and the servants. Bringing the old man to the house of worship was purely a symbolic gesture, for the poor wretch couldn't even remember his name, much less his late wife's.

"I'll have lunch at home and come pick you up to go to Alvarito Certaín's at five o'clock," he said as farewell. He gently shut the bedroom door and I fell asleep again.

I forget what I was dreaming about when violent tremors forced me to sit up. My servant burst into the bedroom with her hair standing on end.

"Earthquake!" she screamed in terror. Yes, the earth was troubling. The city seemed like a carpet someone was shaking. I jumped out of bed and for a second I didn't know what to do. Should we stay inside the apartment, waiting for the danger to pass but risking the fact that the whole building might collapse on top of us, or should we go outside and come what may? Toña, with her hands pressed to her chest, awaited my instructions.

A new round of tremors forced me to choose.

"Let's go outside," I said, and we ran out to the street. Many others from the nearby houses were already there, in their pajamas, carrying children or pets in their arms. The church bells pealed madly, children cried, not knowing the cause of all the uproar, and animals barked or meowed trying to warn their owners about the new tremors to come. A circle of women began to recite a Hail Mary, and the Chocoana immediately joined them. Someone recalled the old prophecy of Father Margallo about the destruction of Santa Fe de Bogotá, and, as if to add fuel to the fire, recited the ominous couplet at the top of his lungs:

On August thirty-one, in a year I will not say
Earthquakes, one by one, will destroy Santa Fe.

Of course, to bring up the famous prophecy by the priest at that moment was absolute nonsense, for it was October and he had predicted that the disaster would take place on the last day of August. But to appeal to people's common sense would have been useless.

Meanwhile ignoring all the danger, the madwoman Margarita crossed the street, sleepy-eyed and screaming without end—as she had done for the last twenty years or so—her cheers for the Liberal Party and her vituperations against the Conservatives. Accustomed to her delirious and almost ubiquitous presence, we ignored her.

Although it seemed that the earthquake had ended, no one dared return to their houses for fear that the worst was yet to come. It was then that I asked myself about where and how Wen might be? Had the quake surprised him at Mass? I didn't have the slightest idea what time it was. I looked around to see if anybody was wearing a watch, and on seeing so many distinguished folk letting themselves be seen in the middle of the street in their pajamas, undershirts, drawers, and night robes, I couldn't help but smile. It seemed we were living in the tropics.

After a while, realizing that the aftershocks had stopped, people got up their nerve to return to their homes. Toña and I began to take inventory of what had been destroyed. Fortunately, the damage inside the apartment wasn't extensive: some pieces of china and a pair of bibelots were smashed to pieces. I tried to phone La Generala to see how things were at the house, but the operator did not respond. I had a cup of coffee, got dressed as fast as I could, and, without shaving, took to the streets again on my bicycle. First, I headed toward La Candelaria to see my family. After confirming that everyone was all right, I continued my rounds. On the way, a beggar was urging passersby to give him more substantial change.

"What do you want so many coins for if the world is coming to an end?" he reasoned loudly.

At the moment I arrived at the Hoyos' residency, Wen and a chauffer, aided by Doña Herminia, were trying to maneuver the stiff body of the grandfather out of the car. I threw down my bicycle and rushed to their aid.

"What happened?" I asked.

"I'll tell you later," Wen said, panting, and then barked an order at his mother. "Twist his leg this way."

At last we were able to get the corpse of the patriarch out of the car and into the house. When we got the body to the bed, the lady, who until then had shown an admirable equanimity, fell into a fit of crying and screaming. The servants were needed to calm her down and convince her to go to her own room. Luckily, the phone was working and we were able to contact the family physician, who suggested that we give my mother-in-law a teaspoon of barbital diluted in a cup of tea and promised to return as soon as all the other urgent petitions allowed him.

After all the commotion passed, and Señora Hoyos was sleeping under the influence of the drug, Wen and I were able to sit down and talk. While we drank hot chocolate and snacked on cheese along with crunchy yucca buns, he told me what had happened at the church.

That Sunday, the Eucharist began as usual, without the slightest indication of what was to come. Despite the fact that it was so early, the chapel's pews were rather full, mostly with early-morning centenarians. Wen held his grandfather on one side and Doña Herminia supported him on the other. The old man, who rarely left his house, wasn't exactly sure where he was and had to be told more than once to be quiet, for he complained about the unbearable cold and called out loudly for someone to bring him a poncho, to the chagrin of his family.

When it came time for Communion, both of them helped him to his feet and almost had to drag him to the altar, where the chaplain Rafael Almansa, a scrawny Franciscan with gray hair and a threadbare blue habit, blessed him with the sign of the cross. Doña Herminia tried to open her father's mouth by force, for he was determined to keep it shut. With Wen's help, she was able to convince him, and he stuck out his long, dirty tongue. And at the moment that the friar was placing the Host on it, the earth shook.

The vaulted ceiling came tumbling down, as did some of the bas-reliefs and cornices, making the faithful howl with panic; they abandoned their pews and fled in packs, following the altar boy. The floor undulated like a raft in a furious sea, and the caryatids and Solomonic pillars ornamented with vines and festoons swayed dangerously. The polychrome high-reliefs of St. Luis of Tolosa, St. Buenaventura, St. Bernardino of Sena, and St. Anthony of Padua shuddered as if the saints wanted to peel themselves from the altar and flee as well. The statues moved from north to south in their niches, performing bizarre genuflections. The statue of St. Victorino also swung its hips, as if it were asking the Virgin to dance a *bambuco* with him. The cross at the top of the main nave came off, fell from on high and narrowly missed crushing Father Almansa to pieces. And just to make the scene a little bit more Dantesque, the church's organ, each of whose pipes is painted with a golden mask, let out harmonious bellows.

"Help! Help!" Señora Hoyos cried out, clinging to her father. But who was going to risk his life to save such an old crock? Worshippers walked among clouds of dust, and like extras in an absurd ballet, tried to dodge the pieces that fell loudly from the ceiling as they pushed and climbed over each other, caught up in the awful chaos, trying to get out of the church and into Real Street.

"Don't panic," said the venerable Almansa, trying to get one of the faithful, who was screeching hysterically, out from under the pentagonal pulpit. "There is no use in despairing."

Wen was able to throw his grandfather over his shoulder and, followed by Doña Herminia, open a path through all the turbulence toward the door. To make matters worse, the old man, who had choked on the Host, was coughing violently and crying out for a glass of water.

When they reached the small plaza in front of the church, the old relic went into convulsions. He spewed out, along with some bile, the piece of the body of Christ given to him during the sacrament, convulsed in a death throe and was finished right there in the midst of the scurrying crowd. Although Father Almansa made it to them as quickly as his arthritic legs and long robes allowed him, he was not able to administer the last rites.

"It took a miracle of God and all the saints to hail down a car to bring us here in that pandemonium," Wen concluded. "What a nightmare!"

What he did not yet know, poor thing, was that the horrible ordeal was just beginning. At one o'clock, after they had had the deceased bathed, perfumed, and in uniform, his many medals pinned to his lapel, another earthquake, more powerful than the one that morning, made the city go mad anew.

We all fled the house, abandoning the corpse, and met up on the street. The ground hopped under our feet, and a nun assured us, crossing herself, that this was divine justice for so many sins. But soon the earth quieted down and we were able to go back inside.

The church bells rang at odd hours the whole day; and five tremors in all shook the capital before it was over. Many were afraid that it would be a repeat of the tragedy of 1917, when an earthquake knocked down the church of Guadalupe and left a dozen dead. But, fortunately, no important structure collapsed, and no one had to be mourned, aside from Doña Herminia's father and a drunkard who committed suicide with a bullet to the temple after the third tremor. Among the masses, it was said that the moon would soon appear in the sky with a tail of fire, transformed into a horrific comet that would crush the earth to pieces, but those who believed this were to be disappointed.

The following morning, the newspaper reported that similar quakes had rocked Medellín, Cali, Cúcuta, and Líbano. Tragedy struck two towns, Gachalá and Medina, which were completely destroyed. Many families from Bogotá decided to leave the city and escape to the country, where they would be safe in the event of another earthquake.

They packed up their belongings in carriages and automobiles and headed out for Tunjuelo, Usaquén, and other such places.

Worried about his loved ones, for in Chiquinquirá there was talk of horrible destruction and many dead, Wen's father left the butler in charge of the hacienda and raced to the capital. When he reached his mansion after a few hours travel, he found his father-in-law laid out beside four candles and his wife distraught.

Half of Bogotá attended the wake. Needless to say, it was a major event that brought together countless characters, headed by the very president of the republic and the mayor, Don Ernesto Sanz de Santamaría. La Generala and the ugly sisters were also there, obviously. My mother grabbed a seat next to Señora Hoyos and made it her task to console her all morning long. The wake transpired with all the customary weeping, hugs, coffees, and chocolates. The ladies then began to gossip about their own matters and the gentlemen gathered in the smoking room and discussed politics, the results at the horse track, and, of course, the notorious robbery at the Bauer jewelry store. Somebody brought up the story that in the middle of the whole disaster, a shameless heretic, of which there were always plenty to go around, had broken into an urn at the Church of San Diego and stolen the tibia bone of the pope and martyr St. Celestino. According to some wicked tongues, after a fruitless search for the relic, aided by parishioners, Father Almansa had ordered a sacristan to clandestinely go to the cemetery and bring back whatever bone he could find to replace the tibia.

"Do you know that my grandfather never touched anyone for fear that he would be infected by some disease?" Wen said in a lowered voice when we went out to the courtyard to get some air. "When I was a child, he never even passed his hands through my hair. I've always wondered how he managed to conceive my mother. Does it smell?"

"No. Smell of what?"

"Death. It's an unmistakable odor, both cloying and tart. As human beings age, they begin to secrete it. And as the years pass, it becomes more and more pronounced, till it is impossible to cover up."

He took out a handkerchief and blew his nose, and suddenly he seemed so adorable that I could not resist the impulse to hug him and plant a kiss on him, taking advantage of the semidarkness and jasmine leaves that shielded us from view. I don't know by what strange miracle Wen was given the gift of aristocratizing everything he does, even blowing his nose. I wouldn't know how to live without him by my side.

We needed umbrellas for the burial. It was drizzling and freezing at the Cementerio Central. We looked like a bunch of well-dressed ravens flitting over the graves. A friend of the deceased, also very old and incoherent, what you might call an illustrious mummy, was in charge of the eulogy. Overcome by violent coughing fits, he delivered a speech full of praise for Wen's grandfather and his venerable lineage. Some of us were afraid that he would drop dead before he was finished and that we would have to go from this burial to another wake. A priest then muttered a short prayer, and, crippled by the cold, finished the ceremony as quickly as he could.

After leaving her father's mortal remains in the tomb, Doña Herminia began to search her storage trunk for mourning clothes for herself, her son, and her husband. Deciding that there weren't enough, she summoned a tailor and designer to show them samples of cloth and to measure all three of them. They would keep a strict mourning for their irreplaceable loss, six months for the husband and son, and an entire year for her. And in the same manner, in keeping with tradition, she began nine nights of prayer for the soul of the departed. But she was not able to complete her novena. On the seventh night, in the middle of an Our Father, she passed out, suffering from fevers that kept her bedridden for three days. In her delirium, she blamed herself for having caused her father's death, forcing him to attend Mass that tragic morning. She only settled down and agreed to have a few spoonfuls of chicken soup when her son sat by her bed and held her hand and spoke to her affectionately.

Little by little, with the amazing abilities cities have for forgetting massacres and national disasters, the shock of the earthquake was relegated to the dustbin of memory. Those who fled to the country to feel safer, returned to their houses in the city and resumed their day-to-day routines.

Doña Herminia recovered from the fevers and abandoned her bed, but she was left thin, haggard, and her skin the worrisome shade of old parchment paper. She fell under a spell of profound sorrow and despondency and did not want to receive the many friends who visited her to inquire about her condition. Since the mere thought of return-ing to the Church of San Diego gave her dizzy spells and severe mi-graines, Father Almansa had to come to the house for her confession. She cried for any reason, and though the cook prepared her favorite dishes with great care, she left the meals untouched, distractedly pushing the food around with her fork. Her most trusted servant em-barrassedly revealed to Wen that in the morning she had to remind her mistress, who had always been a paragon of cleanliness, to per-form her ablutions.

Dr. Hoyos urged his wife to go to their hacienda to relax for a few weeks, convinced that the clean air and morning horse rides (in her youth, it was well known, the señora had been a daring horsewoman) would help in her recovery. The family doctor agreed that a period of time away from Bogotá, enjoying the beautiful scenery and in the healthy company of good rustic people, would help the convalescent regain her will and desire to live, imparting more benefits than any medicine he could prescribe. Moreover, she could pray to the Virgin of Chiquinquirá, who with her customary generosity would certainly grant the señora a quick recovery.

After so much needling, the señora agreed to travel to the family estate, as long as Wenceslao, the light of her life, the person that she loved most in this world, would come with her.

Although he did not talk about it much, Wen had not abandoned his plans to go to the United States and see Eleonora Duse perform. Through the press and details supplied to him by Poncho Zárate, he was up to date on everything about the actress. The night of her debut at the Metropolitan Opera in *The Lady of the Sea,* scalpers had sold tickets for two hundred dollars, and the gringos, mad to see her, snatched them up. It was said that the box office take was an astonish-ing thirty thousand dollars. And thanks to the cursed earthquake and its aftershocks, Wen was not in New York.

He didn't complain about his bad luck, but after five years I knew him well enough to recognize that he was annoyed and waiting impa-tiently for his mother to completely recover before immediately boarding a steamship and crossing the sea. But his duties as a son kept him where he was. Doña Herminia's health was the most important thing. It was impossible for him to leave her weak and disconsolate at a time when she most needed his company and affection. Thus, he could not refuse when she asked him to accompany her to the hacienda. I tried to comfort him by telling him that La Duse's tour would be a long one, and that if we didn't get a chance to see her in New York, we could go to her shows in other cities.

Making the best of the situation, he packed his things, and after reminding me a thousand times to cut out for him any article that appeared in the papers about La Signora, he left for Chiquinquirá with his family. I promised him that I would write dutifully every day, swore not to gaze lasciviously at any man, whether it be Valentino or Vicentini, and assured him that I would come visit him with Esmeralda Gallego.

The saddest day of my life was not one of the many times that I lost a lover. One ends up learning that lovers come and go, and clinging to them doesn't change things, it might even make them more painful. I also learned that although it seems we can't survive good-byes, we not only survive them, but with our astonishing ability to heal, are soon ready for new affairs of the heart.

Perhaps someone might think: the saddest day in an actress's life must have something to do with some tremendous failure on stage. But that wouldn't be right either. I've had plenty of failures throughout my career. It is horrible when an audience is indifferent, or worse, when it boos or catcalls a play you believed in, or a character that you delineated with such care. But oh well, that's the theater! A gamble. A sort of roulette. A Russian roulette, even. Whoever is not willing to risk it, should be doing something else, something more predictable, something less shocking, less startling, less painful.

My most horrible day was not when, during a performance in Verona, I was told of my mother's death, nor the day when we first performed A Doll's House in St. Petersburg, when they informed me of the loss of my father. I loved them both blindly and recklessly, as only a daughter of theater people can love her parents, but ever since I was a girl, I knew that sooner or later they would abandon me, and I began to prepare myself for it early on. Those were terrible days, to be sure, days full of plentiful and salty tears (did you know that the more sorrowful the tears, the saltier they are?), days when memories would come rushing back to make me feel their absence even more, days to remember unfixable moments, things that I might have said or done differently.

On the saddest day of my life I was in Marina di Pisa, a fishing village on the Tuscan coast. It was the day of the death of my firstborn. A little boy. A purply bundle full of wrinkles, *with the face of an old man. Could it have been any other way, after all the suffering as I waited for his birth? I wanted to keep him warm, but there was not an ember of warmth left inside me. I insisted on nourishing him, but perhaps my breast milk was poisoned with rancor. How little time he spent with me, my poor son. Hardly two days. I was so young, so ugly, so stupid. I knew even less than I know now. "Alone, but happy " was my motto, as I had put it plainly to Matilde Serao, with the greatest conviction, thinking that my son's nearness would make me forget his father's betrayal.*

How can I describe the searing grief I felt that day, the feeling of being the victim of such injustice? I perished a thousand times within the space of an hour.

The beastly howls that rose from my throat were held back by my gritted teeth, so that no one would hear them, so that no one would come to separate me from my child, take him from my arms, lock him in a coffin. When I saw that he did not move, did not breathe, that his eyes turned inward, I pressed him to my chest and felt him grow icy, turn into a corpse, into something so foreign, forever mute, forever deaf, blind, and helpless, forever unreachable, a thing that nothing could make alive again, never, nevermore. If I don't make a sound, no one will know, I thought. If I am still and don't cry, they'll never find out. But Matilde found so much silence strange, and she came into my room to see what was wrong. If it wasn't for her, I would have stayed locked in that room for days, rocking in the chair, clinging to my son and not letting go of his decomposing flesh.

Later, at the cemetery, after they had taken him from me and covered him with dirt, I came to understand, shovelful by shovelful, that I would have to learn to live with this grief and that it would never abandon me. And in that sense sorrow has its advantages: from then on I knew that I would never be completely alone. The pain follows you around everywhere, it is always with you, it becomes part of your nature. Sometimes you laugh, you feel buoyant, favored by fortune, you think that you are happy, and perhaps you are. But you don't fool yourself, it is only a reprieve. Grief, hidden from sight, looks on you kindly for the moment.

"And now what, Nennella," Matilde asked after watching me tear off some petals from the flowers that were scattered over the grave and place them in between the pages of my notebook. Matilde, my confidante, my protector, my sometimes hated conscience, my beloved friend. "Now," I said. "Now, we go work." And we took the next train to Turin. When you are the second actress in a company, you don't have the luxury of staying away for too long, for they will forget your face and replace you.

That was the saddest day of my life.

As for the happiest one, it hasn't come yet and I don't think it ever will. That doesn't mean that I haven't had joyous days. The one when I felt the gift for the first time, the magic of becoming another, of forgetting everything and being the character, throwing myself into it and living it with the greatest intensity, that was one of those days. What a revelation! What rapture! And at the same time what a great fear of never again feeling such lightness, such power.

There have also been and are many happy days when, not caring that I was speaking a language that they did not understand, an audience felt what I tried to convey to them, shared in the enchantment of art and the emotions and let me know.

In the same manner, there were also joyous days when I felt loved and understood in the arms of a man. Days when the world seemed to go around a little faster, and with it I, a speck in the universe. The day Enrichetta was married! That simple and discreet wedding caused me unforgettable joy. The same when Halley, my little English boy, my first grandson, was born!

There have been many happy days, but none, I repeat,

that stands out above all the others that is worthy of being classified as the happiest. And I am glad, for I have always, no matter how delicious it proves, distrusted happiness, perhaps because of its ephemeral nature. As opposed to sorrow, which during the course of our long lives we are forced to gobble down in enormous platefuls, happiness was made to be taken in negligible doses, little tiny spoonfuls. Too much happiness is dangerous and can cause irreparable damage. The reason is simple. The human soul, my dear friends, that contraption that Leonardo would have loved to have invented, is made to grieve abundantly, to undergo great sufferings, and to break apart and remake itself time and again, till the end. This is not a merit, it is something intrinsic to its nature. The human soul runs on suffering, sorrow is the fuel that keeps it greased and functioning. And that's as it should be, because when the soul feels joy, it does so in such an intense and furious manner that a simple minute of happiness can feel like a century, and if necessary precautions are not taken, its springs can snap, its secret mechanisms burst from the effect of so much joy. When that happens, the soul collapses, it breaks apart into so many pieces that no one knows how to fit them together again.

One day, in August of 1538, after crossing the mosquito-and serpent-infested jungles of Magdalena, Gonzalo Jiménez de Quesada reached an enormous plain. Happy with the abundance of water and moved by the landscape, which reminded him of his native Granada, he got down from his horse, pulled out a tuft of grass, stabbed the ground three times, and ordered a town to be built on that very spot. His soldiers were quick to obey him and built a dozen straw huts, in memory of the twelve apostles. And so our city was born, founded by someone who, unlike the other barbarous colonists, had a degree in literature.

Since then, Santa Fe de Bogotá lies high on its plateau, the hills of Montserrate and Guadalupe standing guard by its sides, making sure no one bothers her. She sleeps all curled up and dreams of being a great capital so often that she has come to believe her own dreams. But it is just not so. In reality, we live in a dirty and inaccessible village of just two hundred thousand souls. They say, and you don't have to believe me, I am only repeating what I have heard, that two out of every three inhabitants was born here. Río de Janeiro has over a million inhabitants, Buenos Aires almost two. Bogotá, however, unlike its counterparts, refuses to grow. It is as if it can't escape its own lethargy, as if it were afraid of greatness.

I would love to know what goes through the head of a visitor from a civilized nation when he arrives in this town of a thousand hectares. I suppose the first thing that might catch his attention is the enormous number of churches and the arrogance and enthusiasm with which he will be urged to visit all of them in an endless pilgrimage. Begin with a visit to the cathedral, which they say was built on the exact spot where Domingo de las Casas said the first Mass on the day that the city was founded, where you will be spellbound with the statues of the Immaculate and St. Peter and St. Paul high in the façade, their backs to the mountains, and with its Corinthian-style main altar, its choir stalls carved from walnut and mahogany, and its African marble columns sculpted in Paris in the studio of Poussielgue Rusaud. Then go on to La Concepción, the oldest of our churches, and then pass by the Sagrario, Santo Domingo, San Francisco, La Candelaria, Santa Bárbara, El Santuario de la Peña, San Ignacio de Loyola, La Veracruz, La Tercera, Santa Clara, Las Nieves, San Antonio, Las Aguas, San Juan de Dios, Santa Inés, San José, San Agustín, till you come to rest, your feet ruined, in front of the famous image of La Bordadita, a gift from the queen of Spain, now in El Rosario. Are you tired yet? Can't take another step? It doesn't matter; tomorrow we continue our journey, for there are yet many chapels and parishes left to visit. They are everywhere! And all of them with huge noisy bells that toll deafeningly without rhyme or reason, at the slightest pretext: a birth, a death, a wedding.

Sometimes I wonder if the number of churches in a city has anything to do with the number of sins that its inhabitants must repent. If that is the case, then in Bogotá the number of sins per inhabitant must be extremely high, no matter what the propaganda of the Conservative Party (or Catholics, as some prefer to call themselves) says. Or can it be the other way around, that churches exist to exorcise sin and keep it far from their vicinities? In that case, this would be the holiest of capitals.

The second thing someone might notice, whether a foreigner or not, are the unsanitary conditions. Only a sixty-block area has working sewers, so that throughout the rest of the city, there are plenty of pestilent channels, where people put out for all to see, without the slightest shame, their filth. Poor families consider themselves lucky if they have a hole in the ground as a toilet. The majority of people live stacked one atop another in buildings with dozens of rooms, or in rustic shacks with thatched roofs, in dark rooms without windows, a step away from the feces and urine and all other types of crap.

Aqueducts are also conspicuously nonexistent: it is rare for a private residence, and much rarer for a public place, to have running water. In the working-class neighborhoods, long lines form at the public faucets to stock up on the indispensable liquid. Since there are many streets without asphalt or sidewalks, during the rainy season the city becomes a quagmire, a bog that just as easily muddies the hoofs of horses as the espadrilles and jet-black boots of its riders. When the heat comes, clouds of dust form everywhere, as dirt impertinently sneaks in through the nose, looking to rest in the lungs.

It should be said that for those with notable last names—those who prefer to marry their cousins to keep anything foreign at bay and preserve their lineage—that stenchy and unclean capital with its tenements in the barrio of Sans-Facon, its makeshift homes on the shores of the San Francisco River, its prostitutes and street urchins, its lice-infested ponchos and stabbings near Paseo Bolívar does not exist. As if in keeping with the logic of St. Thomas, they do not believe in such a capital because they do not see it, and since they do not wish to know, they simply don't look. That other version of the city is a lie, a fallacious story invented by those in the provinces who envy them and would stop at nothing to discredit them. Why dwell on such backwardness and misery, on the ugly side of things, when there is so much bounty and beauty to extol? The Avenue of the Republic, with its torrent of light streaming from countless lamps suspended over the center of the street on wires hooked to the house façades. The peerless Park of Independence, with its pavilions built for the centenary celebrations, and its pond where ducks swim peacefully around the graceful statue of Rebecca. The parties at the Hotel Granada. Behind us, thankfully, are the days when streetcars were pulled by mules. Now you have to go out on the streets with your eyes peeled, to steer clear of the electric streetcars and the automobiles that fly like arrows in all directions. There are over two hundred cars, sixty motorcycles, and almost nine hundred bicycles. We live in the century of speed. From airplanes to gramophones. Bogotá, provincial? A little village? Prudish? On the contrary. It is a major city. Progressive. The *summum*. And if there is any doubt about it, ask those who arrive from other neighborhoods and other towns, those who admire, dumbstruck, the majesty of the Plaza of Bolívar, the Avenue of Jiménez de Quesada, with its unimaginable width, the posh Echeverry Palace.

I endeavor to become infected by the pretentious crowing all around me, but hard as I try I can't. I watch and I draw my own conclusions. I listen to the irregular beat of the city's heart, which inspires contradictory feelings in me. I am ashamed of it, I despise it, but I also have pity for it, as well as love. Sometimes I think that each day, she, like the men who inhabit her, gulps down great quantities of the impure *aguardiente* sold by gamblers, and that for that reason, she remains stagnant and lethargic, in the throes of a prolonged hangover. Could it be the effects of the cheap booze that hold her back from prosperity and modernization?

So there we are, gazing, much too content, at our own navel, our national heroes twirling the ends of their mustaches, or playing out the endless and tedious quarrel between red and blue infantrymen, the dignified ladies crossing themselves and gossiping about their neighbors. Because you have to remember, in a place so small, everybody knows everything. And, La Generala would add cautiously, from there it spreads. If everyone knew what everybody else was thinking about everything, no one would talk to anyone. If this city insists on continuing to be as smug and insipid, as politically opportunistic and self-absorbed, as stubbornly parochial, one of these days, the entire state of Antioquia, and even the coastal regions, will declare their independence.

Wen laughs at me and says that I am too demanding, that what can you expect of a capital so far from the sea, surrounded by massifs, where culture, science, and progress arrived, year after year, on the back of a mule.

I don't understand the place where I was born and raised. I will never understand it. I have irreconcilable differences with Bogotá. I am attracted to the vibrancy of the primary colors, but in her a dull gray is predominant, from the sky to the clothes we wear, the rich as well as the poor. I am attracted to heat and spontaneity, and here everything is cold, calculated, convenient. I detest our seriousness, our pretensions to elegance, melancholy, and talent. I am annoyed by our little circles of rhymesters, so ridiculously stuck up that they are the laughingstock of the whole country, and by our belief that we are superior, the finest. Superior to whom? Finer than what? Can it be that we really believe we are the Athens of the New World?

"I am tired of Bogotá and all its fashionable types," I said suddenly to Esmeralda Gallego, who had just come from the restroom, after putting a little pinch of powder up her nose, and sat next to me at a table in the Café Windsor. "I would like to have been born somewhere else and been different."

"I'm sick of all of them, too," she said, draping her silk-and-leather coat over a chair. "And where I hate them the most," she said, lowering her voice, "is in bed. They go through life worrying so much about not messing up their hair and about articulating properly without swallowing a single 's,' that, to be honest, it is a feat when they can get an erection. They want to turn everything, even the inconsequential, into a pretext for displaying their exquisiteness and fine judgment. If it was up to them, they would speak in verse, sonnets even."

A waiter served us tea. At the table next to us, two pitiable specimens, dressed in coats, vests, and ties in the strict English style, pontificated in affected voices about literature and politics, stretching the syllables whenever possible. "You sort of want to put them in a cage and exhibit them at the zoo," Wen had said once in a similar situation.

We are surrounded by these fashionable types—*cachacos,* these "perfect citizens" of Bogotá—as well as by would-be *cachacos.* Wherever I look there are one, ten, hundreds of them. All well born, with airs of being great wits, making a great show of their importance and nobility. A true *cachaco* is worldly, traditional, and a bit arrogant. There are young *cachacos* and old *cachacos,* conservatives and liberals, in cassocks and in uniforms, believe it or not, even *cachacos negros.* Of course, *negros* that have been previously refined, like Dr. Robles, who studied at the Colegio del Rosario and, as a lesson to those who don't believe in miracles, ascended to the post of secretary of the treasury in the Parra administration. *Cachacos* are convinced that they are the paragons of civility and grace, the epitome of the Colombian character. Those who come to the city from other places and are able to stock up on the essential doses of honorability, affectation, elegance, and presumptuousness can aspire to greater things, given their proximity to the créme de la créme of their hosts, the *cachacos.*

"And that's who they are, and either they don't know it or they love it. But what about us? Wen, Vengoechea, and I laugh at their customs and we bitch about their ignorance and mindlessness, but although we criticize them and are bent on ridiculing them, although we set ourselves against all their beliefs and norms, we are not any less *cachacos* ourselves. Against our will and disgusted by it, but *cachacos* nonetheless. It's in our blood, a defect, a curse. What the Romans call *fatum*. A ring of fire from which we cannot escape." Esmeralda took tiny sips from her teacup, listening to me with the face of a sphinx. "As an antidote we pretend to be spontaneous and irreverent, but in the end, it is a studied spontaneity and a willful irreverence, both calculated, pure artifice, a replica of carelessness that we put to use with the intent of being, or appearing to be less *cachacos*. But whom are we kidding, for whether we flee to distant lands or we defiantly stay in this dumpy little town, *cachacos* we were born and *cachacos* we will die. That's the way it is, no matter how much it hurts. It's tragic if you think about it."

"Well, let's not exaggerate . . ." Esmeralda comforted me. "It's not that bad. At least on Judgment Day no one will be able to accuse you of not doing everything in your power against your nature." And putting an end to my sermon, which she probably found absurd or too self-important, she changed the subject.

We had come to the Windsor to plan our trip to see Wen. Esmeralda decided that we would take her Fiat to the Hoyos estate, and that she would drive. I warned her that it was a long way to Chiquinquirá. What if something went wrong with the car? Why not bring her chauffeur, Jasón? Who, of course, is a magnificent example of a *cucuteño,* the man from Cúcuta, with a muscular body and cinnamon skin, chatty and impertinent, the opposite of your typical man from the capital. Not paying attention to me, she said that she loved to drive in the country, that in Europe she had gotten used to driving long distances on her own, and that she wasn't worried about mechanical problems, because the car had just had a full checkup. Then she excused herself for having to leave so soon, saying she had to hurry home for she wanted to do a watercolor of the sunset.

Even though she studied painting in Florence and Paris, I have always found Esmeralda's watercolors horrendous. I think that she is more of an artist in the way she lives than in her dwindling forays into the realm of fine arts.

Rich and single, of an unmentionable age somewhere between the epilogue of youth and the prologue of maturity, she does with her life as she wants. Today she is at La Cigarra, the fashionable gathering place, drinking a brandy and chatting about politics, the only woman in a crowd of gentlemen, and tomorrow, if she grows too bored, she will pack and say good-bye to her friends and go to London, or Monte Carlo, or Berlin. An incurable traveler, she has circled the earth a few times and from each journey she returns with antiques and works of art that she never has time to organize and that slowly accumulate in her house in Chapinero, christened "Ali Baba's Cave" by Wen.

Her biography, should someone be inspired to write it, would be full of startling episodes. In some, she would appear sophomoric and pedantic; in most, unwilling to be tied down and an anarchist. High society, which cannot and does not want to ignore her, settles with classifying her as a tad eccentric, and they tolerate her, blaming her sometimes improper behavior on her long stays in Europe and on her vocation as a painter. But in the beginning, Esmeralda Gallego's life was not that much different from that of any other señorita in the capital. She came into the world in the bosom of a wealthy family, and when she was of age entered the Perpetuo Socorro School, where the kind sisters taught her how to pray, speak French, conduct herself at the table, and embroider. Convinced that their little Esmeralda was a veritable gem whom it would be worthwhile to polish in order to find her a first-class husband, the Gallego Quesadas sent her to boarding school in the Swiss Alps, from which she returned just before her twentieth birthday. In the interim, General Gallego had been killed in one of the battles of the War of a Thousand Days, zealously defending the Conservative cause, and his wife, suffering from a rare illness that the doctors could not identify, soon joined him. So, with the exception of an aunt who was a nun, Esmeralda was alone in the world and the inheritor of an immense fortune, with no one to supervise her behavior.

After a year of mourning, during which she dedicated herself to secretly reading *Mud Flower* and *Aura or the Violets* and other novels by Vargas Vila, to playing Liszt on the piano, and to receiving visits from her old friends from school, almost all of them married, the butterfly left her chrysalis behind to begin fluttering in the most elite circles, where she soon came to be known as one of the finest eligible young women in the whole country. The nubile Esmeralda surprised priests and the devout with the generosity of her contributions to good causes, and she listened to the amorous acclamations of the army of men who yearned to drag her to the altar, not especially moved by any of them.

Then one day, sick of Bogotá, realizing that another world existed beyond the plateau, she decided to go on a long and leisurely journey. She showed her first streak of rebelliousness when she would not heed the advice of her confessor that she should invite a respectable señora to go with her, a widow or a spinster who could look after her virtue. Ignoring those who called her behavior unacceptable, she went to the Port of Colombia with only one of her servants accompanying her, and there boarded the steamship *Pérou* of the Compagnie Generale Transatlantique. During her stay in Switzerland, she had only been to towns near Gstaad, but this time she traveled to the major cities of half of Europe, going to museums, taking drawing, painting, and sculpture classes in the academies, helping with theater productions and concerts, and transforming herself, through her exotic beauty and her distinction, into someone who was sought after at the soirées.

In Venice, one morning while she was making a charcoal sketch at the Church of the Redentore, she happened to meet up with a compatriot who was as ugly as he was elegantly dressed, and who had rented a floor in the palace of an Italian noble. After several casual rendezvous in Piazza San Marco and the Teatro Fenice, the sophisticated and somewhat eccentric gentleman invited her for a late-morning snack at his house. He was a misogynist, but he was attracted to the vitality and frankness of the young woman. On the afternoon of their get-together, he pulled out a book from a shelf and autographed it to her in exquisite handwriting. It was then that a stunned Esmeralda realized that she was in the presence of the revered José María Vargas

Vila, who had not until then wanted to reveal his identity. The famous radical introduced her to his secretary-lover-adopted son, a tall Venezuelan with a silly face who gave her a sidelong glance, surprised to see anyone in a skirt in the apartment. During many an afternoon afterward, the aesthete, exhausted by the writing of his new work, relaxed in a gondola with the painter, enjoying the marvels of Renaissance architecture and the dexterity with which the svelte *gondolieri* handled their oars, as he became enmeshed in discussions about art, politics, and religion. True to his ideals, Vargas Vila took any chance he could to rant and rave against the tyrants of America, the imperialist Yankees, and the clergy. Infuriated, he told Esmeralda how, when he was a young professor in Colombia, he had been fired from La Infancia Secondary School for daring to reveal that a Jesuit rector masturbated the adolescents in his office, and he spared no insults for the hypocritical and envious Bogotá society, which chose to denigrate and persecute the accuser, turning a blind eye to the priest's wrongdoing. There is no doubt that the brief but intense time that Esmeralda spent with that extravagantly fashionable fellow—with his sharp tongue, measureless devotion to scandal, and absolute conviction of his own genius—had quite a marked influence on our friend's development.

From Venice she went to Madrid. And unexpectedly, one day before she was supposed to return to South America, as she was eating a plate of fava beans at a restaurant in La Gran Vía, she decided to go to the Middle East. Who or what could get in her way? Without giving it a second thought, she made the change of plans. Something unknown was calling her and she could not resist. The splendor of the mosques made her weep; she crossed deserts from oasis to oasis on the back of a camel, and heard the love songs of the *tuaregs*. It was then that she crossed paths with a handsome sheik who almost convinced her to forget about the West and become his third wife.

On returning to her native city a year after leaving, Esmeralda sat down to think in the solitude of her home, and came to the conclusion that since she had been blessed with so much money, the best thing to do was to squander it as she wished and not put it in the hands of the mercenaries who claimed to want to marry her and watch over it. She decided to take painting more seriously and to remain celibate (her virginity, it should be noted, had already been surrendered to the fascinating Arab with the white turban and the eyes of a falcon), and took it upon herself to enjoy life as she saw fit, deaf to her critics, to any advice, and to all rumors. Around that time, she read *The Soul of the Iris* and wrote a letter to the fondly remembered Vargas Vila, long and full of confessions, which was returned unopened.

Esmeralda was the first woman in Bogotá who dared to ride a bicycle. She was at the conference for women's rights led by Amalia Latorre, a pioneer in her field, at a place in the barrio of La Perseverancia and, surrounded by workers, she called attention to herself by the jangling of her gold bracelets every time someone mentioned the innovative concepts of equality and the right to vote. One morning, staring at herself in the mirror, she felt tired of her long hair, and without hesitating took a pair of scissors and cut it off, becoming the standard bearer for women with short hair. It was rumored that during an especially turbulent part of her life she frequented the seediest taverns in the center of town dressed as a man, and spent her nights, drinking moonshine distilled from corncobs, among the low-class clientele, in the hope of seeing a thug nicknamed Ballbuster, with whom she was in love. Moreover, it was told that she gave champagne to her greyhound Cosette and to her Angora cat who, depending on her mood was called either Bellicose or Paca Heels, and that, accompanied by her two pets and her chauffeur Jasón, Esmeralda marched in the first of May parade, calling for benefits for workers on strike and waving flags on Seventh Street. It was also said, but who can be sure whether it is true, since she sometimes admitted it and sometimes denied it, that during her youth, while in Paris, she had been a concubine of Sir Basel Zahareff, the multimillionaire born in Constantinople, from whose mansion she escaped with her arms full of bruises, on the verge of becoming a morphine addict.

She met Wenceslao Hoyos three years before she met me, at a dinner at the Chilean Embassy. She had just returned from Vienna and was the center of attention because of her black lace dress, her outrageous peacock-feathered headdress, and her reputation for the bizarre. The poetess Lydia Bolena introduced them and they danced all night, delighted with each other, thanking the stars for having found one another. They decided to go to the Salon Olympia the following day to a matinee of the new Mary Pickford film. The enormous theater, with a capacity for five thousand, is peculiar in that the poor do not sit in front of the screen, but instead in seating that has been set up behind the screen, so that they are forced to read the subtitles backward. After the movie, La Gallego and Wenceslao, who we should make clear had seen the subtitles in the proper fashion, walked to a nearby park, strolled under the trees, arm in arm, and stopped by the romantic fountain of Pescado.

Fascinated by his reed-like body, his alabaster skin, his intelligence, his youth, and his beauty, Esmeralda confessed that she was very attracted to him and invited him to an intimate dinner at her house in Chapinero. Anxious to make things clear as soon as possible, Wen explained frankly where his amorous interests lay. And to make her feel better, on intuiting that the world was collapsing around her, he assured her that in the theoretical case that his interests shifted, she would be the first woman he would seek out. La Gallego took the blow like a good boxer. She told him that this wasn't the first time that this had happened to her and that it surely would not be the last. She swore that in the future she would treat him chastely, and so, with a few kisses on the cheek, began their friendship.

We left for Chiquinquirá the following day, Esmeralda behind the wheel and I on the passenger side. She wore a cane-colored georgette dress, white stockings, open-toed high heels, a traveling cap with a gauzy veil, and lapis earrings.

On the road, she told me the gossip that had exploded like a barrelful of gunpowder the night before in the capital. The name of the convent of the Servants of the Resignation, famous for the strictness of its cloister and for the devotion with which the sisters would dedicate themselves to their prayers, was on everybody's tongue because of a scandal of passion.

"I am still amazed," she said. "My aunt has been in the convent for over twenty years and nothing like this has ever, ever happened. The poor soul must be distraught."

Two of the sisters were the protagonists of the lamentable tale. Esmeralda knew one of them, a tall, corpulent, chatty nun, who was the porter at the convent and with whom she crossed paths twice a year when, according to the strict rules of the congregation, she was allowed to visit her aunt.

The nun in question had never given anybody any reason to talk about her, except when they referred to her good personality and her willingness to take charge of the most difficult tasks in the cloister. She had an impressive mezzo voice and was one of the stars of the Servants choir. But one fateful day a novitiate arrived from Cali. A young *mulata* with an enormous derriere, she soon took her vows and increased the number of the brides of the Lord. The porter fell in love with her, unable to hold back her overwhelming feelings, and she began to court the newcomer, who had taken the lovely name of Lilibeth of Jesus. Cautious, knowing the danger of having the other sisters discover the true nature of her affections, she began by giving her flowers and coconut sweets, and later slipped perfumed love notes into her pockets. No one knows if it was in a disastrous moment of weakness, or if she was won over by the abounding attention, but the object of her desire gave in. It was only one night (or so Lilibeth said later), but the encounter, which took place in the darkness of the porter's cell, had a disastrous result: the young nun became pregnant.

For nine months, she hid her shame under the expansive habits. The other sisters did not notice her morning sickness or her lack of appetite when they gathered together at meal times. And though her joyful attitude vanished, giving way to a potent melancholy, the shrewd Mother Superior never suspected a thing, blaming it on those changes in mood that often strike young nuns. Then one night, the entire convent awoke, disturbed at hearing the cries of a newborn. The mother superior went from cell to cell till she found Lilibeth lying in her old bed, a healthy child on her lap and the porter by her side, watching them in a trance.

As much as they pushed her to reveal the name of the father of the girl (for so was the gender of the fruit of her loins), Lilibeth de Jesus did not say a word. The nuns were bewildered and furious. They could not imagine where the seed could have come from. No man had crossed the threshold of their cloister in years, with one exception, the priest who came Sunday after Sunday so that they could confess. But he, due to his saintliness and his status as a nonagenarian, was beyond suspicion. Threats of eternal fire or promises of clemency were of no avail, and the young nun, ignoring their pleas and supplications, held her ground. And no one suspected a thing when her eyes furtively searched for those of the porter with a look of both tenderness and reproach.

"My poor aunt," Esmeralda sighed. "She must have been embarrassed to death."

I asked her about the fate of the unhappy nuns and she shrugged. The porter had taken her own life. One afternoon, worried about her absence during their hymn service, her *compañeras* looked for her everywhere, until they found her in the small room where they kept their cleaning supplies, dead. She had hanged herself with a belt attached to a beam, and half her tongue was lolling out. As they struggled with her sizable figure to take her down, someone announced with a shriek that her private parts were not exactly the same as those of the other Servants. The porter was a hermaphrodite!

"Although I saw her more than once, I never imagined such a thing," Esmeralda said. "It's true, she did have a little mustache, but so many women have that problem."

On hearing about the sad event, Lilibeth confessed what the more astute nuns already knew. The porter was the cause of her motherhood. Despairing and full of shame, the *mulata* fled the convent, taking with her the fruit of her sin, and no one knows where she ended up.

"It's like a novel," I said, wondering how much of the weird story La Gallego had invented in her own little head.

"It's all true," she replied, reading my thoughts, her hands on the steering wheel, her eyes fixed directly on the road ahead. "Nothing but the truth, which is superior by far to the imagination of the most fecund novelist."

In the distance we could see the Hoyos estate. Esmeralda stopped the car so that she could smoke a cigarette before our arrival, knowing that the ill señora very much kept to the old traditions and detested women who smoked. And Esmeralda didn't want to cause a ruckus. By its smell I could tell that her cigarette was marijuana and not tobacco. "So are you going to go see Eleonora Duse?" she asked suddenly, letting out a cloud of smoke through her nose like a dragon and passing me the cigarette.

I answered with an uncertain grunt and said the journey depended on Doña Herminia's recovery. "Wen is dreaming about being at those performances, but even more so about getting an interview in which La Duse would open up her heart," I added. "Maybe if his mother gets better, we will have time to catch her in Boston or Philadelphia. Maybe . . . Who knows?"

A surprise awaited us at the hacienda. The señora looked marvelous, having regained her spirits, and was in an excellent mood; it was Wen who'd had an accident, who required care and attention.

"Don't be alarmed, he's out of danger," the señora said to me, noticing how pale I had turned. "According to the doctor, in four or five weeks he will be his old self, as good as new."

She hurriedly led us to the courtyard, where we found Wenceslao in a reclining chair, with his right leg and left arm in a cast. I ran and knelt by him.

"Are you all right?" I asked, clinging to his good forearm.

"Now I am," he nodded, pouting and almost overcome with emotion. "But when that beast threw me, I didn't think I would make it."

Señora Hoyos and La Gallego, who had maintained a discreet distance while we exchanged our first words, decided it was proper to approach us. Esmeralda hugged her friend and asked for details of the mishap.

Two days before, to please his father, Wen had agreed to accompany him to a livestock sale at a nearby ranch. Since they were going to go there on horseback, the señor chose a magnificent-looking sorrel and threw on it his best saddle. They went to the finca, bought some milking cows and a stud bull, stopped for a moment in Chiquinquirá to get a cake for Doña Herminia, and on the way back tragedy struck.

Some vermin that they couldn't quite make out dashed like lightning across their path, startling Wen's horse, which got up on its hind legs and threw the rider off. The landing was the bad part, for he fell onto a mound of rocks and brambles. When they tried to sit him up, the pain made him let out a string of obscenities. Dr. Hoyos sent one of his workers to the ranch to look for the car that they hardly ever used, and in that vehicle brought his son back to Chiquinquirá, where a doctor set his bones back and put a cast on his leg and his arm.

When she saw the state that Wen was in, Doña Herminia completely forgot about her ills and took over the care of her injured son. To everyone's surprise, her appetite and strength returned and she became once again the active and animated woman she had always been.

"At least I can take solace in the fact that my injury helped to make her better," Wen said, during a moment when the señora had gone to the kitchen to ask for some glasses of orange juice. He wanted to laugh but the pain in his ribs stopped him.

"That's what you get for trying to be such a man," I admonished him.

"Poor Wen," Esmeralda interjected. "And will you have to stay in this far-off place for a month, so removed from civilization and those who so care about you?"

What other choice did he have? His mother insisted that he stay there, afraid that a trip to Bogotá would harm him and delay his recovery. But he suspected that the true cause of her unwillingness to let him return lay elsewhere: as long as he remained in the country, she was not forced to share him with me, or with Esmeralda, or with any of his many acquaintances. Wen would once again be all hers, just as he was as a child, when she could control his every move.

We had lunch with the Hoyos and we stayed a few hours by the side of our injured one, consoling him and assuring him that the four depressing weeks would fly by. Before he knew it, he would be back in the capital dancing the fox-trot.

He nodded with a painful expression on his face. I did not make the slightest allusion to La Duse's tour, not wanting to make things worse, for though the matter wasn't mentioned, I knew that a good part of his sadness came from the frustration of not being able to see her. To distract him, we told him the story of the Servants of the Resignation and the adventures of the Belgian minister's lover.

This time, the Dutchman had fallen head over heels for Florerito, an excellent singer who wasted his talents performing in cafés where there was nothing to be gained either artistically or financially. The only thing was that Florerito, as opposed to many other kids in the city, was immune to the giant's seductions. After futilely sending him a box of chocolates, a beautiful pair of English binoculars, and a gold watch on a chain, the behemoth plunged into a terrible crisis, so bad that the minister became so worried about his lover's well-being and afraid that he would die of sorrow that he went himself to Florerito and begged him to accompany them one afternoon for tea, just tea and nothing else, at the newly opened Ritz Hotel. After much pleading, the singer said yes. When he heard the news, the Dutchman came back to life. But on the afternoon of the tea something unexpected happened: Florerito became smitten with the looks and assured manners of Emil Mayerhans, manager of the Ritz and former director of the Grand Hotel Carlton-Tivoli in Lucerne. The whole situation acquired tragic elements, for Mayerhans was a common, run-of-the-mill kind of guy, a stranger to affairs between individuals of the same sex. Since that day, Florerito had taken refuge in the bottle and in singing ballads of unrequited love.

"We should go before it gets dark," La Gallego said, ending our long talk. So that Wen and I could be alone, she stepped away, pretending to admire the jasmines.

"Will you miss me?" Wen asked.

"It's impossible to miss you more than I already do," I answered.

"I'll do my best to convince my mother to let me return soon," he said. "Perhaps when they take off these things," signaling with his chin to the plaster covering his limbs, "we will still have time for our trip."

I told him that I had a bunch of articles to add to his scrapbook. It was likely that Vicentini would face Pal Moran, a boxer who had just defeated John Shugrue in a sensational match. If the Chilean beat Moran, he would be first in line among the contenders who hoped to challenge Benny Leonard for the world championship.

"And about La Signora, what have you heard?" he said, as if he didn't much care about Vicentini's travails. I told him that she was still in New York, performing Tuesdays and Fridays at the very modern Century Theater, also known as the theater of millionaires, and that, according to Zárate, in two weeks she would leave for Boston. I also told him that to safeguard her from illness and spare her unnecessary physical strain, two porters were going to carry La Duse in a sedan chair from the entrance of Grand Central Terminal to the train that would take her to Boston. When I saw my lover's face brighten with joy and amazement, I forced myself to remember all the details that Zárate had provided for me about this peculiar piece of news. Since it was impossible to find a sedan chair in any of the stores in such a modern metropolis as New York, the prop in question had come from the storage facility of the theater producer David Belasco, who was an old admirer of the actress and also the father-in-law of Morris Gest, the impresario who had convinced her to return to the United States. The chair, as they told the press, had been used years before in a production of *Madame Du Barry.* To the surprise of everyone in the company, Eleonora agreed to the unusual mode of transportation throughout the length of her tour to go to and from the train stations and theaters, on the condition that they remove the gold-leafed decorations that no doubt must have delighted Louis XV's favorite mistress, but for Eleonora, who was well known for a sobriety that bordered on the austere, were much too flamboyant.

"The gringos have many flaws, but they recognize a queen when they see one," the injured Wen sighed and demanded more details about the goings-on of his idol. Of the plays she had performed, which had the demanding New Yorkers liked best? *The Dead City, Ghosts, So It Will Be, The Closed Door* . . . ? Or was it *The Lady of the Sea*?

"They have all been successful," I answered. "Although some cretin wrote a letter to the editor complaining that she hadn't used a wig to hide her gray hair."

"It's like casting pearls before swine," Wen murmured, rolling his eyes, and then he demanded, "What else?"

I wracked my brain trying to remember something not to disappoint him.

"The queen of Hollywood!"

"Swanson?" he yelled. "I can't believe that Gloria Swanson went to see her?"

"And she wept like the Magdalene," I confirmed. "After the performance, she was so ecstatic that she demanded to go backstage to relay her feelings in person, but, sadly, she was informed that La Signora was not accepting visitors."

"Here, we don't even get the papers," Wen cried, sprawling on the chair. "This is the very end of the world."

I tried, as much as I could, to make him feel better. Before leaving, he made me solemnly promise that I would not be alone with Alvarito Certaín, that flirt, who no doubt wanted to take advantage of his absence. I swore, with my hand over my heart, that if Certaín ever wanted to see me, I would make up any excuse to avoid him. I didn't think it right to tell him that he had already visited me two days before. Our get-together, though, was disappointing. Much in keeping with his Apollonian looks, Alvarito was a real piece of marble.

Ever since I was a girl, the stars have fascinated me. My father used to tell me that some nights I would sit on his lap, and spend hours watching them. He would point to them and tell me their names, but I could never memorize them.

Once, a gypsy told me that everything is written in the stars: the past, the present, and the future of the world and its people. It frightened me, and frightens me still every time I hear it. How can the stars, so far away, know so much about our lives? Can it be that they govern our behavior? Is our free will a fiction? That we think we choose or do not choose, when in reality our behavior obeys laws that somehow are dictated by the stars and that we follow them without even being aware of it, without a word of protest?

When I was small I loved to hear my mother sing me a certain little song that I have never heard since. Was it a very old rustic melody that only she remembered? Or had she made it up? She would hold me in her arms and rocked me slowly, back and forth, back and forth, singing to me till I fell asleep on her lap.

> Piccola stella,
> dove vai?
> Stellina, stellina,
> viso di bambina,
> occhi di luce.

I also sang it, without much success, to my own daughter. Enrichetta wasn't too interested in the stars. She liked her dolls, her toy sailboats, or her illustrations of storks perched high on the chimneys.

They say that the Greeks could clearly see gods and animals sketched in the pattern of the stars. They must have had a much more vivid imagination than I do. For, try as I might,

I have never seen the Centaur or Orion. Not even the bears. Arrigo once gave me a book that showed all the constellations. Whatever became of that book?

In years past, when I arrived at a city, I would figure out a way to sneak out from the hotel at night, without anyone seeing me, so that I could walk the streets peacefully. Once, alone in New York, I saw a street vendor screaming his head off, trying to get the attention of passersby. I was curious to see what he was selling, so I stopped to find out. He sold stars. That is, he sold the right to see them up close, to feel like you owned them for a moment. Next to him was an enormous telescope that he rented to anyone who wanted to take a look at the firmament. "Five cents a star!" he yelled. It seemed like a good deal, or at least an original idea. But how could he make a living on a cloudy night, when the storm clouds concealed his merchandise? What could he possibly sell?

By his accent, I could tell that he was Italian. I searched my bag for a coin and gave it to him without saying a word. He adjusted the instrument and let me have a look. I closed one eye and with the other one saw the heavens through the metal tube. Oh, yes, there they were, the stars at hand's reach. I asked the name of the bright one to the East, and he laughed when he heard me speak Italian. "É la stella Polare," he said.

The time for which I had paid a quarter was over right away and I complained that it was too short. "And what else do you want for such a paltry sum," he said shamelessly. "If you want to go on looking, then buy a dollar's worth of stars." I asked him angrily if he took me for a fool, and made it clear that I was not rich. It took a lot of sweat to earn each dollar I made. Besides, who said that the stars were his? What right did he have to profit from them? The stars belonged to God and they were up there so that everyone might enjoy them. At that moment a streetcar passed by, on its side a giant advertisement. It said: THE PASSING STAR, ELEONORA DUSE.

I froze. Was I a star? Was that the reason people paid enormous amounts of money to see me? But whatever the case, I was a passing star, while the others had shone for thousands of years, ignorant of the little habits of man, and they would go on shining for thousands and thousands more.

My anger abated, I asked the vendor if he knew an old lullaby that told the story of a little star. He shrugged. His mother, he answered, had twenty-two children and a drunken husband. He didn't remember her having any time to sing, busy as she was most of the day cleaning fish. Even so, I hummed it for him, just to be sure. "No, no," he said sadly, shaking his head. He didn't know it. Then I told him that I had changed my mind. I would buy fifteen minutes of sky, that is, a dollar's worth of stars. But *niente de inganni!* I didn't want a minute or a star less!

Wen returned to Bogotá to be by my side Wednesday afternoon, right before I came to.

It had struck like lightning. I was eating a mango after
I had finished an article for *Mundo al Día,* and suddenly I was bent
over with stomach pains. Barely able to move, I lay down on the bed
and begged Toña to get my mother as soon as possible. The rest happened in the blink of an eye. La Generala took the apartment by storm,
examined the situation and, on seeing the deplorable state I was
in, pale and horizontal, she had me taken to the hospital in her creaky
coupe. As far as she was concerned, automobiles had not yet been invented. The emergency-room doctor thought that I should be oper-
ated on immediately, but the maker of my days shot back that she was
not going to give over the body of her one and only son to any old
surgeon so that he could slice him up at will. She demanded that they
call Dr. Peñarredonda, who went by the earned nickname of Ace of
the Scalpel, and she forced me to endure the stabbing pains in my
guts till the aforementioned showed up, confirmed the diagnosis, and
ordered them to take me to the operating room.

"Have you ever had surgery?" one of the nurses asked me.

I shook my head.

"Are you allergic to ether?" the young woman went on. "Do you
have any reactions to it?"

"I don't know," I was able to say.

"Well, we don't have time to find out," Peñarredonda interrupted,
coming toward us, and on his command, they covered my face with a

rubber mask. "Breathe slowly and deeply," he said, and more dead than alive, I obeyed.

As I breathed, I thought of how ridiculous I must look with that thing on my face. Not more ridiculous of course than the King of France's twin brother, that poor man that they locked up in a dungeon in a horrifying iron mask. Which Louis was it? XIV or XV? Who had designed that frightening contraption? Or was it conceived, on a whim, by the blacksmith who forged it? I am sure that if the French sovereign had consulted with Wenceslao Hoyos, he would have designed for him a most gorgeous mask in the Venetian style, similar to the one that he used last year for the students' carnival, where we met Jorge Garay, who went to the parade dressed as a fawn, so beautiful that we both fell immediately in love. Oh, Wen, Wen. Why aren't you with me now? All it would take is for you to take one of my hands in yours, which are always so warm, and the pain and the fright would vanish, as would these blinding lights, so white and piercing, theater lights, I am on stage, I am part of a company, I am on Broadway, at the Century, I have just said my line in Italian, without looking at the audience or gesturing too much, as La Signora has warned us about in rehearsal, and in a few minutes she will make her entrance, dressed as Santuzza, but no, she's not here, I'm getting worried, I cast a glance sideways at the other actors, but no one knows what is happening. They, too, are perplexed, the performance has stopped, I think that I should improvise but I don't know what, the audience has noticed that something is wrong, they shift in their seats and begin to whisper, and then, yes, finally, *per carita,* La Duse appears, but she has traded in her costume of a Sicilian peasant for a white uniform with a starched cap. What piece is this where she plays a nurse? Did D'Annunzio write it for her? The tragedienne looks at me, moving her hands in front of my eyes, slowly saying good-bye. She laughs gently.

"He is asleep," she announces.

It was a routine operation. The surgeon buried his scalpel in my flesh, sliced it open, took out what he had to take out, and then closed the wound with some horrific metal clips, but I would not know that till later, since the ether knocked me out for several hours. I asked La Generala if I had talked in my sleep, and her only answer was, "Only absurdities." I don't know when it was that Wen came into the room, all I know is that when I opened my eyes and asked the oft-heard "Where am I?," he was there beside me, and his smile dispelled the last blurring shadows that clouded my consciousness.

"Look what the doctor saved for you," my mother said, displaying a jar of formaldehyde, in which floated my appendix. I shut my eyes, horrified, and did not open them again till La Generala left the room with her little gift.

I looked at Wen. The period of convalescence had done him some good.

"Where are your casts?" I asked.

"I left them at the ranch," he said. "I didn't think that they would be in style here."

And then I was lucid again. I remembered everything in an instant: our plans of going to the United States upon his return from the country; the cabin we had reserved through the travel agency on Florián Street, in the modern and comfortable ocean liner from H. Lindemeyer & Co., our last chance—which my unforseen operation had turned into the impossible dream—of seeing La Duse in Chicago, where she would end her unprecedented tour.

"I am so sorry," I blurted, biting my lower lip in disappointment. "Damn this appendix and its timing!"

He tried to calm me down but I shifted away, in pain under the sheets.

"You should go without me," I urged him. "I don't want to be, nor should I be, a hindrance. Who knows how long it will take me to recover?"

"Stop thinking about it, stop thinking about everything," he said sweetly. "And don't even imagine that I would go to Gringolandia without you. Either we both go or no one goes."

"But . . . what about La Duse?"

"We'll see about it tomorrow," he responded philosophically.

I tried to reply, but the arrival of the ugly sisters interrupted our tête-à-tête. They brought a basket of flowers with a penetrating, perfumy odor, and as soon as they arrived, overwhelmed me with their questions, giggles, and comments, so that after a few minutes I had to shut my eyes. The room began to swirl, their faces lost their shape like reflections in a funhouse mirror, their voices turned into unintelligible chatter, and once again I fell asleep.

It was only after a true battle of wills that, when I was released from the hospital, I was able to go to the *garçonnière* and not to my room in La Candelaria, as La Generala insisted.

Drowning in tears, the señora called me ungrateful and proclaimed that from now on she was not to blame for any relapse that I was to suffer due to lack of proper care. I tried to tell her that Toña would look after me and that Wen would let her know if she was needed, but instead of calming down, she became even more upset.

"If you don't let me take care of you now, as I wish to, and as common sense dictates, don't even think about calling me when you are bent over with pain again." Highly offended, she left without saying good-bye.

At the apartment, convalescence began in between telephone calls from my mother, at every half hour, to see if the wounds showed any signs of infection or if any other problem had presented itself. Her infernal hounding would have tried the patience of a saint, but Wenceslao treated her with utmost friendliness, in such a congenial tone that you would have thought he was courting her.

Once a day, in the afternoons, La Generala burst in like a tornado, always accompanied by one of the ugly sisters, and went about her thorough inspections and then left, but not before berating the *Chocoana* for something and leaving a heap of directions for Wen and me to follow.

I lost a little weight, which, according to my friends who came by the apartment to check up on me, only improved my appearance. Since we had been apart for a few weeks, I ached for Wen's presence, but no matter how much I begged he refused to go to bed with me, afraid that he would damage the wound. Though he did concede, after some pleading, to appease my desires by means of some austere and aseptic manipulations. But better that than nothing.

Esmeralda Gallego, who was out of Bogotá during my stay in the hospital, reappeared looking exquisite in a blue suit, gray stockings, leather gloves of the same shade from Sweden, jet-black shoes, a bell-shaped hat, and a satin bag embroidered with sequins. She brought me a box of chocolates that she and Wen proceeded to devour right under my nose, since Dr. Peñarredonda had forbidden me to have any chocolate.

With her customary imprudence, the first thing she did was to bring up the thorny issue that we tried to keep out of every conversation.

"So, you won't be able to see La Duse," she said out of nowhere.

"No," I responded, shooting her a furious glance. "Her last performance will be in fifteen days. Blame it on my appendix, but we won't be able to see her."

"It's not the fault of anybody's appendix," Wen interjected, turning his back to us and looking for his cigarette case. "Why do we waste our time always trying to find something to blame? It is simply fate, which always refuses to be reined in and forced down roads where it does not want to go."

"I told him a thousand times to go by himself," I explained to Esmeralda. "But he never listens to me."

"And I never will, if you don't stop repeating such stupidities," Wen roared, extremely upset. I curled up in bed. He seemed ready to jump on me and grab me by the throat.

We were silent and uneasy for a few minutes, Wen smoking a *matoaka* (I have never understood his affinity for those disgusting cigarettes), Esmeralda and I transfixed watching the ringlets of smoke, so round, so perfect, that came out of his mouth and floated in the air for a moment before dissolving.

"Why don't the three of us go to Egypt, to see Tutankhamen?" La Gallego proposed unexpectedly, a big smile on her face.

I knew that a British archeologist by the last name of Carter had recently discovered in the Valley of the Kings the tomb of that pharaoh of the eighteenth dynasty, who had died before his twentieth birthday; but not that the government in Cairo had decided to leave the mummy in its gold sarcophagus, so that it would not be desecrated by scientists, and to display it to the public.

"They have put a glass lid on the coffin, so that anyone can see the body of Tutankhamen," she told us.

"Like the glass case where the dwarves put Snow White," I pointed out snidely to bait her.

"Yes, more or less," Esmeralda agreed, unshaken. "It seems that

King Tut was divine—and mummified and everything, he is still quite a beauty. Many, many people are traveling to Luxor to see him. Cheer up!" she insisted. "We'll all go together!"

Wen responded, sarcastically, that in case she wasn't aware, 1923 had been a dreadful year for the economy and that one should think twice before throwing away money on such frivolities. I was very surprised to hear him say this. The day before, talking with some of our visitors, he had mentioned that coffee roasted in a Medellín house, to which his father sold beans that he grew in a ranch near Antioquia, was trading at twenty-one and a half cents in New York and going up, and that this past year, national profits from the export of coffee would surpass five million dollars. And now, in an aggressive manner, he was telling the painter that it seemed a waste of time to make a trip to Egypt only to stand for a couple of minutes next to an embalmed corpse. Not intimidated, Esmeralda argued that she did not see any difference between throwing away money to see an Egyptian mummy and applauding an Italian mummy.

I had to step in between them before something drastic happened.

"Enough," I cried out. "Don't forget that I have just had surgery. Do you want the stitches to pop open?"

They both apologized, but the tension remained. Esmeralda exiled herself to a corner of the room and leafed through a copy of *Cronos,* and Wen ignored her and began to trim his nails. Fortunately, Alvarito Certaín and Juan Vengoechea arrived at that moment, and the heated air cooled off. The new conversation centered on the tragedy of the airship *Dixmude* of the French fleet, which was lost the week before on its way to central Africa. It was all a mystery; after flying over Tunis, the zeppelin had disappeared without a trace. Nothing was known about Captain Rémond de Saint-Amand nor about his fifty crew members.

Taking advantage of the fact that the rest of them were distracted trying to figure out the fate of the *Dixmude* and its shipwrecked airmen, Certaín whispered in my ear that some scars excited him tremendously and that he was dying to see mine. He asked me if it was big or small, but I would not answer him.

The thing is, as far as my wound was concerned, I knew very little. Only once, during my stay in the hospital, did I dare glance at it quickly, and it so unnerved me that I promised myself not to look at it again until it had scarred. Toña took care of cleaning it with soapy water and iodine, following the nurses' directions, and Wen, who loved to lift the bandage and peek, gave me encouraging reports on its healing.

That was for me a rather sad Christmas Eve. Only five days after the operation, my body still felt stiff and I moved only when I had to. Thanks to my deplorable state, it was impossible for Wen and me to go shopping together as we had done in other years, to buy gifts for our friends and loved ones. He took it upon himself to buy presents for my parents, my sisters, my uncles, and my cousins. For Esmeralda, who was obsessed with the stars, we got a sophisticated telescope through which she could watch the firmament from her garden in Chapinero. Before leaving for a remote finca in Girardot where she always spent Christmas, La Gallego sent us via her *Cucuteño* chauffer two identical gold tie pins shaped like beetles. The gifts arrived accompanied by a note which reminded us of our promise to attend her New Year's Eve party, and she demanded that I be recovered by then.

Secretly, I sent Toña to Ricardo Núñez's store to buy a pair of black silk pajamas, which I knew Wen would love. He, in turn, gave me a bottle of my favorite cologne and a French edition of the verses of Rimbaud.

On the twenty-fourth, as is prescribed for such a feast day, Wen and I ate fritters and custard. At night, he went to dinner at his parents'. La Generala insisted I do the same, but not to have to deal with her and the rest of the family I told her that I was afraid that one of my stitches would come off and my guts spill out of the opening. That night I stayed at the *garçonnière,* listening to the *Chocoana*'s distant prayers and to carols sung by children on the street.

The shepherds of Bethlehem
Come adore the Child,
And the Virgin and St. Joseph
Receive them with a smile.
Tarahum, tutatarahum
Tarahum, tutataramam,
Tarahum, tutahum, tutatarahum,
Tarahum, tutataramam . . .

Two days after Christmas, the surgeon came to take out the stitches. La Generala insisted on being there, and there was no way to dissuade her. When Peñarredonda took out the staples from my stomach and announced that I could now walk, I was overcome with a terrible fear. Taking all the necessary precautions, I took some trembling steps around the bedroom, leaning on Wen and my mother.

"In less than a month, you will have forgotten all about the operation," the doctor pronounced. "You'll be able to dance and ride a horse, as if nothing had happened."

Three days later, I gathered up my courage and went outside for the first time after my long seclusion. The morning was cold, and Wen and I, dressed in overcoats and beaver-skin hats, walked slowly to the Colombiana Bookstore. We looked through the new releases and, not finding anything that interested us, left.

"How do you feel?" Wen asked, taking me by the arm.

"Fine," I said. "But it's strange. The smallest thing makes me tired."

On the way back home, we ran into Poncho Zárate, who was wearing new glasses with tortoiseshell frames. His pimply face lit up on seeing us.

"I have news," he sang.

"Vicentini or La Duse?" Wen asked concisely.

"Both."

"Join us for a late breakfast," my lover then ordered.

We found a table at the nearest café and ordered coffee and cheese buns.

"Where do I start?" the journalist asked and, being told Luisito, took a deep breath and let everything out. "He is in Valparaíso, waiting for Bernay, who will travel to Chile to fight him. The press in Santiago announced the fight amid great fanfare and is sure that the gringo is due for a loss. That being said, I wouldn't be so sure."

"Neither would I," Wen confessed, lowering his head. "Vicentini is good, but Bernay is not just any other boxer." He was quiet for a few seconds and then, placing his napkin over his knees, asked with a false indifference, "And what about La Duse?"

"The performances in Chicago have been at the Auditorium, not an empty seat in the house, but the critics have not been kind. The *Daily*

News wrote that *Ghosts* was appalling and they called *The Dead City* a fourth-rate drama, all of which didn't stop audiences from giving her a standing ovation at the end of each performance."

"Well, that we knew," I said disdainfully. Wen said that it didn't surprise him, for in Chicago the press did not care for La Duse. In 1902, the critics had also attacked *Francesca da Rimini.* To perform again in front of those gangsters had been a mistake on the part of La Signora, an error that proved the fineness of her spirit, incapable of holding a grudge.

"This Thursday will be her last performance," Zárate added. "She chose *The Dead City* by D' Annunzio to wind up her tour."

"We knew that also," I said, increasingly dejected.

"And when she was in Washington, the president and the first lady went to see her and invited her to the White House."

"That, too," I confirmed with a weary sigh.

Zárate made a disappointed face and brought up a meeting at the editorial offices as an excuse to leave. When he was out of sight, we couldn't help but laugh at him.

"Today we could have been in Chicago," I said, biting into a cheese bun. "If it wasn't for . . ."

"Don't start with that old song!" Wen emphatically interrupted me.

When we returned to the apartment, Toña said that Señora Esmeralda had called to say that she was back at her house in Chapinero. We got in touch with her to confirm our attendance at the New Year's Eve party and invited her to accompany us on Sunday to a concert at Independence Park where the municipal band would perform the overture to *The Barber of Seville,* but she couldn't, for she was too busy with preparations for the feast.

The party, attended by many distinguished ladies and gentlemen of Bogotá high society, seemed to prove, in the event that anyone still doubted it, that La Gallego was without equal. The gardens of her house, full of flowers and exotic plants, were decorated with garlands of lights that twinkled in the darkness like multicolored fireflies. The servants, dressed in linen tunics, sandals, and red wigs, inspired by the ancient Egyptians, a plain allusion to the trip on which the hostess would embark in a few days, offered the guests, on silver platters, a range of drinks that would satisfy the choosiest among us. An orchestra, atop a stage built for the occasion, reeled off popular tunes throughout the night, which was unusually warm for Bogotá.

After the usual exchange of greetings and compliments on the elegance of our clothes, the guests broke up into smaller groups and we made ourselves comfortable in the fresh night air, seated at one of the tables draped with white tablecloths. Discreet candles, protected by papyrus screens dyed blue, yellow, and red, the colors of the flag, served as light. (These nationalistic streaks in La Gallego exasperated Wen.) We were seated with the ever-present Juan Vengoechea, with Jorge Garay, who that night was breathtaking, and with the poetess Doña Lydia Bolena and her niece, a señorita as thin as the tip of an asparagus.

To be honest, I was a little fed up. Ever since we got out of the taxi, everyone kept asking me how I felt, acting very surprised that I could walk so upright so soon after my surgery. And on top of that there were still a couple of empty places at our table, and I was panicking that the new manager of the streetcar company or some other similar bore would sit with us. So I was relieved when Esmeralda, who looked magnificent in a blindingly white tunic, diamond earrings, and tiara, atop a pair of unbelievable glass heels from Murano, approached our table with a stranger on her arm.

He was a middle-aged man with a body that made obvious his addiction to exercise. His silver hair was combed back and he wore a modern suit, cut flawlessly.

"Let me introduce you to a friend who has returned to the country after a long absence, Aníbal de Montemar," the lady of the house announced, and as she told him our names, I asked Wen who he was.

"An old flame, I imagine," he guessed just before it was his turn to greet the stranger.

Esmeralda excused herself and, leaving us in charge of Montemar, went to greet the minister of Belgium and his lover, who were arriving notoriously late.

"And where are you coming from?" Lydia Bolena inquired, breaking the ice.

"From Boston," the gentleman said in a baritone voice. "I have come back to be reunited with my family and with my country."

And so he told us of how when he was very young ("Let's say two weeks ago last Wednesday," he said enchantingly as a side note) he had left Colombia, fed up with its lack of culture and its politics run by cronyism and caudillos, to make his way in the land of opportunity. Such unthinkable fantasies, he said, had more than been overcome by his determination and will to succeed.

"I am not rich," he clarified. "But what I do have would make me a millionaire here." He burst out laughing and we joined in.

Esmeralda returned, escorted by the Belgian and the Dutchman, and they, too, joined our group. When the giant saw Montemar, it was like watching a block of butter melt in the sunlight. But Wen caught the Dutchman's attention and warned him not to fall under any delusions, since the gentleman was already spoken for, and he pointed with his chin to the hostess. Distressed, the Dutchman relented.

"And how have you found our country?" Garay asked.

"Very backward," Aníbal de Montemar answered, not mincing words. "Backward, and ruined by fanatical and crooked politics, with windows shuttered to the light and wind of civilization." All of us listened closely. "Here, the political parties, instead of developing and progressing, are stagnant in a bog of terminal paralysis, in the fog of superstition. They are tribes ruled by hereditary and irrational aversions."

"Intelligent and fascinating," I whispered in Wen's ear.

"On the day I arrived I decided to go for a walk in the neighborhood where I grew up. I went into a store and confirmed that everything that they sold, from a pin to an umbrella, was imported, because no one has given the slightest thought to our national industry. And then I went to a *chicha* bar and I was offered a drink in which they had dissolved, supposedly as an aphrodisiac, the dust of human bones. Everything is the same! Whether it is the hemp sandals, or the ponchos, or the indifference in the face of poverty, it's all the same. It's as if time had not passed! And even more so for the Indians and the needy who go from here to there looking for solace in church pews."

"But there are also great boulevards and new buildings with many floors," the asparagus dared to say.

"Mirages to fool the unwary. Behind that painted curtain, my dear señorita, the people continue to cling to an archaic morality and to the irrational cult of the ancestry of the illustrious and to a God who is indifferent to suffering," Montemar replied, the trace of a sorrowful smile on his face. "But perhaps it is best if we leave politics and its surrounding reality alone, lest we bore the ladies with those ills that we are forced to live with," he concluded with a gallant note of cynicism.

Vengoechea asked the minister if he had heard anything new about the *Dixmude.* The Belgian put on a serious face and said that it wasn't good. Finally after a week of uncertainty and fruitless searching, they had learned about the fate of the airship and its crew. The story came to light when some fishermen from Sardinia noticed that their nets were heavier than usual and in checking them found, along with countless crustaceans, a lifeless body dressed in a French military uniform, with a gold eagle pinned to his breast. It was the mortal remains of one of the men under the command of Captain Rémond de Saint-Amand! The *Dixmude* had exploded over the Mediterranean and they would never know the cause of the disaster, for no one had survived.

All ten of us looked around dejectedly. "Maybe it would have been wise to continue speaking about politics," Wen noted.

At that moment, the new streetcar manager approached the table and asked La Gallego to dance. She accepted and, inspired by the hostess, the Belgian minister and his lover boy led Señora Bolena and the asparagus to the dance floor. Following which, Vengoechea asked Garay to accompany him for a stroll, and without planning it, we were left alone with Aníbal de Montemar.

The conversation that ensued proved how naive it is to try to trick fate.

"The night before I left America, I saw La Duse," he said out of the blue, just to say something, and I felt a jolt in my spinal column. "You know who she is, right?"

Wen said that not only did we know who she was, but that we knew everything about her. He told the story of her first performance, when she was four, in the touring company run by her father and uncle; of her successes in Turin, where she became a leading actress and her name began to be mentioned with growing interest after her performance in *The Princess of Baghdad;* and of her tempestuous relationship with the poet D'Annunzio, who used her as a model for Foscarina, a character in his novel *The Fire.* When he paused to breathe, I asked Montemar his impression of La Signora.

"From the very beginning of the play, I could not take my eyes off of her," he told us. "She is old, but there is a quiet beauty about her. She began speaking in a hesitant and quiet voice, without moving, almost without gesturing, and like others in the audience, I asked myself naively when she would begin to 'act.' She never, never 'acted,' if, that is, we confine ourselves to the histrionic conventions associated with that verb. The miracle of La Duse, the secret of her art, boils down to simply being natural, to forgetting that there is an enormous audience watching her. Like peeling the rind from a fruit, she has gotten rid of anything superfluous to the art of acting and has kept only what is essential, what is fundamental. That, in my opinion, is her truth."

Wen let him know about our more than once frustrated mission to travel to the United States to see her, and listed each of the obstacles that had hindered us: first, the death of his grandfather and his mother's subsequent grief, the equestrian accident in the country that put him in a most desperate depression for a month and, finally, with the trip already arranged, my unexpected appendicitis, from which I had only begun to recover and which dashed our last hopes of being witness to the great art of La Signora. It was impossible, while still convalescing, to put myself through the ordeal of a train ride to Barranquilla, then the sea crossing to New York, and then another extensive and exhausting train ride to Chicago.

"Señores," Montemar announced, all excited, "I think that you will be very interested in what I have to tell you. From what I can make out, it seems that you have not heard about the extension . . ."

And so we learned that, lured by the bounteous profits that were being reported from her performances, various new producers had put forward a possible extension of the tragedienne's tour after the initial engagement. At first, La Duse didn't seem too enthusiastic, but on the advice of her manager, she listened to their terms, and like the lady that she is, the first thing that she did was to get in touch with Morris Gest and tell him that if he could make an offer to match the others, she would sign with him to prolong her *tournée.* Gest regretted that he could not match the offer of his rivals; his financial situation simply did not allow it. He had under contract the Art Theater of Moscow at the same time as La Duse's company, and he lacked the funds. He wished her the best and left her free to do what she wished. Disappointed, but *les affaires sont les affaires,* La Signora chose the most attractive offer and signed with Fortune Gallo, a countryman of hers who was associated with the famous impresarios the Selwyns.

I put my hand on Wen's knee and felt it trembling.

"That means, Señor de Montemar, that . . ." he tried to finish the sentence but ran out of breath, and the gentleman promptly finished his thought.

"It means that the tour does not end in Chicago as planned. Eleonora Duse's company will continue their performances until March. There are new dates in New Orleans, Los Angeles, San Francisco, Detroit, Indianapolis, and Pittsburgh."

"Are you sure?" I asked. "Absolutely sure?"

"The news was announced the day I boarded the ship in New York."

Wen and I laughed and hugged each other crazily. A sharp pain made me pause and put my hand on my belly: with all the excitement I had forgotten about my recovery.

"I am not through," Montemar said, and we stared at him reverently, as if he were the very oracle at Delphi. "There is one other thing you should know."

"Speak now, or I'll faint right here," Wen urged. "What is this detail that you have saved for last, like a delicious dessert?"

Esmeralda Gallego's friend explained that after her performances in New Orleans and before going on to California, La Duse had agreed to appear, parenthetically, for four nights in another location. She would have to leave the United States and cross the Caribbean.

"Havana?" Wen guessed. "She will perform in Havana?" he repeated skeptically.

"The last week of January," Montemar nodded.

The band abruptly stopped the number they were playing and the conductor announced that there was only one minute left before midnight and the beginning of 1924. In the blink of an eye, a swarm of Egyptians hurriedly filled the champagne glasses, and from the gardens, an explosion of fireworks rose to the heavens heralding the new January.

Wen and I clinked our glasses without taking our eyes off each other and finished off the bubbly liquid.

"And you didn't believe in miracles?" he said.

I was so happy that I didn't know what to say. Burdened by an understandable guilt since my surgery, I felt as if I was Atlas and the weight of the world had been lifted from my shoulders. Montemar's news changed the mood of the party. Our trip was on again. Wen told Vengoechea and Garay and they both congratulated us. Even Esmeralda was happy for us, or at least pretended to be.

"Of course I would have preferred that you came with me to Luxor," she sighed.

The festivities continued until two in the morning, and although I was apprehensive about dancing, I enjoyed watching Wen dance, first with the asparagus and then with a good number of ladies of all different ages. The alcohol and the euphoria over knowing that we would see La Duse made him so crazy that he climbed the stage and, accompanied by the band's pianist, sang loudly, his bedroom eyes on Lydia Bolena.

For you is this spring rose,
Not as lovely, my lady, as you.

La Gallego danced number after number with Montemar and at one point, when he left her alone, I asked her who this heartthrob was.

"An old flame," she confessed.

"Everyone is talking about him," I assured her. "He's the hit of the evening."

Esmeralda nodded, content. She looked at me for a moment, mysterious as a sphinx, and then revealed something very surprising.

"He looks perfect, doesn't he?" she said. "But don't trust appearances, dear Lucho, perfect as he seems, he is tragically flawed." She looked around to make sure that no other ears were listening, took my hand, and so that we could have the utmost privacy, led me to a nearby pergola.

"When Aníbal was a baby, not yet one, his parents took him to the country on vacation. One morning, when his mother was changing his diapers, a goose leapt on him and with one fell peck ripped off his *pipí* and, before anyone could react, swallowed it."

I looked at her suspiciously.

"I swear," she said, bringing her right hand to her heart. "I know for a fact."

I told her that what she just said gave me the shivers.

"You can imagine how I felt when, on our first night of love, Aníbal told me about the tragedy."

"And how did you react?" I inquired.

"Since we were already alone in my bedroom, I made myself do whatever was possible, under the circumstances. He proposed to me, he said that only a woman of my caliber could understand the situation and solace him, and he promised me that once we were married I could do as I pleased. But though I loved him, I couldn't do it. Days later he left, and it wasn't until yesterday that I heard from him and invited him to the *kermesse*."

She put her nose to a gardenia and then, as we headed back to the dance floor, where the victim of the sweet-toothed goose waited for her, all smiles, she whispered, "I hope that you know how to keep a secret. Don't tell anyone, I beg you. Not even that adorable fool who stole your heart."

When the guests began to leave, Esmeralda insisted that Vengoechea, Garay, Wen, and I go home in her Fiat. As soon as we were on the road, our friends fell asleep, but Wen, his emotions still at fever pitch, talked about anything that popped into his head.

"Fate is a cat and we are the mice with which she amuses herself. She grabs us by the tail and, just as we think we are doomed and about to be swallowed whole, she decides, against rhyme and reason, to release us so that we may go our own way."

We agreed that it was necessary to change our itinerary. In deciding to see La Signora, either at the provincial locales during her tour of the southern United States, or at the mythical Antillean capital well known for its vibrant cultural life, we wasted no time in picking the latter. We would enjoy her art in Havana and at the same time come to know that land.

I asked Esmeralda's driver to slow down, for the ride was so bumpy that my wound was hurting.

Then we started playing with dates. It was the first of January. In two weeks, if nothing went wrong (and what could go wrong? hadn't enough gone wrong already?), we could leave. That way we would arrive in Havana a few days before the first performances, to get used to the city, take its pulse.

"Havana," Wen said dreamily. "It was there and not in New York or Chicago where our date was set. Because the same thing has been happening to mankind, a thousand and one times, for millennia, and it still doesn't learn its lesson? Everything is as it is written, what had to be had to be, so that we could see La Duse in Cuba, see her and interview her," he added with determination.

Jasón was dropping everyone off on the front steps of their houses. First, Jorge Garay, who stumbled into the mansion owned by his uncles; then Juan Vengoechea, who was so sleepy he barely said good-bye, and finally we arrived at the *garçonnière.*

"Thank you, Jasón," I said from the sidewalk. "Now you can finally get some rest yourself."

But, to our astonishment, the chauffeur got out of the car, stood in front of us, and looking down at us from his magnificent height, told us that he had instructions from Señorita Gallego to stay with us for the night.

So, he came with us.

I will now draw a veil, discreetly, over the events that took place in our room that early morning. I will only say, since I think it is a proper detail to mention, as it reveals Esmeralda's originality and infinite kindness, that when her chauffeur shed his uniform and jumped into the bed between us, we saw something written in red ink on his manly member, the cryptic message: I4.

"What does that mean?" we asked, dying of curiosity.

Jasón, probably following his boss's order, offered only half a smile as a response. But as it turned out, as a result of a pleasurable exchange of caresses, his stinger began to increase in dimension, and hidden numbers and letters began to emerge from between the I and the 4. And when the chauffeur's scimitar was on display in all its splendor, we could read the message written by Esmeralda Gallego in her unique script. It said: *I hope you like this little present. To both of you, a prosperous 1924.* Such a New Year's Day gift could come only from someone as exceptional as her.

When we awoke, almost before lunch, our dark-haired *Cucuteño* was conspicuously absent.

"Was it a dream?" Wen mused.

"If it was a dream," I said, "now we know what dreams are made of."

That afternoon, Poncho Zárate arrived hurriedly at the *garçonnière,* announcing in a deep voice that he was the bearer of great news. We amused ourselves by going along with him.

"Four performances in the capital of Cuba!" he said, out of breath, throwing himself on the ottoman. "She will open the twenty-seventh of this month at the Teatro Nacional."

"We already know," we responded glacially.

Not everyone becomes a ghost when they die. Most of the dead are bored with this world and are terribly curious to find out what exists in the world beyond. So, without giving it much thought, they leave forever. They go who knows where and never return. But some of the dead like the idea of remaining among the living, mingling with them, whispering in their ears, interfering with their choices. Sometimes they try to help. Sometimes they seek vengeance. There are some noble ones, but these are in the minority. Most of them are to be feared, and if you are not careful, they will fill your head with horrible thoughts.

I know this because all the great Italian actresses are ghosts. Adelaide Ristori, Clementina Cazzola, Carlotta Marchionni, Fanny Sadowski, Celestina Paladini . . . Some nights they come and visit me in my room. I ask Désirée and Maria to leave then, and I make up something that needs to be done, inventing anything so that I will be left alone with the ghosts.

They sit around me and we have tea. They pretend to drink, but their cups remain full. They talk (that is, they move their lips as if they were talking), but no sound comes out. Of course, I don't have to hear them to know what they are saying. I know them well. Each one has her own personality, her own obsessions. All of them look horrific. With their once magnificent hair sparse and disheveled. With their caked-on makeup with which they try to hide their decomposing flesh. Dressed in the rags that were once magnificent apparel.

Although it has been years since I last performed in *The Lady of the Camellias*, La Cazzola continues to give me advice on how to improve my death scene, which she thinks weak, very weak, a real disaster! And who better than her to point this out? She, who after playing Marquerite Gautier hundreds of times, died from tuberculosis in real life! For her part, La Sadowski laughs at the chastity of my Marguerite. "She was a nobody. A puttana. And you, Eleonora, play her as if she were a virgin," she pronounces and then asks us if we remember the night that she kissed Armand so true to life that the authorities in Milan fined her for immoral conduct and threatened to shut down the theater if the scandal was repeated. Of course they remembered. All of us remembered. Forgetfulness is an art we have no talent for.

And, of course, they talk of men. Husbands and lovers. They are so bold as to make a list of mine and then go on to evaluate them. La Ristori, who is the worst, reads the names one by one, and the others offer their opinions.

"Martino Cafiero."

"A conquistadore di donne."

"Tebaldo Checchi."

"The cuckold."

"Well, he was sort of a dope."

"Fabio Andó."

"Now, he was handsome."

"Not just handsome, gorgeous."

"The only time, Eleonora, that the man on top of you was well planted there."

"Mario Praga."

"That's a lie!" I jump up furious, taking their bait. "There was never anything between us. We were friends, just friends."

"Arrigo Boito."

"Boring."

"A saint, according to her."

"Did he ever finish that opera he was supposedly working on?"

"The one about Nero? Of course not."

"Gabriele D'Annunzio."

"His head, beautiful. His body, loathsome."

"Oh yes, those narrow shoulders, those wide hips."

"He almost ruined her career with those morbid plays."

"A charlatan."

"An egomaniac."

"How could you have so lost your mind and humiliated yourself?"

"So many times performing in *La locandiera* and you didn't learn anything from Mirandolina."

"Now she knew how to treat a man, the bread in one hand, the stick in the other."

"What did you see in D'Annunzio, woman? Was it made of gold or something?"

I blush and they laugh loudly.

Can you believe that they go to the theater sometimes? They watch me closely, with a mixture of envy and contempt. On those occasions, I try to ignore them, for I know that they want to make me nervous, so that I forget a line or lose my concentration. I make sure not to look at them, but I know they are there. Observing me, judging me, heckling me.

"I would have done that differently." "Too discreet and subdued for my taste. No fire, no heat." "Poor Eleonora, so untalented and so persevering." "She had to invent another way of acting, because she couldn't do it like it's supposed to be done."

They look at me, judge me, criticize me. They laugh at my sunken cheeks and at my colorless lips. At my wrinkled skin, the dark circles under my eyes, my dull hair. What's wrong with my face? My face is the card with which I introduce myself. The script of the years on it is who I am.

Adelaide Ristori says that an actress should know when to retire, which is an art, for the passing of time, as we know, is very deceiving. She abandoned the stage while still young. Or when at least she still looked young, which is one and the same thing. She married the Marquis Capranica del Grillo and from then on went to the theater only on special occasions, or to performances by old colleagues, or to the opening night of some promising beginner. . . . They all agree, one should retire in one's prime and not one's sunset. "Or die while at the top," Clementina Cazzolla adds very convincingly.

The night of my first performance in Havana, La Ristori appeared out of nowhere in the dressing room to tell me that she had performed in that theater. And where haven't you performed? I thought. The witch was a pioneer of *tournées* to distant continents. Wherever I went, she had already been there, packing in the theaters. When she saw me urgently suck oxygen from the tank, she asked with a hypocritical uneasiness, "Till when, *cara Eleonora*, till when?" "Till I can't anymore, Adelaide. You had the Capranica's palace, I have nothing." When I answered her, María, who was combing my hair, looked at me with concern, thinking that I was talking to myself.

7

Havana?" my mother said after I told her that Wen and I would soon be on our way to that city.

Against all expectations (I expected a torrential scolding about the untimeliness of the voyage, given my recent recovery from appendicitis), she held back and nodded slowly, pensively, and then hid her face in her knitting. I looked with surprise at Lucrecia, the oldest of the ugly sisters, and she shrugged, an ambivalent smile on her face. My in-laws likewise did not present any obstacles for our trip, because Wen decided that it was "none of their business."

Wen had no problems reserving a luxury cabin on the Swedish liner *Fynlandia.* The ship would leave the Port of Colombia on January 12, and after making a stop in Colón, would arrive in the Cuban capital.

During the days prior to our departure from Bogotá, poor Vicentini was relegated to a humiliating second-class status, while La Duse took up all of our attention. Well aware that aside from her native language La Duse only spoke French, Wenceslao decided that since neither of us spoke Dante's language, we should practice Hugo's with the goal of being able to speak fluently to La Signora. He was still convinced that no matter how much she despised the press, we would get to interview her and draw from her secrets that would make reporters in Gringolandia and the Old World die from envy. So, to the astonishment of the *Chocoana,* we spoke to each other in French most of the time, and addressed her in the same language as well.

"*Toña, chérie, il nous faudrait quelque chose de léger pour diner, au contraire nous arriverons gros comme des cochons à La Habana.*"

"Blessed Mother of God, Señorito Wen, speak to me in Christian!"

"Tu ne trouves pas qu'elle est bien bête, cette nègresse? C'est quand même incroyable: même en nous écoutant toute la journée, elle n'arrive pas à apprendre un mot."

"Laisse-la tranquille avec sa cuisine."

A few days after I informed La Generala about our trip, I received a concise letter in her own hand in which she asked that I pay her a visit at five that afternoon. After crossing the main hallway of the mansion in La Candelaria, I headed for the parlor thinking she would receive me there, but the servant who answered the door said that La Señora wanted to see me in the study. That made me a bit curious.

As soon as I walked in, three pairs of eyes were fixed on me. The mother of the ugly sisters was accompanied by her two brothers, Manolo and Melitón, which made me even more intrigued.

"Sit down, son," La Generala ordered, pointing to a comfortable armchair, after I had kissed her and shaken hands with my uncles.

I obeyed without saying a word and sat down before them like a defendant in front of a tribunal. The Reyeses were more stuck-up and circumspect than usual, and though I scrutinized their faces to try to guess what was coming, I could discern nothing.

"Tea?"

"Yes, please."

We all watched in silence as my mother poured the golden infusion, added a spoonful of sugar, stirred it delicately, and handed me the cup along with a small napkin. I took one sip and dared to ask, "Can someone please tell me what all this is about?"

La Generala and Manolo watched Melitón, and the oldest of my uncles let out a deep sigh, stopped twirling the ends of his mustache, and reluctantly assumed responsibility for explaining things.

"We wanted to see you, Lucho, to speak with you about a very sensitive matter, which is of extreme importance to this family, and is somewhat connected to the trip on which you are about to embark."

In the minutes that followed, Melitón spoke of a thousand and one things in his exuberant manner, the language florid and cryptic, without ever making up his mind to address the question directly. I was starting to lose my patience when Manolo, suddenly emboldened, grabbed the story away from him and, to the relief of his two siblings, went straight to the point.

"It's about your Uncle Misael, Lucho."

"You heard from him?" I said, intrigued.

"Yes. And we need for you to go see him."

I giggled nervously and reminded them that I was going to the capital of Cuba and not to Copenhagen, where for many years, almost thirty now, my third uncle had lived.

Manolo tried to come up with a proper response, but on realizing that no one could hear the words he was saying, he raised his eyebrows in a helpless gesture, asking the others for help. Melitón sank in his chair, counting himself out, so it was up to La Generala, a fire in her eyes, to take charge.

"Your uncle has never lived in Copenhagen," she blurted out. "It was something we concocted to stop others from talking."

"And the box of tin soldiers that he sent me as a gift?" I insisted. That had been the favorite toy of my childhood: I loved the idea of a barracks where twenty-five rough and valiant soldiers lived, not a woman in sight, and I would invent all types of adventures for them.

"The soldiers came from a toy store in London where I ordered them," Melitón confessed in a raggedy voice.

Once the doors of the secret sprung open, other declarations came pouring out. The much-talked-about uncle, of whom all that was left was a sepia photograph in which he appeared as a scrawny boy with a pensive face, of whom I had nothing but a blurry memory—probably from my imagination and not my memory, since he had left Bogotá when I was still small. Having supposedly replanted his roots in Denmark, where all the nephews and friends of the family had been told he went, amid the snow and the swans, enjoying life, the forgotten and faded away uncle, was now revealed to me in his true guise: a profligate, a reprobate, and the shame of the Reyes clan.

According to his sister and brothers, when he was twenty-five, Misael, the only one of them who was still single, was a bum in the habit of throwing away his money on betting and gambling. His father, who had faith that his son would come to his senses and become a decent man, endured this, as terrible as it was for him, stoically. But there was one instance where the young man so disappointed the patriarch (no one ever found out the exact nature of the disappointment) that he couldn't hold back, and in a fury he slapped his son and threatened to disown him if he didn't once and for all put an end to his abominable behavior. For a while, it seemed, the black sheep complied with the old man's wishes, but as soon as he could he fled from the house, taking with him only two changes of clothes in an old suitcase, without leaving a farewell note. The parents thought that he had left in a passing fit of anger and would soon return begging for forgiveness. But it did not happen.

Three months later, the patriarch, desperate over the disappearance of the son who, in spite of it all (and no one explained to me what this *all* was about, either), was his favorite, hired a private investigator to discover his whereabouts.

To prevent a scandal, the police were never informed about the disappearance, nor were close friends, who were told that Misael was spending some time in Antioquia, on a ranch owned by Carmen del Viboral. After countless inquiries, the detective confirmed that the youngest brother had boarded in La Dorada a steamship that was headed for Cuba. The father then became hopeful and entrusted the detective with a huge sum of money to go to the island, find his youngest, and convince him to return; but as soon as the detective had the money in his pocket, he was never heard from again.

Nothing else was known about the case until, two years later, two different travelers returning from Gringolandia said that they had seen him in Havana during the docking of their ships there. Both accounts, though contradictory in nature, came from very reliable sources, which made them all the more disturbing. A widow, good friend of my late grandmother, swore that she had run into him in the area around the bay. It was late afternoon, and the young man, very elegant, tanned, and smoking a cigar, was in a car with a blonde who had the unmistakable air of a cocotte. On recognizing the widow, the wayward soul lifted his straw hat and saluted her with a mocking gesture, the car never slowing down. Some weeks later, the other person, one of Misael's professors of ethics during his years in school, also said he saw him, but under very different circumstances. According to this version, Misael was walking along the streets near the cathedral in the middle of a Holy Week procession, dressed in a filthy penitent's habit and carrying an enormous cross. A hood hid his face, but at a certain moment it fell back from his head and allowed the stupefied traveler to recognize him. The youngest of the Reyeses, bone-thin and with a three-day beard, wore no shoes and his feet were covered with sores. He was the very image of dirtiness and neglect. In his eyes, the witness insisted as he told the tale, there was not a trace of the intelligence and pugnacity that had marked him when he lived in Bogotá. The gentleman began to follow him, in the hope of talking to him and finding out some details of his life in Cuba, but as they arrived at the cathedral plaza, a throng of worshippers came between them and in the blink of an eye he had lost him.

The Reyeses pretended to laugh at such stories, which they called ridiculous fictions, continuing to insist that their absent son was in the countryside, tired of his spurious life of debauchery and now entirely dedicated to meditation and the writing of a book.

"*Papá* tried to find him once more, this time through a lawyer in Havana that someone had recommended," La Generala recalled. "The lawyer confirmed that in fact Misael was living there. He also found out that he was in good health and employed by some government ministry, but that he was absolutely opposed to renewing any sort of contact with us. He had made up his mind to have a new life, and he did not want any of us interfering. Your grandfather, Lucho, wrote the lawyer, begging for Misael's address, who knows why, maybe to go see him, but received in reply a letter informing him that the lawyer had passed away and that his nephew who took over the firm had no information about the case. *Papá,* God rest his soul, died soon afterwards, and although the doctors said that it was his liver, I know that it was grief that killed him. It was then that, to safeguard the family's honor, we began telling whomever asked that our brother was in Copenhagen, where fate smiled on him. With a few postcards and the presents that he apparently sent his nephews conveniently brought to the attention of anyone with the tendency to gossip, it was more than enough to make the news spread and be accepted as fact by almost everyone. And then time passed, and time, my Lucho, lets everything be forgotten."

My mother turned toward an armoire, opened a drawer, pulled out a photograph, and showed it to me.

"It was taken right before he fled," she said to me.

I looked at the picture, confused and full of emotion. A young man with unruly hair and pale skin looked back at me, his expression an odd mixture of audacity and pessimism. I searched my memory, trying to remember some detail of that face, some word he had spoken, some gesture, but this proved useless. I was about to say that I looked like him but what I said was, "And why are you telling me this now, after so many years?" I wanted to return the picture to La Generala, but she had her hands intertwined, and did not seem too concerned with taking it back. "Wouldn't it be better just to leave the uncle alone now that everyone has forgotten him?"

Melitón pulled out a paper from the same drawer and held it out to me.

"Read this and you will understand."

It was a letter postmarked in Havana some five months prior. It had been written in green ink on the stationery of the Hotel Perla de Cuba, and it said:

Melitón, Manolo and Maria, my brothers and sister,

Throughout all these years I have spared you the disappointment of having to hear from me and believe me, if I knew of any other way out of this, I wouldn't be writing to you. But I have no other choice. I urgently need as much money as possible. Robbed of my inheritance, I can turn to no one else but you. It is a very serious issue, a matter of life and death. As you can see, despite all the years of silence, I don't forget you.

The Unexpected One

"The Unexpected One?" I said, thinking that I should say that I found my uncle's handwriting horrendous. "That's what you called him?"

"It was a private joke," Melitón clarified. "By the time he came into this world, we did not think that we would have any more siblings. The stork brought him to us on a whim."

"He signed the letter that way," La Generala added, "so that we would know it was him."

"Did you answer him?"

"Twice, with no reply," Melitón said.

"Were you going to send him the money?" I insisted.

"We want to give him *his* money," my mother declared.

And so I found out that despite the threats and tantrums, our grandfather Reyes never disowned his unruly son. When his will was read, it confirmed that indeed, part of his riches went to The Unexpected One.

"And for twenty years you didn't lift a finger to give him that heap of money?" I was shocked. "Maybe he is living in abject misery, who knows in what condition, unaware of his fortune. This is shameful!"

My uncles could not look at me, and La Generala took a few steps away from me. Then, without anyone having to say anything out loud, I knew the mission with which they were entrusting me. I should take advantage of my stay in Havana to find out the whereabouts of my uncle Misael Reyes and let him know that in Bogotá a great inheritance awaited him.

"But how am I going to find him? Havana is not some little village," I protested, pointing out that what Wenceslao and I had planned was a pleasure trip, and that a refined aesthetic experience would run the risk of turning into an arduous and stressful search. "And even if I were to bump into someone who introduced himself with that name, how would I know for sure that it was him and not an impostor?"

"You will find him," my mother assured me, not listening to my protests. "I am sure that you will run into Misael." And with an enthusiastic flair, she handed back to me the photograph and the letter that I had set on the ebony writing desk. "You know, sometimes I look at you and it is as if I had him right here in front of me, as he was in those days before he fled."

"Does he look like him to you, Luis?" my uncle Melitón said.

"Very much so," Manolo agreed.

"Neither of you has any idea how *much* he looks like him," La Generala interjected, staring at me fixedly.

And then they inundated me with ideas of how I might come upon my lost uncle, and then they let me in on secrets and clues that would allow me, if I found him, to dispel any doubt about his identity. And lastly, they made me promise not to reveal the secret to anyone. When I returned to the *garçonnière*, I told Wenceslao everything.

I explained that I had said yes just to be rid of them, but that I wasn't going to ruin our trip by playing Sherlock Holmes in Havana. I sensed something dark and disturbing about the whole thing. Without lifting his eyes from the scrapbook with the silver and mother-of-pearl cover, where he was inserting some clippings supplied to him by the loyal Zárate, he listened to my complaints without seeming too interested.

"You like to turn everything into a tragedy," he said. "I don't think that it would be such a big deal to find your uncle. How old is he?"

"He's over fifty, I think," I said as I did the math and showed him the photograph. He was dumbfounded by how alike we looked, and made clear, getting right to the point, his thoughts on the nature of the "problem" that had made The Unexpected One break from his family and start a new life. If his escape was due to what we both suspected, that man of flawless features and strong-willed appearance must have suffered the unmentionable in the suffocating Bogotá of the turn of the century.

"Maybe we will find him at a box in the theater, cheering on La Duse," Wen declared in a joking manner and put an end to the discussion. Although I tried to forget about the matter, an inexplicable anxiety made my stomach jump.

As absurd as it might seem, even as we put the last touches on the preparations for our trip, Esmeralda Gallego did not stop trying to convince us to go with her to Egypt. She only gave in when we showed her the ticket for the *Fynlandia.* She would leave Bogotá a week after us, but by air.

On Saturday the fifth of January, at eleven-thirty in the morning, a plane piloted by an intrepid twenty-six-year-old named Camilo Daza had flown over Bogotá. Overnight, the young man had become very famous for being the first Colombian to have dared to fly a plane over the capital.

We had only to see the photographs of the young man from the paeans published in all the papers, in which he appeared very handsome, in suit and tie, leaning on his plane *Bolívar,* to understand Esmeralda Gallego's sudden interest in aeronautics.

"You should think twice about this," Wen insisted on the afternoon that she came to the *garçonnière* to say good-bye to us, sporting a mink boa around her neck and a blue-velvet top hat on her head. "They have yet to finish inventing those things. The air is for the birds, not for you. Don't be stubborn, woman."

"Camilo Daza learned to fly in the United States and he is an ace," she bragged, mocking what she thought was our inexcusable dullness. "He has flown a thousand times with passengers without a single problem."

"And who says," her friend grumbled, "that the problem won't present itself in flight one thousand and one?"

"My darling, you won't make me change my mind. I will fly to Barranquilla, and then, when I arrive in Luxor and am standing in front of Tutankhamen, I will kiss his golden sarcophagus in your name."

That afternoon, Esmeralda wanted to visit the central market, and we went along, though not without protesting. Jasón, who kept the masses at bay by glaring at them with a severe expression, joined us and we followed Esmeralda, making sure not to fall behind and, at the same time, not to soil our shoes with the mud, or the rotted rinds, or the blood of animals. As if she were a servant and not an elegant and cultured lady, the jewel of all the best salons in the capital, La Gallego moved among the vendors, testing the quality of grains and the freshness of the vegetables, and inquiring about the price of hammocks and sisal ropes and saddlecloths. We stopped for a moment, near where a curious crowd gathered around a pair: one was a chubby Amerindian, the other, a tall man of mixed Negro and Indian origin who shouted at the top of his voice about the benefits of an ointment that he had brought all the way from his indigenous Guajira, a miraculous drug capable of curing countless ailments.

Then we came upon a barefoot boy who, surrounded by rabbits and hens, papayas and yuccas, sold pieces of red paper with poems painted on them. Due to the fact that his most likely buyers could not read, the lad screamed out poems like "Farewell to Mother," or "My Beloved Fatherland," and urged the people to purchase those that they preferred.

After dithering over a poem about a marriage among the poor, and another one about a soldier who promises to return to his beloved's window, our friend ended up buying, for a cent, a work titled "The Blind Guitarist."

Suddenly, Esmeralda put a hand over her heart and made her way forward, like a zombie, toward an old man caked in dirt turning the handles of a miniature organ. On top of the organ, two parakeets, one blue, the other yellow, waited for anyone who wanted to know their fortune. And that someone had just arrived, a lunatic painter who handed the organ player the astounding sum of one peso and took the cards that one of the birds, the sky-blue one, handed her with its beak.

"There are journeys that never end," she read, choked with emotion, "and journeys that are always beginning." And it was then that we found out that our little outing, while seemingly senseless, had a secret purpose connected with an old longing. Years before, when she was a girl, Esmeralda, unknown to her parents, had gone to the market with one of the cooks, and she had wanted a parakeet to reveal her fortune, but the cook had considered it a waste of money and did not give her the coin. The memory of that frustration had been with her ever since.

"Well, she has pulled out the thorn," Wen uttered, drying up a fat tear on her face with a hankie. "If only everything were so easy!"

The old man, still stunned by the outrageous sum he had been paid and frightened that she might regret her generosity, demanded that the "gentlemen" also find out their fortunes. Although it seemed to us like the height of stupidity, Wen and I took the cards that at the beck of their master the trained birds handed us. By coincidence, both of us got the same message, written in an irregular script with spelling errors. "Jelousy is a germ dat eats up the heart." Since neither of us is jealous, the fortune disappointed us.

So, finally, we were able to leave that hell and return to the apartment.

After long hugs, we said good-bye to our favorite jewel. With one of her incomparable guffaws, Esmeralda was able to fight back the tears that were threatening to ruin her makeup, and she promised to be back by midyear so that we could celebrate, in a party that will go down in history, my thirty-fourth birthday. After her visit to Luxor, she would spend some time in Constantinople and Stromboli, and on the way back stop in Paris to update her wardrobe. She wished us luck with the Italian mummy and ordered Jasón to start up the Fiat.

"I will miss you," my lover called out as the car rode away.

The following morning we left for Barranquilla. I'll skip the details of our farewell with friends and family at the train station. Suffice it to say that before we boarded, La Generala and my uncles pulled me aside to give me some final directions. I couldn't help feeling like a secret agent entrusted with a difficult mission.

"Do all you can to find him, my Lucho," La Generala urged me. "And take good care of yourself."

Melitón slipped a wallet into my jacket pocket. It was bulging with dollars.

"You know I don't need money," I protested.

"It's so you don't skimp on the expenses of the search," Manolo assured me. "And so that you get a little something for yourself."

I was going to protest again, but changed my mind when I heard the train whistle. I hugged La Generala and the ugly sisters, my uncles and their wives, Doña Herminia and my father-in-law, and then Alvarito Certaín, Vengoechea, Jorge Garay, the blond Romero Villa, and Poncho Zárate, who arrived at the last minute, just in time to show us the morning edition of *El Tiempo*, where he happened to see us mentioned under the headline "Off They Go." "The distinguished gentlemen Wenceslao Hoyos and Lucho Belalcázar leave today for Barranquilla, en route to Havana, where pressing matters beckon them." With another whistle, the conductor announced our imminent departure. I forced Wen away from his mother, who was weeping as if he were being deported to Siberia and she was never going to see him again, and dragged him toward the compartment that we had reserved. The train began to move slowly as we still said our last good-byes.

"What a nightmare," I snorted.

We took our seats and tried to relax.

"Are you happy?" I asked my darling, taking his hand.

"So happy, it all seems untrue," he said, with that disarming frankness of his.

But not five minutes had gone by when something unexpected shattered our peace. The train came to a sudden halt, braking abruptly, and we stuck our heads out the window to investigate.

"What happened?" Wen yelled to one of the workers who had disembarked to see what was wrong.

"There is an old woman in the middle of the track and she won't move," the man explained. "But don't worry, they are making her move."

And then we saw the perpetrator. A slight woman, dressed in black, with gray, unkempt hair, was approaching us, walking near the cars and screaming obscenities addressed at the Conservative Party. We recognized her immediately, for we were tired of seeing her roam the streets of Bogotá: It was none other than Mad Margarita, the unfortunate schoolteacher from Fusagasugá, who had lost her mind when her son perished in battle during the War of a Thousand Days. I was unaware that her delirium now entailed stopping train traffic. When she passed by our car, she stopped and smiled coyly, as if apologizing for the disturbance caused by her ramblings.

"Señora Margarita, this cannot be allowed," I scolded her sweetly, as if she were a little girl. "Go home, please."

Embarrassed, she gave in, and on seeing the locomotive pulling behind it, with a monumental effort, the cars replete with passengers, she came dangerously close to our window. "Tell her that Lauro, her little boy, sent you," she insisted.

We left the old woman's figure behind and returned to our seats.

"What do you think she meant by that?" I asked, intrigued.

"Forget it. She herself doesn't know what she means."

The journey was exhausting, but we reminded ourselves that of all the possible ways it was the quickest. Not counting Camilo Daza's airplane, of course, but getting into one of those contraptions was a risk that we were not willing to take. Leave it to La Gallego, who did things so crazy that they would make Mad Margarita seem sane. We talked, and read, and enjoyed the victuals prepared for us by the kind Toña and then slept, and after talking and eating and sleeping a number of times, like an endless ritual, the thickening warm air let us know that we were nearing Barranquilla.

The first time Enrichetta saw a statue she thought that it was a real naked woman. She was almost three, and her father and I were convinced that she was the most intelligent child in the world. On that day, in the park, she began tugging at my hand very excitedly so that I would look at the very strange lady. When I explained to her, amused, that it wasn't a signorina but a sculpture, a piece of marble that an artist had carved and given beautiful shape, she didn't believe me. Teobaldo had to carry her over and make her caress, at first frightened, but later with unabashed delight, the body of the signorina smoothed by many years of rain and wind.

"She is made of stone," she conceded dejectedly, but immediately added: "She is made of stone, but she is alive."

Teobaldo and I laughed and, not to disillusion her, told her that yes, she was alive.

After we left, I turned around to look at the sculpture one last time and had the impression that, a prisoner in her body as we are in ours, the marble figure watched us with her hollowed eyes as we moved away.

Sometimes, in gardens, in fountains, I watch the statues with envy and think that within their still and enduring beauty, a living soul circulates, continually renewing itself. They should be happy, for they enjoy inertia and flux at once. They should, but likely they are not. They must envy us our ability to do what is prohibited to them: to go from one place to another as we wish. I would gladly change such "fate" for the tranquil peace of any statue.

My life has been nothing else but a never-ending journey, an endless traveling. Always roaming, from a very tender age, at first in trains and rundown cars, then later in fancy automobiles and ocean liners, crossing the countryside, deserts, and oceans. I envy things that stay in their place like trees, with their roots sunk into the profundity of the earth.

My grandfather, the great Luigi Duse, was one of the great performers of Venetian comedy, and his theater in Padua bore his name. He was famous, but he died a ruin, having lost everything, even his theater. Alessandro and Enrico, his sons, put together a touring company but had to replace the comedies with dramas, for neither had inherited the comic ability of the old man.

Theirs was a third-class company, the type that is rarely seen in important cities. Alessandro, my father, met a peasant girl on tour, married her, and put her on stage. Then I was born. My first memories are not of images or voices, but of a sound: the clatter of the cart in which the actors went from town to town.

Once, in Padua, my father and I stopped for a few weeks at an inn. My mother was in the hospital and we would visit her in the afternoons. Afterwards, Papa left me alone in the room and headed for the theater. Poor man. He hated acting. He had a horrible memory and often forgot his lines. What he liked was painting, mixing the colors with brushes and applying them to a canvas or a piece of wood.

The owner of the inn, who had only had boys and they were already grown, took a liking to me. One day, she knocked on the door of our room and gave me a doll. She told me that she had saved it from when she herself was a little girl. She had found it in the bottom of a large chest and wanted to know if I would like to keep it. It was lovely, with a porcelain face and a body made of cloth, with blond ringlets and a long, embroidered batiste dress that smelled like camphor. I had some toys, but nothing like that doll. I loved her from the moment that I first held her. I hugged her so tightly that my father scolded me.

When the engagements in Padua ended, Mama was discharged from the hospital and rejoined us. She was thin and pale, as usual. My mother no longer acted, her appearance was dreadful, and she coughed all the time. She was in charge of mending the costumes. All day long, there was a needle in her hand. But, at night, after she had fallen asleep, my father would secretly undo her work and sew the costumes right. He didn't want the other women to complain. Mama was never much of a seamstress.

I helped my parents pack and put the suitcases in the truck with those of the other actors. Then we walked to the station.

"Where is your doll, Eleonora?" Mama asked as we were boarding the train. "Did you leave it in the room?"

I didn't answer, the train was about to leave and we hurriedly climbed aboard to take our seats. I had not forgotten my doll, obviously. I had left her on the bed, lying on a pillow, neatly covered by a blanket to protect her from the cold.

"Who knows when you will ever have another one," my aunt Theresa whined.

"I still have her," I said in her ear. "But she stayed home."

I did the same thing with Enrichetta as I had done with that old doll: as soon as she was old enough, I looked for a good boarding school. She would suffer, naturally, but not as much as the daughter of actors. I wasn't willing to have history repeat itself. For years, I was able to hide what I did from her. We would meet up someplace, during her vacations, and we would be happy during those weeks. Afterwards, she would return to school and I would return to the road, one trip linking with another. My poor daughter, if I did her wrong it was to avoid a greater wrong. "Never live apart from your children," I advised her. "Not even for one day. Don't make the same mistake as your mother."

Enrichetta never wants to talk about those days. She shrugs. "I survived," she says whenever I bring it up. Does she blame me, perhaps? Children are our prey till they are old enough to become in their own way our predators. It is horrible, having to make decisions for them, risking that one day they will reproach us for what we did with their lives.

Mama held on that winter in which I gave up my doll,

and one more, and then she could no longer be with us. She stayed in Bologna, waiting for us, and there she died. We mourned her, buried her, and continued our travels. Life, for some, is a journey. Not figuratively, but literally—literally oppressive and exhausting.

8

The sultanic Barranquilla on the Magdalena welcomed us with a temperature of 36 degrees centigrade and a station crowded with people of all races and mixtures, dressed in bright colors, yelling, sweating profusely, and gesturing in exaggerated manner. The contrast with the chilly, circumspect, and dull-gray capital was so shocking that for a moment we couldn't seem to move, afraid that we would be swallowed by the whirlwind of voices, color, and activity that boiled under the crackling sun and clear sky.

We stayed in a small hotel recommended by Vengoechea, and the owner, swallowing all his s's in the local accent, recommended the best shops in the city. We dedicated the next few hours to buying clothes suitable for the Caribbean. Our heavy costumes from Bogotá made us an ideal target for mockery, and the Barranquillans, with their characteristic tactlessness, made no effort to hide their stares and sarcastic remarks. When we finally shed our old clothes, I felt a sense of relief that must be what a snake experiences when it sheds its old skin.

If Bogotá seems atrocious to me, then Barranquilla, for opposite reasons, is equally atrocious. Everything is odious there. The noise, the sweat, the dust, the lack of common courtesy from both the lower and upper classes, the base politicking pushed to unimaginable extremes, the irrational hostility for anything connected to the capital, the unhealthiness, the rivers that run through the streets every time it rains, with a brutal and overwhelming force, bringing everything, absolutely everything, to a halt. And yet, like it or not, if you want to escape to the world, you need to come here. Situated on the left bank of the Magdalena, and some, if I remember correctly, ten or twenty kilometers from the Atlantic Ocean, Barranquilla is at once a fluvial, a maritime, and an aerial port, the golden gate of Colombia.

"I have discovered something," Wenceslao announced the following day, as we rode in a taxi to the home of a novelist whom I had corresponded with and was curious to meet. "I only like the coastals when they are far away from the coast."

Abraham Zacarías López-Penha was a writer pretty much ignored in Bogotá. When, by pure chance, his novel *The Shadow's Bride* fell into my hands, I took it upon myself to find out more about him and to get his address, and I learned that he was an erudite and trustworthy person who didn't hide his obsession with spiritualism. I wrote him and told him how much his book had captured my interest, and he responded with an invitation to visit him whenever I could. With his brother David, and along with hundreds of others Sephardic Jews, he had come to live in Colombia from Curaçao. In addition to being a poet and novelist, he was a mathematician, a cotton farmer, and an esteemed *kadosch* of the Free Masons.

The writer, a lean and elegant man, some sixty years old, radiated a pleasant air of inner peace, and greeted us warmly but without embarrassing overfamiliarities. In spite of his cordiality, in his composed manners you could see the desire to keep a certain distance. He invited us to try the local beer, and let us admire his incredible library, composed mostly of esoteric volumes.

He asked how we liked the city, and on realizing that we did not know what to say, afraid that if we spoke the truth it would not be courteous, he burst out laughing. Barranquilla, he said, is like one of these girls who when you least expect it has a growth spurt.

"It has grown so rapidly and disproportionately that it doesn't feel right in its own skin," he ascertained. "But it will get used to it. You have to remember, my friends, that its population, which was forty thousand only a quarter century ago, is now over one hundred and twenty thousand souls. Neither construction nor other services have been able to develop as quickly. Yet I'll venture to guess that in the middle of this mishmash of Colombians from different regions, of

Germans and Syrians, of Italians and Lebanese, the modern world will arrive in this country."

He sent for his car and, chauffeured by an expressionless driver who never took his eyes off the road, he took us on a tour of the city, north and south, east and west. The barrio of San Roque and the Jewish Alley; the Prado, a new district destined to become the most aristocratic in Barranquilla; the famous soap factory La Cubana; the elitist Colegio Alemán and the just as exclusive Club Barranquilla; the ostentatious Palacio la Aduana, which anyone could mistake for the Parthenon; Dr. Krufer's modern clinic; the central boulevard with its palm trees, its almonds, and its flowering *cámbulos,* busy day and night, for unlike in Bogotá, where the bustle of the city dies with dusk, in Barranquilla night is experienced with particular intensity; the river port . . .

López-Penha was sorry that our stay was so brief, he stressed that on our next visit we should take a boat up the Magdalena, for the fishing in the wide river was a fascinating experience. Especially if we took one of those strapping hunks with us to bait our hooks, I thought as I watched the tough fishermen, in their shorts and with their muscular arms, emptying their boats of a day's work.

A meager steamship with a large paddle wheel arrived from La Dorada. Its passengers, who by all accounts seemed to lack the funds to buy tickets on one of the ships from Colombia Railways & Navigation or the Compañía Antioqueña de Transporte, disembarked from the cargo ships, relieved after an eight-hour and almost-eight-hundred-kilometer journey on the river. We overheard remarks that a treacherous sandbank had interrupted their trip for a couple of days, so the crew was unloading boxes of any supplies that might spoil.

A little later, we went to a seedy restaurant run by a pair of witches named Marie and Sylvie, who said they were French. Astonished at seeing that one of them had her teeth in an abominable condition and that the other wouldn't take her index finger out of her nose, we asked López-Penha why he had brought us there. He explained that although they were pigs and they treated their customers like dirt, the two old women were expert arepa makers.

125

"I have the luxury of living anywhere in the world I choose," the Sephardi said while we ate our arepas, which were good, granted, but not so good as to have to put up with such Furies, "but, and don't ask me why, because I don't know the answer, I chose this place. Or did it choose me?"

He insisted that we move from the hotel to his house, where we would have first-class accommodations, and on not being able to convince us he tried to get us to promise that we would accompany him that night to the house of one of his best friends. Wen and I looked at each other furtively, not knowing how to respond. We didn't want to disappoint him, but at the same time we were worried about the prospect of staying up all night, as the following day we were due to leave early for the Port of Colombia.

"I'll have you back in the hotel before midnight," the novelist promised, reading our thoughts.

We accepted the invitation in the face of such perseverance. López-Penha dropped us off at the hotel, warning us that he would return for us exactly at eight. Back in the room Wen jumped in the shower and I followed him.

"Is it my imagination or do we smell funny?" he asked, sniffing his body and then mine.

The so-called "smell" was a dandy's euphemism. In truth, we stank. There was a foul odor emanating from our underarms that stuck to every centimeter of our skin. Only after scrubbing once and again with soap were we able to rid ourselves of it. In Havana, we would find out that this funk is called *grajo* and that it is the result of strolling through Caribbean streets without wearing the proper deodorant. Since our sweat glands were not accustomed to overwork in Bogotá, thanks to the cold, it was a lesson that we would have to learn.

After the shower and some erotic frolicking under a cold stream of water, we rushed to get ready. With a punctuality that is likely very unusual in Barranquilla, López-Penha arrived to pick us up at the exact hour. The car took us to a house on the outskirts of the city. On the way, the novelist told us that his friend was throwing an intimate dinner party to celebrate his twentieth wedding anniversary. Nothing major, just a few guests. The marriage, he said, had scandalized the prudish society of the coast; it was uncommon for a man of such high standing to become attached to a circus performer and, not content to simply have an affair with her, to take her to the altar.

The house was dark and quiet. As soon as our companion rang the bell, a hunchbacked servant who was also missing an eye opened the door. Lighting the way with a candelabra, she led us into the living room.

"The señor will be right with you," the phantom muttered, and leaving the candles on the table, vanished.

"There's no electricity?" I asked, somewhat surprised.

"Nacianceno doesn't like such artifices," López-Penha responded.

"Your friend is a writer also?" Wen wondered.

"Not even close. He is a scientist. The most talented hypnotist who has ever lived."

"A hypnotist?" I screamed out, unable to contain myself.

"An explorer of consciousness, if you like," a voice replied. And, by some dark curtains that we couldn't make out fully because of the lack of light, we saw Próspero Nacianceno. Much later, when Wen and I tried to remember what he looked like, we realized, perplexed, that all we could remember was that he was short, with blue eyes, and in tails. As unbelievable as it may sound, we couldn't pinpoint if he was fat or thin, light or dark-haired, with an eagle or a Roman nose, or with thick or thin lips. We did recall that he was a gentleman with flawless manners and he received us as if we were old friends.

Then we heard the doorbell again.

Led in by the same servant, two middle-aged ladies entered the room. The first was overly made up, with her hair curled extensively. She could hardly breathe inside her green, corseted dress, which would have been suitable for a cancan dancer in the time of Toulouse-Lautrec. The other one, very pale, subdued, and distracted, as distinct from her friend, was dressed in gray, with a tiny felt hat, and had her white hair in a bun.

After the customary introductions we learned that the extroverted one went by the name of Melusina Jaramillo and was an equestrian performer in the circus, while her quiet companion, named Asmania, was in charge of the acrobats' costumes and little was said about her life except that she had been a beautiful and enchanting young woman and that she had been married to a conjurer named Pailock, who made her disappear in front of audiences. They were both best friends of the lady of the house.

Don Próspero imagined that we must be starving, which was true, so he led us to a dining room profusely lit by candles.

"Where's Sobeida?" Melusina said softly.

"She'll be here," our host responded, and then, very amused, recounted that she had already tried on half a dozen dresses and had not been happy with any of them.

"Men will never understand, no matter how much they try, the intricacies of the female spirit," a high-pitched voice called out.

The voice belonged, of course, to Señora Nacianceno, who descended the marble staircase with a studied slowness. She wore a tight-fitting black satin dress, with a sapphire brooch in the shape of a rose on her breast. We almost fainted from the shock of seeing that the lady's cheeks and chin were covered with a chestnut beard. Before we could recover or hide our reactions, she walked toward us and reached out her hand heavy with rings, so we would kiss it.

"It seems that no one warned you that when I met my husband I was the bearded lady for the Pubillones Circus," she said in a mocking tone, and gave the Jew a recriminatory tap with the handle of her fan. "My forgetful Abraham Zacarías, you would have been to blame if these young men passed out before the evening started."

She kissed her friends effusively, and, as if it were a throne, took her seat at the head of the table. At her chair, which was made of a gorgeous wood, she looked truly like a queen, upright and sure of herself. In spite of her beard—or perhaps because of it, I couldn't tell for sure—her face, with its Ethiopian features and ivory tonalities, seemed especially beautiful.

"Welcome," she said, raising a glass and inviting us to toast. Although I hadn't noticed when the monstrous servant had poured us some white wine, we quickly raised our glasses also.

"To our first twenty years of happiness," Próspero toasted.

"To love, that like the hare leaps up when least expected," Melusina Jaramillo added with a conspirational wink toward the hosts.

The antique china seemed to have come from a castle in a fairy tale, and the meal (mostly seafood, although there was also some chicken and heavily seasoned lamb) surprised us with its abundance and tastiness. We ate, entertained by Sobeida and Melusina's stories about their life in the circus, before the former fell in love with the wealthy Barranquillan and abandoned her art. Throughout the dinner, the lady in gray never relinquished her muteness and limited herself to listening closely and timidly smiling when the rest of us teetered with laughter. Behind Asmania's apparent serenity, I saw a deep suffering, a devastating and perennial anguish that couldn't be expressed in words.

The hosts regretted that another one of their great friends, Manuel Cervera, couldn't be with them that evening. He had contracted food poisoning from a fish stew and was recovering.

"Manolito is nuts," Nacianceno explained. "An incorrigible bohemian. He lives in the Lebanese barrio and his dream is to have that little piece of Barranquilla secede from the republic."

"Is it true that he collects castanets, dead ladies' hands, love letters that have been returned to him, and other such stuff?" Melusina asked, her mouth full.

"Among other things," López-Penha confirmed.

After a delicious dessert, *la señora* and her friends excused themselves to put the final touches on a little surprise that they wanted to present to us and on which they wanted to spare no detail. For his part, Próspero Nacianceno invited all the gentlemen to follow him to the *fumoir* and there offered us cigars and cigarillos of the finest quality. As we merrily smoked, we talked about literature, music, painting, and, since it couldn't be avoided, politics. At times we could hear the distant laughter of Sobeida and Melusina. Our trip came up in conversation also, and it made López-Penha recall his modernist youth, the years in which he had published some of his poetry in Cuban magazines like *La Habana Elegante, Gris y Azul,* and *Las Tres Américas.* During that time, he remembered he had kept an extensive correspondence with a pair of talented poets named Carlos Pío Uhrbach and Juana Borrero.

"It was to her, who had been so fascinated with my Breton ballad 'Yvonne' that she used that pseudonym to sign her letters, that my 'Dance of Havana' was dedicated, and to him, another poem whose title I can't remember," he said.

When we offered to visit them on his part when we were there, he smiled ironically.

"Impossible. They both died in the flower of their youth. Their souls were too pure: their time with us fleeting."

Suddenly, Nacianceno looked at his watch, stood up, and said:

"Since Abraham has already informed me that you must leave early, and we still have to attend to the ladies' surprise, it's time to take care of our business."

On noticing our confused expressions, he laughed.

"I am talking about our hypnosis session," he clarified. "Sit right here if you will, Señor Belalcázar," he told me, pointing to a comfortable chair.

I tried to protest and make clear to him that it must be some kind of misunderstanding, that I had never been hypnotized and had no interest in undergoing an experience of such a nature; but, not paying me any mind, López-Penha guided me to the spot suggested by the hypnotist and tried to put me at ease, explaining that it was a once-in-a-lifetime experience for which I would be eternally grateful. I looked at Wen, at once amused, desperate, and resigned, and he nodded, which gave me courage to go on.

Standing in front of me, Nacianceno took out from his vest pocket a small, diamond-shaped mirror and told me to look at it and concentrate on its sparkling.

"You will sleep, you will immediately fall asleep," he whispered. "You are already asleep, my friend, already . . ."

What happened then I recount as I was later told about it by Wenceslao. After a few seconds of watching the little mirror dancing slowly in front of my eyes, I fell into a deep stupor.

The explorer of consciousness asked me to return to the days of my childhood and tell him about my fears, and I promptly complied.

I spoke, according to Wen, of countless phantoms. Of the runaway mule that roamed the narrow streets of La Candelaria in the middle of the night, disturbing the sleep of all with its horrific whinnies and trailed by its own turbulent wake, of the specter from Las Aguas, the repulsive apparition who had once been a graceful and flirtatious woman, but who one day committed the sacrilege of comparing the beauty of her hair with that of the Virgin of Las Aguas, and it then turned into a tangle of foul and slimy serpents. Of Saint Victorino's light, which lay in wait in the darkness, until some unbeliever dared summon it with a whistle and then was struck suddenly with a devastating death as a lesson to the arrogant, and of the spirit of Don Ángel Ley, the gallant captain in the viceroy's guard, who lost his mind one morning after prayers, when he came across a burial and, upon asking who the deceased was, saw his own body laid out in the coffin, a sword buried in him, while a voice from beyond the grave answered his question: "A sinner named Ángel Ley."

"But is there anything that you fear more than these specters, Luchito?"

My voice, and Wenceslao got goose bumps all over his body as he told me, unexpectedly became that of a child, and on my face there rose the confused emotions of a three-year-old.

"I . . . I . . . don't know," I hesitated.

"Tell me, my child, no one else will know," Don Próspero insisted. "It will be a secret between us."

"I am afraid of my mother when she gets impatient, when she knits her brow and looks at me with her falcon eyes. I am afraid of my father. So big, so fat, and so busy with his own matters that he only remembers that I exist to scream at me about something. I am afraid that one day Toña will leave and I will be without her. I am afraid of my cousins when they play games, because they become animals that push, hit, and bite. I am afraid of strangers who come to the door and want to put me in a bag and take me away forever," I said, all at once.

"But those are small fears and I am after a bigger one," he persisted. "What are you afraid of above all else?"

"I . . . I . . . don't know."

"Of course you know, and you should tell me," the enchanter uttered brusquely, and then, softening his tone, added: "Who or what causes you the greatest terror, Luchito?"

"My . . . my uncle."

"Which uncle? What is his name?"

"M . . . M . . . Misael. That's him. The youngest one. The one I like to secretly watch through the keyhole when he bathes in *Papá's* house. The one who plays with his thing when he's inside the porcelain bathtub, thinking that no one sees him, till it grows, not even imagining that I am watching. The one with the slender body covered in silky hair that I would love to caress with the tips of my fingers. The one who wets my ears with his cologne so that his smell will be with me all day, wherever I go. The one I am both afraid of and attracted to. When Uncle Misael carries me, I undo the knot of his tie and awkwardly pull at his chest hairs. When I refuse to eat my soup and Uncle announces that he will feed me, I open my mouth without complaining, so that the spoon held in his hand may penetrate it, and I hold on to the utensil between my tongue and my palate, I wait ages before I let it go and then gladly swallow the liquid so that I can feel its warmth run down my esophagus. I like when my uncle kisses me and when he tickles me with his thin mustache; I like when he chases me from room to room of the house in La Candelaria and when he finally grabs me and holds me tightly in his sinewy arms. I like the tiny blue veins that I can just make out underneath the milkiness of his skin. My uncle is a thousand times more beautiful than the image of the Christ of Las Limpias that my mother has in her room and a hundred thousand times more beautiful than the angels on the stamps glued on the top of Toña's bench. Why am I afraid of my uncle, who pampers me and spoils me so? Why am I afraid of him if he has never scolded me, or threatened me, or been anything but sweet and tender? Why is it, that when I am in bed, in the darkness, in the middle of the night, I scream as if some great danger, which I can't explain, more terrifying than the runaway mule, or the specter of Las Aguas, or Saint Victorino's light, or the phantom of Don Ángel, were upon me? No, it is not my uncle whom I fear. It is not him, disturbing, but innocent and respectful as he is. It's me I fear, the man who lives in me, whom I sense inside me; the man lying in wait, with infinite patience, till my child's body matures so that he may hatch and make himself known, to be like him, as adorable and tender as he is, as pretty and seductive, as different and as much like him as he is and to give in to the temptations of the flesh."

Wen tells me that at the end of my soliloquy I collapsed onto the chair and wept silently till all my anguish had vanished and I was calm, clean, and pure, as if bathed by a light.

"Now, I will wake you," the hypnotist announced. "When you open your eyes, you will not remember anything you have said, but the fear of confronting your uncle will have disappeared. Perhaps he, too, without knowing it, is waiting for you. There are different ways of being someone's father or someone's son. He is your father, your mirror, and you are his reflection, his natural continuation, his son. It'll be good that after so long you will be able to embrace and get to know each other again."

With a great yawn, I came to. I thought that I had slept for hours, but the hands on the clock told the truth: the session had lasted half an hour.

"Wasn't it truly marvelous?" the Sephardi said, grabbing my hand, and I returned his grasp out of mere courtesy for I had no idea what had transpired during the lapse of time. At that moment, Señora Asmania appeared at the door and, with a little gesture of her head, asked us to follow her.

We went into a room furnished with lurid-colored damask furniture, Arabian carpets, and decorated with tinfoil half-moons. Incense burned in its four corners, giving off a fine aroma that was difficult to describe. To the beat of the oriental music from a wind-up gramophone, Sobeida and Melusina appeared dressed as houries. They wore anklets, pants made of transparent muslin, tight vests trimmed with bugles and sequins, and translucent veils over their faces. They pushed between them an enormous hulking thing covered in linen. They placed it in the center of the room and danced around it, wiggling their bellies almost indecently.

When the music stopped, the sensuous Sobeida stepped forward and stood in front of her husband. Taking off the veil that hid her beard, she wet her sweet and flushed lips with the end of her tongue, kissed the fingers of her right hand and put them on Don Próspero's mouth. Then we heard the beating of a drum and Melusina, with a quick swipe, pulled away the cloth to let us see the contraption underneath. It was a guillotine, something I considered inappropriate in that *Thousand and One Nights* scenario. The rest of the scene took place in a whirl, in much less time than it will take me to tell it: Sobeida placed her beautiful head in the lower part of the device, and she gazed in rapture at the hypnotist and exclaimed, "Praise be to you, my love, sole owner of my destiny, the most powerful and benevolent among men! May my head be ripped from my body, my lord, if ever you doubt that my passion for you is eternal."

She had barely finished the last word of her sinuous speech when Melusina put the contraption to work, and the sharp blade severed, in one swoop, the neck of the bearded lady, splashing us with warm, dark, sticky blood. Before passing out, I thought I saw the discreet Asmania, laughing maliciously, pick up the decapitated head and put it on a tray.

When I came to, everyone had surrounded me, alarmed, as Asmania administered smelling salts. I was relieved to see that Nacianceno's wife still had her head attached to her body, not a scratch on her neck.

"I think he's going to be all right," Melusina Jaramillo concluded, not being able to hide her laughter.

"I hope that Señor Belalcázar can forgive our little games," Sobeida said. "It's innocent fun, but sometimes it may prove a little shocking to someone who is . . ." I thought for sure that she was going to say, "a *cachaco*," but she chose instead a less wounding term . . . "not from here."

They said their farewells, wishing us a great vacation in Havana. López-Penha, after predicting that our trip would go very well, apologized for not being able to accompany us to the hotel for he still had some matters to take care of with Don Próspero. His driver, who could match Asmania in his muteness, would take us back.

"All that stuff I said when I was hypnotized, can it be true?" I asked Wen on the way back, upon learning what had happened in the hypnotist's *fumoir.* "I don't remember any such things about my uncle. Not once, till La Generala summoned me, did I even suspect that we had a similar limp or that I feared him. The truth is that I barely remembered him!"

"Maybe you needed to forget those things for specific reasons," he suggested. "But you are now grown up and have nothing to fear. Besides, I am with you and I'll protect you."

We slept in each other's arms, and, due to the heat, naked, with the windows wide open. It is quite a liberating sensation not to have to curl up under heavy blankets all night.

In the morning, as we devoured a sumptuous breakfast, we went over all that had happened the night before. We agreed that the ceremony of the decapitation had been *bouleversant,* we laughed at Don Próspero's obsession with beards and regretted that Esmeralda hadn't had a chance to enjoy the unusual evening because of her obsession with going to Egypt. We headed to the Montoya Station and boarded the express to the Port of Colombia. Once there, we had no problem finding the pier where the liner *Fynlandia* was moored. Captain Hort Ferk welcomed us in person as we boarded. He was an imposing Swede who, as we found out later, had just returned from the capital where he had met with the president of the republic.

We loved our cabin, and after a stroll on the deck we confirmed that the boat was completely full and was a sort of floating Tower of Babel.

That afternoon we set sail.

"Adieu, la Colombie," Wen said as he looked off into the distance, leaning on the railing, the wind passing through his hair, so that he seemed irresistibly like some romantic poet. *"Dans quelques jours nous serons enfin devant la plus grande actrice de tous les temps . . . Avec le pardon de Madame Bernhardt."*

PART TWO

Havana
January through February 1924

Of my mysterious life,
So dark and full of woe,
You will hear a tale of something
That will freeze your very soul.

Your cheeks, the color of rose,
Will turn gaunt as it unfolds,
As you hear this strange tale
That will freeze your very soul.

Julián del Casal

Because you boys,
When you get together . . .

Bola de Nieve

Each city has its own personality, each deals with you in its own way. Some welcome you as soon as you arrive, showering you with blessings. They are patient, friendly, loving. Other cities loathe you at first sight. You have not even introduced yourself; have not had the chance to cause offense, but it hardly matters. They reject you—you awaken in them an unnatural hatred. They growl at you through clenched teeth, and at the first chance would sink them into you, forcing you to flee.

Whoever thinks that a city is but a conglomeration of houses, public buildings, factories, parks, statues, fountains, streets, cars, of people that come and go obsessed with their own problems, is mistaken. Cities are gigantic creatures that breathe silently.

When I arrive at a city, I'm careful not to be fooled by first impressions. I have learned to be guided by other signals that better reveal its true nature. Smells, for example. Smells betray a city. So does a certain pulse that comes from deep within and that you feel between your toes.

Sometimes, I come upon a new city and I feel as if I were a part of it, as if I have always lived there. In other cities, I feel extraneous, a foreigner, a speck of dust in its eye. As soon as the city becomes aware of my presence, it gets all worked up, it weeps and gets insulted, and looks for a way to be rid of me. Only when it sees that I am not afraid does it consider tolerating me. But woe is me, if I grow too trusting. I never let my guard down, for the city waits in ambush, and if the right moment comes I will pay dearly for my arrogance.

As a rule, I distrust cities. I don't feel tied down to any one of them. I am, to put it plainly, from nowhere. I was born in a hotel room in Vigevano. My parents arrived there a few days before my birth and left a few days afterwards, never to return. The cathedral is pretty, with an impressive duomo. And that is that.

Some cities cause spasms of the soul; others, a measureless peace. Chicago despises me, although I have to admit, the hatred is reciprocal: I, too, detest it. Christiania, on the other hand, is compassionate. The night that I tried to visit Ibsen there, his wife informed me that it was impossible, that he was on his deathbed. Christiania shared in my sorrow as I stood for many hours outside the playwright's home, braving the wintry air, keeping a watch on the light from his window, while he suffered without knowing that I had traveled all the way to Norway to thank him for reinventing the theater.

Venice for me is almost always Gabriele—Gabriele and I in a gondola, admiring the domes of churches in those bright days when he loved me. Venice is our first night together in that penthouse apartment at the Palazzo Barbaro-Wolkoof.

Montevideo is desolate and mournful. There, those of us in Rossi's company witnessed the death of one of our own: Diotti. He was ravaged by fevers, far away from his loved ones. It was sudden and devastating. Montevideo is the grave of a youth, one far too young, who had never done any harm in this world; Montevideo is the letter that Rossi sent to a mother, breaking the news. Why were my prayers not answered?

Vienna is a fusion of sounds: waltzes, applause, crystal. Alexandria is a giant bazaar, foul and dirty, full of dazed people who smoke incessantly. Paris is the abode of The Magnificent One. Paris belongs to Sarah. Despite the show of public devotion for me, I always feel like a stranger there. Paris, always loyal to the fiery redhead, watches me with disdain, as if trying to make me understand that I am nothing, an impostor.

Berlin is Robi Mendelssohn's laugh—my dear Jew, the most generous man in the world. They say that he was secretly in love with me, though I swear, if it was true, he never once acted on it. He was my friend, almost a brother. When he died, his widow Giulietta, withdrew her friendship. She made accusations, imagining that Robi and I were lovers. I had never noticed before how jealous she had always been of me.

Good God! I loved her like a daughter. It was I, after all, who first introduced them.

Lisbon is an endless stupor. There, one morning, in the vicinity of the Torre de Belém, an elderly gentleman, very well dressed and sporting a monocle, stopped me. I was annoyed. I thought that it might be someone who had seen my pictures in the papers, but I soon realized that he had no idea who I was. The gentleman warily assured me that he had just heard a voice with a message for me.

I looked him up and down, wondering if he was mad; but, unwavering, he added that he had a gift for hearing voices and that it was his duty to relay each message to its rightful recipient. If, for some reason, he failed to fulfill his obligations, he would fall victim to horrible earaches that no doctor could manage to alleviate. Would I allow him then to convey the message? I agreed to listen to him, firstly because I did not want to be at blame for his earaches, and secondly because I figured that it was the quickest way to get rid of him. So then he blurted out: "You have two arms and you need them both. If you had to cut one off, which one would you choose?" I was going to answer something, I don't remember what, but he stopped me with a gesture, and explained that his work was done once he had revealed his message. He bowed respectfully and walked away, twirling his cane.

Months later, Enrichetta summoned me urgently to Berlin. She was already a young woman, and someone, a poisonous soul, had put in her hands Il fuoco. She told me that she was hurt and humiliated, not so much by Gabriele's novel, for it was a work worthy of the scoundrel who was its author, but for my own lack of self-pride. How could I stay with a man who wrote with such cruelty about me? I tried to deflate the issue, pointing out that La Foscarina was a character in a novel and not me, but she only shot me an icy stare.

"Fine, Enrichetta," I said, having no other choice, "you are a grown woman and you are going to have to understand.

I have two arms. You are one of them, the other one is D'Annunzio, and I can't cut either one of them off without it killing
me." Just as I finished uttering the last word, as my daughter
fell into my arms weeping, I remembered the gentleman from
Lisbon and I realized for the first time that that afternoon he
had been speaking to me in Portuguese the entire time. How
in the hell was I able to understand him? Lisbon is always for
me that eccentric gentleman who wandered through the city,
passing on messages to others.

And what about Havana? What memories do I have of
her, of her combination of exquisiteness and savagery? What
will she transform herself into in my thoughts, this magnificent
place that serves as a bridge between two worlds? The weeks
that I have lived here will be compressed into just a few images. A boat crossing the bay perhaps. Seagulls cawing above
me. The tempting, the alluring, whatever it is that drags us toward the mystery that is the power of the sea. Calloused hands
beating on drums. No, no. Havana will be two young,
charming gentlemen, determined against the odds to rip these
faded memories from me.

The first days aboard the *Fynlandia,* the stopover at Puerto Colón, and the last leg toward Havana, were rather dull.

The crew was a swarm of creatures with hair the color of wheat; and in size and appearance they seemed to have all been descended from the Norse god Odin himself. They were trained in the art of attending the passengers with the utmost courtesy, but always at a cool distance. On confirming that it was absurd to expect the slightest measure of human warmth from these Scandinavians, and that our smiles and suggestive looks were dashed against shields forged with some secret and impenetrable metal, we gave up on our fantasy of seducing them.

We devoted ourselves instead to watching the passengers, but could not find in them anything worth our efforts. They were mostly old Jewish men, bearded and in threadbare coats; plump matrons; newlywed couples; and unbearable children who ran all over the place pursued by their governesses.

The second night aboard, Captain Hort Ferk invited us to a banquet and we sat at his table in the ship's dining room. Like the rest of the invited guests (an Argentinean couple who were touring the world celebrating their silver anniversary, a Polish conductor with an unpronounceable last name, and a certain Miss Eppleton, an old maid), we outdid ourselves praising the chef, who had prepared, in our honor, fish in a white sauce, stuffed with almonds and walnuts. To be honest, the fish was tasteless and the whole evening rather pathetic. The Argentinean husband spent the whole night pointing out to us the beauty of women and wisecracking, again and again, how lucky we were to be traveling without our wives. The *gringa* recounted ad nauseam the tale of one of her cousins who was going to join her fiancé but disappeared during the sinking of the *Titanic.* And to top off the intolerable, nightmarish evening, the hardworking Vikings in charge of serving us seemed more delicious than ever.

The third day, after breakfast, I decided to stay in bed and began to read a novel by Valle-Inclán. Wenceslao, who had not given up on his quest to find among the passengers at least one tidbit that he could sink his teeth into, went to make his rounds. I was lost in my reading when he returned triumphantly.

"Well?" I asked, leaving the Marquis of Bradomín in the middle of a love scene.

"We have one of ours aboard," he announced.

"How could you not have noticed before?" I asked, excited, sitting up on the bed and throwing *Sonata de primavera* aside.

"He has not been feeling well, so he has never been to the dining room." And then, telegram-style, he caught me up on all he had learned: "Cuban. Twenty-seven years old. Returning from Argentina from visiting an aunt. Rich, well-educated, confident and . . ."

Without even letting him finish his report, I insisted that I be introduced. With a mysterious smile, he consented and led me to the bow of the ship, where a stranger looked out at the horizon. On hearing us, he turned, and I was face to face with Emilio De la Cruz. I almost stumbled and fell over into the sea. Wen's description was missing a final and very important detail: ugly. Though I don't think that word completely captures it. More than ugly, though that he was, hands down, Emilio was a rare bird—a freak of nature. Scrawny, haggard, with tiny eyes and the dramatic face of a monkey, he was a very rare bird indeed. What saved him from being a complete disaster was that he was terribly charming. Like Wen, he was an only child, and only for the sake of pleasing his father, a wealthy landowner in Ciego de Ávila, he had studied law. The diploma, duly signed by the esteemed rector of the University of Havana, hung on a wall in the dining room of his father's house. In return, Emilito received a monthly stipend that allowed him to live comfortably, devoted, as he himself told us, to doing nothing, fluttering from party to party and generously repaying his lovers for their attentions.

From that morning on we were inseparable. Our first Cuban friend made up for his lack of good looks with lively conversation, a good sense of humor when it came to Argentinean marriages, and a worldly self-assurance that made evident not only that he was well bred, but that he was used to moving in exclusive circles. Soon we stopped being the Señores Hoyos, Belalcázar, and De la Cruz and became simply Wen, Lucho, and Emilito.

At Emilio's suggestion, we spent our mornings sunbathing on the deck. Emilio and Wen entertained themselves by observing the passengers, guessing where they were going and for what reason, and making up countless gruesome tales about them. They made fun of the garish outfits of the nouveau riche ladies, and of the mustaches and protruding bellies of their husbands. They toyed with Miss Eppleton, telling her of succulent mangoes that grew on vines and watermelons that hung from the branches of trees and ripened in the sun. And they felt no shame about slandering Captain Ferk, concocting for him a romantic affair with a rabbi.

Another thing they loved to do was to ring the service bell so that one of the Vikings would appear and in perfect English ask us what we wanted. To which De la Cruz, knowing that Scandinavians rarely spoke our language, would answer in Spanish under his breath, "To have my way with you, my darling." Or "To eat you alive, my angel." We would burst out laughing like spoiled brats before ordering lemonade or a glass of red wine.

The Cubano shared Wen's fascination with boxers. He knew who Luis Vicentini was, of course, and had to admit that his looks, as rough as they were childlike, were appealing; but, and in this he agreed with me, Vicentini wasn't as superbly wonderful as my lover imagined. His favorite—and this before his trip to Argentina—was his compatriot named Fello Rodríguez, also known as the Tiger of Havana.

"He's not all that good in the ring," he informed us, "but he sure is good to look at."

However, during his stay in that southerly country, he had discovered in the pages of the daily *Clarin* the existence of a young boxer of just nineteen tender years, a native of Georgia and named Young Stribling. If the pictures corresponded at all with what he was like in the flesh, then the precious *gringo* would, without a doubt, take over the most prominent spot on his altar.

Since Emilio was returning home after a two-month stay at his aunt's husband's ranch, he did not know anything about Eleonora Duse's visit. Wen, very pleased, provided him all the details of the engagement. Our homely friend listened attentively, careful not to betray his ignorance on the topic; for, unless I am wholly mistaken, he had not a clue as to who was the Italian actress who inspired us to cross the ocean. Later, he promised us that he would buy a ticket to go see La Signora, and then recited the names of all the great personalities that had performed in Havana: Anna Pavlova, Enrico Caruso, Sergei Rachmaninoff, Titta Ruffo, Encarnación López "La Argentinita," Ignacio Paderewski, María Guerrero, and, of course, the incomparable, the superhuman, the divine Bernhardt . . .

That string of pretentious epithets preceding the name of his idol's rival so irked Wen that, oozing venom but not losing his composure, he said that although he had never managed to see the French tragedienne act, he had read various critics who called her bombastic, pompous, exaggerated in her gestures, not to mention the ones that called her a whorish old woman who appeared on stage with her scandalous red wigs and a thick coat of makeup to hide her wrinkled face. Far from being upset by these comments, De la Cruz confirmed them, enjoying himself in recalling that six years before, when he went to the performances of Bernhardt's second and last season in Cuba, he had been bewildered to see the old woman, who could have been knitting stockings for her great-grandchildren, attempt to perform *The Death of Cleopatra,* or *Joan of Arc,* or *The Lady of the Camellias.* Not once, he went on, could he recognize in such a human ruin the sensuous queen of the Nile, or the maiden of Orléans, or the consumptive, seductive courtesan of Paris. His statement made Wen jump up from his lounge chair and hug him effusively.

"La Duse is the opposite pole of La Bernhardt, my friend," he said to the startled De la Cruz. "She detests artifice and loves, as no one else, moderation and restraint. Sarah, that witch, accused her of stealing her repertoire. But could it be that plays produced by the pen of a genius belong to one interpreter alone? Each actress is free to choose, among the many, those she desires, and to give her flesh and soul to the characters to make them real." His eyes seemed like two embers, and the zeal with which he spoke made me think that if he put his mind to it he could be quite a defense lawyer. "That La Bernhardt lost her mind when Eleonora interpreted *The Lady of the Camellias, Magda,* and *The Wife of Claude* in the Paris theaters seems, no matter which way you look at it, a little suspicious. For if, in reality, the Frenchwoman had accomplished something incomparable in her performance of those roles, far from being bothered that the Italian was performing them in a mediocre, in her judgment, fashion, it should have made her *happy,* for the comparison would only emphasize her supposed histrionic superiority. But instead she would become annoyed any time Eleonora performed one of the plays that, presumptuously, she thought were hers, and she would stomp and curse and swear out of that toothless mouth. There had to be a *reason.* Don't you think?"

We made sure to quickly agree and, to prevent the start of another disquisition in defense of La Duse, Emilito immersed himself in a thorough description of the pampa and the abundant gauchos who are spread throughout it—strong, hairy men, fearless and with magnetic eyes—a sort of giant species of men who devour their meat almost raw and are able to wrestle a bull one-on-one and come out victorious.

"And did you ever run into a certain Martín Fierro?" Wen asked, forgetting for a moment about his revered Eleonora.

"Quite a few times," De la Cruz confirmed and his cheeks reddened with pleasure while I thought that, almost certainly, the encounters must have taken place in darkness, so that the gauchos would not have to suffer the horror of looking at his face. "At one point, I was about to let them brand my haunches with their hot irons."

We got off at the Port of Colón, but after ten minutes I grew bored and told them that I would be returning to the boat. The shacks and surrounding nature seemed to lack all interest and it only took one quick look for me to realize that the same was true with the natives. Faced with so much filth, heat, and misery, I chose to remain aboard with my Valle-Inclan novel, ensconced in the Gaetani Palace with María del Rosario and Bradomín. Wenceslao, however, went into town with Emilito and made him dizzy with a patriotic tirade about how the *gringos* had treacherously ripped this piece off the map of Colombia to invent the Republic of Panama so they could build the canal that makes them such lucrative profits. They returned with a basket of ripened and feverish fruits that I didn't even want to taste. They, however, ate bananas, tangerines, and slices of papaya and watermelon till they were sated, and had even invited Miss Eppleton to their little feast.

When the *Fynlandia* set its course for the Island, Havana became the principal topic of our conversations. De la Cruz inquired if we had a reservation at any hotel, and when we told him we didn't, he offered to recommend an excellent one. He asked discreetly how much we were willing to spend. "As much as it takes to feel comfortable in a first-class establishment," Wen said haughtily, and Emilio then suggested, without hesitating, that in that case the ideal place would be the Seville-Biltmore, a hotel with all comforts imaginable, near the ocean and most of the places of interest. That didn't mean, he made clear, that places which were less expensive but which would make our stay pleasant, didn't exist. But the hotel he had recommended was very chic and very much in fashion. And furthermore, they had just added a tower that made it the tallest building in the capital. "So we will stay there," I said, putting an end to the subject and without asking, so as not to have it seem important, the nightly rate.

De la Cruz also lectured us about the historic and recreational places that we must visit, like the Cathedral, the Centro Gallego, the gardens at the Tropical Brewery, the beaches at Marianao, and the university stadium, which was used by thousands of students to exercise; all this, of course, without mentioning other destinations, *non sanctos,* about which he would fill us in at the appropriate time . . . for although the primary objective of our visit was to attend La Duse's performances in El Nacional, we would spend our mornings, afternoons, and late nights enjoying ourselves and open to meeting colorful characters.

The night of Monday the twenty-first of January, Wen and I stayed up late, I reading and he writing letters to his mother and to Juanma Vengoechea, which he was going to send as soon as we set foot in Havana. He asked if I wasn't going to write to La Generala, and I told him that I would rather send a telegram. According to our calculations, around that time La Gallego would be making her triumphal entry into Barranquilla in the plane *Bolívar,* and if she wasn't already en route to New York, from where she would take another boat to Suez, she would soon be. I looked out the porthole of our cabin and saw the sea, inky and calm, with an enormous round moon that looked like a bright arepa. If the captain was true to his word, first thing in the morning we would be in the capital of Cuba.

Hort Ferk didn't let us down. Before seven, on a splendid morning of blue skies without a trace of clouds, the *Fynlandia* made its way into the neck of the Bay of Havana, which is a mere three hundred meters wide and famous for its treacherous ways with ships with deep drafts. A little tugboat sailed ahead, indicating the route, to prevent an accident. Five years before, the liner *Valvarena* was wrecked when it tried to enter the bay during a tropical storm. On the deck with the other passengers, we watched, astonished at the abrupt bluffs on the bay floor that allowed access to the port. The city sparkled with a golden light, and De la Cruz, still sleepy-eyed, for whom crossing the mouth of that bay lacked any sort of surprise, pointed out the sharks that prowled around the ship.

"Whoever falls in won't live to tell the tale," he said, and we gulped as we watched those brownish-gray bodies, with their tough and lustrous skins, that appeared and disappeared with such ease. "Of course, you are going to have to find some nice Chinese joint to try shark-fin soup," Emilio proposed. "It's delicious," he added, not noticing the faces of disgust we were all making.

As the *Fynlandia* advanced, many fishing trawlers passed by her. Some were going out to sea and the others, the bulk of them, were returning from their nightly tasks bringing back fresh fish that merchants would bid on. In the boats, some of the men and kids waved back at the children and adults who greeted them from the ship, but most of the workers, consumed by their work, seemed not to notice the hands, the handkerchiefs, and the hats that were raised toward them.

"El Morro," De la Cruz announced, pointing at the castle with an enormous lighthouse that rose from a limestone cliff, on the left bank of the entrance to the bay; then, turning theatrically in the opposite direction, he said, "La Punta," and pointed to a fortress with thick walls, a watchtower, and large, rusted cannons, built also right on the sea centuries before, to protect the town from the threat of pirates. On the stones of the fort, a group of cadets energized their muscles with jumping jacks and other calisthenics. "Ladies and gentlemen, you have reached San Cristóbal de La Habana," the Cuban announced with open arms, using the city's full name.

A third fortress, La Cabaña, appeared on the top of a hill to the north. Once we were told that it was a military prison, the cute little windows on its walls didn't seem so amusing.

Seagulls and gannets flew over the ship, committed apparently to welcoming us with their shrieks, but suddenly dove into the choppy sea after some fish, betraying their true intentions.

"La Fuerza," the expert continued and invited us to admire the citadel with battlements on each of its four corners, a drawbridge and deep wraparound moat, which rose a few meters from the *malecón*. From atop the belltower, a weather vane in the shape of a woman seemed to greet us.

"When the English invaded us in days of yore, all this was turned to dust and we had to rebuild it," De la Cruz told us, pointing at all the buildings. "For, in case you didn't know it, our people were once upon a time British subjects. Too bad that they returned us to Spain in exchange for Florida," he remarked, "otherwise we would now speak perfect English, we would drink tea at five, with our pinkies in the air, and we wouldn't have so much of the stinking Spanish in us."

The smell of the port came upon us suddenly, like a slap: a penetrating mix, the same all over the globe, of salt residue, rancid onion, pitch, fish brine, rotting wood, and urine. An unpleasant smell that you take in with every breath and that, for some incomprehensible reason, you begin to appreciate after a couple of days of enjoying the sea air. Once the ship had crossed through the narrow access path, the bay opened up unexpectedly, full of generosity, allowing us to see the many cargo and fishing schooners and small domestic steamships that zigzagged on the bay. The longshoremen, mostly blacks and *mestizos,* pulled out bales from the holds of the boats and carried them on their backs to the solid footing of the port.

De la Cruz said that the name of the fishing enclave on the hillside in the left bank was Casablanca. Beyond the other bank, which was full

of houses where importers and exporters kept their goods, and of es-
tablishments catering to seamen, the city was scattered. As the *Fynlandia* docked in the pier of San Francisco, we were able to make out
the convent of the same name; the graceful Mercury who adorned the
dome of the Commerce Guild; people walking in all directions;
houses, cafés, and bars; a labyrinth of narrow streets; streetcars, automobiles, and horse-drawn carts. Periodic gusts of odd sounds
reached us: automobile horns, the cries of fishmongers and lottery
salesmen, dismembered chords of music. The city simmered like a
thick stew cooked under the torrid sun. Just as when we had gotten
off the train in Barranquilla, I had the feeling that the Cuban capital
could also gobble us up if it wanted to, open its enormous dogfish
jaws and swallow us, intruders who had just arrived with the hopes of
sniffing its tail, whole, without leaving a single trace.

After going through the unavoidable process of customs and immigration, we were out on the street following Emilio De la Cruz. A
swarm of beggars and trinket-sellers descended upon us, but our
guide made them back off with a disdainful gesture. A delight of a
man ran up to him, screaming his name, gave him a hug, and took his
luggage.

"These gentlemen are my friends and we will drop them off at the
corner of Trocadero and Zulueta," Emilio told him, and while we
walked behind the man, who had also taken charge of our luggage, he
told us that Pancho, whom he had known since they were kids, was his
uncle's bodyguard and chauffeur. His uncle owned grocery stores
and had just successfully begun his political career.

The De la Cruz family automobile ("one of many," the driver made
clear in passing) was parked nearby. Dazed by the crowd, the noise,
and the unmerciful rays of the sun, we hurried to get into the stunning, six-cylinder Cleveland. Pancho fit in our bags as best as he could
and made the car fly through the avenue.

"After you check into the hotel, you can eat and rest awhile,"
Emilio recommended, "but be ready at three, when I'll come to pick
you up to show you around."

We said yes like automatons, and a few moments later the car
stopped suddenly, the brakes screeching loudly, at a stately hotel with
an exotic, Moorish-style façade and a tower of, I can't recall, eight or

nine stories. A group of employees hurried out to the lobby of the Seville-Biltmore to take care of the luggage, with a kindness bordering on obsequiousness.

That the place was chic—not just in style, but modern—we got two proofs in less than a minute. The first was when the receptionist did not even bat an eye when we requested only one bed, as wide as possible; and the second, when as we signed the guest book, we saw coming out of the elevator, thin and dressed in lilac silk, an orchid on her breast, none other than the most beautiful Gloria Swanson. A man was there to meet her, and as if he were handling a crystal figurine, led her daintily toward the tables of the tiled interior courtyard.

"Pinch me," I asked Wen, not able to believe that the Hollywood star that I had so often seen on the screen at the Salon Olympia was no more than a few steps away from me, sipping from a straw a yellow drink garnished with an orange slice. "Not so hard, you bitch," I cried with clenched teeth, rubbing the hurt spot.

The bellboy called us with a respectful "This way, gentlemen," and led, toward their spacious room on the second floor, the two provincials recently arrived from whatever third-rate country where seeing the great Swanson in the flesh would have been inconceivable.

The room, cozy and tastefully furnished, had a window facing east, which we opened. A wave of sunlight flooded the four walls, and we quickly put away all our things in the drawers of the wardrobe. From between the pages of one of the books that I brought, an envelope containing a letter from my uncles to the Colombian consul stuck out. On seeing it, I remembered the task that I tried to keep far away from my thoughts. I wasn't, of course, going to ruin the celebration of our arrival by thinking of my wayward uncle: there was plenty of time to deal with that disagreeable mess.

We took a reviving bath and, realizing that it was still long before noon, decided to explore the neighborhood at our own risk. There was no better time, the concierge suggested, to take a stroll on the Prado, only half a block away, and so there we headed, fumbling, getting used to moving in that shimmering, almost palpable, light that draws the contours of houses and ignites them in surprising colors.

The wide boulevard, shaded by two rows of laurels, seduced us on first sight. But on coming closer and seeing the bronze lions on their stone pedestals, their jaws open and their manes unkempt, half asleep in the flaming heat, on passing the womanly iron streetlamps on each corner, each with five bulbs, on coming upon the marble benches where passersby sat to enjoy the shade and listen to one another's stories, on discovering the whimsical arabesques that drew themselves on the granite ground when the light filtered through the leaves of poplars and then came undone, we fell hopelessly in love with the tree-lined street.

"I doubt that such an enchanting place exists in any other city," Wen ventured to say. And, knowing better, I didn't argue.

We made our way slowly through the walkway, toward the sea, ignoring the cars that passed by us on the parallel roads. On each side of those roads, in the adjacent sidewalks, life unfolded with a boisterous and dizzying speed. The boulevard, however, is a haven, with its own tempo, more pleasing for the newly arrived because, before jumping headlong into the torrent of the city, it allows them to get used to the furious rhythm in stages. And so we learned, without the aid of guides or go-betweens, that the Prado is a sort of river with a wide, dry bed, and that like all rivers it perishes in the sea.

At the end of the avenue, near the statue of the poet who, before dying in front of the firing squad, wrote a few verses dedicated to a swallow, we ran into a sad, immense, and unattractive jailhouse. Looking away from its walls crowded with barred windows, we turned our attention to a square with tall columns surrounded by wrought-iron benches. There, we guessed, a band performed evening concerts, maybe on Sundays. Later we strolled on the esplanade of La Punta and, coming closer to the *malecón* that spreads toward the west, we again admired the wonders of that fort and of El Morro. Waves crashed against the stone wall where we had stopped, and one of them, breaking with undue force, splashed on us. I tasted the sea on my lips and felt the sentimental urge to kiss Wen and steal the salt from his lips.

Afterwards, we decided to go back on the boulevard and retrace our steps toward the opposite end. On each street crossing, we stood again in ceremony under the lions that watched over each corner, who, so imposing and full of themselves, did not even glance at us. We walked on and on, taking great delight in the buildings on each side, most of them great residences of two or more floors, with ornate balconies and façades. We imagined that it would be possible to make that whole journey sheltering ourselves from the sun or the rain in the immense portals of many columns.

On reaching Neptuno, the Prado ceased to be an oasis of pedestrians and became a wide, noisy street, lacking any charm, aside from the magnificent houses that lined it. Crossing the street diagonally, we came upon the busy Parque Central and a statue of José Martí, ardently preaching, surrounded by ridiculous sculptures and bas-reliefs reminiscent of the *Iliad,* which were supposed to represent the motherland, honor, courage, and other such stupidities. The poor apostle ranted and ranted from his pedestal, the whole day long, and not a single passerby seemed interested in what he said.

The wooden and wrought-iron benches spread among the fountains, the palm trees, and fig trees enticed us to take a break and, since the infernal heat was beginning to take its toll, we grabbed one of them. It was only briefly, because a couple of kids, who approached us offering to shine our shoes and who apparently didn't know the meaning of the word "no," scared us away.

We continued our pilgrimage, and our next stop was in front of a large fountain, on which a beautiful Indian made of white Carrara marble, with a quiver full of arrows and a feathered headdress held in one hand the shield of the city, and in the other a horn of plenty. At her feet, four dolphins, smitten with their mistress, shot out from their mouths thin streams of water and leapt upwards, trying to escape the black-green moss in which they were entrapped. "Weep no more, dolphins of the fountain, on the gray cup of old stone," I mused, staring at them, not quite sure who dictated those mysterious words to me. If I had paper and pencil in hand, I would have written a poem right on the spot. "Noble Havana," so the fountain was named, reminded us on that morning—as if the walk from one end of the Prado to the other hadn't already convinced us—that we were on an isle very different from our mound-surrounded Bogotá, a place so full of life that, for obvious reasons, it was known as the Pearl of the Antilles.

Wen, weary with so much beauty and novelty, proposed that we should gather our strength, and taking up the Prado again (Neptuno, Virtudes, Ánimas, Trocadero—the names of the streets seemed less strange now), dazed by the car horns and the cries with which street merchants announced the sale of fruits and sweets, we returned to the Seville-Biltmore.

During lunch we reconfirmed the cosmopolitan nature of the hotel. Many of the guests were foreigners, mostly *gringos*. We secretly wished to run into La Swanson again, to observe her more closely, but the celluloid diva was nowhere to be seen. Wen ordered a lamb chop with mint and roasted tomatoes, while I, since after our little adventure I felt like exploring all aspects of the Island, took the recommendation of our chubby and obsequious waiter and ordered slices of fried pork, a dish called "Moors and Christians" (a divine metaphor for what was simply rice and black beans!), and yucca so strongly seasoned with garlic that as soon as the meal was done I rushed to wash my mouth frenetically. Our time, which at first had seemed short, allowed us to take a look at a map of the city and even to take a nap on the softened sheets of the canopied bed.

When Emilio De la Cruz came to pick us up, and we let him know that the Prado no longer held any secrets for us, he burst out laughing and said we were impatient and unfaithful. In his company, we went deep into the ancient heart of the capital. We didn't stay on one single street, but instead roamed from O'Reilly to San Ignacio and from Obrapía to Mercaderes, chatting animatedly and stopping each time we came upon something we deemed worthy of stopping for: the cathedral with its uneven towers; the plazas framed by the colonial palaces; the embroidered railing, called "neighbor guard," which separated one balcony from another; the colorful *mediopuntos*—stained-glass semicircular windows—of some mansion for rent.

If that second go-round lacked the intensity and magic of our morning adventure, it served to confirm something that we had often heard: that Cuban men are divine.

"Well, *some of them,*" our ugly Emilito pointed out playfully. And I cruelly thought how every rule has an exception.

Not knowing how we got there, we suddenly found ourselves again strolling on the walkway guarded by lions and we stopped at El Anón del Prado. De la Cruz thought it a sin if we returned to the hotel without tasting the fruit sorbets that they sold in that establishment, and it didn't take much to convince us. It was at El Anón, as we savored our ice creams with our little silver spoons, where snidely he proposed that if we weren't all that tired and the adventure tempted us, we should go with him to a variety theater for single men.

"I can't guarantee you that the show itself will please you," he warned us, "but I can guarantee that the audience will be a feast for the eyes."

He offered to come pick us up, but we told him we'd rather go on our own to start to feel more at home in the city. He agreed and said that the theater was very close to the hotel. Nevertheless, since it would be dark out, he recommended that we arrange for a fiacre. "A taxi," he explained, "that's what we call them here."

We asked for the address.

"On the corner of Consulado and Virtudes," he answered. "But all you have to say is the Alhambra."

I don't like it when they speak ill of Sarah in my presence. The great ones always deserve respect. She had her flaws, many flaws, but it is thanks to her that I came to understand that the theater is an eternal longing to reach distant places, and that it was worth dedicating your whole life to it.

I saw her for the first time when I had just become a leading actress. The world-famous Sarah, who was touring Europe with her company, agreed to come to Turin only if they put at her disposal the Carignano. They almost drove Rossi mad, till he agreed to interrupt his season and grant a few dates to the Frenchwoman. They refurbished the old theater in a rush, and my dressing room was transformed into a sort of bedchamber in the Palace of Versailles. They announced the performances: The Lady of the Camellias, The Sphinx, Adriana Lecouvreur, and Frou-frou, and, despite the fact that seats were very expensive, there was much anticipation and the shows quickly sold out.

Ten days before opening night, trunks and cages with animals began to arrive. And finally Bernhardt appeared, with her fiery long locks and that mouth that looked like a mailbox that had just been painted red, and with a cub lion and her young Greek husband.

I saw every show. But more than seeing her, I studied her. They said she was a genius. And she was, without a doubt, in her own way. Extraordinary and one-of-a-kind. Her enunciation was incoherent, she walked on the stage like a rocket about to take off, and she knitted her brow in an exaggerated manner.

Sarah was always herself. She never stopped being La Bernhardt, no matter what role she took on. She was too striking, too captivating and forceful to submit to someone else. She lacked the necessary humility to disappear behind a character. It was Sarah whom Armand fell in love with, not Marguerite.

She didn't become a character, she substituted for it. The set was horrible, and the actors on stage with her very ordinary. But why waste money on hiring other reputable actors? At the end of the day, the audience paid their money to see Bernhardt. As long as she performed well—and of course she did!—that was all that mattered.

One night, Rossi dragged me to the dressing rooms and, putting me face-to-face with The Magnificent One, explained to her that I was the principal actress of La Compagnia della Citta di Torino. I saluted her, blushing and with a little bow. I was so nervous that I didn't even dare look up at her. I doubt if she looked at me.

When she left Turin followed by her entourage, her trunks, and her zoo, everything changed for me. Her power, her magic, had marked me. I knew what I wanted: to put myself in the service of art and of beauty. To be free, to be great. Great like her, but not her. To win the right to do as I wanted, and not what rules imposed on me. I realized that to achieve this, I needed to overcome my insecurities and lack of confidence.

Sara was beautiful? I, too, could be, if I wanted to. Sara was moving? I, too, would make audiences vibrate with emotion, but in a whole other manner. I didn't quite know how, wasn't yet sure what that manner would be. The only thing that was clear to me at that time was that I would not try to imitate her, instead I would do the opposite. She was an explosion of feelings? I would be the soul of moderation. She recited? I would speak. She underlined? I would insinuate. Rossi wasn't sure if I was joking or if I had taken leave of my senses when I proposed that we should resume our season with The Lady of the Camellias and that I would play the lead.

"Do you want to burn down my Carignano?" he whimpered and forced me to do Let's Get a Divorce.

But that summer, in Rome, I got my way. For the first time I confronted him and I said either we do Dumas fils or we do nothing. My sudden firmness made him relent. I wanted to bring to life the same characters the Frenchwoman did, and risk comparison.

On returning to Turin, we started with Frou-frou. "Dangerous," many said. How dare we stage one of Sarah's successes, with her own season so fresh in the mind still? The theater was packed. I suppose the audience came to witness a disaster. They came to laugh at me and left applauding me. The same happened when an emboldened Rossi agreed to stage The Lady of the Camellias.

I saw Sarah again fifteen years later, in different circumstances.

She herself convinced Schurmann, who had been her producer and was then mine, to book me for an engagement in her theater. I hesitated before accepting. I had waited for that moment a long time, and when it finally came, I was afraid. To perform in the French capital, in none other than the Renaissance, was to enter a wolves' lair. In the home of The Magnificent Sarah! The biggest wolf. The critics had already begun comparing us. In England, Bernard Shaw had published an article about us, in which he compared our methods of acting and ended up preferring mine. Someone told me that when they read it to her, La Bernhardt had a fit of rage. Could I survive the battering of her fans, which were numbered in the thousands in Paris?

To stall, I came up with all types of excuses and demands. I told Gabriele that I would only go if he would write a play that I could perform for the first time there. And he did it! I asked Andó if he would put off all his engagements for a couple of weeks to come on stage with me in the part of Armando Duval, and to my surprise he said yes. He was already forty-seven years old, but he was still the best leading actor in Italy. I saw that I had no choice. Sooner or later it would happen. I told Schurmann that I would do it.

The first thing I did when I got to Paris was to buy new chiffons at Worth. All dressed up, I put my courage to the *sticking place and went off to meet Sarah, who had cut short a tour of Brussels to come welcome me. As can be expected, she did not remember our meeting in Turin and I didn't want to bring it up. She embraced me effusively (why did everything have to be so theatrical with her?) and overwhelmed me with her compliments. She was gentle, and by all appearances very caring and protective of me; but when I got to the theater I found her dressing room locked so that I had no choice but to take refuge in an uncomfortable and smelly one at the end of the hall.*

Although some considered it a type of suicide, I chose The Lady of the Camellias to open.

I have rarely felt as nervous as I did that night. All of Paris was at the Renaissance. The Princess Mathilde Bonaparte. The widow of Dumas fils. Bizet's widow. And an army of critics headed by the influential and paunchy Sarcey, all with their eyes fixed on me. In a box, trying at all costs to call attention to herself, with an enormous crown of flowers and her hands crowded with glimmering rings, was Sarah. This did not make me feel any better. I should admit that it was a terrible performance. One of the worst of my life. The critics were cold. The same thing happened a few days later, when I performed Magda. With Cavalleria rusticana and The Wife of Claudius the press treated me a little better.

And then the witch, not happy with having been witness to my failure, tried to get us to perform together in a charity event that would raise funds for a monument to Dumas fils. Her devilish plan consisted of a performance of The Lady of the Camellias. She, the last two acts; me, the second and third. Or the two that had come off the worst at my opening night. She announced her idea to the press, and I had no choice but to go along. But that being so, I refused to perform what she had so perfidiously chosen. I said that I would do the second act of The Wife of Claudius and refused to be convinced otherwise.

To my surprise (and Sarah's surprise, I imagine), it was a complete success. When, days later, I did that play again, Parisians went crazy and paid up to two hundred and fifty francs for a seat. They had "discovered" my style. And suddenly, they loved me.

Sarah left for London, furious, and there she avenged herself by making poisonous comments to the press. "Eleonora Duse traverses roads that have been opened up by others," she said. "It is true that she never imitates: she plants flowers where others have planted trees and trees where others have planted flowers. She has done nothing but to use someone else's gloves and put them on inside out," she declared. "She is a great actress, even perhaps one of the greatest, but she is not an artist," she concluded.

To finish off the visit, I debuted without much ado the play that D'Annunzio had written for me. And I was about to return to Italy when Sarcey thought that I should offer one special event, a matinee by invitation only, so all the theater people would have a chance to see me. Since there was no way to convince Sarah to rent us the Renaissance, Schurmann found the Théâtre de la Porte Saint-Martin. That afternoon was my revenge. I began with *Cavalleria rusticana*, then performed the fifth act of *The Lady of the Camellias* and, to finish off, the second act of *The Wife of Claudius*. The horrible Sarcey, whom I so feared, said his farewells with an article in *Les Temps* in which he declared that I was returning to Italy victorious and leaving an example for French actors that they would do well to take advantage of . . . I imagine The Magnificent One never forgave him.

Oh, Sarah, Sarah . . . True to herself till the very end. I learned so much from her! She was my inspiration, the one who spurred me to the top. Where is she now? Who knows! But in any case, I am sure that she doesn't roam the Comédie Française or the Renaissance like a nostalgic phantom. I'm inclined to believe that at this moment she is walking on stage, there in the depths of hell, amid sulfurous clouds and the bubbling cauldrons of oils where sinners are boiled. With her bright red hair in complex braids, The Divine One recites her lines. Always beautiful and seductive, she performs for Astaroth and Asmodeo, the great dukes of the underworld, and for hundreds of incubi and succubi who beat the ground with their tridents to celebrate her art.

2

I impatiently checked my pocket watch, the one Wen gave me on our first anniversary, engraved on the back with *Forever*. It was time for the show, and many of us in the audience shifted restlessly in our seats.

Wenceslao and I, both dressed in white head to toe, had arrived thirty minutes before in a car that the concierge at the Seville-Biltmore had called for us. During the short ride, the driver, a greasy and impudent Spaniard from Asturias, tried as hard as he could to engage us in conversation. But after asking us where we were from, how long we had been in the city, if we were brothers (I have no idea why people think that!), and what did we think of Havana, all of which questions we answered coldly with as few words as possible, he gave up. As revenge for our aristocratic silence, he charged us, we realized later, much more than the trip actually cost.

Emilio De la Cruz was already waiting for us under the marquee, surrounded by colorful posters, other passersby, and peanut and lottery salesmen; he, too, was dressed in white, his hair shiny with gel. In spite of having spent whole days with him while on board the *Fynlandia,* each time I saw him it took me a while to get used to his ugliness. On seeing us, he ran toward us, waving the tickets in his hand. There was no way to get him to accept money from us, he insisted that we were to be his guests that night, and he let us know that if we continued to protest he would take it as an insult. After looking at some of the photographs on display near the front door, we entered the theater chatting amiably.

The rug, a fiery red, matched the stage curtain. Although it was early, and they had only rung the first bell, the theater was almost full. We asked Monkeyface if such a large audience was normal and he responded, smiling, that if we were to go into any of the important theaters at that time, they would be just as lively.

"Cubans love the theater," he pronounced with evident pride. "They especially love this one."

We found three empty seats and made ourselves comfortable, De la Cruz on my right and Wenceslao on my left.

All around us, people continued to talk and smoke. In the row in front of us, a handful of very vivacious young men, mostly dark-haired and well-fed, traded jokes, gossip, and political comments, seasoning them with riotous laughter. Not content to just gab with each other or with their nearby friends, they stood up to grab the attention of others a few rows away, yelling without the least embarrassment and underlining certain phrases with winks, gestures, and waving of their arms. On more than one occasion, some of them became aware of the astonishment with which we watched them, and smiled at us from ear to ear before resuming their conversations, completely undisturbed.

The second bell announced that there was five minutes left before curtain time. While I pretended to listen to Emilio De la Cruz, who was enthusiastically suggesting to me that we should prolong our stay so that we could enjoy the upcoming Carnival, celebrated on three consecutive Sundays, out of the corner of my eye I watched a fluttery and impassioned Wenceslao make the moves on his neighbor. The boy next to him had opened his legs in such a manner that his right knee grazed, as if casually, my lover's left knee. Blond and blue-eyed, he would have been handsome if not for his protruding teeth and his large, fan-like ears. He asked Wen who knows what, and my darling, overcome by a sudden loquacity that would have astonished the driver from Asturias, began a fervent conversation with him. I took a deep breath and told myself that my lover was an honest-to-goodness tramp.

Wen cannot for the life of him resist the temptation to flirt with whatever member of the male sex gives him the slightest provocation. I am a little choosier and it annoys me when certain characters, who fall without a doubt under the category of strange ones, even so much as look at me. Wen disagrees, asserting that ignoring the come-ons of the ugly is an act not only in bad taste, but also revealing of a lack of sensibility. Sometimes I don't know whether to attribute such an attitude to his lecherous nature, compared to which my needs seem prudish, or to a mixture of pity and generosity, befitting a good Samaritan, which stops him from chilling any such aspirants with a deadly look or obvious signs of revulsion.

Whatever the case, to me it doesn't make sense, so taking my eyes away from the knocking knees I shifted my attention to the rest of the scene.

Not one more soul could fit into the one-hundred-and-fifty-seat orchestra. With a gesture of his chin, Emilito pointed to the "henhouse," the upper tier of the theater. There, the smoke was thicker and the ruckus louder.

"If I wasn't afraid of lice and fleas, I would go up there with the workers without even thinking about it. You come upon such showpieces!" he remarked with a roguish wink, and then added in a low voice: "It's not for nothing that they call that section 'paradise'!"

At that instant the young man seated next to Wenceslao whispered something apparently very funny in his ear, for the estimable Señor Hoyos let out a guffaw unthinkable in any theater in Bogotá. The two seemed to be enjoying each other all the more, and the initial contact at the knees had now extended to the calves.

"Wenceslao is very friendly," De la Cruz pointed out with a dash of venom, to bait me.

"Oh yes," I agreed, not giving the matter interest.

"How long have you been together?" he wondered.

"Very long," I answered, feigning boredom and rolling my eyes. "When we met, they were just starting to build the pyramid at Cheops," I went on, and as soon as ugly boy turned his head, I pinched Wen's thigh.

In the pit, the musicians were gathering in their places and readying their instruments, music sheets, and *particellas.* And then, an explosion was heard in the distance.

"Don't be startled," Monkeyface assured us. "It's the nine o'clock cannon. Every night it is fired from El Morro so people can set their clocks."

A second later, we heard the ringing of a bell, followed by three rings separated by small pauses, and the houselights darkened gradually. As soon as this happened, the conversations all drew to a close. In response to a signal from the conductor, the orchestra began to play a sort of overture, a rhythmic melody.

"Don't even think about doing anything with that oddball," I whispered to Wen.

"I find him attractive," he replied.

"He has terrible teeth," I retorted.

"Do I need him for a toothpaste ad?"

"And what about those ears?" I added sarcastically.

"You're too demanding," he protested.

"And you are very generous," I concluded, barely whispering, for the formerly riotous young men from the row in front were shushing us. The curtains were raised with the last bars of the melody, allowing us to see a marvelous scene that was greeted with applause.

The stage was set with a rental house very similar to those we had seen during our walk with Emilio in the narrow streets of the old city. No detail was lacking to give the appearance of reality: the multicolored *mediopuntos,* the windows with carved-wood spindles, the rundown furniture, the ornamental plants in porcelain vases, and the white sheets hung to dry on a clothes line. The appearance of the actors was the cause for another round of applause.

"This play opened many years ago and since the first day it has been very successful," Monkeyface explained. "If they close it down, people insist that it reopen."

The plot, sprinkled with music and double-entendre jokes, was very simple, not to say ordinary. Two medical students named Arturo and Rodolfo share a room in the terrace of a tenement. Because of the meager monthly stipends sent to them by their families from the interior of the Island, they find themselves in a bind, without a dime to eat. To make things worse, one of Rodolfo's cousins, whom they call Pachencho, lives with them as a guest, without contributing a thing to the depleted reserves of the young men. The future doctors decide that Pachencho should pretend to die so they can set up his funeral and in that way round up some money from their charitable neighbors. They even get Don Pepe, an old loan shark, famous in the neighborhood for his miserliness, to be moved by the death, and he lends them some money at just forty percent interest.

When the "deceased's" girlfriend, the *mulata* Rosalía, walked on stage with her hands on her waist and shaking her hips shamelessly, half the audience couldn't contain themselves, jumping from their seats and clapping and whistling and yelling remarks at the actress that verged on the obscene and that she endured complacently.

"That's Blanquita Becerra," Emilito revealed with a trace of reverence. "Some prefer La Sorg, but for me, Blanquita is the queen of the Alhambra, especially when she plays a *mulata*."

We nodded, inferring that La Sorg was another female figure in the company, and returned our attention to the stage. The actress greeted her admirers respectfully, put her hands on her breasts as if she were holding them in so they wouldn't pop out of their provocative brassiere, and waited till they quieted down to recite her first lines. In a booming voice, she let it be known that she was heartbroken over the death of Pachencho, for even if they had quarreled the night before, the deceased had stolen her heart. She announced that she would give the students twenty pesos, which took her many hours of work to save, to contribute to the cost of the burial and, initiating another round of catcalls, she alluringly reached in between her breasts and pulled out the wrinkled bills.

La Becerra's movements were so exaggerated and her voice so shrill and unpleasant that I looked at Wen as if saying, "If this is the best one, I don't want to see the others." He nodded. The grazing with his neighbor not only had continued but had extended to the forearm and the shoulder, so that they seemed like Siamese twins.

The comedy's action lurched on: a third of the jokes we couldn't hear for all the racket, another third we didn't get, and the last third we thought atrociously vulgar. In spite of this, we forced ourselves to laugh once in a while. Like everybody else there, De la Cruz and the boy with the huge teeth filled the hall with their guffaws and clapped loudly in praise of the antics of the actors, especially of the one known as "El Gallego," a Spaniard with a beret, mustache, and flushed cheeks, and another one who, in black face and dark gloves, played a negro, director of The Eternal Life funeral parlor, who thought himself very smart and educated but blurted out malapropisms right and left.

Truth be told, there was little difference between the behavior of the elegant gentlemen in the orchestra, with their straw hats with black bands resting on their thighs, and the rabble-rousers in the gallery. Notwithstanding their social positions, the quality of their wardrobes, and the amount of money that they carried in their pockets, they all seemed to greatly enjoy that sequence of put downs and womanly wigglings.

The story of Pachencho and his accomplices unfolded predictably; after a series of misunderstandings, Rosalía discovers that she has been the victim of a fraud, and the three crafty rogues are unmasked. But their neighbors forgive them and the lovers resume their romance. To finish off the production, the cast danced an ardent rumba with a catchy refrain, to which the audience joined in singing.

> *Tin Tan, you ate and then you ran,*
> *Tin Tan, you ate and then you ran.*

Heeding the adage "When in Rome, do as the Romans," we stood up for the final ovation and tried to shake our hips a little bit to the rhythm of the rumba, even though we never understood who was the Tin Tan mentioned in the song, for no character who had come on stage had such a name, or what eating and then running had to do with it.

There was an intermission, and Emilio suggested that we step outside to stretch. Almost unwillingly, Wenceslao forced himself to unlatch from his Siamese twin, who stayed in his seat looking up at him like a slaughtered lamb, and follow us out to the lobby. Once there, I took out my silver cigarette case and offered it to De la Cruz. With a contemptuous smile, he forced me to put it away and took out of his jacket a small case of homemade cigars. Soon the whole place was full of smoke. I am not exaggerating when I say we could barely see our faces.

The audience chatted about some of the best scenes in the comedy and enjoyed themselves repeating some of the allusions to the state of national politics. While Emilio talked to us about *Automobile Madness, Christopher Columbus Gallego,* and other very funny plays that, if we liked, we could see during the next few days, Wen and I traded elbow jabs to point out certain smokers who were especially fine-looking.

We were surprised to find out that there were three shows each night at the Alhambra.

"Those who have to get up early come to the first show," our guide said. "But if I can, I always come to the eleven o'clock show, the performances are always the best."

"Doesn't it end too late?" Wen protested.

"Late?" the Cuban laughed. "You have to get used to the pulse of this city. Here the good stuff doesn't start till midnight . . ."

Suddenly, De la Cruz excused himself and went over to greet some friends at the opposite end of the lobby. I thought I saw, through the spirals of smoke, two silhouettes that turned toward us, and almost as if by habit I took a deep breath and stuck out my chest.

"My eyes are burning," Wen complained. "Let's go back in."

"You are in a hurry to return to Señor Ears?" I said sarcastically.

"I'm serious," he said with an annoyed gesture, taking my arm. "Let's go."

I made a signal to Emilio and we went back in the theater making our way slowly through the swarm of people, trying not to brush up against any cigarettes. From the back of the orchestra, we could see the Siamese twin who had not moved from his seat. I admitted that seen from behind and from far away, he wasn't bad. He had broad shoulders and a strong neck, but those teeth, and, on top of that, that horrific set of ears!

"His legs are very hard," Wen mentioned, trying to assuage me. "And I think he's hairy."

"How do you know?" I inquired, sneering. "Are you psychic? Do you have X-ray vision? Or perhaps you asked him?"

"I said, *I think,*" he answered, without becoming agitated, and smiled at Emilio De la Cruz, who was coming toward us. "Besides, you should see his shoes," he added nonchalantly and moved on, heading to our row.

I asked what was so special about them.

"They are enormous," he reported with malice, and stared at me for a moment, putting an end to the discussion.

Emilio told us that his friends wanted to meet us and proposed that we go out for drinks after the show. He said they were pleasant and well-mannered and, as if baiting us, said that one of them was also a great fan of La Duse and was up to date on all the happenings during her *tournée*. We told him it was an excellent idea.

Wen had one last magisterial move waiting for me. When it came time to sit down, he didn't go to the seat he had been in before, but sat in mine. With an obsequious display, he signaled toward the empty seat, next to the cluster of teeth. Trying not to seem disconcerted, I accepted the challenge and settled myself in the banquette, very careful to keep a prudent distance between the petrified Siamese twin, who could not understand what had happened, and myself.

The second half of the show consisted of a series of dances performed by chorus girls with short hair and even shorter skirts, and of songs presented by the *vedettes*. One of the choreographies took place on a ship in the high seas that had unexpectedly run into a tempest of lightning, thunder, and great waves that splashed on the dancers dressed as sailors and made them appear to lose their balance and show off their goods to the delighted audience. We were astonished at the quality of the illusions, and Monkeyface let us know that they were the work of the ingenuous Pepito Gomiz, the famous Catalan set designer. He assured us that Gomiz was capable of transforming, right in front of the eyes of the audience, a miserable little shack into a lavish mansion, or of simulating with an incredible realism a car crash or a train coming out of a tunnel, and that in large part the successes at the Alhambra were due to his overflowing imagination.

The eruption of women onto the stage produced in most of the males in the audience a condition that can be compared to epilepsy. They jumped in their seats, slapped others near them to call attention to some details of the ladies' anatomies, and their eyes shone with a boundless lubricity. I tried to set aside my natural prejudices and assay, in a cold and objective manner, the qualities that came together to raise such exultation. For they must have something, I reasoned, and I took up the task of studying them with a scientific eye. Opulent bosoms, waists like Greek amphorae, ample hips, chubby calves. That and tons of makeup covering eyebrows, eyelids, chins, and mouths. Try as I might, I could not find one fascinating thing in them.

Blanquita reappeared, dressed not as a crude *mulata,* like in the comedy, but as a true queen, and she roused the people anew. This time, the soprano did not resort to the swaying of her hips or the showing of her abundant breasts to get the gentlemen all worked up; instead she appealed to their patriotism in a vehement rendition of a song that spoke of "Cuba, the envy of all, paradise before the fall."

While La Becerra shouted herself hoarse, making sure the orchestra didn't drown her out, I felt Señor Ears' leg barely grazing mine. I let him, without giving away the slightest sign of either rejection or consent, and tried to look, discreetly, at his lower extremities. Wen wasn't wrong: the guy had a pair of legs that, imprisoned in the white cloth of his pants, looked like Theban columns. Without looking at him, pretending to be absorbed in watching the singer, I pressed as much of my body as I could next to his and felt as if I had grazed a live wire. Something similar must have happened to my neighbor, for just at that moment he took the hat that had been resting on his knees and used it to cover up the promising promontory that was rising from between his thighs. We looked at each other in complicity and he offered me a smile that in spite of revealing all his teeth, did not seem as shocking. It's true that his teeth stood out, but at least they were white and in good condition, I reconsidered, proud of my sudden largesse, and, as far as the ears were concerned, I consoled myself with the fact that sometimes a chink on a block of marble, or a crack on a piece of beautiful wood served, by mode of contrast, to highlight the splendor of the rest of the piece. Wen watched me out of the corner of his eye and nodded to let me know he was in agreement.

"And what is your name?" I asked the blond boy, my voice hoarse with excitement.

"Paco Pla," he answered, pressing his lips to my ear.

When we left the theater, a line of men was waiting to go into the next show, which would be the musical *The Isle of the Parrots.* Señor Ears walked between Wenceslao and me, and our *cicerone* was a little startled when I blurted out, shamelessly, that Paco would be coming with us.

"Of course," he was able to say, and without recovering completely, led us to the corner, where his friends awaited us. Now if he was quite surprised on seeing us take with us, without the slightest hesitation, our little conquest from the Alhambra, much more so—doubly so—were Wen and I surprised on discovering that his friends were a light-skinned *mulato* and a negro, both very charming and handsome. If the sight of individuals of such races were curiosity enough in the Indianized Bogotá, having any exchange, on a level of equality and camaraderie, with them was downright unthinkable. I have to admit that with the exception of Toña, the *Chocoana,* I had never before spoken with a negro. I had not dealt much with *mulatos* either, certainly not with one of such distinguished manners and choice vocabulary, who, to our great surprise, came from an excellent family, worked as a pharmacist, and wrote poetry.

Once the introductions were done, De la Cruz asked us to board his automobile, a four-door Dodge Brothers that was parked nearby, and started discussing with his countrymen where would be the best place to have a drink and talk for a little while. The young Pla timidly suggested the Café Inglaterra, but Bartolomé Valdivieso—that was the *mulato*'s name—suggested that it would be better if we went to the open air of the Prado, and so there we headed. The owner of the vehicle, who had not been working long as a chauffeur, drove clinging to the steering wheel, stiffer than a wooden doll, and his experience was cause for many jocular remarks about the danger we were in. Through a conversation that Emilio was having with the negro, we learned that his name was Agustín Miraflores, also known as Scissors, and that he worked in a fashionable tailor shop on O'Reilly Street. It was no wonder, I told myself, he wore his elegant suit with such ease, as if he were born in it. Talking to the pharmacist, Cluster of Teeth revealed that he was a university student and a rowing enthusiast. "That explains the body," Wen said with a look, and I nodded.

The so-called open air turned out to be a series of small cafés, one right next to the other, near the area of the Prado adjoining Parque Central. The place we went to was full to the hilt, but all we had to do for a table was slide a tip to one of the waiters. An all-women musical group called the Álvarez Sisters performed *danzóns* and *guarachas,* and several couples danced gracefully. Everyone wanted beer and, following their suggestion that we should not wait till our second day in Cuba to taste La Tropical, we ordered the same. Although in theory it was winter in Havana, it was very warm. We swallowed the cold, frothy liquid bottoms up and it produced a restorative feeling of freshness. They drank from the bottles, saying it tasted better that way; we, of course, chose to drink from our glasses.

"So the whole purpose of your trip is to see La Duse?" Bartolomé exclaimed, opening up a subject that, as we were told, interested him tremendously.

"To see La Duse . . . and to be with Cubans," Wenceslao corrected him, in a mischievous tone, after draining his glass. A little foam mustache graced his upper lip. I was going to take out my handkerchief and offer it to him, but beating me to it, the negro took his out swiftly and wiped Wen's mouth with it.

"And what do you think so far, of Cubans?" Agustín asked, putting away his handkerchief.

"*Chusquísimos,*" I answered, and on seeing that they didn't understand the meaning of the word, I had to explain to them that it meant "most lovely," and during the next few minutes the conversation turned to the different words for saying the same thing in Colombian and on the Island.

But Wen wasn't ready to dismiss the topic of the actress's visit and interrogated the pharmacist, who, without having to be begged, shared the latest news with us. If there were no complications, the tragedienne would arrive at the port in the steamship *Tivives* on Saturday the twenty-sixth of February, coming from New Orleans. With her would be her company, which consisted of about twenty people, as well as the voluminous cargo of costumes and stage sets. However, he said, it was almost certain that the organizer of the tour, the impresario Fortune Gallo, would arrive a couple of days earlier so that he himself could make sure that everything was ready to receive La Signora properly. Bartolomé boasted about personally knowing Fortune Gallo, an Italian-American who had on previous occasions presented high-quality operas in Havana, and he expected to meet and come to know La Duse through him. His dream was to hand her a sonnet he was composing that he was thinking of titling "To Eleonora the Sublime." I noticed that Wen, without being able to help it, arched an eyebrow and, trying to hide his interest, asked the poet where the actress would be staying.

"I still haven't been able to find out. It is a very closely guarded secret," the young man said. "Nevertheless, I am inclined to say that she will be staying at the Inglaterra."

"All she would have to do is cross San Rafael Street to be in the theater," the tailor agreed and he explained to us that it was one of the best hotels in the country.

"*The* best," the *mulato* corrected him.

"Maybe not quite," the blond boy interrupted. "What about the Almendares?"

De la Cruz settled the incipient argument by saying that, in his opinion, the Almendares was the most luxurious of the modern hotels and that the Inglaterra, built fifty years before, the most renowned of the older ones.

"What I can tell you for sure," Bartolomé continued, "is that there will be four performances, with a two-day rest after each one, to recover. She brings with her *Spettri, La città morta, La donna del mare,* and *La porta chiusa,* which she will open with two days after her arrival."

De la Cruz, Agustín, and Paco were very impressed with the *mulato's* Italian pronunciation, and Bartolomé, lowering his eyes modestly, admitted that for three weeks he had been taking classes with a merchant from Naples so that he would be able to understand the greatest possible number of words uttered by La Signora on stage and to be able to greet her in her native tongue.

Monkeyface pointed out, very much enjoying himself, that it seemed as if all the great ladies of the international stage had conspired to appear in Havana at the same time: Esperanza Iris was singing at the Payret; Mimí Aguglia was performing at the Martí; Josefina Ruiz del Castillo was finishing off her stay at the Principal de la Comedia on the twenty-seventh, and María Tubau would then open in the same theater. Moreover, after a period of rest for medical reasons, Luz Gil would return to the Cubano with her Arquímides Pous's company and, though she was a local star, the soprano was a great draw. And if that were not enough, the imminent arrival of Margarita Xirgu from Lima had just been announced. The Catalan's visit to the Nacional had been postponed two weeks to cede those dates to La Signora. Would La Duse be able to fill the house, competing with such eminent figures?

"For God's sake, Emilito! None of those others are competition for Eleonora," Bartolomé thundered, rolling his eyes, and Wenceslao jumped to his aid:

"We are not talking about an ordinary actress here, we are talking about a legend."

"Fortunately, Titta Ruffo has just finished his performances at the opera house and has left for Cienfuegos," the tailor said.

Wen lamented not having arrived earlier to hear the celebrated baritone perform *André Chenier* at the Nacional. Almost without even being aware of it, we finished our third round of Tropicals, which the waiter had placed in front of us with the utmost discretion, and unanimously called for a fourth round.

"The funny thing with beers is that you have to get up and urinate so often to make room for the others," the tailor joked, and leaving his chair he headed for the bathroom. Paco Pla and Wenceslao followed him.

De la Cruz took advantage of the negro's absence to tell me that if we needed fine clothes, up to date and suitable for life in Havana, we should go to La Boston, the tailor shop where Agustín worked. The *mulato* nodded, casting a lenient eye at the clothes from Barranquilla that I wore, and he agreed that there was no better tailor, with first-class materials and a fair price. His father, who was very particular about his wardrobe, did not even want to hear word of any other tailor but Agustín's boss, and he ordered all his clothes as well as those of his sons from there. Emilito let me know that Bartolomé's father was the famous General Valdivieso, a hero in the War of Independence, now wholly dedicated to politics and with a seat in the Senate.

"The Conservative or the Liberal Party?" I asked.

"Neither," the pharmacist-bard responded, and in a mocking tone explained to me that his father belonged to the Popular Party, invented in a hurry some years back by one Alfredo Zayas, with the aim of rising to the presidency of the Republic. "Everyone knows it as the 'Party of the Few,' " he added, giggling with Monkeyface.

"I thought Zayas was a liberal," I remarked.

"He is, in a way, since it was with the support of the previous president, who was a liberal and pulled hundreds of shady deals to help him, that he gained power," De la Cruz explained. "But when he wasn't able to obtain his own party's candidacy he was forced to create the Popular Party."

"Zayas is a shameless crook, that is what he is," the *mulato* proclaimed. "A rake and a thief."

"Like all of them," the other one added calmly.

The three who were in the bathroom returned, laughing noisily. I noticed though, that Wen was a little pale. Quickly and discreetly, he brought me up to date on his findings:

"The rower magnificent, the negro impressive!"

I gulped, and knowing that what I was about to say was proof of my scurrilous *cachaco*ness, I couldn't help but give voice to my doubts.

"But . . . a negro?" I whispered, troubled. "He is so snub-nosed that his voice seems to be plugged up."

"You'll see," he replied, annoyed and defiant, and on realizing that a reproachful silence had settled in, he began to speak in a loud voice about a movie La Duse had made, which, though it was never shown in Colombia, he knew was titled *Ashes*.

"Oh, yes, *Cenere*," Valdivieso recalled, taking a chance to practice his Italian. "They haven't shown it here, either."

Two or three bottles of beer and several trips to the bathroom later, our tongues were loosened enough to talk about all sorts of details about the life led by those of us in the "club," as De la Cruz put it, in Bogotá. They were horrified to learn that we had no cafés opened all hours of the night and no theaters where only men attended. They almost felt sorry for us for the restrictions and discretions we were forced to observe and urged us to enjoy our stay in their country to the fullest.

"Here, if you're not on the ground, you're in the air," Paco Pla assured us. "Be suspicious of anyone who still lives with his mother, knows how to cook, and has pretty handwriting."

"If *maricones* could fly," Emilito mused, "you wouldn't be able to see the sun over Cuba."

And they began to talk of the enormous number of journalists, professors, artists, judges, athletes, merchants, doctors, policemen, priests, and politicians whom they knew for certain to belong to the "club," and the number of other characters, even greater, who came under suspicion. In this last category, they included brothers, cousins, uncles, in-laws, and even grandfathers.

"Look, my old man used to say, 'Any hole gets the milk,' " the negro murmured, in a confidential aside to me. "I myself have a missus and three little ones: two girls and a boy who is just turning one. Just because sometimes you want to be with a man doesn't mean that you are bent!"

I nodded, a bit shocked, and told him that I agreed.

Then the four of them wanted to know how our kind was referred to in Colombia. With a little effort, aside from the well-known femme, pederast, sodomite, and queen, we came up with some other appellatives, like donkey rider, butterfly, watchmaker, and girly boy. They, on the other hand, came out with an enormous list that grew and grew, with roars of laughter that got progressively louder: bird, hummingbird, sparrow, duck, goosy, hen, dovey, mule, filly, cow, snapper, stone bass, puff, weakling, cracked, cracked in the shaft, cracked in the ass, uncorked, disher, ballwarmer, boy whore, girl, baby girl, young lady, señorita, miss, madam, she, woman, dame, matron, refined young man, pretty boy, doll, nympho, queer, flutter-flutter, ass sniffer, tail breaker, spinner, between the lines, confused one, unclear one, twisted, magician (because he makes it disappear), he-who-swallows, milkchugger, swordeater, tubeswallower, tubeblower, cocksucker, sticklicker, lollipopper, softwrist, pillow kisser, wing flapper, water bottle, past the rock, ass taker, assifier, brokeass, openass, rare bird, softy, soft in the legs, soft in the butt, feather, feathered one, he's on the other team, from across the street, plays the bottom half, jumps rope, has his problem, drops the soap, has his witness, is suspicious, his ice cream melts, he likes to play the organ, has songs within him, he's family, from around here, same company, from the Salvation Army, and, of course, *maricón,* first in all its different categories: *maricón* from the soul; up the ass; closeted; all out; jewelry-wearing; old-fashioned; championship class; day after day; hook, line, and sinker; and then its variations: *marica, mariquita, maricona, mariconcito,* and *mariconsón.* We found the varieties of name very revealing.

The ladies of the band had already finished when De la Cruz excused himself and went to the bathroom.

"You must be very exhausted," Paco Pla said to us abruptly. "If you want, I'll accompany you to the hotel."

"I will, too," Bartolomé exclaimed, grabbing his hat.

"And so will I," Scissors interjected, getting up. "The sooner the better."

"Should we wait for Emilio?" I asked hesitantly.

"I think not," Wenceslao replied.

We left some bills on the table and we hurried out of there before Monkeyface returned. I myself thought that it was unforgivably rude to do this to a person who had been so kind and generous with us, and I let Wen know it in a low voice. He replied that, yes, De la Cruz had been a dear and obliging, but not so much as to sleep with him. "These three, on the other hand . . . hmmm . . . I can eat them alive," he hinted.

Paco, Agustín, and Bartolomé walked behind us, like an honor guard. I couldn't tell for sure if they heard us or not, for when alcohol takes over, you can speak at the top of your lungs and think that you are whispering. The hotel was closer than we imagined, and we were there in no time. The doorman held the front door open for us. But if all things signaled that this was the time to say our farewells, none of our three guardian angels were ready to cede the battle and retire.

Convinced that his age bestowed on him special privileges, the blond boy, with a grand audacity, invited himself to accompany us to our room.

"I, too, would like to come," the *mulato* declared, not holding back.

"Don't forget my invitation to this party," the negro begged comically.

I took Wenceslao by the arm, past the doorman who was yawning and waiting for us to say our good-byes, and spoke to him privately.

"What's wrong?" he asked me impatiently. "Is it the negro?"

"No, no . . ." I stuttered. "It's just that . . ." Oh, how I cursed my so often repudiated *cachaco* upper-class nature that, without my being able to prevent it, reared its head at the worst times! "We have never done it with three at the same time," I said, trying to hide my nervousness.

"There is a first for everything," he said insolently.

He made a half turn and, heading toward the triumvirate of our suitors, asked them to come closer.

"We'll have the last drink upstairs!" he proposed and, past the good-natured and understanding looks from the doorman, up we all went.

I had, rather as is my custom, not slowed down to record intimate details or anything that may cause others discomfort, but I can't go on without saying that it was a memorable evening.

It is no wonder that those who are dedicated to the occult pay special attention to the secrets of numerology. Numbers are there, whether we know it or not, in all aspects of our life. They are keys, and can lead us toward unforeseen paths, change everything, transform actions that have been repeated a thousand times into events full of surprises. That in fortune-telling three is a number venerated by the ancients, a triangle in which the active and the passive produce through their interaction the neutral, was something both of us knew very well and had experimented with; but the magic of five, up to then unknown to us, revealed itself to us that night in Havana. Five, the end result of the sum of two and three, or, in other words, of duality and contradiction and of balance and harmony, it is synonymous with madness, passion, and instability. As soon as the impeccable white suits were nothing more than a bundle in the middle of the room, we understood why. If for cabalists the triad represents perfect equilibrium, the union of intelligence, the soul, and matter, the pentagon, on the other hand, has at its heart versatility; it is pure mercury, all colors, the urge for change, the seed of disorder. It is a chaos that, in complete contradiction to its nature, seeks complete knowledge. Five stands as the doorway to intemperate fantasies; it is an explosive coupling where desire guides the four elemental forces: an outrageous figure, ruled by instinct, and one has to be careful with it, because it can prove as harmful as it is pleasurable.

The first Cuban night turned out to be a *lectio magistralis* on sensuality, a true Caribbean orgy. Our bodies wrapped around one another in all possible combinations and past my mouth went a parade of napes, backs, calves, chests, knees, butts, bellies, and anonymous phalluses that I sucked, chomped on, and licked fervently and indiscriminately. In the darkness, with my eyes closed, I tried to guess who each delicious piece could belong to. Did this ribcage or these splendid haunches form part of Paco's anatomy, or Agustín's, or perhaps Bartolomé's? There wasn't time for conjectures, because a hand that, of course, I couldn't identify either, held me, impatiently and trembling, by the jaw and led my mouth to another place. In the middle of this bacchanal, someone came upon the scar from my operation and carefully dedicated himself to wetting it with saliva. I touched the head and discovered by the frizzy hair, like very thin wires, that it was the tailor.

The whole thing went on longer than I thought we could withstand. Each time the passion seemed, at last, soothed, a spark was enough, a mere graze, for the flames to come alive and the fire to crackle anew and, in spite of having surrendered, we took up the sweet combat again. I still don't understand how the guests of the other one hundred and fifty rooms didn't complain to the manager about the chorus of panting, gasping, nervous laughter, and death cries. The blond boy happened to be rather loud, and on more than one occasion we had to put a pillow over his face to drown out his moans.

As if the wide bed were an experiment table in a scientist's lab and we outstanding students eager for knowledge, Wen and I were able to confirm that the epidermis of whites, *mulatos,* and negros smelled and tasted differently, that each yielded to the touch its own peculiar sensations not at all like the other, and that even the same portion of skin of a certain body allows for different textures if it is caressed with the tips of the fingers or with the tongue. If the rower's equipment had been classified by Wen as magnificent, and the tailor's, without the slightest bit of exaggeration, as impressive, the pharmacist's package didn't suffer from comparison to his contenders, in fact it triumphed, making it worthy of the qualifier "colossal." At the end of the day, its eminence made sense: through the *mulato*'s veins coursed, two in one, the best of the blood of two races. The swords were grabbed, crossed, and plunged once and again, and we had little doubt that they were forged with top-quality metals, for they gave scant sign of deterioration and never lost their impressive solidity. If she wished, Esmeralda Gallego could have written on any of them not just a greeting, but an entire letter, complete with postscript.

Oh, the wonders of five: freedom, variety, E natural and C sharp; the five-pointed star that is a symbol for the human body. Five are the senses; five the wounds our Lord suffered on the cross; on the fifth day, according to Genesis, the animals were created. Five, full of rapid and lively vibrations. Infinite circular five that returns to itself in a *ritornello* each time that is multiplied: $5 \times 5 = 25$; $25 \times 5 = 125$; $125 \times 5 = 625. \ldots$ According to my dear Pythagoras, three is being, movement, and speech: what holds the world together, congruence with the excellent, the number of shape and form, for a body can no longer exist but in three dimensions, the joy and abundance given to us by Jupiter; but the number five—and if you doubt me, ask Aristarchus of Samos—who will not let me lie, is the biggest mystery, what is prohibited, what grates us with temptation, the expanding and mutable many, the attraction and sensual magnetism with which the planet Mercury governs us. And that little secret, my friend, I did not find in an Egyptian temple that sheltered the secrets of the telamons, but in room 221 ($2 + 2 + 1 = 5$) of the Seville-Biltmore Hotel, in Havana, on the unforgettable and torrid early morning of the twenty-third ($2 + 3 = 5$) of January.

At six in the morning, just as we had finally laid our heads down, exhausted from a bout that had lasted several hours, Scissors jumped out of bed and into his pants at full speed. I think that I was the only one to notice.

"*Mi negra* believes in live and let live, as long as I am a good husband and always get back before daybreak," he explained with a smile. He finished dressing hurriedly and left the room with a cordial "See you around."

Wenceslao was snoring, pressed to the pharmacist's back, and I asked myself if they were both dreaming, a duet, about La Duse. Before he had fallen asleep, General Valdivieso's son had promised us to bring us his sonnet so that we could look at it and help him choose, from all the different versions of the text, the most extravagant one. As for me, before laying my head on the formidable chest of Señor Ears (who in the end wasn't all that hairy) and falling into a deep sleep, I felt one last pang of guilt thinking of Emilio De la

Cruz's astonished face on returning from the bathroom and finding the table that we had only minutes before left empty. What excuse are we to make when we see him again? I asked myself, worried; but sleep, powerful and impatient, dragged me into its realm before I could come up with an answer.

I have parroted the words of others for so many years that I am no longer sure when I speak if the words are mine or they are lines that, without even realizing it, I have stolen from one of the characters I have brought to life. I don't know if they are original thoughts or phrases I have tucked away in some recess of my mind that all of a sudden leap to my tongue.

The words get all tangled up in my head like strands of yarn in a drawer. And, in spite of everything, I have never felt as clear and sure as I do tonight.

That last phrase, for example! I could swear that I have heard it before. I can't recall whether from my own mouth or the mouth of another. Is it Eleonora who speaks or Marguerite Gautier? Francesca da Rimini, Frou-Frou? Maybe Trovaldo's Nora? Can it be that with the passing of time I have become these women? Can it be that a little of each of them has dissolved in me, in the stuff of which I am made, mixing in with my way of being, with my way of seeing things, contaminating it, adulterating my nature, clouding it? How can one possibly know?

Ever since I came into this world I have lived within words, from them, learning to subjugate their savage nature, looking to domesticate them, and I must confess that they arouse in me a great suspicion. They are unruly and traitorous. You can never, never be certain that they are on your side, for the first chance they get they will sell you out, betray you. It's not that they are good or that they are evil. They are what they are, little detachments of ourselves, an inexhaustible fountain of quarrels and misunderstandings because they are made in the image of those who utter them.

They have but been pronounced and you realize that you have chosen wrongly, that they weren't what you meant at all to express your feelings. And if you write them down, it is worse. They stay on the paper like guilt, laughing at you, forcing you to cross them out, to break them, to repent.

Words are polymorphous. If you watch them closely, you will notice that they have a certain weight, size, temperature, but in a second they will undergo a mutation and become something else. Fortunately they neither smell nor taste like anything. They are also colorless. Whoever thinks differently is a hopeless romantic trying to make everything beautiful.

There are a thousand ways to say each word, even the simplest ones, and ten thousand ways to misunderstand them. That is why, if it is difficult to create a phrase that makes sense, it is much more difficult to repeat it onstage, to exactly capture just what a character is trying to say when she uses them. In my judgment, mankind irrefutably proved its devotion to folly by choosing words, among the myriad other possibilities offered by God, as the tool with which to communicate.

During my second tour of the United States, Schurmann and some of his friends insisted that I meet Thomas Alva Edison, who by that time had patented over a thousand inventions. They took me to his laboratory in a place in New Jersey called West Orange, where I found out that the famous gentleman was a little bit deaf. I thanked him for his inventions, especially what he had contributed to better stage lighting, and he tried to explain to me the principles of the incandescent bulb.

Before leaving, Schurmann's friends insisted that I leave a recording of my voice in Mr. Edison's famous phonograph.

"You will be immortalized," they assured me. "And others will be able to enjoy your art in posterity."

I was hesitant, for speaking lines into a machine seemed to me the height of absurdity, but they so begged that I agreed, not to seem rude. One of the genius's assistants brought a wax cylinder and proceeded with great celerity to set everything up. At the signal from Mr. Edison, I recited the last lines that Dumas fils put in the mouth of Marguerite, with coughs and death throes included.

When I finished, they all seemed very impressed, especially the inventor. Later I found out that they would do the same thing with whatever eminent figure from literature, music, the theater, and politics passed through there. Mr. Edison had an extensive collection of phonographic recordings that was not lacking, of course, Sarah's voice, reciting *The Lady of the Camellias* as well! What a failure of the imagination on my part! Had I known it, I would have opted for *Heimal* or *The Wife of Claudius* instead, just for variation.

They forced me to listen to the product of our experiment. They put the phonograph on some other gadget, made it go around, put a needle to it, and all eyes were fixed on me. As if emitting from a grotto, through the speaker we heard a listless and distant voice that stubbornly mimicked the way I spoke.

What left Edison troubled, Schurmann astonished, and his friends flushed, was that the words were not the same. Instead of the lines from Dumas fils that I had just recorded, that replica of my voice spoke some ancient and rather obscene Neopolitan verses.

We endured the poem till its end, with the stupid hope that, once finished, the machine would reproduce my true words, but what was heard, from the end of the cylinder, was a series of German words that sounded like harsh barking. Realizing that they were still watching, I smiled resignedly.

Edison made it a point to viciously scold his young assistant. Pale and disconcerted, he called him stupid, and blamed the "error" on some distraction on his part. But the young man did not remain quiet. Respectful, with firmness, he stressed once and again that on his part there had been no mistake. Everything was done as it should have been! As strange as it might seem, it was that exact cylinder on which we had just recorded. If the lady said one thing and the phonograph insisted on repeating another, it was not his fault!

My friends tried to soothe Edison, who told his assistant to leave and later, going out of his way to make excuses, said, "This has never happened! It is inconceivable!" He urged me to do it again. This time he would put his trust in no one; he would handle the gadget himself.

I turned down his invitation, claiming that I had to rest my voice before rehearsal. Once was enough. Words had once again proved their untamable nature. I did not want to risk it again.

3

In the roof garden of the Seville-Biltmore, as we sipped on a refreshing lemonade frappe at a table with a view of the sea, we went over the papers of that Wednesday, the twenty-third of January. All of them carried the same news on the front page. "The Great Leader of the Bolsheviks Deceased," "Mourning in Russia," "The Genius of the Worker's Revolution Is No More," "The Communist Lenin Is Dead" . . . Since we did not much care about that topic, we looked for the pages that talked about Eleonora Duse's arrival and carried recent photographs.

The pictures not only showed La Signora's autumnal beauty but the spirituality that she radiated and that revolved around her in a nimbus of serenity and absorption. The woman was at peace with herself, in spite of her many troubles and conflicts. The deceptions in love, the public's ungratefulness, the nightmare of war, and the financial difficulties had left prominent marks on her character, making her modest, wise, and patient. Or, at least, that is what the photographs revealed.

The *Diario de la Marina,* the dean of the Havana press, confirmed that her first show would be the twenty-eighth of January, coinciding with the seventy-first anniversary of the birth of José Martí, and it proclaimed: "La Duse's art is the eloquence of a glance, the inflection of a word; it is a gesture, a pause. Her profound and subtle intelligence delves into words till it finds in them their most hidden sense, and thus compresses in each phrase infinite meanings." On another page, there was an article reprinted from *The Evening Telegram* where, among other things, it was maintained that: "The potentiality of La Duse's art has not only not diminished, but it has increased, if increase is possible in any art that, like hers, has bordered on the limits of genius."

For its part, *El Heraldo* included the opinions of the theater critic of *The Globe,* from New York, who, as well as crowning La Signora "the first actress of the world," spared no praise for her. "The art of the brilliant actress can be characterized as such: it is the triumph of the spirit over matter. The audience is baffled in the face of such a highly innovative example of authenticity and simplicity. It is astonishing to find oneself in the presence of an actress who does not use paint or cover her face with makeup and, nevertheless, always seems young in her words, her manners, and her movement. La Duse possesses the secret of eternal youth. To watch her and to hear her is to witness how the spirit is capable of never aging." In another article, the paper added: "The arrival of La Duse is the topic of the day. If her performances have been received as a momentous event by Americans, through whose country parade the world's greatest artists, to us her visit offers one added bonus: the fact that the illustrious tragedienne has never passed through our city and there had been little hope that it would ever happen."

El País printed the price of a seasonal ticket for all four shows. The *grille* seats cost two hundred pesos, the box seats on the first and second floor one hundred and fifty, and on the third floor a hundred. The individual ticket, which was paid for separately, on the day of the show, cost five pesos a performance. Taking into account that the Cuban peso was worth a dollar, the prices seemed astronomical.

"In Bogotá, only you would pay such prices," I remarked.

"But we are in Cuba," Wen replied. "Listen to what the papers say," and he read another fragment from the article in *El País.* "The box office at the Teatro Nacional had been flooded with those seeking tickets. The box seats are almost sold out. And the orchestra seats will soon be also."

I wondered out loud whether it would be wiser to buy a box on the first floor or orchestra seats, which cost a little bit less (forty each with the price of general admission included, I pointed out). And moreover, I added, why would we want a box with four seats? My reasonings were refuted one by one. Wen absolutely refused even the possibility of considering orchestra seats and plainly said that after traveling so far to see La Signora perform, he wanted to see her from a prime spot. Since I didn't feel like arguing about it, I told him that we would get tickets for wherever he pleased.

"A box on the first level," he decided. "And I think that we should take care of it right away."

I suggested that we call Señor Pedrito Varela who, according to the papers, was in charge of selling the tickets for the series. His number was A-4864. But Wen, who on that Monday had woken up on the wrong side of the bed, said that a theater could have many boxes on the first level, some good, some all right, and many dreadful, and fearful that they would not give him a preferred seat, said we should take care of it in person. We were close to the theater, he pointed out. If we just kept on walking, we would run into it in fifteen minutes. After going up to the room to refill our wallets and to put away in the scrapbook with the silver and mother-of-pearl cover the clippings of photographs and news items about La Duse's imminent arrival, we went out.

We loved the façade of the Nacional, replete with columns, arcades, balconies, gargoyles, and statues and said that judging by its exterior it seemed a very opulent temple to Thalia. We reached Pedrito Varela's little office, in the bowels of the building, at the same time as a very elegant woman dressed in pearl gray. Someone who worked there asked us to take a seat on one of the benches, left some papers on top of a very disorganized desk, and went searching for Varela. While we waited, I took the time to furtively observe the lady who was sitting in front of us. She was thin and of medium height, with oblique Chinese eyes, and I guessed that she was about sixty years old. Her black hair was up in a bun held in place with tortoiseshell hair clips, and there were silver strands visible. Sitting upright, her hands full of rings and resting on her lap, she looked off into the distance at some undetermined point, like a Buddha, absorbed in thought. Wenceslao interrupted my examination to show me a picture of Eleonora Duse that he had just found on a small table, half-hidden by a copy of the magazine *Social.* As we looked at it, a tiny individual with a bow tie burst into the office.

"Good morning, madam. Good morning, gentlemen," he said in a high-pitched voice and went to his desk in a hurry. "Sorry for the delay. I'll be right with you."

He had barely sat down when another person came into the office. He was a healthy-looking man about our age, so smug and arrogant that I was overcome with a desire to kick him in the ass. In a drawling voice he offered his "Good morning" and, without even looking at any of us who were waiting, went straight to the man in charge of tickets, who made sure to greet him very effusively and to ask him how his mother was doing.

"She is wonderful, thank God," the dandy answered and then added with a pretentious Castilian accent. "I am counting off the minutes, Pedrito. I need the best box seat from which to see La Duse."

"As you wish, my good man," Varela answered, sweet as molasses, and easing down into his chair opened up the notebook where he kept track of each ticket sold.

Infuriated, as if someone had just lit a torch to his behind, Wenceslao stood next to the newcomer and, deliberately ignoring him, addressed the man in charge of the tickets in his best interpretation of a mortally offended *cachaco.*

"You will take care of this gentleman after you have taken care of us, for neither the lady . . ." he pointed to the Chinese lady, who had just taken a sandalwood fan out of her purse and waved it with an exasperating slowness as she impassively watched the scene, "nor we," he pointed at me, "are here for our health."

Varela was so surprised he did not even try to respond. Flattening both hands on the desk and leaning toward him, Wen asked, this time in the voice of a general: "Do you understand or do I have to repeat myself?"

So red it seemed he was going to suffer a heart attack, Varela looked at the fop not knowing what to do, begging for his help. Feigning an indifference that the trembling of his hand grasping the onyx handle of his cane and the bulging of the veins on his neck made difficult to believe, the fop retorted:

"There is no hurry, Pedrito. I will send someone with the money," and turning on his heel, raising his chin as high as possible, he left the room, but not before muttering for all of us to hear, "Hope all goes well!"

For a fleeting moment we remained still and silent. But as soon as the steps of the "good gentleman" going down the stairs faded out, the old woman began to fan herself with an extraordinary quickness, and the four of us breathed in unison.

Pedrito Varela dried the sweat that drenched his brow, gathered himself, and putting his most friendly foot forward, addressed Wen, who was still standing by the desk.

"And how can I be of help to you, my good man?"

"Take care of the lady first, please," Wen responded in a caustic voice, and, with an obsequious gesture, invited her to approach the table. As she was being taken care of, he came and sat by me again. "Who the hell does he think he is?" he muttered.

"All right, that's enough," I said, trying to calm him down. "You put him in his place."

Soon, the Chinese lady lowered her head in a gesture of farewell and left with her tickets. Since Wen was still upset and didn't want to have to undergo another fight, I took charge of the transaction and sat in front of Varela.

"We want a box on the first level," I said.

"The best one," my lover added from his spot, almost as a threat.

Varela nodded, his eyes fixed on his notebook, and he showed me a seating chart where the sold seats were marked with red Xs. I noticed that the papers were exaggerating a bit when they said all four shows would be sold out soon, and I handed the chart to Wenceslao so that he could make the choice.

"I think this one," he said, handing me back the paper, and I pointed out the spot to Varela.

"If I may, I would suggest this other seat," the ticketmaster said in a mellifluous tone, as I counted out one hundred and fifty dollars in crisp bills and put it in front of him. "It's a much better spot, with a perfect view of the stage."

I looked at Wen inquiringly.

"Fine," he agreed.

After asking our names and writing them down in his book, he told us that the *Diario de la Marina* was going to publish a piece with the names of all those who bought series tickets and wanted to know if we would give our authorizations to have our names mentioned. I looked at Wen again to see what he thought, and he nodded, shrugging his shoulders. Before we left, Varela tried to apologize for the altercation. Putting out my hand, I said that he should forget it happened. But Wen, who was not ready to offer his forgiveness just like that, confined himself to muttering a distant "Thank you," before turning his back to him.

Outside, it was pouring and we could not leave the building.

"For more than ten minutes now, you have had an enemy in Havana," a female voice declared from behind us. On turning, we saw the lady with the fan. Her lips were pressed into a thin, expressionless line, but she teased us with her oblique eyes. "You have offended Don Olavo Vázquez Garralaga and that, my friends, is going to cost you," she added solemnly, arching her very thin eyebrows.

We asked who so-and-so was and, letting her mouth break into a smile, she said: "A poet." And straightaway she clarified: "Or at least that's what he wants to make us believe."

She told us her name was María de Lachambre and, on confirming that, as she had suspected, we were foreigners recently arrived in the city, she doubly appreciated our "unusual and impromptu show of gentlemanliness." A rented Ford stopped at the sidewalk and the lady, making a signal to the driver so that he would hold up, asked us if she could take us to our hotel. The three of us climbed into the car, and on the way she explained to us that Vázquez Garralaga, a writer very much in fashion, was accustomed to being respected and spoiled everywhere he went. And as for Varela, he wasn't a bad sort, notwithstanding his obsequiousness, a flaw, she pointed out, pretty common in our times. "You have taught both of them a great lesson," she proclaimed. We exchanged some more words, during which the topic of La Duse came up again, and then we said our farewells until the night of the twenty-eighth.

As we stepped out of the car, we almost ran into Emilio De la Cruz, who was just at that moment arriving at the Seville-Biltmore underneath an enormous umbrella. Seeing him right in front of us, so unexpectedly, we were mortified, not knowing what to tell him to justify our rude disappearance the night before. Fortunately, it was not necessary to invent any excuses: Emilito, displaying a generosity and sense of understanding that was far greater than his ugliness, congratulated us for what he called our "orgiastic Havana debut." Relieved, we invited him to have lunch with us and he made no excuses.

As we ate, we told him that we had already bought tickets for all four of La Signora's performances and we told him not to even think of wasting money on buying one, for he could have one of the seats in our box and invite whomever he wanted. Wen told him about our run-in with Vázquez Garralaga and what the Asian woman had told us about him later. De la Cruz was delighted.

"There isn't much to say about Olavito, except that he is spoiled and that he writes cloying verses, that he thinks himself God's gift to the world and has a frighteningly long tongue. Most likely at this moment he is finding out your names so that he can put you at the head of his black list. Instead of looking for a husband, as he should, he spends the whole damn day with his poetry and, since his father has all the money in the world, every year he publishes several books here and in Paris. You will grow weary of seeing him everywhere, always very exquisitely dressed, accompanied by his mother, like a girl," he remarked disdainfully. "But the real character in the story you have told me is not Olavito . . ." and before continuing, he made a dramatic pause, "but María Cay, La Generala Lachambre."

He informed us that the lady in question, the widow of a Spanish military man, wasn't Chinese, as we thought, but half Japanese, and that she was well known for having been one of the most beautiful women in Havana, a muse to many famous poets.

"Her father was chancellor of the imperial consulate of Japan in Havana," he told us. "They say that Julián del Casal was in love with her and that when Rubén Darío saw her, the same thing happened. You know how those modernists went crazy over anything Oriental!"

Once we had finished lunch, we went back out, since it had stopped raining. De la Cruz said that that night he had to have dinner with his uncles, but he asked us not to make any plans for Thursday, for he would like to take us out to the country, to go to the theater and then an amusement park.

Before leaving, he gave us directions on how to get to La Boston, at 88 O'Reilly, and off we went in search of a new wardrobe. Scissors, who did not expect to run into two members of the bacchanal so soon, was taken by surprise. A little disturbed, his manner very ceremonious and professional, he helped us choose the cloth for our suits. Under the attentive gaze of the shop's owner, he took down our measurements, taking care to touch only what was essential, and promised us that although he had many orders pending, he would make sure that our clothes would be ready as soon as possible.

"Gentlemen of your standing cannot go around Havana dressed any old way," was his not-too-flattering farewell.

There is no doubt that Cubans are obsessed with fine clothes. Emilito had already mentioned it during our crossing: they would rather eat boiled sweet potatoes for a month if they had to, as long as they could step out of the house dressed to the nines.

On leaving La Boston, we headed for a nearby street that ran parallel to it, Obispo, and we walked a few blocks heading away from the sea, to visit La Moderna Poesía and find out if it deserved its excellent reputation as a bookstore. It did, without a doubt. The variety in the selection of books, from all the great capitals, was astonishing. Wen took the opportunity, with a malicious curiosity, to ask to see the work of Vázquez Garralaga and the employee brought to him an impressive pile of books that had been exquisitely published, explaining that these were just the more recent ones, and that if we wanted to see previous works, they also had those available. We took a look through the pages and quickly became convinced that the style of the poet was an admixture of tears, triviality, and syrup. And just as we were ready to rush out of there, a pretty young woman dressed in blue crepe, with an old woman on her arm, closed in on us.

"Pardon me, gentlemen," the young woman remarked, blushing to the roots of her short hair. "My aunt and I have noticed that you are foreigners and that you are lovers of poetry and I would . . . we would like to invite you to a soirée. I hope you can come!" And without even giving us a chance to say a word, she placed in my hand a cream-colored envelope and, dragging the old woman, moved hurriedly away from us. But before leaving, the girl turned around and said cunningly, "Olavo is not the only one who publishes books in Cuba!"

Surprised and knowing that other clients were watching us, we opened the envelope and found inside an announcement printed in gold letters.

"Señorita Graziella Gerbelasa is one of the most talented writers on the Island," the employee who was attending us revealed. "Her first two collections, *The Woodwork of the Soul* and *The Bliss of Torture,* have been very well received. Would you like to see them?"

We told him not to bother, and he added that the following Monday, on José Martí's birthday, there would be a celebration for the publication of her new book.

The announcement we had just received mentioned the title of the new work, *The Reliquary.* And it included the place and time that the party would take place. We looked at each other, amused, and remarked on how that kind of spontaneity was impossible in prudish Bogotá, where people were very wary of even talking to strangers.

The thundershower had left a muggy heat in its wake, so we decided that an ice cream break at El Anón would best suit us, and off we went to the Prado to wet our whistles. Then, our feet aching, we returned to the hotel.

Paco Pla was waiting for us in the lobby. In the daylight, he seemed younger and blonder, and his ears, if it were possible, even more striking. He told us that he had come from studying Latin with a fellow student all morning and that he was thinking of going to the university's sports field to do a little exercise. Would we like to come with him if we weren't doing anything? Without even thinking about it, we said yes and were out in the street again, one on each side of him.

You can easily pick out the streetcars in Havana, the rower explained to us, for they are painted different colors, depending on their routes. The *vedado* to Muelle de Luz is white and green, the *vedado* to San Juan de Dios white and red, and the *vedado* to Marianao white on white. We got on one that was white, yellow, and white on Havana Street and were lucky enough to find some empty seats. "There are some days when they are so full that you get dizzy with the smell of the riffraff, but you can't ask for much more for five cents," Paco remarked. Whispering, he said that the night before had been marvelous. And he was longing to repeat the experience . . . if possible without any others. He was greedy and wanted us all to himself, and he smiled, displaying his cluster of teeth.

The stadium at the university was crowded, and seeing myself surrounded by so many young men, so graceful and full of life, I told myself that if heaven did exist it would be some place like this. Gymnasts, tennis players, fencers, runners, javelin and disc throwers, boxers, baseball, volleyball, and basketball players, and all other types of athletes flocked by us, chatting in loud voices, joking around carelessly, drying their sweat with small towels and wearing sport clothes that left their torsos, arms, and legs visible.

The young men of this Island have made a vocation of gliding, a profession of swaying. There is something airy about their movements, in the sinuous, almost awkward manner with which they carry themselves. Where does that unwieldy and involuntary voluptuousness that comes to life with a mere glance, a touch, come from? Perfection does not matter at all; it's as if the heat and the proximity to the sea had blurred the traditional norms of measuring the beautiful and these had been replaced by more primitive notions, where the sensual imposes itself on the intellectualization of beauty.

As I thought about all this, I was struck by an incomprehensible melancholy, and mimicking the fox in the fable, I consoled myself with the fact that the grapes were still not sweet.

Señor Ears headed for the locker room to change his clothes, and we told him that we would wait for him in the bleachers. He returned after a little while, wearing a pair of shorts and a tank top, accompanied by other athletes dressed (or should I say undressed?) in the same manner, to whom we were introduced. Some of them studied architecture, like him, others studied medicine or the law. The group was grilling us with questions about Bogotá when a young, dark-haired man approached us in an energetic manner to tell his friends of a certain meeting that had been called due to the death of Lenin. On catching sight of such a specimen, all the rest of them—Big Teeth and those around us, the sportsmen that came and went out of the locker rooms and *vestiaires,* those who prowled around us, those who circled the track with great speed, those who dueled with foils and swords, those who flew over the vault, those who boxed, those who lifted weights, those who hurled discs and javelins, those who hit balls with bats or rackets or who jumped in the air to put them through hoops—all of them, all of them without exception, were scattered and turned into smoke and disappeared so that all that was left intact was that stunning man who was saying something about a brotherly coming together between workers and students, that wonder who good-naturedly extended his hand and crushed ours.

I'll try to describe him, though I should warn beforehand that my words will not be able reproduce with exactitude what my dazzled eyes, forgetting to blink, took in.

Dark hair, thick and curly but kept away from the brow and thrown back, though it seemed no comb had ever been able to tame it, crowned the head of this sort of Caribbean demigod; the brow rested on a pair of bushy eyebrows, impeccably arched: the eyebrows of a Moor that, with just a bit of furrowing, came together. The coffee-colored eyes, large and of penetrating look, a bit sunken, were protected by long, silky eyelashes. It was enough to look at them to know that they belonged to a strong personality that did not know what it was to give in to adversity. A lover of classic features, a purist, would say that his eagle nose was off, since it widened at the base, betraying a sign of *mestizo* blood. But, although veering from the classic Hellenic model, it fit just right on the slightly too oval face. His nose gave way to one of those mouths that seemed to have been made for kissing; thick, fresh lips, a provocative and sensual mouth from whose corners there could hang a perfect smile. If I needed to say anything about his teeth, straight and very white, it would be that anyone, without complaint, would offer up his arms and thighs to them. His ears? Perfect, with lobes that seemed to invite caresses. His chin and jaw, in spite of being shaven, suggested the presence of a thick beard, the color of old bronze, on the soft skin. A long neck, robust and with pliant tendons, held up this exceptional head. The body, a little taller than normal, hinted at hard and fibrous limbs under his suit.

Wen says, and I have to believe him, because I did not hear a thing, except the cymbals and flutes that angels played above my head, that one of the students had asked the dark-haired man, in a derisive tone, why he wasn't in mourning for Lenin, and the man had answered:

"You do not know what a great loss mankind has suffered." He told me, moreover, that the young man had expressed much interest in talking to us so that we could bring him up to date on information about the workers and university students in Colombia. Fortunately, some friends called him and he had to say his good-byes quickly. I say that it was fortunate that he parted from us, because had he stayed longer I don't think that I would have been able to withstand such great beauty. Once he was far enough away, sprinting with such vigorous strides that we were able to guess the contours of his firm and lively ass, I had to sit down on the bleachers, because I was at the point of fainting. My temple was throbbing, and Wen, fearing I would go into shock, fanned me with his hat.

"Are you all right?" Paco said, and seeing that I couldn't even answer him, asked one of the students who was in his third year of medical school to take my pulse. It was out of control. They brought me a glass of water, which I drank slowly, surrounded by worried faces, and little by little I came back to my senses. Once I could speak, I went out of my way to convince them that I was fine: it was just a dizzy spell caused by the heat.

"Or the change in altitude," Wen intervened, helping me to put them at ease.

Finally, we were able to convince each of them to return to their favorite sport and leave us alone in the bleachers. Wen admitted that he, too, had been very impressed by the dark-haired apparition. I asked him if he had mentioned his name.

"Of course, he even asked where we were staying," he answered. "It's just that you were as flustered as I've ever seen you."

"Well," I defended myself, "have you ever seen anyone so divine in all your life?"

"Yes," he replied, upset. "You."

"Aside from me, silly," and, lowering my voice, I insisted: "Wasn't he supernaturally attractive?"

"The man is Beauty itself," he admitted, rolling his eyes. "But don't get your hopes up."

"Why? It's true he did seem a little sad about the death of the Soviet czar, but his sorrow will pass, no?"

"Have you lost your mind?" Wen proclaimed, outraged. "Didn't you see his wife standing right there next to him? She was stuck to him the whole time, like a leech."

I swore to him on the sacred sacraments that I had not noticed any female presence. What wife? From what hellish hole had she escaped with the sole purpose of making our lives bitter? Wen was struck with a fit of laughter, and he assured me that I even shook her hand when the Beauty had introduced us and told us they had just married. I said that that Adonis could have been accompanied not by a single wife but by a whole harem of women, and I would have noticed only him.

"What's his name?" I insisted.

"Julio Antonio Mella, if I recall correctly."

Soon, Cluster of Teeth finished his exercising and, sweating and all worked up, came towards the bleachers where we waited for him. We urged him to shower quickly, because we were atrociously hungry and wanted to invite him out to eat with us. Truth be told, we were just impatient to wheedle information out of him.

We didn't want to go back by streetcar, so we took a taxi, asking the driver to take us to the Morro and on the way subjecting the student to an honest-to-goodness interrogation. Paco Pla provided us with more facts than we were expecting. Since the lives of other students were a frequent topic of discussion in university classrooms and the motivation for gossip and loose talk, he knew everything about Mella. And they had been team members in the four-man regatta in Cienfuegos in 1921, where they took the gold medal. It seemed that on top of all his other occupations, that gorgeous man also found time to practice swimming, basketball, and canoeing.

Julio Antonio Mella was the soul of the university and one of its most fancied bodies. Not yet twenty-one (because of his physique, we had guessed he was three or four years older), he was well known for his revolutionary impulses and his capacity to lead. His real name was Nicanor, and his surname McPartland, his mother's last name; she was an Irishwoman, who, in one of those twists of fate common in life, shacked up with a Dominican tailor who lived in the city. Beauty and his younger brother, Cecilio, were the fruit of that illegitimate love. When Julio Antonio was six, his mother decided to go live in New

Orleans, and left the children with her lover. Mella attended parochial schools and then matriculated in the well-known Newton Academy. At eighteen, he began his study of law, and soon attracted attention with his aggressiveness and his gifts as an orator. He was one of the leaders of the student protest against bestowing the title of professor *honoris causa* on the Yankee ambassador Enoch Crowder, which the rector had been considering. It was not long before he became editor in chief of the magazine *Alma Mater.*

When the University Federation was established, he took the position of secretary. A year later, better known and putting all his charms to use, he won the presidency and began creating a student congress. In that conclave, to the scandal of many, Mella was able to pass a motion that censured religious education. At around that time, having begun to frequent the labor unions and to associate with leaders of the workers, he got it into his head that the student congress should send a message of solidarity to the Workers' Federation of Havana. And, needless to say, he succeeded. His great achievement of 1923 was to set up on campus the José Martí Popular University, where the workers studied after their day jobs.

"To tell you the truth," Paco concluded, "I am afraid that Julio Antonio will not last long as student president."

"Why?" Wen asked.

"People complain that each day he cares less about the university's problems, and that he is too involved in the problems of the working class. There are a lot of questions being asked. Some say that he is a Communist."

"And in the midst of all this commotion, he continues to study?"

"And has excellent grades, despite the animosity that more than one professor feel toward him," Pla remarked. "It was precisely in one of those law-school classrooms that he met Oliva Zaldívar, the woman he married." He paused, for a moment of suspense, expecting a new set of questions. I don't know if we were put off by the mention of the wife or if our thirst to find out more had been sated, but there were no more questions. We asked him to suggest a place where the food was good and then went off to the restaurant at the Hotel Lafayette.

When it came time for dessert, so that our guest would not get any false expectations, Wen said that he had an atrocious headache and that the only thing he wanted to do was to lie down and rest. Although the rower put up a great struggle we were able to get him on the first red-and-white streetcar that came by, promising that very soon we would offer him the night that he was dreaming about. I don't know if I was seeing things, but as he waved good-bye, standing next to the conductor, his ears seemed to be drooping from dejection.

At the hotel, two surprises awaited us. The first was a note in a handwriting full of arabesques on a sheet of perfumed paper. For a moment, I had the crazy idea that it might be from the wacky Gerbelasa. But no, it was from Madame Lachambre, inviting us to tea on Friday, at the Ideal Room. The second surprise was that Bartolomé Valdivieso was seated in the lobby, a thick notebook on his lap, waiting for us.

"We got rid of one to run into another," I whispered as we made our way toward him, pretending we were delighted to see him. "This is torment!"

Since we didn't have the slightest desire to bring him up to the room, we decided to receive him right there. The pharmacist, true to his word, brought with him the sonnet in progress, "To Eleonora the Sublime." The thick book he carried contained, recorded in his hand and in emerald ink, almost four hundred different versions of the work. Sometimes the differences were obvious, sometimes minimal. However, with a poem dedicated to an actress of La Duse's magnitude, the selection of any one syllable, the apparently simple substitution of one term for another, could prove crucial. Since we had promised him that we would help him with this task, we suggested that he leave the notebook with us and that we would go over its contents later, in the calm of our room. But the *mulato,* courteous but intransigent, insisted that he would rather read the different versions out loud, so that we could weigh the pros and the cons of each one together.

Not having an alternative, we moved to a quiet corner and asked one of the good-looking waiters to bring us three coffees, Bartolomé's full-strength and ours diluted a bit with hot water. Gathering all our patience and good will, and inwardly cursing the moment we offered our help, we readied ourselves to listen to his verse.

The truth was, Bartolomé's sonnet wasn't exactly bad: if one had to characterize it, one would go back and forth between two other words: horrible and pathetic. When studied impartially, it did comply with much of the requisites of that type of lyrical poem. The problem was that in those fourteen lines, in all their variations and combinations that the author read to us with just the right emphasis, there were assembled the greatest number of absurdities and barbarities imaginable.

The first stanza, the only one of which there were no other versions, since, according to the pharmacist, it was sturdy and served as a perfect foundation for the architecture of the poem, was a glimpse, of what was to follow.

> *Oh, towering monument,*
> *Your creation conquers eternity,*
> *Your gifts will live in posterity,*
> *Alone engraved in the firmament.*

With the first line of the second stanza, things got a little more complicated, and so began our analysis of the endless and maddening possibilities. What seemed better to begin that section: "Chained to enchantment like a dream"? Or "Eternalized by a funereal scream"? Or, perhaps, "There is, about you, an eternal gleam"? Whatever decision he made, it would give rise to new problems due to its relation to the three following lines. For example, let's say the *mulato* decided to use the last of these three examples (something that was not likely, because he defended, with a vehemence probably best reserved for a better cause, the second example), the stanza could read as follows.

> *There is about you an eternal gleam,*
> *That glows in the amethyst sky;*
> *And from your throne you cannot espy*
> *Those that with your offerings teem.*

But why put The Sublime One glowing in the skies? we asked ourselves. Wouldn't it be better, perhaps, to get rid of the second line of that hypothetical stanza, and put in its place something more evocative of the ethereal nature that critics assigned to her gestures? Like

"Your movements are beautiful and spry." And, of course, "Through the ages you flutter and you fly" wasn't a horrible option, if we thought of ages as transmitting that solid feeling of perdurability, and of the verbs "flutter" and "fly," on the other hand, as conveying that willingness to search everywhere for perfection, not resting on one's laurels, that was so much a part of La Signora's wisdom. After almost an hour of knocking our heads with all the possibilities, we came to the conclusion that the following alternative was the best of all and, for a moment, it became my favorite:

> *Living on in a fever of dreams,*
> *Through the ages you burst with your cries.*
> *Thespis makes sure your glory never dies,*
> *As you sift the truth from what it seems.*

Only for a moment, of course, because after a little while, another stanza became my favorite.

> *Trapped in a labyrinth of dreams,*
> *A thorn you reveal in your soul.*
> *Glorious Melpomene, as a whole,*
> *Your beauty rattles eternity's beams.*

Suddenly, Bartolomé Valdivieso began to look desperately through his scribbled notebook, till he came upon a stanza that he had completely forgotten about, written the night before in the throes of insomnia. He read it in a tremulous voice and then fixed his eyes on us, awaiting our verdict.

> *How many nymphs have you outshone,*
> *As, one by one, you darkened them?*
> *Oh, Eleonora, flawless as a gem,*
> *Listen, listen, when for you I groan.*

We both told him it was magnificent. Wen had only one suggestion: the fourth line should read, "From the heavens your light is on loan," which I considered an improvement over the other last line. As for me, although I agreed, I suggested some minor changes to the second and third lines. Both suggestions were accepted enthusiastically, and, at least for that night, the stanza was done.

But going on to the tercets, I thought I would go mad. The *mulato,* having worked on the poem for many weeks, had woven a fathomless web of alternatives. One verb called for another and so on: to row or to cling could become, according to the necessities of the meter, clap, snap, trap, flap, or lie, fly, dry, try, cry. Not satisfied with the material that he had amassed, the band continued to compose new lines in situ, as he was inspired to fill up the last pages of the notebook. As time passed, choosing anything became very complicated, with the endless possibilities of combinations in the damn little sonnet seeming infinite.

More than once I wanted to clench my fists and scream, out of pure and simple desperation. I think I held back because Wenceslao glared at me, begging me to keep my patience. What would the beautiful Gloria Swanson, who perhaps might be having a drink in the roof garden, say if she passed by there and saw me losing my composure? How could we explain to the star, to the rest of the guests, and to Mister Jouffret, manager of the Seville-Biltmore, that the pharmacist, who had driven us to the edge of madness, was to blame? Finally, Valdivieso seemed to have settled on an ending for "To Eleonora the Sublime":

> *Your art, Duse! Of embossed gold,*
> *Has brilliantly endured tests new and old,*
> *Has sifted the precious from the moss.*
>
> *Without sinking to flattery, I raise my brow,*
> *Just a messenger, with a message in tow,*
> *With nothing to offer but humble applause.*

To finish up, rhyming "moss" with "applause" seemed to me unacceptable. But, on seeing that it was already midnight, I took a deep breath and held back my criticisms. I even nodded vehemently in response to Wen's comment that, as it was, the sonnet was ready to be presented to its recipient. By that point, I couldn't tell you which one of the versions we had deemed acceptable.

Bartolomé told us that he planned to hire a calligrapher to copy the verses on parchment; then he would roll it up and tie it with a golden thread and slip it into a crocodile-skin case.

"I hope that my voice doesn't tremble when, before leaving the poem in the hands of Her Eminence, I read it to her," he exclaimed. "I don't know how to thank you for your help!" he added, overcome with emotion.

To my astonishment, Wenceslao suggested a possible way for him to repay us: once the sonnet had been read, the pharmacist could perhaps convince La Signora to grant us an interview. Surprised by the request, since he didn't know anything about our secret aspirations, the *mulato* assured us that he would do whatever he could to smooth the thorny path toward the actress. Fortune Gallo was supposed to arrive at the port from Indianapolis a day before Eleonora, on the twenty-fifth. After much begging, he had managed to get his father to cable him and invite him to dinner on the day of his arrival, and the impresario had accepted. During the reception, Bartolomé planned to rip from him the promise that he would help him convince the actress to listen to his sonnet.

And just as he was saying good-bye, the senator's son remembered something very important: it had been confirmed that the Inglaterra was the hotel where the tragedienne would be staying. She had reserved several suites on the fourth floor, the ones that faced San Rafael Street.

That night, perhaps due to a day so rich with events, I had a troubling nightmare; but the morning after, though I racked my brain, I couldn't tell Wen about it at all. All I remembered was unconnected images, in which there appeared, mounted on the horses of a *carrousel,* Mella, Graziella Gerbelasa, Vázquez Garralaga, the negro, the One with the Teeth, and the pharmacist. They went up and down, around and around, while in a box at the Teatro Nacional, Señora Cay pretended to conduct the orchestra, using her fan as a baton, and an enormous chorus of young athletes, spread out on the seats of the orchestra, recited like a litany the depressing "To Eleonora the Sublime." When Wen asked me what role I played in the oneiric witches' Sabbath, I couldn't answer him.

Love. Love. How boring!

Why does the whole world always want to talk about love? Why do people insist on believing that it is the axis around which existence rotates? I should first make clear that I have nothing against it. I loved and was loved (though I fear that I loved more than those who loved me), but love has not been, like some think, the motor that drove my steps through life, nor my principal preoccupation; instead, it was but a temporary affliction. Affliction, yes, because if you ask me, love is nothing but a disturbance, a change in our natural state, an ailment that, if it goes on too long, wears out and lays waste to the body as well as the spirit.

Love is a terrible, dangerous illness. I imagine that doctors don't finally admit its pathological qualities so as not to cause problems. Can you imagine how quickly the clinics and hospitals would fill up? Perhaps such a crisis, as they often do, would force a qualitative leap, a step forward in the evolution of humanity. If they decided to include love among the epidemics (putting it on the same level with measles, typhus, and influenza), science would abandon its odious fixations and would muster up the courage to find an antidote, some medicine that would cure it or, at least, serve to alleviate its sorrows, a kind of negative elixir d'amour.

Pills for unrequited love! Ointments to keep it at bay! More than one pharmacist would fill his coffers with gold selling such remedies.

I first found love in the theater. Vicarious loves, passions on loan, so to speak. The first time that I suffered from its effects in the flesh was for a man who did not deserve the tears I shed for him. It was a disastrous debut. Then there were other loves, not too many, thankfully; all of them, in their own way, tormenting.

Sarah used to say that the heart of a woman should be a

portable lamp, to plug it in wherever there was electricity when one needed light. And to be able to turn it off later, just at the right moment, whenever it was most convenient. She also said that with love, the briefer it is the better, else we run the risk of it stealing our judgment and our liberty. Was she right? I couldn't tell you for sure. For her love was a sport. For me it is a sort of cult. She was cynical but wise. Whereas I, when it came to love, was far too romantic and foolish. Who knows about one woman's happiness? Where did I come to know it? When? How? With whom?

Oh, love: the eternal paradox. I yearned for it and feared it. I enjoyed it and cursed it. Wretched is she who never knew it; wretched, too, she that had it and wanted to cling to it irrationally. We run after love, unsatisfied and needy, and on catching up with it, oh, how it makes us suffer! Love, love . . . I don't have anything against it, I'll say again, but I wish that they would stop idealizing it, place it where it rightfully belongs. In between pneumonia and erysipelas wouldn't be a bad spot, for example.

We were still in bed when Monkeyface came to pick us up. Our trip proved a delight: his uncle's ranch in Arroyo Naranjo was a small paradise full of fountains, fruit trees, and servants that were entirely devoted to spoiling the señorito and pleasing his guests. Since the owners of the property came on very few occasions, to celebrate a birthday or a wedding anniversary, our visit was a momentous event. A chubby black maid, who reminded us of Toña, chased a piglet around the patio and, paying little heed to its squeals of terror, slit its neck right in front of us, with a smile on her face that was almost childish. Although we were overcome by the scene, it didn't, a little bit later, stop us from chewing on the crispy, burnt skin.

As night fell, we returned to the city, red from the sun and carrying a basket of mangoes, guavas, oranges, and pineapples. Emilito asked us to be ready at eight-thirty to go see Josefina Cruz del Castillo, who that night was performing in *Let's Get a Divorce* at the Principal de la Comedia, and later to accompany him to Havana Park. Before going up to our room, we had an ingenious idea of what to do with our fruit: we asked for a card and sent the basket, together with some laudatory remarks, to Gloria Swanson's suite.

I got in the shower right away, for I felt grimy with the sweat and dust of the trip, and afterward, while Wen showered, I looked through the pages of the daily *La Discusión* that I had picked up in the lobby.

Lenin's death was still news. As if it were not enough to have delayed the announcement of their leader's passing away for twenty-four hours, the Soviet Congress had decided to put off the funeral till Saturday, so that the workers and folk from the country who wanted to see the body up close had time to travel to Moscow. The paper also said that eleven physicians had performed the autopsy on the Bolshevik and that the death certificate had been signed by four professors, four doctors, and the national health commissar. Since sorrows never come alone, it was rumored that the other great Russian leader, Leon Trotsky, was also suffering from a serious illness. What would Mella think about all this? I rested my head on the back of the armchair and closed my eyes to imagine Mella deep in thought, his beautiful eyebrows of an Arab prince brought close together, his mouth pressed with worry. I imagined that I approached the young man on tiptoes and pressed my cheek to his, before pecking his ear with a kiss. At that moment, Wen came out of the bathroom and I had to spread the newspaper on my lap to hide my excitement. I was definitely obsessed with the dark-haired beauty. I would even become a Communist, if need be, if that's what it took for us to have a little fling.

Let's Get a Divorce, with Ruiz del Castillo, was no great thing. Wenceslao arrived at the theater already biased against her, for the play had been one of the great successes of Eleonora Duse's youth, and he loved categorizing the poor Spanish actress as unconvincing, a screamer, and over the top. The performance did not seem so bad either to Monkeyface or to me, but we egged him on to keep him happy. Just as the curtain dropped on the last act, we ran out of the Ánimas theater without even applauding Josefina and climbed back into the indefatigable De la Cruz's Dodge Brothers. Since it was already ten-thirty, we asked him if it was appropriate to go to an amusement park at such an hour.

"Remember, this is not Bogotá," he replied mockingly, as he pressed down on the accelerator and drove us to Havana Park. It ended up being a great fair, packed with visitors attracted by the dancing and the gambling. We strolled from one place to another, under garlands of colorful lights, overwhelmed by the shouting and the music that whimsically intermingled. For a reasonable sum, we saw the lady with no arms but with hands: a well-proportioned young woman, dressed elegantly, whose hands were stuck to her shoulders. In spite of such an inconvenience, the lady showed the curious onlookers that she was able to use a typewriter and perform her *toilette* with her feet. Then we went into the covered wagon of the man of rubber, an individual with the ability to stretch his skin as if it were elastic. Although Wen and Emilito tried to convince me to go in with them into the booth of the serpent woman, who, according to what they said, had no spinal column, I told them I would rather wait outside by the dais, where a band of midgets played all kinds of musical instruments and danced and sang and boxed. What I did agree to see was a show by the Kellvints, a group of intrepid acrobats who hurled themselves from one hundred forty feet in the air, landing in a tank full of flaming oil. Was it some kind of trick or a true feat? I was so stunned that I couldn't tell for sure.

That night we fell unto our marriage bed dead from exhaustion. We didn't even notice that someone had slipped a card underneath our door, signed by La Swanson, in which she thanked us for the "delightful fruits" and invited us to have breakfast with her the following morning at exactly eight. When we found the message it was already past nine and both of us wanted to beat our heads against the walls. To miss out on such an opportunity! Now that was bad luck!

Wen insisted that we should go to the Colombian Consulate General that morning with the message from Melitón and Manolo. "The sooner we get that over with, the better," he said, and he almost had to drag me to number 22 on Cuba Street, where the offices of the consulate were located. Apparently, Dr. García Benitez had nothing to keep him entertained that morning, so he received us effusively. He asked how things were in Bogotá, wanted to know about the well-being of all sorts of people, told us the particulars of the titanic efforts that Minister Gutiérrez Lee, as well as himself, was making to introduce Cubans to the pleasures of the coffee from our land, and, lastly, he read closely the letter we had given him as soon as we walked into his office. As his eyes passed over the lines, his expression became serious and he shook his head in a concerned manner.

"Your uncles, Señor Belalcázar, want me to help you locate the whereabouts of Don Misael Reyes, but I am afraid that I cannot do much to help you," he stated. "They had written me before asking for news about their brother, and I see that I must repeat to you what I wrote back to them then: I have no idea where he is. In the period that

I have been here he has never come to the consulate or the legation or communicated with us. All my investigations through other countrymen who live on the Island came up with nothing. Who knows, after so much time, if someone using such a name arrived in this country three decades ago? In the immigration archives (which, it should be said, are not very trustworthy) the name Misael Reyes does not appear."

"Maybe he changed his name and secretly lives under another name," Wen guessed, making evident his love for cheap serial dramas.

"And what exactly would my uncle be hiding from?" I interjected, losing my patience.

"They have put you in charge of a difficult mission, Señor Belalcázar," the consul concluded. "If I may, I would suggest that you take out an ad in a newspaper. Perhaps that way, if your uncle actually lives in Havana, he might agree to see you. Another option is to go to the police and pursue an investigation with all the powers of the law."

And then he broke into an interminable monologue about the seeds of Cuban tobacco, and the samples of *caña japonesa* and *yerba elefante* that he had sent to Santander, about the differences between Havana and Bogotá and how much he missed his native land. After this little lecture, we were finally able to say our good-byes and flee the consulate. Wen asked me what I was going to do and I didn't know what to say. Neither of García Benitez's suggestions seemed too attractive. To publish an ad in a newspaper telling an uncle who had disappeared thirty years ago that I needed to speak to him urgently seemed a little too much out of a novel, and the notion of getting the police involved I liked even less.

For the moment, I decided that we go to Perla de Cuba. The letter sent by Misael to his siblings was written on a sheet of paper with a letterhead from that hotel, and although the consul said that his investigations there had proved fruitless, I wanted to see for myself. And so, like a pair of detectives, we walked into Perla de Cuba, on Amistad, only three blocks from the Prado, and we made them look up the name of The Unexpected One in the guest register of the period between June and July of 1923; but, if we were to believe their records, during that time no one named Misael Reyes had stayed there.

On leaving the hotel, I felt like a complete idiot. Just because someone had written a note with their letterhead on top, did that have to mean he stayed there? He could have gotten hold of the paper in countless ways . . .

"But then, why did he give this address as a way to get in touch with him?" my lover asked. "It doesn't make sense."

Yes, it was all absurd, and I cursed out loud. To dispel my bad mood, Wenceslao proposed that we lunch at the Inglaterra. I agreed to go, not suspecting what he was up to, but it didn't take me long to find out. As soon as we got to the hotel, where, according to the *mulato* pharmacist, La Duse would be staying, he went to the reception desk and subjected one of the employees to the third degree. He wanted to know exactly which rooms La Signora would be occupying and to book for us one that would be the nearest possible. At first, the man was reticent about giving up any information, but a little cash softened him up and he told Wen as much as he wanted to know. La Duse would be staying there for two weeks, accompanied by Katherine Garnett, an English aristocrat who was a close friend of hers, and two employees. The rest of the company would be staying in another hotel, also near the theater, but not so expensive.

By the time we sat down to eat lunch, we already had a reservation at the Inglaterra, a room with a view of San Rafael Street, next door to La Duse's room.

"I hope that you don't mind leaving the Seville," Wen said when everything had been set. "For our plans, it is better that we stay here."

I told him that I didn't care one way or the other and asked him what time we would be moving.

"After we finish this," he answered, pointing to the dishes in front of us, and he reminded me that that afternoon we were to have tea with the Chinese lady.

Since they were used to the comings and goings of tourists, they didn't pay much attention to our quick departure from the Seville-Biltmore. As I paid the bill, I saw Gloria Swanson for the last time; she was, by chance, also leaving the hotel. The queen of Hollywood, escorted by an entourage of maids, journalists, and fans descended the stairs on the way to the street. She turned for a moment to look at me, made a disappointed gesture with her heart-shaped mouth, and said good-bye with the ring and index fingers of her right hand. I mechanically responded with my own farewell, surely looking like a moron. When I told Wen about it, he didn't believe me.

We went by car to the Inglaterra and barely had time to drop off our luggage in our room before we had to leave hurriedly for the Ideal Room, which fortunately was nearby.

Generala Lachambre, or María Cay, was already seated at one of the tables in the tea salon when we arrived, right on time for our date but out of breath. She was wearing a Prussian-blue dress made of charmeuse, and a double-strand pearl necklace. She reached out her hand so we could kiss it and, as if she had known us all our lives, began pointing out the other ladies present and joking about them.

"The fat one in red, choking on that enormous *biscuit glacé,* she drinks several cups of vinegar each day in hopes of losing weight," she exclaimed, her imperturbable features losing none of their cunning. "And that other one, the peroxide blonde, brushes her eyelashes with cod liver oil in hopes that they will grow. Oh, you don't believe me?" she asked Wen, who was smiling skeptically. "Go near her under some pretext and see if you don't smell it."

Located on Galiano, the Ideal Room is the most elegant tea salon in the city. Its ceilings and walls are decorated with Art Nouveau motifs, and wherever you look there are pots filled with flowers. That afternoon, the room was filled with ladies and their gentlemen, who were mostly young and all dressed up very fashionably; they devoured the sweets and ice creams that were the specialty of the house and chatted frenziedly.

"I don't understand how some women dare to go out in American clothes," La Cay exclaimed. "To me those rags are no different than what they gave slaves to wear. They couldn't be more . . . rustic."

"Your dress is beautiful," Wen flattered her.

"It's from Au Petit Paris. I buy my summer hats from the Trapié Sisters and the shoes in Trianón."

Throughout the lighthearted conversation in which we talked about everything, including the, according to Wen, disastrous performance by Josefina Ruiz del Castillo in *Let's Get a Divorce,* we drank our teas.

A tall, thin, young man entered the establishment and came over to say hello to Madame Lachambre. "Pablo Álvarez de Cañas, social chronicler for *El País*," she announced and, after introducing us, told the gentleman the reason for our visit. The newly arrived guest said something to the effect that to see La Duse on stage was worth any sacrifice and, after saying his good-byes, headed for one of the few empty spots. "Attention, the show is about to start!" La Cay mused and urged us not to take our eyes off the pair of youngsters at a table in the back.

It was a girl of some twenty-odd years, scrawny and with a sulking disposition, and her brother, younger than she, extremely pale and with dark hair. "They are the Loynaz Muñozes," our Asian friend pointed out. "The girl, who is called Dulce María and writes poetry, happened to fall in love with Pablito, a nobody, and her mother and grandmother, who are from one of the poshest families on the Island, almost had seizures. They moved heaven and earth till they broke up their rich heiress from the penniless newspaperman. It was incredibly ugly! I know it firsthand. Troy was burning!" This Dulce María suddenly recognized her old flame and became visibly nervous. Álvarez de Cañas said hello to her with a circumspect nod of his head. Not appreciating this show of civility, the young woman whispered something to her companion, grabbed her purse, and they both left the place quickly. Wen and I, speechless, watched the scene without much discretion. But I noticed that we weren't the only ones: an anticipative silence had fallen over the Ideal Room. Only with the departure of the siblings did conversations resume. "Poor girl and poor Pablo, who adores her without hope," the Chinese lady remarked in epilogue as she let out a sigh.

"And the brother, what is his name?" Wen tried to ascertain, kicking me under the table to let me know that he thought the boy quite a muffin. "That is Carlos Manuel," our informant revealed. "Very handsome, no?" We nodded solemnly, though I was telling myself: not quite as handsome as Julio Antonio Mella. "It seems that all of the Loynaz Muñozes are a little bit eccentric, if not outright mad," La Cay added and, when we asked her why, she told us that they had taken all electric bulbs out of their bedrooms and preferred to light them with candles; that they had a garden with exotic plants where spider monkeys from the jungles of Venezuela, flamingoes, cockatoos, and royal white turkeys wandered about; that they ate their dinner at dawn and slept during the day; and that they wrote poetry and paid the owner of the corner store to pretend to be a Russian Orthodox priest when they presented him to their friends. Dulce María seemed to be the one who was most normal, but the other siblings—Enrique, Carlos Manuel, and Flor—were quite unique. Enrique, who was the second oldest, was also a poet, a very good one, according to the few who had had the privilege to read his work; according to the lady, he was more beautiful than the Loynaz we had seen, but so shy that he would only present himself to strangers in a suit of Tartar armor. Carlos Manuel was a musician and a polyglot, who had an excessive fascination with black magic and occult books, and who at dusk liked to stroll through the garden in a monk's habit. As for the youngest one, the fifteen-year-old Flor, she was well known for being rebellious and willful and wore high leather boots trimmed with otter skin, and one day when the family chauffeur was distracted eating corn fritters, she had stolen the car and, behind the wheel herself, taken it for a joy ride all over the Vedado neighborhood. The mother, who was divorced from General Loynaz del Castillo, had ceded to her children an entire wing of the mansion that they shared, so that she could remain, as much as possible, removed from all their strangeness. In truth, it was a miracle that we had been able to see two of them, for they almost always remained locked up in the huge house, where professors in all fields came to instruct them.

The gossip about the owner of Pablo Álvarez de Cañas's heart and her brothers, though fascinating, didn't really spark my interest and, though there were fans in every corner of the room, I began to feel short of breath. Suddenly, Señora Lachambre cut short her chatter, took a fan from her purse (not the same one as the of the morning with the theater tickets, but a bigger one) and as she waved, alternating between herself and me, she looked me in the eyes with an earnestness that contrasted with the lightness of her previous comments.

"The resemblance is so striking that it can't be a coincidence," she said. "Pardon my rudeness, Señor Belalcázar, but do you know Misael Reyes?"

Wen choked on his tea and began to cough loudly, spraying us. Trying to hide my confusion, I told her that not only did I know him, but that, more important, he was my uncle on my mother's side and that I needed to see him urgently.

Although, from all appearances, the lady did not like to show her feelings in public, my reply moved her. The corner of her mouth began to shake uncontrollably and, to hide it, she brought the linen napkin to her face. When she brought it down, the shaking had stopped.

"His nephew," she murmured, forcing a smile.

Wen, who can sometimes be phenomenally impertinent, didn't wait for María Cay's explanation, but barraged her with questions. When and how had she met my uncle? What was her current relationship with him? What did he do? And, most important, where could we find him? I could hardly get him to shut up. We were going to have news about my disappeared uncle from a most unexpected source.

I took out the photograph that I had slipped into my jacket that morning before visiting the consul and handed it to the lady. She held it out with the tips of her fingers, studied it carefully, and, as she handed it back, said, "I imagine that you have heard of Julián del Casal."

Wenceslao and I exchanged confused looks, but we nodded eagerly. Of course: Julián del Casal, the modernist. He and Ruben Darío had written admiring verses to a young and beautiful María Cay that, try as we might, we could not see in the person sitting in front of us. But what in the hell did Casal, dead for so many years, just as the Nicaraguan bard was dead, have to do with Misael Reyes? What was she getting at? Did the old woman have a screw loose?

"When I met Julián, in February of 1890, I felt as if I were drowning in his turquoise eyes." The evocative tone gave way to an expression of disdain and annoyance. "You don't see eyes like that anymore; today men have eyes that seem to have been made in a factory, like the eyes of dolls," she grumbled and, on noticing our frustration, made a gesture asking us to have patience. "Don't you worry, I am not senile. When you tell a story, the proper thing to do is to start from the beginning, and in the beginning there was Julián, with his paleness, so unusual in the tropics, his awkward gait, his sadness, and his eyes, his amazing eyes capable of seducing, without even wanting to, any woman."

She told us that she had met him at a masquerade party, in the mansion of Pérez de la Riva. Her brother Raoul Cay, who was a book critic for the literary magazines and defended Casal's talent tooth and claw, did the honors.

"I was dressed as a Japanese woman, with a beautiful kimono and a paper umbrella," she remembered. "I felt ridiculous atop an enormous pair of wooden sandals, but truth be told I was the hit of the party, they toasted me like mad."

Julián del Casal wrote an account of the evening for *La Discusión* and made reference to her grace and beauty with passionate praise. Some days after, the "Japanese woman" sent him a copy of the photograph that, to please her father, she had taken before going to the ball. She thought she would die when she found out, from Raoul, that the poet had written some verses inspired by the photograph.

"Maybe you know the poem. It's called 'Kakemono.' " We told her we didn't, and, as if this were impossible to believe, she recited a fragment from memory: " 'At the sight of your beauty so portrayed, my ills were all forgotten . . . ' " We told her again that we didn't know it, and she pursed her lips, disappointed.

The daughter of the ex-chancellor of the Empire of the Sun fell for the friend of her brother's, who wrote a different kind of poetry and, like Baudelaire, was always dressed in black. She couldn't care less about any of Raoul's other friends, literary young men and bohemians who met every afternoon from two to five as a literary circle at La Galería Literaria on Aguiar Street; but whatever had to do with that newspaperman, who lived in that tiny room above the bookstore, without any income but what he made from his position as a chronicler and copy editor at *La Discusión* and for the collaborations published in *La Habana Elegante, El Fígaro,* and *La Caricatura,* interested her immensely. She found out, always through Raoul, that Casal called his diminutive and lugubrious room "my cell," that he liked to surround himself with fake Chinese objects, that he was very proud of his small collection of the works of the French poets, and that he mended his torn suits and sewed the buttons on himself. All this moved her to tears and caused her absurd fits of shaking. Around that time, the young man had already published his first book, *Leaves to the Wind,* which pleased many but disappointed some others, and was writing the poetry that would make up his second, *Snow.* "Because snow, like poetry, is fleeting, a thing of winter, the place where I find myself in my own life," our friend exclaimed, repeating the words of the poet.

"For several months, for almost a year, we played a game of cat and mouse. All of Havana was telling Raoul that Casal was crazy about me and he would repeat it to me, very amused, thinking that I would never fall in love with such a poor boy, and that if I did make such a mistake, our father would be sure to pull me by the ears and bring me back to my senses. When we happened to run into each other in some place, however, Julián treated me with an icy courtesy that I could not quite understand. I found myself obliged to play the role of an unattainable beloved, in spite of the fact that I fervently yearned that he would dare woo me. Although I was careful that neither my father nor Raoul would notice, I lost my mind over that man, I would have done anything he asked of me. The passion that the poet supposedly felt for me became a topic of conversation in every gathering and soirée. I played the part, but every time that I looked into those greenish-blue eyes, I wanted to dive into them and never emerge. I didn't understand any of it, but when he dedicated 'Cameo' to me and published it in *El Fígaro,* it was as if someone, perhaps a kind Oriental deity, removed the blindfold from my eyes. On reading it, I realized not only that Julián had never loved me, but that he never would."

"And why did you reach that conclusion?" Wen dared to interrupt her.

"I would have to have been stupid or slow not to realize it, my dear. The poem left no room for doubt. After referring to my beauty, capable of making anyone go out of their mind with pleasure, and praising my sculptural breasts, my voice with the accent of a siren, my mouth made with the fiery blood of a strawberry, the rosy jasper of my brow and the black curls of my hair, how do you think he finished?"

Wen and I made faces as if we did not have the slightest clue, and La Cay recited, not too pleased, the last lines of the poem:

> *I cannot love you. Your beauty binds*
> *Me in rings of absolute tedium.*

Where on this earth is he who finds
A heart as cold and as dead as mine?

Those words fell on me like a bucket of cold water. Absolute tedium! Julián's heart was made of ice, of snow, like his poem: it was a piece of tin, that not even her splendid beauty, praised by all, could cause to beat. When they saw each other again, María Cay, swallowing and feigning a delight that she was far from feeling, reproached him ironically: "I didn't expect such a beautiful frog as a gift, my good sir," to which the writer, overcome with nerves, could not respond.

"And then I did whatever I had to, to get him out of my head," she continued. "I began to fantasize about a man who wanted a woman of flesh and blood and not one who adored a photograph of me dressed up as a Japanese woman but who found it impossible to flirt with me. I painfully understood that Julian, in the same manner that he had persisted in describing landscapes and distant and exotic objects in his poetry, could only love imaginary women and sing of nonexistent passions. He was addicted to the spirals of blue smoke from sandalwood, to opal, to portraits of chrysanthemums, cranes, and pagodas. I forced myself away from him and, as time passed, convinced myself that I didn't care about him."

"But of course you still did care about him," Wen commented, listening to her story entranced, his elbows on the table and his chin resting on his palms.

I gave him a withering look. If he kept egging her on, our Asian friend would never get to the part about Misael Reyes, and as for me, I had grown tired of her love story with the modernist a long time ago, no matter what intensity of turquoise his eyes might have been. I yawned discreetly, to see if it would inspire her to get to the point, but La Cay hardly noticed and serenely continued her tale.

For months she avoided Casal, and it was around that time that General Lachambre began to court her, with the consent of the ex-chancellor. After they were already engaged and a few months before the wedding, she saw the author of *Snow* again. It was the end of July 1892. Raoul had invited Ruben Darío, who was passing through Havana, for dinner, and the Nicaraguan had insisted that Julián also come to the banquet.

"My brother asked me to go with guests to the room where the distinctions awarded to our daddy by the Chinese Empire were displayed. Dario loved the *kakemonos* and *surimonos,* the little lacquer boxes, the ivory figurines, and my father's antique arms collection. Raoul and he doubled over with laughter when Casal, forgetting his famous pessimism on finding himself amid all these things that transported him to another world, wrapped himself in silk mantles and made whimsical turbans for his head. Soon Daddy came in, accompanied by General Lachambre, whom he introduced to the guests. 'This is my daughter's fiancé,' he said. I was surprised to find myself gauging Julián's reaction and lamenting the fact that it did not seem to cause him one bit of sadness or dismay to meet the man who would be my husband. I realized then that though I had painstakingly tried to bury all my feelings for him, they were still very much alive. A rage burned within me. Why was I still hurt by the mere proximity of this idiot who could neither know how nor was able to love me? I was so upset that I almost asked the general to push up the date of our wedding. I needed to become Señora Lachambre as soon as possible."

On noticing how I was fidgeting, the lady begged me to be calm, for my uncle was just about to appear in the story.

"I saw him again the following year, after I was already married. Raoul had invited us to a party, and in the dining room, chatting with a dozen other writers, was Casal."

Since her brother had told her that he was suffering from some lung ailment, she courteously inquired about his health. Julián told her that ever since he had moved to a room on the terrace of Domingo Malpica's house he felt better. That night, one of the guests, Aniceto Valdivia (the same gentleman who, years before, on returning from Europe, had put in Casal's hands the works of Rimbaud, Verlaine, and Mallarmé) attended the party accompanied by a young man from Bogotá who had recently arrived in the country.

"When they told me that his name was Misael Reyes," the Chinese lady remembered, "I could only think of responding with something silly and obvious: that he had an archangel's name. Misael is Micael and Micael is Michael, he of the fiery sword and saffron hair and emerald-green wings, he who most resembles God."

As María spoke to him, the young man smiled, as if distracted, and the general's wife noticed that his glance shifted furtively toward Julián, who was chatting with the old man Cay, Raoul, and Ramón Meza on the other side of the room. An hour later, very discreetly, the young Colombian and the poet left together. She was the only one who saw them leave, for she had been watching them all night like a veteran spy, noticing first the shy giggles that they exchanged and the passionate conversation in which they became engaged, forgetting about everybody else.

Very early the following morning, Señora Lachambre made up whatever pretext to leave the house and impetuously made her way to the Malpica residence on Virtudes Street. She went up the spiral staircase that led to the terrace as fast as she could, and half-heartedly knocked on the door to Julián's room. After waiting for a few seconds that seemed like centuries, she heard a chair move, and then some footsteps, and finally the poet opened the door. It was clear that he had just awoken and had not yet washed his face. His hair was a mess, and he wore a penitent's white, coarse-wool smock. Although La Cay had heard about this eccentricity of his, the outfit still surprised her. Casal held in his hand a poem that he had recently written, and she was able to see the title: "A Request." Making a superhuman effort, she was able to say something like: "You're going to think that I am crazy for . . ." but she couldn't finish her thought on noticing that behind him, wrapped in a sheet and rubbing his eyes, was the young man from Colombia. Everything seemed to indicate that, this time at least, the poet had preferred the natural to the artificial.

"I was frozen there watching them, as confused as they were, and when I was able to get my bearings again, I turned around and went down the stairs three at a time, regretting that I had been so impulsive and crazy."

After that, for as long as Julián del Casal was alive, he and the foreigner were inseparable. Any time that the general's wife spoke to her brother Raoul or to one of the writers or journalists from the *La Habana Elegante* circle, she found a way to ask about Julián and always, always, the name of the Colombian would come up alongside his. Some spoke of their friendship as something most natural; others, however, spoke of it seasoning their comments with a pinch of malice.

And so, in this manner, she knew that Misael Reyes had been with Casal when, hoping to recuperate from lung tumors, he went to Yaguajay, to visit his sister Carmelina for a few weeks. Each day frailer of health, he was able to finish his third and last book, *Busts and Verses,* turn it in to the publisher, and go over the proofs with the help of his young friend.

"Do you know how Casal died?" La Cay asked and, not waiting for a reply, fearing not only that we would say we didn't know but that we didn't care, she kept on speaking. "He was at a dinner in the home of Dr. Lucas de los Santos Lamadrid, seated next to Misael, of course, when one of the guests told a joke. They say that it wasn't an especially funny joke, but he found it hilarious. He laughed so hard that he had an aneurysm; he spit out a mouthful of blood and fell over on the table, to the horror of everybody present. For Julián to die laughing, he who had been so melancholy, so neurotic always . . . what a vile paradox! I am convinced that if he had somehow known what was going to happen he would have committed suicide the night before so as not to come off as ridiculous."

The burial was quite an occasion. The poet's friends paid for everything, and, as they say in Cuba, they threw the house out the window. The deceased, who had long lived with major privations and financial difficulties, could count on the luxurious funeral services of the House of Guillot. Since no one knew where to lay his remains, one of his best friends, Rosell Saurí, offered a place in his family's mausoleum in the cemetery, at the end of the central, tree-lined path, to the right. They took the coffin all the way there, in a Philadelphia-model hearse, pulled by three pairs of black horses.

Some weeks later, Señora Lachambre saw Misael Reyes on Concordia Street. He was so thin and haggard that she almost didn't recognize him. It was he who noticed her and almost burst into tears. They went into a café and she forced him to eat something. At first, the Colombian refused but afterwards began to eat with the voracity of one who has not had any food in a long time.

" 'Oh, María,' he said to me in his funny accent, 'only you can understand what I am going through, only you.' "

We waited silently for the lady to go on. But upon putting back on the inexpressive mask that she had lost when telling of the death of the poet, she merely added in a neutral voice:

"End of story."

"And what happened with my uncle?" I asked.

"I don't know exactly," she declared. "Can you believe that after that I never saw him again? It seems to me that one time Raoul told me that the Colombian had descended to the pits of hell, but I never understood what he meant by that and, given my state as a respectable married woman, it wasn't really fitting for me to ask any further questions."

Wen was as frustrated as I was. I felt like slapping the Chinese lady for forcing us to listen to that endless, melodramatic story without ever getting to what we were really interested in: what had happened to Misael Reyes. When we asked her who might know of his whereabouts, she shrugged. "Perhaps Count Kostia," she ventured. On noticing our surprise, she made clear that it wasn't a Russian noble but a pseudonym used by the poet and playwright Aniceto Valdivia as a byline for his newspaper stories in days gone by. It was through him that my uncle had met Casal; it wasn't absurd to think then that Misael had kept in touch with him, or, at least, that Count might know where to find him. La Cay warned us that the gentleman was rather old and that he was well known for his temper tantrums. To make matters worse, some days he behaved very peculiarly: lolling about the house in diapers and showing off the Great Cross of St. Olaf that King Haakon VII had decorated him with when he had served as the Cuban ambassador to Norway, and at the first moment the servants would take their eyes off him he would go out in the streets in such a getup. María couldn't guarantee that Casal's and Misael's friend would agree to see us, but she promised to get in touch with him and do all she could to help us.

We said good-bye to her and on leaving the Ideal Room, just as we were to go our different ways, Wen grabbed her by the arm and asked what she felt for my uncle. Hate, perhaps?

"No, not hate. Pity maybe. What I can tell you is that I envied him," she confessed. "Envy him still. Profoundly."

We took the first taxi that came by, and when we got to our room we called Emilito De la Cruz and Bartolomé Valdivieso to let them know that we had switched hotels. The latter listened to us hurriedly, as he was very nervous: just at that moment he was leaving to pick up Fortune Gallo to take him out to dinner.

That night we went to the Martí to see Mimí Aguglia, who was opening her second season with the premiere of *The Lady X,* a play about a woman gnawed by addiction and adversity. On noticing that the posters at the entrance of the theater called the actress a brilliant tragedienne, "the most illustrious in the world," Wen went in with his mind made up that everything would be horrible and, in effect, he did find everything abominable. Beginning with the uncomfortable seats, followed by the costumes and scenery, and ending with Aguglia her-self, who performed in Spanish. Eleonora's countrywoman, to be truthful, wasn't as bad as Wen made her out to be from the moment she walked on stage, but the actors who performed with her, all Cuban, were among the worst.

It didn't take us long to realize that Mimi had many admirers in Ha-vana, for she was given ovations various times during the course of the play. Every time the audience applauded in the middle of a scene, Wen would become furious in his seat, muttering insults at the crowd. But when, during one of the intermissions, we found out that the following week the actress would perform in *Fedora* and *The Lady of the Camellias,* La Duse's paladin began to foam at the mouth like a rabid dog.

"How dare she!" he reviled, almost screaming, not caring about others who were chatting in the lobby and casting reproachful glances his way. "*Fedora* and *The Lady of the Camellias* belong to La Signora, and to put them on while she is performing in another the-ater only a few blocks away, is a provocation and a sacrilege!"

I was about to tell him that I didn't see what the big deal was. Didn't his beloved Eleonora do exactly the same thing when she brought with her to Paris a repertoire made up of all of Bernhardt's successes? But I held my tongue to prevent another furious outburst. It didn't even help when I pointed out a good-looking audience member and told Wen that the fellow resembled Vicentini. Not even by mentioning the Chilean could I get him to put an end to his diatribe.

"Aguglia is worse than Josefina Ruiz del Castillo . . . which is saying a lot!" he roared like a judge pronouncing an irrevocable sentence. "Thank goodness that La Duse arrives tomorrow and all these second-class divas will find out what true greatness is."

That night I couldn't sleep. The following day we would go to the port, to wait for La Signora, and I was very tense about it. Wen, on the other hand, snored enthusiastically.

I was under the impression that I had finally fallen asleep when, at exactly seven in the morning, the phone woke me. It was María Cay to say that Count Kostia refused to see us, but that after much entreating, he had agreed to put us in contact with someone who knew how to reach my uncle. We had to be patient: he would get in touch with us to tell us what we should do.

I had just hung up when the phone rang again. I picked up the receiver in a nasty mood. This time it was the pharmacist.

"Signor Gallo was very pleasant and he promised that he would do what he could so I could meet La Duse and read her my sonnet," he exclaimed, euphoric, and then made one last inquiry about "To Eleonora the Sublime." "What sounds better, Luchito: 'sifted the precious from the moss' or 'has made a triumph of loss'? Be honest, for the love of God, I am about to send it to the calligrapher."

At night, in the silence and the emptiness, I sometimes hear life pass by with such a horrible murmur that I would do anything not to have to hear it. . . .

There were nights when I would stay on the stage after finishing a performance. I would not leave after the final curtain. I would remain still, quiet, till everyone had left. Everyone, the audience, the members of the company, the theater employees. I was sure that when I was alone in the darkness I would begin to feel better.

In Mrs. Alving's house, near the fjord, or in poor blind Anna's, next to what had been the great Micenas. Any place would suit, any refuge as long as I didn't have to go back to the hotel room. Of course, this is a fantasy that I have never tried to put into practice, something that I seldom talk about. Neither Désirée nor María would allow me to stay the night on the stage. If I tried it, they would drag me by force to the hotel and, ignoring my protests, force me into bed. The bed where, covered by a sheet up to her chin and with eyes wide open, Eleonora spends a good deal of her night thinking of the horror of the day that has ended and the horror of the day to come, where she will have to, in order to live and because of living, still squeeze her heart, exhausted as it might seem.

Wretched Eleonora, who was born to imitate life but never possess it! When will the fifth act of her existence come to an end?

So that those hours pass by quickly, Eleonora has invented some tricks. She calls them "time traps." They are not completely successful, but at least they help to ease the wait. Night is a large, dark paradise that one must cross barefoot, at the mercy of rats and memory. Eleonora imagines, for example, all the people that have lain in that bed before her. She tries to visualize them. Businessmen. Widows traveling. All different sorts of couples: secret lovers, newlyweds, married folks who each make themselves comfortable on the far side of the mattress. For each of those characters she invents a face, the sound of a voice, a manner of moving. And a history.

Other times she chooses a country or a city to which she has never been and tries to imagine, down to its most trivial details, its houses, its streets, its people, its customs, its landscape, not allowing her mind to wander in any other direction.

It's all about fantasies, about inventing people and places. To imagine, not to remember. Years before, she would choose some child and entertain herself imagining what would become of her when she grew older. How many lives did she conceive for her goddaughter, Mendelssohn's daughter! And for her grandchildren, Hugh and Eleonora! But there are no children close to her anymore. They have all grown up into men and women. They are far away and live their own lives, somewhat gray but real. Eleonora wants to declare a truce, she wants to sleep but she can't. Sometimes the lack of air makes it impossible; other times an upcoming tour, the prospect of getting on a train or a boat. But generally it is exhaustion that keeps her awake.

Oh, if only everything had already happened. But the Earth continues on its disciplined rounds every twenty-four hours. It never stops and neither do we. We wake up each morning and we fulfill, whether we like it or not, our obligations, we nourish the body, even when we don't want to, so it doesn't grow feeble, and then we go to bed, to rest from the fatigue and prepare us for the next one. We go on, even when we have no faith or hope. The reason? I don't know. Inertia, maybe. Or perhaps because, when everything is said and done, we are nothing more than a species of sophisticated automatons.

Do you understand then why, if it were possible, I would stay on the stage even after the play was over? There, inside *whatever character I am playing, protected by her skin, suffering her ills, but safe from the night, from solitude, from myself.*

What a dangerous thing life is, my friends! What a dangerous and persistent thing!

5

And so the fragile woman, the one in a black suit and hat, and gloves just as dark, the one who covered her face with a veil to keep it from the glances of the snoops, was she, Eleonora Duse. Although I knew that she was an old woman and I was tired of listening to Wen speak about the austerity of her wardrobe, on seeing her I felt something that, if it wasn't a letdown, very much resembled one.

We were at the San Francisco pier, the same one where we had arrived at the Island fours days before, four days that because of their intense nature seemed like a month. We had arrived there early, impatiently waiting, among many others, for the arrival of the *Tivives,* which was scheduled to arrive at nine in the morning and did not appear until past eleven. La Signora could not have chosen a more rotten day to arrive: the skies were overcast and threatened at any moment, perhaps as punishment for our curiosity, to open up with a downpour.

During the wait, we heard countless stories related to La Duse. A pack of lies mostly, according to Wen. A newspaperman reported that one of the things that the legend insisted upon was to have a tank of oxygen in her dressing room, for many times she was short of breath during the performances. Fortune Gallo nervously paced the pier from one end to the other, frequently checking his watch.

Finally, the *Tivives* docked. The seamen took hold of the ropes to secure the craft to the stakes. We all craned our necks, trying to make out the actress. Ten minutes passed before the first passengers started to disembark, embarrassed by all the people.

Suddenly, somebody let out a warning yell: La Signora was descending the ship's staircase, holding the arm of one of the twenty or so members of her company. She was overtly plain, her *toilette* almost Franciscan. A very elegant lady of aristocratic bearing followed behind her. We took for granted that it was Katherine Garnett, the English friend who would be staying with her. Behind them were two other ladies, Désirée Wertheimstein, her secretary, who for many years had traveled with her everywhere, and María Avogadro, her maid.

The producer of the tour made his way forward to greet his artist. But without stopping, La Duse barely grazed Gallo's outstretched hands and continued in a hurry behind the men who opened the way for her.

As she got closer, we got up on our tiptoes to see her better. She was shorter than I had imagined. I strained to see her hands (so famous since D'Annunzio had invented the epithet "she of the beautiful hands"), but the shawl that was draped over her shoulders prevented me. However, just at the moment that the actress passed in front of us, dodging the reporters who asked her what it felt like to be visiting Havana for the first time and what she thought about Mussolini, the photographers who harassed her to pose for their cameras, and we, who watched her as if she were a circus act and not a respectable and circumspect lady who could very well be our mother, an unexpected gust of sea air shook the tulle of her hat and we were able to catch a glimpse of her pallid, sharp-featured countenance, the sunken eyes, enormous and sad, and the dirty-white hair gathered at the nape. She looked like an aged and exhausted church mouse.

Following the directions that Gallo called out, the caravan headed toward a car parked near the walkway. As soon as La Signora, the Englishwoman, the secretary, and the maid got in, and the impresario settled in between them, the chauffeur put the car in gear and it went off into the distance amid the protests and jeering of the gathered press.

Stunned by the way the actress had ignored them, vanishing without even making a statement, the majority of the reporters left cursing her name. Who did she think she was? Royalty or something, how obnoxious! How different from the *divette* Esperanza Iris, who arrived lavishing smiles on everyone, posing for photographers and signing autographs for her hundreds of admirers. Damn that vain old hag! To hell with her!

Other reporters, more stubborn or perhaps fearful of a reprimand if they returned empty-handed, began to interview the other Italians about any nonsense that came into their heads. On realizing that one of them, tall with greased hair, dressed in a cigar-colored gabardine was the lead actor Memo Benassi, they took countless pictures of him. None of which, as far as we could confirm, were published later. Someone said that the actor was in negotiation with a company in Hollywood to make a film with Pola Negri.

The actors did not take long in getting into other cars and disappearing as well. Little by little, things returned to normal on the wharf. We stayed fixed in our spot till two young prostitutes, both heavily made up, and a hunchback whom they called Rigoletto, started to watch us, whispering and laughing, so we decided it was time to get out of there.

"Did you notice that she wore no earrings?" I remarked on our way back to the hotel. "And it seems that the story about her having to be carried about in a chair is not true."

Since I got no response, I remained silent, knowing that my friend's brain was working at a vertiginous speed, looking for a way to get by the barrier of protection that La Signora had raised around her person, searching for any means to open a gap in that barricade to gain access to that privacy which she so jealously guarded.

What stratagems were being plotted inside that head? I asked myself. Was he planning to gain access to the tragedienne in the same manner as Valdivieso, through Fortune Gallo? Or was he thinking of making use of the spell he cast over women to win the good will of those who protected Eleonora, and get one of these to help us? But which one? Miss Garnett who walked beside her, pointing out the bumps and dips in the walkway, and saying things to her that no one could hear? Or one of the guardians that walked behind her, watching her back like a pair of Cerberuses, and casting admonishing glances before them and behind them?

That Saturday, as we were leaving for the port, we had seen various floral arrangements in the hallway of the hotel. They were on the floor, by the door of the room where La Duse would be staying, waiting to be taken in. Wen began to look through the cards attached to the larger arrangements. One of them was from the minister of the Italian delegation and it was engraved with the republic's coat of arms; another one said *Cara Eleonora, benvenuta* and was signed by Fortune Gallo; but the arrangement that topped them all, which was composed of red roses, lilies, and anthuriums was sent by the obnoxious Olavo Vázquez Garralaga. His note read: *Per l'immensa Eleonora, che viene ad arricchire il cuore dei cubani con la sua arte.*

Just as I was telling Wenceslao that it was an unpardonable error on our behalf not to have sent flowers, he ran into our room toward the desk. I watched him from the doorway, at first not having the slightest idea what he was up to, scribbling some lines on a card, but soon enough understanding what he was planning: without the slightest scruple, he tore the poet's card to pieces and replaced it with the one that he had just written.

"Ready?" he asked, not feeling guilty at all, as he made his way toward the elevator.

"What did you write?" I inquired.

"A message of adoration signed by two Colombians who had crossed the sea to applaud her art."

On returning to the Inglaterra after La Duse's arrival, Wenceslao investigated with Regla, the *mulata* maid who was in charge of the fourth floor, what had become of the star and her retinue. Regla, at first hesitant to give away any details, was without delay bribed with a single bill that was certainly worth two weeks' salary for her. It disappeared down her cleavage, and the knot in her tongue came undone right away. Lowering her voice, with a mysterious air, she began to blab.

The first thing La Signora did on entering the room was to lift the veil from her hat and order that the shutters on the balconies facing the ruckus of San Rafael be closed. Then she put on some eyeglasses and went, inch by inch, through the rooms, followed by her secretary and maid, examining everything carefully and passing her index finger over the surface of the wood, searching for the smallest speck of dust. She sat on her bed to see if the mattress was firm, and sunk her hands into the pillows to see if they were soft. She tested the lights on the ceilings and lamps to make sure they would turn on without

problem, that the pressure and the temperature of the water coming
out of the bathroom faucets was adequate, and that the bell for calling
on service worked as it should. She noticed, too, the width of the armoire, the depth of the drawers, and the efficiency of the front-door
lock, which could be double-bolted. Lastly, she straightened by a tad
one of the pictures that hung in the entrance. The ritual complete, she
let out a breath, nodded, and collapsed, exhausted, in a rocking chair.
And then her people began to flutter from one room to another, opening suitcases and hanging dresses. Suddenly, on noticing the maid's
presence, they stopped their work and told her, in a clumsy Spanish,
that she was excused and that she would be called if needed.

"What about the cards with the flowers?" Wen asked the *mulata*.
"Did La Signora read them?"

The maid gulped, made a face as if it were a great effort to remember, and then answered, sadly, no. Noticing how Wenceslao bit his
lower lip, disappointed, she consoled him by saying that maybe La
Signora read them after she had left the room.

"Listen to what I am saying, Regla," my lover demanded in a soft
but intimidating voice. "I want you to keep me informed of everything
that happens in those rooms," and he pointed to the opposite wall.
"You already know how generous I can be with those who are good to
me: let it be known that you will not regret it."

So it was in that fashion that the *mulata,* who couldn't stop nodding
and muttering "Yes, sir" and "As you say, señor," became his main spy,
although not the only one. That afternoon, as I was going out for a
stroll in the neighborhood, Wen took it upon himself to go all over the
hotel, recruiting, thanks to bills handed out furtively here and there,
an army of squealers that included elevator men, concierges, bell-
boys, phone operators, laundry and cleaning personnel, a clerk, and
an assistant chef. On meeting up with me, he was exhausted but
happy. His confidants had promised him to keep him up to date about
everything relating to Eleonora: visitors, calls, meals, whims, and
everything else.

I told him about a scoop that I had just found out from Pedrito
Varela on the steps of the Teatro Nacional. La Duse's premiere would
no longer be Monday the twenty-eighth. At the request of the actress,

it would be moved to Tuesday. La Signora was very upset and the customs agents in New Orleans were to blame: the idiots, unwilling until the very last minute to allow the company to take the stage sets out of the country only to bring them back in fifteen days later, had ruined her nerves. By postponing for twenty-four hours the first performance, which, according to what had been announced, was *The Closed Door,* the tragedienne could rest a bit and calm down. Oh, and as far as the oxygen tank in her dressing room, it was true; Varela himself had helped put it there.

That night, Emilio De la Cruz picked us up to go to a black-tie party given by a friend of his, which would be attended by "half of Havana."

"We're going to have a lot of fun," he guaranteed us, pressing down on the car's accelerator and driving us to a neighborhood we did not yet know: El Almendares. There, near the river of the same name, was the home of the Montes de Oca. During the ride over, he remarked that the couple was so wealthy that their only pastime in life was to find ways to throw away their exorbitant inheritance. Not even the crisis of the famished livestock, which had ruined so many fortunes, had made them cut back on their way of life.

When we arrived, the *kermesse* was at its peak. Anything that shone or had any worth in the capital was congregated under this roof. The guests numbered over two hundred, and among them we spied Pablo Álvarez de Cañas, who as a solace for the truncated romance with the Loynaz girl, was dancing with a mummy daubed with face paint.

"That fat one over there is Pablito's rival," our *cicerone* whispered. "Not in love," he clarified, "but in matters of journalism." And he made us go with him to meet Fontana, the social chronicler for the *Diario de la Marina.* He, too, was an admirer of La Duse and he told us about the visit that the main figures in the company had made to the newspaper's office that afternoon.

"The manager, who is called Guido Carreras, is very pleasant and chatty, and I found the Señoritas Morino very cute and cosmopolitan," Fontana said. "The one I found intolerable was the lead actor."

My lover asked him what was wrong with Memo Benassi and the columnist made a disagreeable face.

"He's very . . . *postalita. Postalita, pujón y sangregorda!*"

Wenceslao and I exchanged glances not understanding these Cubanisms, so De la Cruz translated the diatribe. *Postalita* is synonymous with haughty, vain, and conceited. *Pujón* is one who tries, without much success, to be funny. And you call *sangregorda* anyone who lacks grace or the slightest bit of common affection.

"In Cuba we forgive any flaw," the fat man said, "except for one: to be *pesao*." Which was anyone who made themselves unbearable through the aforementioned.

La Duse, true to her habits, had refused to go to the newspaper. Carreras apologized for her, explaining that she was tired from the trip and reminding them that La Signora would rather be seen on stage. Although they tried to hide their disappointment, the editor of the *Diario,* its publisher, and the Ichasos, León and Francisco, assistant editor and theater critic respectively, found the rudeness very upsetting.

Then Fontana changed the topic, telling about the project that Mina López-Salmón de Buffin was brewing. In honor of La Duse, and with the aim of raising funds for the *crèche* Buffin, the lady was going to throw a fantastic costume ball at the Teatro Nacional.

And just at that moment, Madame Buffin approached us in the arms of a listless young man who walked dragging his feet. She was a ham whose age was difficult to guess, lavishly fleshy, but Wen was dazzled by her diamond tiara, which made her seem a queen, and by her white damask dress that fit her like a glove. As soon as Fontana and De la Cruz told her who we were ("two gentlemen from very wealthy Colombian families of superior lineage"), she treated us like old friends.

"You cannot miss the Ball of a Thousand and One Nights for anything in the world," she warned us. "It will be a grand event."

She told us that Dr. Habib Steffano, an accomplished Arabic man of letters, president of the National Academy of Damascus, and the old secretary of King Faisal I, was serving as her consultant for the ball to have an authentic Oriental feel. She had still not decided who would play the roles of the skillful Scheherezade and the caliph Harun-ar-Rashid, but the names of various candidates were being bandied about. The selection was not only difficult but also a very delicate matter, for she did not want to hurt any feelings.

"If it was up to me," Wen interrupted her. "Scheherezade would have already been chosen."

"And who would it be, if I might ask?"

"You, of course."

The lady blushed and, after thanking him for the compliment, argued, modestly, that in the city there were many señoras and señoritas who were capable of seducing the caliph with their *charme.* As far as Eleonora Duse was concerned, she and Dr. Steffano were going to write her a letter asking her to do them the honor of serving on the jury that would award the prizes for best costumes. They were aware that the actress was not wont to go to parties, but they were sure that, since this was a tribute paid to her by the city of Havana, she would make an exception.

"Excusez-moi!" Madame Buffin exclaimed, bringing her hand to her brow. "I have not introduced you to Señor Dalmau!"

We shook the gelatinous right hand of her companion and found out right away that he was from a good family, a draftsman and designer, who had just returned to the Island after living for two years in Europe. Aurelio Dalmau had worked in Paris with the Folies Bergères and, to please Mina, was designing the outfits that the houris would wear for the Ball of a Thousand and One Nights.

"I have a lot of work to do, but if you like I can take care of your costumes," he proposed, looking us up and down and licking his lips like an asp. "You would make a marvelous Sinbad," he said to Wenceslao and then, fixing his eyes on me, added: "You I see as an afreet, with fiery red crepe pantaloons, a short leather vest with no shirt underneath, with a silver band on your arm."

We made no reply and, on realizing that the idea of wearing costumes didn't really excite us, Mina de Buffin said that it wasn't necessary to come to the ball in a costume. The president of the republic and his wife, for example, would attend dressed as Christians.

When Madame Buffin and Dalmau left, Fontana went off about the young man's awful taste, doubted that he ever had anything to do with the Folies, and advised us that, if we wanted to wear costumes to the ball, we should go see Ana María Borrero, who was a stupendous designer and was making outfits for the extras in the tableau Ali Baba and the Forty Thieves.

"If not, you can buy them in El Encanto, where there are many beautiful pieces, or, if not, at Fin de Siglo, where they are priced better, and so be it," he concluded.

Glass in hand, Emilio led us through the rooms, introducing us to dozens of guests whose names we could not remember. Since we were fresh meat, many covetous glances fell upon us.

"Good God, look who's here!" De la Cruz said suddenly, and with a sinister expression on his hideous face led us to a small room where, far away from the music and the noise, a handful of guests chatted animatedly. "Olavito, I want you to meet two friends of mine," he squealed loudly and, before we could flee, we found ourselves in front of Vázquez Garralaga.

However awkward it may have been for us, I imagine that it must have been worse for him. I blushed on recalling how Wenceslao had stolen his flowers and I felt like slapping Monkeyface. While the poet remained stiff, not knowing what to do, the lady next to him broke the ice telling us she was his mother, and she gave us her hand.

"Don't be a jerk, Olavo," Emilio kidded him. "It seems that you really went overboard at Pedrito Varela's office, but what's done is done."

The mother elbowed her child in the ribs, urging him to make peace and to quit being so melodramatic, and the rhymster conceded to reach out a hand to us that was as cold and stiff as Lenin's, when we shook it.

"Delighted to meet you, gentlemen," he gabbled in a dignified manner. "I hope that there are no ill feelings and that . . ."

"Oh, enough of this, what ill feelings," Monkeyface interrupted, and he forced us to hug as a symbol of everything being "water under the bridge."

Soon, we were chatting like old friends. And although Olavo agreed with Wen that Josefina Ruiz del Castillo was nothing to write home about, his thoughts about Aguglia were different. However, he might agree with the fact that to advertise her as the greatest living tragedienne was quite audacious, though he did find her very talented and multifaceted. Did we know, for example, that she had a lovely mezzo voice and that weeks before she had sung opposite Titta Ruffo at the Nacional? But when all was said, his favorite was Esperanza Iris. Had we not gone to the Payret to see her in *The Merry Widow, The*

Countess of Montmartre, or any other of her many creations? How could we not have gone yet? We would make plans to go together. He went to her performances two or three times a week: he loved operettas and Iris's company performed with exquisite taste.

"What about Maria Tubau, the Spaniard who is premiering next week, what do you know about her?" Wen asked him, using the formal *usted.*

"Oh, please, why are you being so proper, so formal with me, you are going to make me feel old!" the poet quipped and then remarked that La Tubau (the younger one, because the other one, her famous compatriot and namesake María Álvarez Tubau, had been dead for ten years) had just arrived from Mexico, where she had caused an uproar. "According to the press, she is a delight, but we will have to wait to make up our minds when she performs at the Principal de la Comedia, because as you know the papers love everything."

Even your poetry, I thought.

We laughed, we drank, we danced with Señora Garralaga, flirted with a boy who bore a slight resemblance to Mella, and did everything possible to keep our distance from Aurelio Dalmau, who somehow made it so that he bumped into us every five minutes and stared at us with the eyes of a slaughtered lamb.

At midnight, the owner of the house asked for silence so that the artistic *intermezzo* could begin. In a grandiose tone, he announced that the bard Vázquez Garralaga would delight us with some of his creations, and Olavito took the stage at once. As he passed by us, Wen, feeling extremely cruel, asked him to recite the poem dedicated to Madame Butterfly and, without needing to be asked again, the author began to recite the garbage that had almost given us a seizure at La Moderna Poesía:

> *On the way to a pagoda full of light,*
> *Overcome by an unnatural fury*
> *A foreigner walked without taking his sight,*
> *From a geisha he held arm in arm.*

Afraid that we would burst out laughing, we discreetly moved away and found refuge on the terrace. There we discovered, alone in a corner, Graziella Gerbelasa, who, with her eyes fixed on the heavens, repeated in a low and monotonous tone, like a lunatic: "I detest him, I detest him, I detest him, I detest him . . ." Since we thought it rude to interrupt her litany, we turned around and returned to the main room just in time to hear that last stanza of Olavo's poem:

> *Oh my forbidden Japanese girl,*
> *As untouchable as a wound.*
> *Why spin my life into a whirl,*
> *Why, Butterfly, love whom you can't?*

Amid a round of applause, and after taking a deep bow, Vázquez Garralaga made his way to where his mother awaited him, brimming with pride. As he passed by us, Wen put a hand on him and whispered hypocritically: "Marvelous."

To continue the feast, the host announced another surprise: the daughter of the immortal Ignacio Cervantes, the beloved María, was among us, prepared to regale us with the best of her musical repertoire. A woman with her hair garçon-style sat in front of the grand piano, and Wen and I looked at each other in horror. We were just about to turn around and escape to the delivering grace of the terrace when we were paralyzed by some rhythmical chords.

As her hand frolicked on the ivories, the lady let the audience know that the song she was going to play had been composed by her father when she was a little girl. In a perfectly pitched voice full of cunning, she began to sing.

> *To my father's mill,*
> *There we will convene,*
> *And you'll peel the sugar cane*
> *And I'll suck it clean.*
>
> *For the Cubana when you meet her,*
> *For the Cubana when you meet her,*
> *Than sugar is sweeter,*
> *Than sugar is sweeter,*
> *Than sugar is sweeter,*
> *Sugar and honey.*

María Cervantes soon had the audience in her pocket with her irresistible charm.

She looked like a lady and played like a virtuoso, but as she mischievously crooned those lyrics about peeling the sugar cane and sucking it clean, the double entendre was unmistakable even to the most angelic of beings, and the guests couldn't hold back their malicious laughs. I told myself that, in the end, that was the secret essence of the Island: a perfect mixture of the sophisticated and the vulgar, an endless parade of contrasts. Ruffo's arias and the primitive and sultry rhythm of the Negro drums; the high-class guests at the Seville-Biltmore and the riffraff tenants at the Jesús el Monte; the French perfumes at Fin de Siglo and the stinking espadrilles of the Spaniards; the poetry of Casal and the longshoremen's jargon at the port. If you mix the ingredients in the right proportions, add salt and pepper to taste, cook it in the tropical sun, there you have the Island on a platter.

On finishing "My Father's Mill," the artist was rewarded with an enthusiastic round of applause. And then, leaving Wen and me in shock, she announced that she wanted to dedicate her next piece to two gentlemen recently arrived from the lands washed by the Tequendama: two distinguished young men who were livening up the party and Havana with their presence. She cast a cunning look our way, and we wanted the earth to swallow us. She started the song, marking time with the snap of flirtatious air kisses cast our way.

To conclude with a flair, La Cervantes sang "The Girl From Camagüey," and the audience went crazy:

> *I don't want a rich lover*
> *I don't want him to be pretty or vain,*
> *I want a loving lover.*
> *And as he won't lie, it won't be a pain.*
>
> *I'm honest, I'm a woman,*
> *I live my life with loving,*
> *I'm Cubana and I need a man*
> *In Camagüey that's how it is.*

After the singer's propaganda on our behalf, a horde of the daughters of Eve descended upon us to claim us as dates for the ball. Lucky

Wen was able to slip away and pretended to chat with Vázquez Garralaga and his mother; but I had to dance with a bunch of ladies with
illustrious last names and withstand, with a grimace frozen on my
face that must have only vaguely resembled a smile, the flirtations,
come-ons, and insinuations. In the end, I fell into the arms of a
preened and chubby woman, who almost made me pass out when she
told me in a seductive voice that she was Esperanza Iris and that she
expected my "buddy" and me at the revival of one of her great triumphs, the zarzuela *Benamor*. The Mexican star held me so tightly
against her breast that I was afraid that she wanted to suffocate me.

On our way back to the Inglaterra, Wen was lost in his thoughts and
long-faced. I didn't want to ask the cause of his silence in front of
Emilio De la Cruz, but as soon as we were alone in our room, I forced
him to speak.

"I told Olavito about our wish to interview La Duse, and he said
that he had written a play in five acts called *The Victim of His Sin*," he
hiccupped, on the verge of tears.

"And?" I asked, not knowing what was so horrible.

"He wants to offer it to La Signora, through the Italian ambassador,
so that she adds it to her repertoire," he concluded, grabbing me by
the neck and breaking into sobs.

He was completely drunk. I led him to bed and took off his clothes
as best as I could. The phone rang and I threw myself on the gadget
wondering who would be so inconsiderate as to call at three-thirty in
the morning. "Hello," I exclaimed. At first, there was a silence, then a
resounding cough, and finally, from the other end of the line there
came a coarse and circumspect voice.

"Señor Belalcázar?"

"This is he. Who is calling?"

"It is Count Kostia."

I was very close to either laughing or crying. What kind of lunatic
chose such an hour to call someone he has never met? My God, what a
delirious country we had come to! I made an effort to sound normal.

"Yes, Señora Lachambre mentioned that you might . . ."

The old man did not allow me to continue. He cut me off sharply.
"Tomorrow go to 187 Águila Street and ask for Fan Ya Ling."

"There they will tell me who . . ."

"You need to go before noon!" he interrupted me again.

"Did Señora Cay explain to you that . . . ? "

"And don't tell anyone that I called you!" he added most rudely, with that warning putting an end to our little chat.

I heard a metallic noise and realized that the count had hung up. I did the same and, as I began to undress, I wondered if I would remember the address the following morning or if it would be wiser to be safe and write it down. In case memory failed, I wrote it down on the first thing I found, on the back of the invitation that Graziella Gerbelasa had given us in the bookstore.

I put out the lights and tried to sleep, but a rhythmic small noise that I couldn't identify, kept me up. At first, I thought that it was coming from the street, but outside it was quiet. I paid closer attention and discovered that the noise was coming from the adjacent room. I got out of bed and put my ear to the wall, to listen better. It was someone snoring, without a doubt, a refined and elegant snore, uncannily syncopated and musical, like a muted instrument. At the risk of being accused of sacrilege, the following day I would let Wenceslao know of my discovery: La Duse snored.

If one of my closest friends, Lougné-Poe, could hear me, he would warn you not to be fooled by either my querulous tone or by my frailty. According to him, my appearance is misleading. He says I have the strength of ten men and that I will bury everyone who surrounds me. I hope he is wrong!

"You should live and work and not just sit there pondering and brooding over unsolvable mysteries," he says to me. And also that so much dying with Marguerite Gautier has made me mournful. That just as others are addicted to alcohol and hallucinogens, I am to melancholy.

And could it be any other way? I ask. Can you expect anything else from a woman who was pushed onto the stage at four, who was hit on the knees with a stick to make her cry, from someone who is ill more often than she is well and who, of the two hundred or so plays that she has performed in over the course of her life, only cares for ten? And yet, in spite of everything, that tragic haze that reporters like to talk about so much is not so thick as to prevent her from enjoying herself once in a while.

One time we were in a financial jam and Lougné, who was the director of the company then, insisted, against my wishes, that we revive Fedora, since it always filled the house. I tried to refuse to do it and to get him to change his mind by inventing a hundred excuses, but in the end I had to give in. "Fine," I said eventually, adopting the pose of the martyr. "I'll do what you say." Since I had not done the play in a few years, he offered to bring me the script. "No!" I cut him off with a distressing scream, as if I were the very Fedora speaking. "You can force me to perform in the play again, but never to reread it!" We glared at each other seriously, and then suddenly we burst out laughing. We laughed for five minutes. I had to hold on to my stomach: I thought that I was coming undone from the inside.

"Eleonora Giulia Amalia," Lougné exclaimed after a

while, when he was able to speak again, because I had been christened with all those names. "This is the first time since the day I met you that I have heard you laugh as it should be. I have seen you shed dozens of tears hundreds of times, on and off the stage; I have seen you switch rooms in a hotel five times in a day because none of them met your requirements; I have even seen you play a part in Italian while the rest of the cast played their parts in French; but laugh, no, I have never heard you laugh, and don't get mad at what I am about to say, but for a tragedienne you do it very well!"

Laughing is healthy; there is no doubt about that. Perhaps if I did it more often, Désirée and María could throw away countless bottles of medicine. Sure, I would like to laugh more often. But what am I to do? You laugh about something, or with someone. If not, you are a sort of idiot, it is impossible to go through life drooling and laughing at everything. . . .

on't try to intimidate me, I am a lawyer and I know my rights!"
Wenceslao declared, trying to seem sure of himself, but he
couldn't fool me. He was scared, pale, and trembling: he was
just as frightened or even more so than I, and it was natural. Never
before had we set foot in a police station and much less as suspects.
Our premiere could not have been more unpleasant. The headquarters of the Havana secret police, located at 5 Tacón Street, a few steps
from the Avenida del Puerto, is a gloomy, terrifying building, a
labyrinth of dirty offices capable of intimidating anyone, full of men
who watch you rancorously, assuming that you are a heartless criminal until proven otherwise.

The furniture in the small room they led us into consisted of a table
with cigarette burns and water rings and the four wooden chairs on
which we were seated: us on one side, the detectives on the other. The
walls, empty and not painted, with greenish moisture stains, lacked
windows; the air was stuffy, difficult to breathe, and all that hung
from the high ceiling for illumination was a single bulb. In one corner,
there was a disgusting spittoon and near it I saw a prowling cockroach. For a moment I thought that if these men decided to beat us to
death, no one outside would know. Our screams of pain would remain
trapped inside the enclosure, bouncing from one wall to the other,
without penetrating the walls, till they dissolved.

"You have made a mistake, gentlemen," I said with as much composure as I could muster. "Call the Colombian consulate. We are respectable and have traveled to Havana to see the performances of
Eleonora Duse."

One of the agents, the so-called Aquiles de la Osa, tilted his head and laughed sarcastically, keeping his eyes on us.

"Where were you last night?" he asked. "Because you weren't at the Inglaterra."

I was sick of that question, which had been asked again and again during the two hours that we had spent there. I repeated, for the tenth time, the same answer. "We were, till dawn, in a series of brothels."

"The addresses," the other detective, Ignacio Falero, demanded for the tenth time in a monotonous tone and, lighting a cigarette, sucked in the smoke forcefully and blew it out through his nose. As distinct from his partner, who was tall and well built, with a mustache, abundant dark hair, and the air of a movie star, he was short and bald, potbellied but strong as a bull.

"How can we possibly remember everywhere we went?" Wenceslao exploded. "They were houses of vice and sin. We were drunk, my friends! Inebriated! Trashed! When one drinks too much liquor, he loses a sense of time and space. The mind becomes clouded, the reason obfuscated, and one is incapable of remembering exactly where he was and what he did," and sliding the wooden chair on which he was seated back he kicked the table. "Enough! I can't stand this vile interrogation!" he screamed. "I demand a lawyer!"

"And why do you need one?" the one who smoked said, unperturbed by the outburst.

Wen turned purple and opened his mouth to answer, but at that moment a new person burst into the room. Because of the hurry with which all the detectives got to their feet, we realized he was their superior. Being neither timid nor remiss, I addressed the newly arrived gentleman.

"There has been some confusion here. You are following a mistaken lead. We are not delinquents."

Ignoring my complaint, he introduced himself as Pompilio Ramos, assistant inspector, and, reaching into the pocket of his jacket with great care, he pulled out a paper and spread it in front of us.

"Did you write this message, Señor Belalcázar?" he asked with a weary expression.

My body went cold when I recognized my handwriting, and I couldn't muster an answer.

"Yes, he wrote that message," Wenceslao exclaimed, belligerently coming to my defense. "What about it?"

The detectives all looked at each other and the assistant inspector nodded. At the same instant, Falero threw the butt of his cigarette on the floor and stepped on it.

"Up, gentlemen!" he ordered. "We are going to take a little walk."

Almost paralyzed with fear, lightly shoved by the agents, we followed Pompilio Ramos through the offices and hallways, watched from behind by two others. Outside it was pouring. La Duse, I thought as if I didn't have more important things to worry about, is probably furious about having to rehearse on such a dismal day. The policemen put us in the car and we rode off. The streets were empty.

"With all this rain, the celebration for Marti's anniversary is fucked," Aquiles de la Osa uttered.

"Where are we going?" I muttered.

"Don't you know," Ignacio Falero, who was driving, replied sarcastically. "To Campanario and Salud. Do you remember that address?"

Since the assistant inspector had his eyes so fixed on me that it bordered on rudeness, I put my head back on the car seat and closed my eyes. I couldn't believe what was happening. How did we get into this nightmare? How had my note gotten into the hands of these thugs? Ever since I was a child I have felt a profound aversion, a real phobia, to the police, whether they be secret police or in uniforms, and the threat of a scandal, of our pictures splattered in the newspapers, had me very upset. I regretted having followed Count Kostia's instructions so closely. It was because of him, and because of the queerness of my Uncle Misael, that we were in this mess, the seriousness of which I had yet to figure out. In any case, what I was sure of was that we should not reveal the place where we spent the night.

I felt Wenceslao's fingers secretly graze mine, trying to instill calm and assurance through his touch. But if the discreet caress was also meant for me to open my eyes and look at him, I must have disappointed him, because I kept my eyes tightly shut. I wasn't calm. How could I be?

Very still, and trying to breathe as slowly as possible, I tried to reconstruct the events that had ended with our arrest.

Everything started on Sunday morning, at 187 Águila. There, in the middle of Chinatown, near the corner of Dragones, in between a tenement house and a laundry, there is (or there was, you will see soon enough why I make this distinction) a small store called El Crisantemo Dorado. As we opened the door and walked inside, a small bell rang softly and melodiously, announcing our entrance to the owner. But, in spite of the warning, no one came out to greet us.

When our eyes got used to the darkness of the place, we realized that we were surrounded by display cases in which were exhibited, without any rhyme or reason, the most unique objects: parasols, Buddhas of all different sizes and material, embroidered slippers, ointments made from the marrow of lions and the claws of leopards, fans made from sandalwood and paper, different types of vases and porcelain spoons, antique books, tea tins, a palanquin, and countless figurines made from bamboo, ebony, cherry, terracotta, ivory, jade, and volcanic rock. The colorful store, where it was impossible to move an arm or a foot without running the risk of knocking into some piece and shattering it, was a sort of combination pharmacy and the Celestial Empire art shop.

On one of the shelves, Wen found an exquisite blue cut-glass flask and picked it up with great care to examine it closer. The container was full of a brown powder and it lacked any identifying label. Taking off the top and smelling the contents, we were able to confirm that it had no smell. Rather imprudently, I stuck my pinky in the flask and put a bit of the powder on the tip of my tongue: it was also flavorless.

"Canthalides," a voice revealed suddenly, and as we tried to figure out where it came from, its owner added, in a mangled Spanish, that cantharides, or Spanish fly, was the best medicine for the bladder and that he had it not only in powder, but in liquid, ointment, and poultice. How would the gentlemen like it? Which of the two needs the miraculous medicine, imported all the way from Canton? The gaunt figure of a Chinese man advanced toward us, materializing from the shadows. I figured that he must be some ninety years old; he walked bent over at the waist, there were pimples on the delicate skin of his face, and his beard was made up of long, scant, white strands.

Since I remained frozen, not because of the surprise but because of the disgust at having tasted those pulverized cockroaches, it was Wen who greeted the old man, explained that, fortunately, neither of us needed this or any other medicine, and the purpose of our visit was to see a person named Fan Ya Ling.

The *Chino* let out a series of plaintive, slow guffaws and let us know that it was he we were looking for and that he was at our service.

"The count told us to come see you," Wenceslao continued. "We thought he might have warned you."

"Which count you speak?" Fan Ya Ling replied with an amused expression and grabbed the blue crystal flask and put it back in its place.

I decided to join the conversation, to clarify things by getting to the point.

"We need to see Señor Misael Reyes," I said.

The shopkeeper nodded and let out a "Hmmm!" that we didn't know how to interpret and, moving toward a rustic wooden bench near the door, he settled himself in it with great difficulty. Suddenly, a cat that we had all this time thought was made of porcelain came to life, leaped from the top of the armoire and, shooting past us like an arrow, landed on the lap of the old man, who began to caress its back with great care. He was so focused on passing the end of his fingers over the arched spine of the feline that Wen gave me a worried look, thinking he might have forgotten about us.

"Can you help us, señor?" I didn't know how to address him. Would Fan be his first name and Ya Ling his last name?

"Can, goal man, of coulse can," he replied and, throwing off the animal, which went to hide in a corner, he gestured for us to come closer, which we did without hesitation.

In his hacked language, substituting the *r* and the *d* with an *l,* the old man told us to be at the Teatro *Chino* on Zanja Street at eight o'clock that night. It was necessary for one of us ("goal man, you," he said, pointing at me with his fan) to wear a carnation in his lapel. Because we could not understand half of the things that he was saying and we made him repeat some words several times, he began to get angry and to click his tongue to let us know how upset he was. Finally, good or not, we were able to understand, or thought we understood, his directions: we were to enter the theater and wait with the other members of the audience for someone to approach us to take us to my uncle.

"And does it have to be at night?" Wen thought to ask. "It's that we had plans to see Esperanza Iris in *Benamor,*" he explained. "Couldn't you tell that person to take us right now?"

Fan Ya Ling whacked himself on the thigh with his fan, irate, and let out an unintelligible whammy of a word, *"Tuniamacalimbambó."*

I appeased him and, after assuring him that we would be in the theater at the said hour, with the flower in the lapel, and saying our gracious farewells, we left El Crisantemo Dorado.

"What a crotchety old geezer!" Wen groaned.

We walked on Dragones Street, which was very busy. Chinatown in Havana is a mixture of penetrating aromas, for the most part unpleasant, which float in the air and assault the unwary passerby: rotting vegetables, sea food, incense, oils, dirty clothes. I asked Wen how anybody could live there without being made dizzy by them. "They are used to it," he guessed. On crossing Amistad we found ourselves in a small market. Several vendors had taken over the sidewalks and offered a great variety of vegetables, fish, meats, and fruits. An anthill of clients (white, black, and *mestizo*) checked out the merchandise and haggled with the Chinese for lower prices. It was there, amid baskets replete with eels and shark fins, amid the carrots, the sesame, the parsley, and the radishes, that I found the one person I least expected to see in that place. Although he had his back to us, I recognized him immediately. I called Wenceslao, who at the moment was asking a herbalist questions, to warn him.

The force of our glances was such that Julio Antonio Mella turned around, holding on to a bunch of cilantro and a stinky fish wrapped in yellow paper, and he gave us a marvelous smile. He greeted us in a familiar fashion and remarked that the day before he had been at the Seville-Biltmore and had been very disappointed when he found out that we were no longer staying there.

"I thought you had returned to Colombia!" he exclaimed.

When we explained to him that we had moved to the Inglaterra, he raised his eyebrows and remarked, jokingly, that he had never had the luxury to sleep in a bed-of-roses hotel. Not even on his honeymoon! I forced myself to overlook the unfortunate observation he had made in mentioning the wife whose existence I chose to ignore, and I asked him if he lived close by.

"Yes," he answered. "May I invite you for some coffee?"

He paid for the cilantro with some coins and headed, with a nimble step, up the street. Wen and I walked beside him, hypnotized. Seeing his virile stride, with not a care in the world, so sure of himself, I understood clearly that this dark-haired marvel was the eighth wonder of the world, a living work of art, a blanket of flesh that anyone would love to wrap himself in on cold nights. Mella spoke enthusiastically about Chinese cuisine and its rare and delicious courses made with ingredients unheard of in Western kitchens, such as castor oil and peas.

"In the restaurants of this neighborhood, I devour whatever is put in front of me. But I never ask what I am eating," he said. "That way there are no disagreeable surprises," and he laughed heartily.

I discreetly slowed my pace to be able to properly appreciate that dreamy ass. The vision of that ass that I imagined under the cloth of his pants, round and compact, covered with light hairs, transported me to heaven. If Wen hadn't turned around and called on me to catch up, I would have stayed right there, floating on Dragones Street.

We followed Julio Antonio into an alleyway, where he stopped in front of an ancient three-story building. He asked me to hold his fish, looked for his keys in his pockets and, minutes later, we were inside the second-floor apartment. It was narrow, and the living room was decorated atrociously, I thought, but it was clean and tidy.

"Hello, we have company," the Adonis shouted, closing the door behind him and gesturing for us to be seated. A thin old woman dressed very simply came out from one of the rooms. Mella put a hand on her shoulders and informed us that the señora was Oliva's grandmother. The woman took the groceries and headed for the kitchen to make our coffee.

The student fell into a rocking chair, his muscular legs open.

"So, what is going on in your country?" he asked, watching us eagerly.

Suddenly, I thought it would be funny if I told him about our séances with Esmeralda Gallego, of the parties at the house of the Belgian minister, and of our romps with Vengoechea through the nocturnal and perverse Bogotá. What would the leader of the university student body, who surely wanted to hear a tale of social protests and political demonstrations, have thought had he heard about all the foolishness that made up our day-to-day life?

"But tell me something, don't just sit there," he insisted.

As I thought of ways to get out of this one, Wen took charge and, to my surprise, began a detailed report on the situation with the students and the proletariat in Colombia. I don't know how much of it was true, but it sounded convincing. About the university, he stated, nothing of much interest to tell, for the students and the professors both seemed as if they were living in another century, ignorant of the ways of the nation; among the workers and the labor unions, however, the situation was very different. He talked about the emerging textile industry in Medellín, of the migrant workers of Magdalena, and of the oil laborers of Barrancabermeja; he spoke about strikes of the workers at the slaughterhouse in Medellín, of the tailors in Armenia, and of the taxi drivers in Manizales, and he spoke of the parades on the first of May, when artisans and workers took to the streets with placards reading "Liberty, equality, and fraternity" and singing *La Marseillaise.* Mella listened to Wen fascinated, encouraging him, with his attention, to add details and elucidations.

To conclude, and leaving me completely astonished, Wenceslao made the young man think that we were sympathizers with the Communist group that had just been founded by workers and intellectuals connected to the launderer Silvestre Savitski. He assured him that the Russian immigrant, a Bolshevik of pure stock, kept us up to date on the triumphs of the Soviet Revolution.

"The Socialist ideas are gaining ground in Colombia," my lover stated gravely. "But, unfortunately, Pancho Villa is better known than Lenin."

The mention of the Bolshevik led us to talk about his death and, in particular, about the fate of his body. I said that I didn't agree with those who wanted his body mummified and put on display forever. I did share the opinion of the health commissioner, however, who was an advocate of preserving the remains for a while, so that they could be incinerated when construction of the crematorium in Moscow was finished. In that way the Russian people, who thought cremation was heretical and ungodly, would be shown a clear example of cleanliness.

"Poor Lenin," Wen murmured, looking sad. "Some want to turn him into a mummy, others want to burn him."

Our student said that he agreed with the idea of preserving the body of the leader and displaying it to the public in a mausoleum.

"Would not the Christians have done the same with the body of Jesus, their most valuable relic?" he argued. "The way I see things, Lenin is another Christ: the true redeemer of humanity."

And he mentioned that a group of surgeons had just submitted a petition to the Supreme Soviet to let the science of anatomy take advantage of this unique opportunity to study the cerebral structure of one of the greatest minds of all time. He told us also that a mass rally was planned in Paris at Place Saint-Denis to pay him honors, and in Havana the communist group of the Workers' Federation was preparing a tribute.

"It's next Sunday. We are working so that the greatest number of students will attend. I am going to be one of the speakers. I hope you will be there!"

I guaranteed, staring at him spellbound, that we would be in the first row.

At that instant, the old woman returned with three cups on a tray. One had the handle chipped and Julio made sure he grabbed it.

"Hmmmm," he breathed in, bringing it to his nose. "It smells delicious." And after tasting the coffee, which to us tasted like a nasty concoction, taken straight from a witch's cauldron, he added ecstatically: "The dark nectar of the white gods!"

We nodded and did all we could to swallow the brew. When the grandmother of the luckiest woman in the world returned to the kitchen with the cups, Mella picked up where we had left off and began to describe to us the agitated, in his opinion, state of the Island.

"There is more corruption than you can imagine. At the time when the price of sugar was sky high and we had money to burn, a private company bought the ancient convent of Santa Clara for less than a million pesos; and Zaya's money-grabbing administration just bought it for more than two million. Now that's doing business!" he roared. "Our little country is a mecca of degeneracy and a backyard for the Yankees. So many years of struggle and of much blood spilt to end up with the Platt Amendment shoved up . . . er, down our throat."

When we asked him what the amendment was, he looked at us in surprise at our great ignorance. In 1901, the neighbors to the North had insisted on an amendment to the constitution that would transform Cuba into a republic: the famous Platt Amendment. That document gave the United States the right to occupy the Island any time they thought it was threatened.

"It's like giving a neighbor the key to your house so that he can do with it as he pleases," he summed up. "The sun doesn't rise here without Crowder's consent. He is the Yankee ambassador."

He told us also of a national movement of veterans and patriots, which brought together weary fighters from the Wars of Independence and young people desirous of positive change in their country, and which was challenging the government, insisting on reforms and a curb to political crookedness. In recent years, some armed insurrections had been aborted, but as the saying goes, where there is smoke there is fire. And some spark could yet catch on.

He paused and a cuckoo clock announced that it was noon. Mella said that Oliva should arrive at any moment and would we stay and have lunch with them. "Where three can eat, so can five," he reasoned. The prospect of seeing him beside his little wife chilled the blood in my veins, so we told him we needed to return to the hotel.

"But we can meet up tomorrow," Wen proposed and immediately added, "I have yet to tell you about either the exploitation of the workers in the banana plantations or the streetcar strike in Bogotá in 1910!"

Julio Antonio's beautiful eyes sparkled with curiosity and he accepted our proposal to get together again—not Monday, as Wenceslao had wanted, for that day he was going to be busy with the preparations for the meeting-tribute to Lenin, but early morning Tuesday. We agreed to get together at nine in the lobby of the Inglaterra.

"And if you feel like it, we can go to the beach," my lover suggested with an apparent innocence. "So, aside from talking, maybe we can swim a bit."

I couldn't help but let my eyes wander to the chest of the dark-haired beauty; and on imagining him naked, my mouth began to water.

"Agreed," the young man said.

We said good-bye to Oliva's grandmother, who came out of the kitchen for the third time, drying her hands on her apron, and we left the apartment, but not before Mella once more crushed our fingers as a sign of friendship and gave us unexpected bear hugs.

On the way back, I mentioned to Wen that he had behaved like a true revolutionary. "Where did you get all those facts? I thought that you only read the news that pertained to La Duse or Luis Vicentini."

He shrugged and replied mysteriously.

"You, Lucho Belalcázar, do not know me as well as you think you do."

At the hotel, a pile of Vázquez Garralaga's books had been left for us. There were twenty in all, each with a syrupy dedication.

"Olavito adores us," I remarked teasingly, putting the books away in a drawer.

Wen's spies didn't take long to bring him up to date on La Signora's activities that day. At midmorning she had crossed the street accompanied by Fortune Gallo and her friend Katherine Garnett, to see the inside of the Teatro Nacional. Although she was still dressed in black and wearing a veil, she seemed cheerful, perhaps because it was a sunny day and the meteorological observatory in Casablanca predicted that the weather would remain good.

She had found the theater beautiful. *Che bello! Che bellezza!* A group of workers, under the supervision of the company's manager, had already begun putting in place the set of *The Closed Door.* Monday morning the cast would get together to rehearse. On returning to her room, Eleonora asked for a lettuce salad, a chicken leg, and a glass of wine to be brought up to her. The Englishwoman, on the other hand, was in the restaurant, eating lunch alone.

Five minutes later we were at a table near Katherine Garnett and, I don't remember under what pretext, the distinguished, sincere, and irresistible Wenceslao Hoyos was initiating a pleasant chat with her, taking great pains to use his best English. He pretended not to have the slightest idea who the lady was and, on hearing that she was in Havana in the company of the tragedienne, put on such a natural expression of surprise that had La Duse witnessed the scene, she would have signed him up for her company right then and there.

The outcome of that first meeting was that they agreed to take a stroll together that same afternoon. Naively, I thought that I could take advantage of the solitude to rest and read a little Bourget. Fate, however, had something else in mind for me. I was already in bed, in my undergarments, when reception rang to announce that Bartolomé Valdivieso was here for a visit. I gave permission for him to come up to the fourth floor, and the *mulato* came in holding a cardboard box. A bit disappointed that Wenceslao wasn't there, he showed me the crocodile-skin case and the parchment on which was transcribed, in the meticulous strokes of a calligrapher, the definitive version of "To Eleonora the Sublime." I congratulated him and asked if Fortune Gallo had arranged the meeting with the tragedienne already.

"Not yet," he replied with a sigh. "In his opinion it is better to wait till after the premiere, when La Signora will be calmer."

The visit from the son of General Valdivieso lasted an hour, during which time we tried to keep ourselves entertained as best as possible. But something strange was going on with me: even though we fooled around on top of the bedspread, sometimes with the *mulato*'s body on top of me, sometimes underneath me, engaged in a kind of Greco-Roman struggle, I was like an ice floe. I couldn't focus on the matter. Every time I closed my eyes, the image of Mella appeared in my mind and I grew colder and colder. Finally, I begged the pharmacist to postpone the transaction for another time, I just wasn't up to it. He consented, not trying to hide his annoyance, and in a jiffy he was gone.

When Wenceslao returned, in a state of euphoria, he found me under the covers up to my neck, exhausted and a bit depressed. I told him what had happened and, seated on the edge of the bed, he admonished me in the tone one might use to scold a child.

"You are obsessed with the revolutionary," he assessed. "And it is very likely that he will leave you all dressed up with nowhere to go. The best thing to do is to get him out of your head."

"Never!" I replied. "That dark beauty will fall even if I have to recite the *Communist Manifesto* for him from memory."

"Yeah sure," he laughed. "I'll see that when it snows in Havana."

"If God gives me life, health, and license, who are you to say we won't hit the lottery?" I said stubbornly and asked him if he was with me or against me.

"Of course I am with you, love of my loves," he assured me, and kissed me. "But I don't like you falling to pieces for any little thing."

I was about to say that Mella was a far cry from any little thing, but changed my mind and asked him about his stroll with La Garnett. His face brightened.

"We are like bread and butter already," he said. "I told her about my admiration for La Duse and how excited I was, for, in a couple of days, the dream of seeing her on stage would become reality. Can you believe that the Englishwoman lent her one hundred thousand liras last year so that she could act in London? La Duse has just finished paying her back with the profits from this tour. The last producers paid her two thousand five hundred dollars for each performance and this one pays her three thousand."

"That's a fortune!"

"Not really, if you take into account that she has to pay the salaries and the expenses of the company: ships, trains, hotels, food . . ."

The Englishwoman was very interested in seeing the scrapbook dedicated to La Duse and had insinuated that perhaps she could get him into the theater to see a rehearsal.

"And did you say anything about the interview?" I inquired.

"I didn't want to push my luck," he answered. "Everything in its own time. If she suspects that my friendship is opportunistic, she might get upset."

I told him what *el mulato* said about his dealings with Fortune Gallo, and he put his arms around me.

"If Bartolomé is able to get to her with his horrendous sonnet and speaks to her favorably about us, and if Vázquez Garralaga does the same when, because of the good offices of the Italian ambassador, he presents her his play, and, on top of all this, if we count on the help of the Englishwoman, who is so close to her, it is impossible she will refuse to see us," he fantasized.

At that moment, we heard a soft knocking on the door. Regla, the chambermaid, was a bundle of nerves as she came in, bearing some papers.

"She wants these telegrams sent out," she whispered.

Wen grabbed the papers from her hand and we read them together. La Signora wrote in a large and ornamental script, in lively strokes.

The messages, in French, were to people in North American cities, except for one addressed to her daughter Enrichetta in London. That one declared that she was in Havana, that the weather was bearable and the city beautiful. It ended up saying that she liked the place and that there she would throw four soirées.

"Four parties?" I asked, intrigued.

"She must mean performances," he replied and gave back the papers to the *mulata*, who left the room like a possessed soul, without even saying good-bye. Following which, scissors in hand, Wen gave himself over to the task of checking the newspapers, piled up on a chair, in search of new clippings for his collection. In the *Diario de la Marina* he found a list of those who had already picked up their tickets for all four performances, and in it, our names.

At eight, after apologizing to Vázquez Garralaga for not going with him to the Payret due to unforeseen circumstances, we were in the Teatro *Chino*. Following Fan Ya Ling's directions, I had a carnation in my lapel. The play to be performed that night was called *Man Tan Pei Pin Koc Nag*, which, the Chinese man who sold us the tickets told us meant *The Fate of a Flower*. Before going in, I asked how long the performance lasted and he made me feel better when he said it was "sholt, vely sholt."

In that place full of yellow folk with slanted eyes, we were, due to our physiognomies and elegant attires, two strange birds. It stunk of fried food and smelly clothes. Surrounding us, the audience ate all kinds of food and we truly felt like flies in a bowl of milk. The curtain was raised and the stage, without a backdrop, was bare. A gong that made us jump in our hard seats signaled the beginning of the performance.

The worst nightmare would seem like a fairy tale compared with what we had to sit through. The lights came up precariously and two men dressed in colorful costumes appeared and began to talk (in Chinese, logically), sing, mime, and execute with their flexible bodies all sorts of acrobatic feats. The action, it seemed, took place in ancient times, but we couldn't understand anything. The scenes were all disjointed, some short, some overwhelmingly long, and always, at the end, the actors would leave the stage in a stately manner. For each new appearance they would be dressed differently, each costume more luxurious than the one before. A sort of props manager dressed in civilian clothes walked on and off the stage whenever he pleased, putting on the floor the few objects necessary for the presentation and then taking them when they were no longer needed, these interruptions not seeming to bother the audience at all.

"What time is it?" Wen whispered, and I showed him my watch, which said nine. "Show your carnation, I beg of you."

The arrival of some actresses broke up the monotony. If the men moved by leaping like monkeys, the ladies, on the other hand, advanced on the stage with much primness, their legs pressed together and their feet dragging. Their makeup, caked on exaggeratedly, made them look like dolls, and on parting their vermilion-colored lips they revealed several golden teeth.

A dragon burst unto the scene and an actor confronted him with a sword, singing. And about the song, what can I say? The first thing would be to ask if that annoying succession of squeals, more reminiscent of a cat in heat than of a human being, could be classified as such. None of the artists let out their voices with their mouths open, projecting it from the soft palate, but instead did it in an absurd manner, with their lips closed and their throats vibrating. Wen and I endured it, incredulous and exasperated, wanting to cover our ears. The musical accompaniment didn't make things much better.

The orchestra was composed of four Asians who played, tirelessly, a flute, a sort of banjo, a drum, and some loud cymbals. Each one played his instrument whenever he felt like it, without a trace of order or harmony.

The actors leaped and flipped as if they were colorful windmills, and they howled like demons; the cymbal player clashed the metal plates in the noisiest way possible; the drum and the banjo went out of their way to contribute to the chaos, and the flutist, a true sadist, let out an unbearable whistle, shrill and piercing, that came in through the ears and advanced, unstoppable, toward the brain, where it would plunge like a sharpened drill.

At ten o'clock I didn't know if I could stand it anymore, and I started to have serious doubts about the Chinese man from El Crisantemo Dorado, thinking he had pulled our leg, but I didn't want to let Wenceslao in on my fears. At eleven, incapable of paying attention to what was happening on stage, I began to fear that the performance would go on *ad infinitum,* without even granting us the respite of an intermission. As for Wen, I don't know if he was sleeping or pretending, his head had fallen on his chest, and although he jumped up each time the man with the cymbals did his thing, his eyes were stubbornly shut. As unbelievable as it may seem, the people around us seemed to be enjoying the performance: they welcomed each speech with laughter or exclamations of anger depending on the context, clapped at the end of dances, and continued chewing with their inexhaustible mandibles sweets, fruits, fritters, peanuts, stalks of celery, and carrots pulled out from seemingly bottomless paper bags.

At the moment I was about to wake Wenceslao to flee from that Oriental inferno, I felt someone tap me on the back. A Chinese man whose features I didn't get to make out said to follow him and headed for the exit. Without paying heed to the heirs of the Celestial Empire who surrounded us, we made our way toward the aisle and out to the street.

At the door of the theater, a fat individual awaited us and all we had to do was look at him once to see that he wasn't a pure Chinese. The flattened nose and the curly hair betrayed a mixing of races. He said he was called José Chiang and, not beating around the bush, asked us for five pesos for taking us to Misael Reyes. I was about to take out my wallet and give it to him, but something made me pause and I told him that I would give it to him when we got there. Apparently he found this funny, because with a mockingly courteous gesture, he signaled the way. The three of us went farther into Chinatown, which at nighttime, shadowy and with few pedestrians, seemed nothing like the place we had visited that morning.

This guy was a chatterbox and immediately he drew us into conversation. When he asked us if we had enjoyed the performance, and Wenceslao, trying to be polite, said that yes, especially the actresses, who were very pretty, José let out a guffaw, putting his hands on his enormous belly so that it wouldn't flop up and down.

"They were men dressed as women!" he explained, and we didn't have any choice but to laugh with him.

Out of nowhere, he began to talk about Fan Ya Ling. The old man had arrived in Cuba on a ship to work as a coolie in the sugarcane fields. The contract, for eight years, stipulated that he would be paid six pesos a month, money that he never saw; it was written also that he would be fed wholeheartedly, and he almost died from hunger, building with others from the Celestial Empire a sugar mill. But, even with all this, he had managed to survive and prosper.

"That guy is a fireball," Chiang said. "You have to watch it with him, because he can cast an evil eye in the fabric of your soul. And Chinese curses are the worst! Even Negroes fear them! Because they are cast through smoke, and no one can undo them."

We were walking in the middle of the street and our steps resonated on the asphalt almost supernaturally.

"Are we almost there?" I asked our guide, afraid that he was setting a trap for us.

"We're just beginning," the half-breed joked and, pointing to a hovel on the way, he said that if some day we needed some Bengalese opium or some cannabis, we could find it there. Of course, if we called him ahead of time, he could get us the best prices. "Have you heard the story of Li Tie Kouai?" he said out of nowhere and, ascertaining that we hadn't, began to narrate. "Li Tie Kouai was a man who grew bored with drinking, whoring, and living the wild life and went to live by himself on top of a mountain. Through the years, he became famous for his wisdom, and a young man climbed the mountain to learn his lessons and become his disciple. One afternoon, Li Tie Kouai had a hunch that his mother, whom he had not seen in many years, was not doing well, so he decided to visit her, but only in his spirit. 'You will take care of my body until I return in seven days,' he instructed his student. His soul separated from his body, which remained stiff and cold under a tree, and he went to look in on the old woman. Then, a week passed and since the teacher remained frozen stiff, the man thought that he was dead, and so he grew bored with the whole affair and left the place. But lo and behold, on the ninth night, Li Tie Kouai returned, looking for his body, and couldn't find it anywhere. Finally, after searching the entire mountaintop like a madman, he came upon a pile of guts and skin and bones. A tiger had devoured him! Imagine that! He was as enraged as can be, and rightfully so! Do you know what it is for a soul to live without a body? It's hell! Not knowing what to do, the spirit began to search for another body to settle into and had the luck to find a lame beggar who had just kicked the bucket. Without thinking about it twice, he got in and lived a long life."

Wenceslao and I glanced at each other, trying to find the moral in this little tale or what it had to do with us.

"It's a nice legend," I remarked.

"It's not a legend," José Chiang replied, becoming serious. "It's something that happened many years ago. Fan Ya Ling told me about it," and he stopped in front of a huge wooden door in a building on the corner. The meager light of a streetlight lengthened our shadows phantasmagorically. "We are here," he announced, pointing to the door of the mansion. "It has been a pleasure to serve you, gentlemen," and he reached out an open hand, expecting his payment.

I handed him the bill and he gestured for us to knock. As I did it, he quickly turned around and, without saying good-bye, disappeared into the fog. We waited a few minutes and there was no answer.

"Do it again," Wen whispered, looking around in all directions. "I don't like this place. What if they want to kill us?"

"Be quiet, you'll jinx us saying things like that," I said and knocked again, more forcefully. And right away the door half-opened.

"Come in," said a man's voice.

I felt my heart skip a beat and, pushed by Wenceslao, I stepped into the darkened house. He followed me, his hand holding onto my belt.

"This way. Careful!" the voice warned us.

We heard footsteps and followed them toward a hallway.

"Stop."

A light went on and I looked for the figure of the man hoping to see my uncle, but I was to be disappointed. What I found instead was a young, attractive Oriental who, something rare in his race, was rather tall. He wore a loose silk shirt and dark pants.

"Who is Señor Reyes's nephew?" he asked calmly, signaling for us to take a seat. He spoke perfect Spanish, though with a light accent that sounded like an Englishman's. The living room was a mix of antiques, and Art Nouveau French furniture, with rugs, Gobelin tapestries, mirrors, lacquered screens, and porcelain cups and jars all arranged exquisitely.

"I am," I answered, sitting next to Wen on the Empire-style sofa. "And you are, good sir?"

"My name is Mei Feng," he said, keeping his eyes on me as he settled into an armchair. "I am your uncle's secretary . . . or his chambermaid." And then, after a pause, he added with a melancholic irony, "I have never been quite sure myself."

There was an uncomfortable silence that Mei Feng broke by asking us whether we wanted anything to drink. A whiskey? Something less strong; a brandy, perhaps? I accepted the brandy and Wen wanted two fingers of aged Bacardí rum. As Mei Feng headed for the bar to make the drinks, I wondered whether it would be wise to ask him where The Unexpected One was and when we would be able, finally, to see his face. However, I remembered all the havoc caused by Li Tie Kouai's disciple's lack of patience and opted to wait for the explanation that, sooner or later, had to be given to us.

"Your uncle is sort of a hermit," the man remarked with a trace of mockery in his voice, deftly pouring drinks. "One of the few people that he visits is Count Kostia and that, truthfully, doesn't happen very often. He prefers his friends to come here. It's a beautiful house, no? I never get tired of so many lovely things and I very much enjoy listening to him talk about them. Each object has its own story and important reason for being with him."

He handed us the drinks and returned to his chair.

"But," he said, "I hate to inform you that Señor Reyes is not here."

"But you just said that he never leaves the house," Wen protested. "Where is he?"

"I don't know. I am as perplexed as you are. I went to the movie theater to see Gloria Swanson in *Under the Whip,* and when I returned, a few hours ago, I was surprised to see that he wasn't here. And even more surprised that he hadn't left a message. Something unexpected must have come up."

"Can we wait for him?" I ventured.

"Of course," Mei Feng asserted. "You can wait for him as long as you like. Maybe he will be back soon."

We were silent for a while.

"But it could be that he doesn't return tonight," he warned us in a neutral tone, his eyes fixed on the rug.

"My uncle was expecting me, right?"

The secretary nodded several times.

"Yes. He was very moved and was very much looking forward to seeing you. He said that when he lived in Bogotá you were his youngest nephew, and his favorite."

Wen asked him why Count Kostia hadn't given him our phone number so he could call us. The *Chino* tried to hide a smile and chose not to answer. Then he continued his story.

"Señor Misael told me about the houses and the people in La Candelaria, about the barren plateau and the earthquakes. I must admit I was surprised: he had never spoken to me about that time in his life. Truthfully, he doesn't speak much," Mei Feng lowered his eyes, "especially about the past."

I got my courage up and peppered him with questions. Each one was answered immediately.

"Why had my uncle written to his siblings on the Perla de Cuba stationery?"

"Because at that time a close friend of his worked in the hotel and could bring him any letter addressed to him there."

"Why then didn't he answer the one that my mother and uncles wrote to him?"

"Because he had a falling out with that same person who worked at the Perla de Cuba, and perhaps out of spite he didn't give your uncle the letter."

"What does my uncle do?"

"He is a businessman."

"How long have you worked for him?"

"Long."

"Why so much secrecy? Neither the consulate, nor the police know a thing about him. What's he hiding from? Why?"

"I think that Señor Reyes should answer that one."

Wen started to move around the room, looking at the art objects up close. I noticed that Mei Feng was watching him out of the corner of his eye, afraid that he would shatter one of the antique, and surely priceless, Chinese vases atop one of the tables. Without getting up, he explained that green was the predominant color of the porcelain pieces that the potters baked in ovens called *kilu,* during the long reign of Emperor Hang-Hsi, a contemporary of Louis XIV. The red, deep-rose, and golden vases were from the period in which Chen Lung reigned over the Celestial Empire. Wasn't it peculiar that in such different cultures, artists would choose the same colors? For in Paris as well, during the time of Louis XV, du Barry rose was the color of choice.

"Look at this, Lucho," my lover remarked, stepping away from the vases, tired I suppose of know-it-all's commentary, and standing in front of a frame on the mantelpiece. I promptly went and stood next to him. In the simple, embossed gold frame there was not a portrait, as I had imagined. Behind the glass, there was the manuscript of a sonnet. In the lower corner, it was signed by the author, Julián del Casal, with the year in which he had written it, 1893, and under it all, in his sinewy script, his dedication: "To Misael, the archangel, just in time."

It was a love poem, the same one that Casal held in his hands the morning that María Cay knocked at his door, at the terrace on Virtudes Street, and caught him with the Colombian.

Supplication

Let me rest near the warmth of your face
The heart that will forever be amiss,
With the perfumy fever of your first kiss,
With the soft pressure of your first embrace.

I fell from grace bound in mighty ropes,
But by your side I now freely return,
As the imprisoned swan one day will turn
To the soft nest on its native slopes.

I want to find in you my squandered peace,
And surrender within your crimson lips
And into the rapture of your radiant eyes.

My soul I'll forsake to you piece by piece,
Like the moon when it hides in the eclipse,
Like the stars as dawn awakes the skies.

"It's beautiful, isn't it? It's in his book *Busts and Verses,*" Mei Feng informed us from his spot. "It was published without the dedication, of course."

As soon as we returned to the sofa, the secretary got up and went to the gramophone. He put on some blues, at low volume, and said that it was the favorite record of the owner of the house. He would listen to it again and again, without growing tired of it. "I don't understand how it is not scratched," he said. The title of the song was "Down-hearted Blues" and it was performed by a singer named Bessie Smith. The young man returned to his armchair and we listened in silence, enjoying the woman's smooth, sensual voice and the piano in the background. When it was finished, we remained quiet, without uttering a word for half an hour, after which I asked the young man for pen and paper. He quickly brought it to me and I wrote my uncle a note. I wrote down my first and last names, the phone number of the Inglaterra Hotel, the number of our room, and a terse message: "Call me if you want to see me." Then we got up.

"We are going," I announced, giving the message to the secretary. "Tell my uncle that if he wants to see me, I have left all the information there for him to contact me."

Mei Feng nodded and, with a stolid face, led us with a light to the door. Once there, he pointed the way we should take to hit the main street where we could easily find a taxi.

"I am sorry that you made the trip for no reason," he whispered before disappearing behind the huge door.

We walked. The night was a little frightening, but a few blocks away we grabbed a taxi. Without consulting me, Wen told the driver to take us to the corner of Colón and Crespo. During one of our strolls, Emilito De la Cruz had pointed to a house out of which was run a male brothel. "Guys for guys," he remarked, raising his eyebrows. "It's a phenomenal spot. I feel that I can't even describe it. It is not to be missed." With his incredible sense of orientation, Wen found the place, which had a red light burning in one of the front windows, and we went in a little past one in the morning.

"Welcome, señores," a tall, well-built, dark-skinned man received us. He had the face of a criminal but was dressed like a gentleman.

When we left that seedy den, at eight in the morning, exhausted and bleary-eyed, with our wallets empty, we had to agree with De la Cruz that this was a place out of the ordinary: sordid and full of temptations, conceived to make real the most perverted fantasies. Needless to say, for that night at least the leader of the university students was erased completely from my mind.

The lobby of the Inglaterra was empty with the exception of two men, one very tall and the other one short, both in dark suits and felt hats. On seeing us arrive, they stood up and quickly moved toward us, just at the moment that the employee at the reception desk informed us that they had called from La Boston to say that we needed to go try on the clothes they were making for us.

"Secret police," one of the men said, showing us identification. "You have to come with us."

In my life, there have been five important men. That's not a lot when you think how long I have lived. But people talk, people invent things, and you have no choice but to make a thing into what it is not. If you were to listen to the lies that circulate about me, you would think I was a devourer of lovers. Someone who is insatiable, or something like it.

The first one was Marino Cafiero, a well-known journalist from a good family, who dressed nicely, had good manners, and knew how to talk. He was well educated, or at least I thought so at the time. In any case, he dazzled me. It didn't take much for him to seduce me. I was young, with no experience other than the lovers' roles I'd played, and I had never had such a gallant, perfumed, and generous man by my side.

I succumbed to his attentions with an astonishing ease. It was the first time I had been courted. I couldn't believe my luck! I, the graceless, withdrawn Eleonora, was finally called upon by someone. And it wasn't just anyone who claimed me, but Cafiero, the conqueror of actresses, a worldly man. How could I not give myself to him, completely and gratefully? Later I have asked myself if the swiftness of my surrender, the speed with which I capitulated, wasn't because of the nature of what I practiced. Did I intuit, perhaps, that the only way to represent in a truthful fashion a woman overcome with passion was to experience that passion? "Oh, this is love?" I thought when he took me in his arms. "This is the feeling that exalts heroines, that makes them suffer, to waste away like candles, betray their virtue and their husbands and even lose their minds?" I loved him, fleetingly and uncontrollably, almost to the edge of hysteria. Like any romantic young woman bent upon elevating to the category of sublime passion what was for him nothing but a common adventure. I even continued to care for him, with a sharp and continuous love, when Rossi's company moved to Turin and, to my surprise, my lover did nothing to try to keep me from going.

When we saw each other again, a few weeks later, and I told him directly that I was pregnant, he went pale with fright, but was careful not to mention marriage. He did offer to pay the costs of the delivery. "Not necessary," I said, trying to keep my composure, and I ran out so that he would not see me cry. I had that child, and God took him from me.

A year later, in Florence, I was married to Teobaldo Checchi, an actor in Rossi's company. Not a great artist, but a magnificent person. At that time, what I needed was to feel protected, and he not only offered me security, but convinced me that I had the talent to go places. I don't regret what I did, but I would not marry again for all the gold in the world. To a sensible woman, getting married is like jumping into a river in the middle of the winter, a thing you don't do twice.

I don't include my husband, rest his soul, in my list of lovers. I never loved him. What I felt for him, at most, was a resigned affection. He paid my debts, bought me dresses, took care of me when I was sick, and freed me from worry. If a dog gets lost and has the luck to come upon a new master who offers him food and a home, he is obligated to show gratitude. The same happened to me. As long as it lasted, I was a good wife. I even thought about abandoning the theater, renouncing everything, when Enrichetta was born, but I was under contract to travel to Montevideo so I gave up the idea. "You can't leave Rossi without a leading actress," Teobaldo himself advised me, and we boarded a ship for South America. My first visit abroad.

Since the crossing was long (twenty-six endless days), we took the opportunity to rehearse aboard. And then, as if I weren't tired of having him at my side, a light shone in front of me and I fell before it, overcome as if by divine revelation with how beautiful, captivating, and adorable Flavio Andó was.

He was the third. The third man in my life. What demeanor, what a mouth, what a mustache! And what eyes, always drowsy but capable of melting you like butter with a look. I dare not say that it was love. I think it was more like a collision, a fit. It was a blustery, reckless, adulterous passion, which the company knew about at once and Teobaldo not long after. My husband, my solace! made the decision to stay in Buenos Aires to finish the tournée. He left me alone. We never separated legally, before the law we continued to be man and wife till the day of his death. A little after returning to Italy, I was already tired of Andó. He was as attractive as he was dumb! But oh how the ladies sighed when the peacock took me in his arms on stage and kissed me rabidly.

Later, Boito appeared and I fell like a devotee before his dignity, his renown, his wisdom. It was absolute. I loved him voraciously, desperately, though he was never all mine. He was older than I, had his circle of aristocratic friends, chains that bound him to a sentimental past that he could not renounce, a whole existence from which I was excluded. But even then, the part of him that did belong to me was enough to ennoble me, to make me feel, for the first time, dignified, uncontaminated, proud, beautiful. By his side, I understood what it meant to pursue an aesthetic ideal. I asked him about everything. We wrote each other often, and whenever it was possible we would spend a few days together. Sometimes I dreamed about the future and imagined a little house in the country, with three windows. In one, Boito's beautiful head was visible, in the other one I, and in the last one was the girl. Enrichetta loved him also. He treated her with delicacy, advised her like a father, and helped me keep her away from the fatal heritage of the theater.

Poor Arrigo! He idolized Verdi! I never confessed to him, out of pity, that I preferred Wagner. He never understood the work of Ibsen, whom he called disdainfully "the pharmacist." He said that his plays were coarse and without poetry. When I premiered A Doll's House at the Filodrammatici in

Milan, he almost stopped talking to me. He was very disappointed. With the years, our meetings and letters became fewer and farther between, and slowly he ceased to be a man and became, in my eyes, a superior spirit, an object of veneration. The saint.

And, to wrap things up, D'Annunzio appeared. My last love and the most devastating one.

Five men. Five only. Fortunately.

7

It took me a while to figure it out, but I finally understood that the substance that was smeared on the walls and that I almost stained my clothes with (granular and viscous like pâté, the color somewhere between gray and rose) was the crushed brain of Mei Feng. I'll never eat brains again, I thought, and I made a superhuman effort not to vomit.

The living room of my uncle's house seemed some other place: rugs, furniture, and cushions all out of place, as if a tornado had passed through there after we had left. Miraculously, two jars that had fallen to the floor were still unscathed. The upholstery on the Empire sofa, however, was ruined by the copious bloodstains.

The body of The Unexpected One's secretary or chambermaid was laid out on the floor near one of the folding screens, around him a red puddle, half coagulated. The sheet that covered him wasn't big enough and his legs were visible from the knees down. Pompilio Ramos lifted the cover and pressed us to look at him.

"Do you recognize him?" he said.

Although the moment wasn't exactly right for quibbles about linguistics, it was evident that the verb the assistant inspector of the secret police had used to formulate the question wasn't exactly adequate. Could anyone *recognize* the young Asian of normal features, smooth skin, and plentiful, blackthorn-colored hair, in the remains of that skull? The proper word perhaps would have been "guess." Can you *guess* who it is? Yes, Señor Ramos, with a little effort we can guess that that head, ripped open by a bullet to the temple, belonged to Mei Feng, that that viscous dark blood, those brains, the splinters of bone and particles of skin scattered on the floor, splashed on the walls and furniture belonged to him. It was the first disfigured corpse that I had seen in my life, and the experience proved hair-raising. Despite their rigidity, the eyes and mouth of the cadaver displayed an amused expression of surprise, of someone who couldn't believe what had happened.

"Do you recognize him?" the assistant inspector insisted.

Wenceslao responded that yes, we did recognize him. I couldn't help it, my knees went weak and I had to race, followed by one of the detectives, to the bathroom. I stuck my head in the toilet and threw up so long and hard that I thought I would heave out my entrails. Afterwards I went to the sink, washed my mouth, and splashed my face with water. Aquiles de la Osa handed me a towel with an inscrutable expression on his face.

"You don't think that we killed him, do you?" I asked him as I dried my face.

"In this profession, one only believes in what can be proven," he answered. "And the fact is that the murdered man had a note in his pocket written by you."

When we returned to the living room, the unfortunate Mei Feng was being wheeled out, on the way to a morgue, and the forensic doctor was informing the assistant inspector, Ignacio Falero, and a pale and disengaged Wenceslao Hoyos that in his judgment the crime had been committed between four and five in the morning.

"What is strange is that none of the neighbors called the police," he whispered.

"Bah!" Pompilio Ramos responded. "A shot here or a shot there in the middle of the night, who cares about such things in Chinatown?"

Wenceslao dropped on one end of the sofa, not worrying about the blood. A bony old maid came out of one of the interior rooms, very frightened, led by a policeman who held onto one of her skeletal arms. Her name was Atanasia and she was the one who had found the young man's unbrained body on arriving at the house early morning to attend, as usual, to her cleaning and cooking duties.

"One more question, señora, and then you may go in peace," the

assistant inspector promised. "Do you remember these two gentlemen?" And he pointed at us.

The old woman fixed her owl eyes on us and swore on the Virgin of
Cobre that she did not know who we were.

"All right," Ramos said, addressing his detectives. "I think that it is
time to return to home base." And, looking at both of us, he added, "I
imagine that after seeing this enlightening spectacle our Colombian
friends will have much to tell us."

In another room of police headquarters that was, if it were possible, more dismal than the first, Wenceslao and I were submitted to a
thorough new round of interrogation. This time a stenographer
copied our answers at an unbelievable speed. Desirous to return to
the hotel as soon as possible, we told them everything relating to Misael Reyes, trying not to leave out any detail, no matter how irrelevant
it might seem: the charge of my family to find his whereabouts, the
godlike help of Señora Cay, the call from Count Kostia, the trips to El
Crisantemo Dorado and the Teatro *Chino,* the visit to my uncle's house
and meeting the late Mei Feng. To conclude, we insisted arduously
that we were innocent. But even if the detectives began to treat us a
little bit more familiarly and Ignacio Falero even offered us cigarettes,
you didn't have to be too smart to realize that the absence of an alibi
was what was keeping us from escaping that spider's web. Wen and I
still had not mentioned that the "series of brothels" we had visited
was in fact one male brothel, afraid of the consequences such a thing
could bring if publicized.

Pompilio Ramos reappeared with the news that Inspector Donato
Cubas wanted to see us in his office. The two detectives looked at him,
surprised, and the assistant inspector, shrugging his shoulders, made
a face as if he didn't understand what was going on. The office they
took us to was a bit more seemly, with windows facing out onto the
street, through which we could see that it had stopped raining and
that a pusillanimous sun was trying to peek through the storm clouds.
Aside from the said Cubas, who was better dressed and seemed better
mannered than his underlings, there were two other individuals
there: the Colombian consul in Havana and the person who, worried
about our disappearance and through various inquiries, first through

the workers in the Inglaterra and then at the headquarters of the secret police, had asked for the diplomat's help: Emilito De la Cruz. On
seeing him, I wanted to wrap my arms around him and I became convinced that he was as good as he was ugly.

The consul pleaded effusively on our part, giving the inspector his
word of honor that we were from good families. He stated for the
record that this past Friday we had sought his help in finding Misael
Reyes. It had been only by chance that we had visited the scene of the
crime a few hours before the crime had been perpetrated. "A terrible
coincidence," he insisted. Moreover, in the hypothetical case that we
had any motive to murder the Oriental, would we be so stupid as to
leave a note on him in our own handwriting and with all our information? Two sensible people would never act in such an obtuse manner.

Donato Cubas nodded gravely and agreed with the consul, but immediately got to the heart of the matter. Where were we when the
bloody deed had been done? Who could testify to the fact that we
were indeed far from the scene of the crime?

"The gentlemen assure me that they spent the night going from
brothel to brothel, which makes sense, since they are young and Havana has an army of sinful women ready to bring joy to anyone who
solicits their services," the inspector said. "If only they could remember the location of some of the houses that they visited so we could
verify what they say . . ."

One address and the name of at least one witness was all that was
needed to resolve the issue. It looked like it was necessary to confess
the truth.

"I think that the Señores Belalcázar and Hoyos would be more comfortable if they could speak to the inspector alone," De la Cruz declared and, without waiting for the consul's permission, led him out
of the office.

"All right," Cubas sighed. "What's going on? Where were you last
night?"

I gulped before answering. "In a house on Colón Street."

The inspector gestured impatiently: this detail helped very little,
in Colón there was a proliferation of whorehouses. Could we recall
the cross streets!

"On the corner of Colón and Crespo," I stammered and, wanting to put an end to the whole sordid affair, I gave him all the details that I could remember. "It was an old house, three floors, with a door knocker in the shape of a paw and a seedy bar out in front called El Complaciente."

"Holy shit!" Cubas blurted out, staring at us. "That place is a den of sodomites! Are you sure that that's where you were?" On seeing us nod, he snorted and yelled for Detective De la Osa, who quickly appeared. "Aquiles, go to Azuquita's house and find out when these two were there." Then, turning toward us, he asked us for the names of anyone in the brothel that we had had relations with.

We mentioned Stew, Crybaby, and Stiff Yucca, among others. Detective Aquiles, who was taking notes in a tiny notebook, let us know with a gesture that that was enough. Then they put us in a room where we could await the results of the investigation with the Colombian consul and Emilito and, twenty-five minutes later, we were saying good-bye to the agents.

"I hope that if your uncle tries to get in touch with you, you won't keep it from us," the inspector suggested. "As you can imagine, his disappearance makes him a prime suspect."

I left the secret police headquarters reeling: aside from everything we had been through, now it was possible that I was the nephew of a murderer. We took a taxi with Emilito and the consul and, on the way, the former brought us up to date on the details of the Oriental's death that he had been able to wheedle out of the agents. As strange as it may seem, nothing of value was missing from the house, so theft was ruled out as a motive. One thing that was significant was that Atanasia, the maid, who swore she had no idea where her boss was, insisted on calling him Ismael and not Misael.

"The maid told them about a man, a Frenchman it seems, who had come to the house daily during the last few weeks. She didn't know his name, because it was the deceased who always received him at the door and led him to Señor Reyes's office. She only saw him glancingly as she went about her cleaning duties."

One afternoon when she dared ask Mei Feng the reason for the stranger's frequent and prolonged visits, he looked at her viciously and answered: "Business."

Emilito, Wenceslao, and I got out on the corner of Prado and San

Rafael. As a way of saying his good-byes, Dr. García Benítez advised us to be a little more prudent about our nightly excursions and went on his way. We raced to the elevator of the Inglaterra and, once in our room, we told Monkeyface everything we had left out about our adventure.

"My advice is that you forget about your uncle," he said, getting right to the point. "I'm sorry Lucho, but it seems that the guy is involved in some strange business and you can get yourself in a real mess, without even knowing it."

And he added something that he hadn't wanted to say in front of the diplomat: according to Atanasia, Mei Feng didn't much care for the visitor who locked himself with the owner of the house in the office. Maybe it was a crime of passion.

Lying on the bed with his feet in my lap so I could massage them, Wen began to speculate on the situation. Why so much mystery around The Unexpected One? Why did neither the secret police nor the consulate have any information about him? Was he running from the law and is that why he had to live in the shadows, hiding from everyone? Was my uncle a professional criminal, a swindler? Was he a bank robber? Or maybe he dealt in contraband? But what kind of contraband? Liquor? Probably not. Narcotics, then? Arms? I remembered the unsuccessful uprisings that Mella told us about and thought that someone had to supply the weapons and ammunition to the rebels. De la Cruz guessed that maybe the contraband was actually Chinos.

"Orientals?" I repeated, pushing aside my lover's feet. "What does that mean?"

Emilito explained that, for some years now, the Cuban government had prohibited the entrance of Chinese immigrants. Suddenly I realized that during our testimony to Aquiles de la Osa and Ignacio Falero, neither Wen nor I had mentioned José Chiang, the fat man who had led us to my uncle's house. We alluded to him in vague terms ("a chubby guy," "a person who seemed *mestizo,* half Chinese, half black") without giving his name. Would it be wise to contact the detectives, or should we leave things as they were, not poking our nose into the hornet's nest? With great effort, I picked up the thread of Monkeyface's narrative. In spite of the proscription, he stated, the number of

Chinese people continued to grow in the capital and in the inland cities. There were rumors of ships that arrived clandestinely and dropped off loads of Chinos on the Havana coast. Good portions of those immigrants were "imported" by smugglers whom they then paid a portion of their monthly salaries. All this sounded like a cheap novel, so I let Sherlock Holmes and Dr. Watson know that as far as I was concerned there was a simpler explanation to everything. Maybe my uncle didn't have anything to do with Mei Feng's death and was out of town on business.

"Oh, you stupid boy!" Wen exploded, losing his patience. "Don't come to me with all this your innocent uncle crap! If your uncle were clean, he would show his face and not stay hiding who knows where. And don't you find it suspicious that the murderer took precisely what he took?"

I asked him what he was talking about and he looked at me incredulously.

"The picture frame, my darling," he said. "The one with the poem. Didn't you notice that it wasn't there?"

No, I hadn't noticed, and neither had Atanasia, apparently. Could its theft be an important detail in solving the case? Oh, I was tired of all of this; everything was too complicated and mixed up for me. I sighed deeply and, on seeing that De la Cruz and Wen continued with their digressions, I begged for mercy and headed for the bathroom. Let each one take care of his own thing. Let Donato Cubas and his boys worry about catching the murderer, whoever it may be. For us it was better to turn the page and forget about the whole affair. As I took a shower, I heard them talking on the phone to Vázquez Garralaga, arranging to get together for Graziella Gerbelasa's reading.

"Don't count on me," I warned them when I came back into the room in my bedclothes. "I'll stay here resting, I need it."

My comment went in one ear and out the other.

"What's wrong is that you must be starving to death!" De la Cruz exclaimed. "With a full stomach, things will seem different." And with two lively pats, he pushed Wen toward the bathroom. "Go now, wash the *grajo* off you and get all pretty, I am taking you out to a fascinating spot for lunch."

The place in question was the renowned and very modern Almendares Hotel, and Emilio was right, for after wolfing down some plantain chips and a baked lobster, accompanied by a few glasses of good wine, and some slices of guava with cheese as a finale, I joyfully welcomed the idea of crossing half of Havana to the Casino Español, where at six in the afternoon there would be a party to celebrate Gerbelasa's new work.

The hall chosen for the occasion was overwhelmingly splendorous. Its magnificent columns, walls, and floors were all marble, and it was decorated with various baskets of white dahlias, sweet peas, and sprays of tuberose.

"I'll be damned if those flowers are not from El Clavel," Emilito whispered ecstatically.

Monkeyface told us the names of the various writers gathered there. Present were Fernando Ortiz, president of the Economic Society of the Nation's Friends; José María Chacón y Calvo, director of the Society of Conferences and founder of the Society of Cuban Folklore; Miguel del Carrión, author of the controversial novels *Upright Women* and *Impure Women,* which we should read as soon as possible; and José Manuel Carbonell, a much-sought-after poet thanks to the success of *Crests.* Enrique Uhthoff, the journalist and creator of the libretto for the operetta *The Girl Lupe,* which would soon premiere with Esperanza Iris, had come to the party in the company of the *divette* and paraded her around the premises, bloated with pride, greeting his friends and urging them to attend the premiere.

Among the young intellectuals, our guardian angel spotted Jorge Mañach, José Antonio Fernández de Castro, Alejo Carpentier, and Rubén Martínez Villena, who was picked by Wen, without the slightest hesitation, as the most attractive one in the group: so fair-skinned and with those beautiful green eyes. Since I still had Mella stuck inside my head, I couldn't care less for any of them. De la Cruz assured us that not since the function in honor of the Duvan Turzoff's Russian company, during which several of the writers present gave speeches, had there been so many luminaries together under one roof. "If the building collapses, it will be the end of Cuban literature," he added jokingly. There also abounded many señoras and señoritas of the highest society, showing off their silk dresses, their jewels, their hairdos and, taking advantage of the chill in the air, their fur coats.

We moved in among the faction of guests and discovered that, for the most part, the conversations had little to do with art. Some mentioned the symbolic burial of Lenin (because, in the end, those who were set on mummifying him had gotten their way and were hurriedly building a mausoleum, right next to the fortress of the Kremlin, to preserve him there) and the homage that the Russian railroad workers had paid him by stopping all trains at the same time for five minutes. Others talked about the imminent arrival on the Island of Mrs. Carrie Chapman Catt, founder and president for twenty years of the International Woman Suffrage Alliance and the ruckus that her visit would certainly cause in the national ladies' associations. Various people who were congregated around Fernando Ortiz exchanged opinions about the possible annexation by the United States of the Isle of Pines and the force that the colony of Bostonians living there was rounding up.

Of course there were some who preferred to talk about less significant matters, like, for example, about the lion Samson of the Santos and Artigas Circus, who had become the star of the day when he escaped from his cage in Santiago de Cuba. The ladies gossiped about Mina López-Salmón de Buffin's Ball of a Thousand and One Nights and of the spectacular costumes, which were closely guarded secrets, that would be worn by the Marquise of Villalta, Catalina Lasa de Pedro, and Chichita Grau del Valle, as well as about the sensuality exuded by Adelaide and Hughes, members of a dance team that performed Apache dances each night at the Casino Nacional, much better, any way you looked at it, than Leonor and Maurice, the duo who danced at the Almendares Hotel.

For his part, Martínez Villena made reference to the next meeting between the Scorpions and the Lions, the two most popular baseball teams, at Almendares Park. Wenceslao, approaching the young man, introduced himself most courteously and let it be known that, even if in Colombia the sport he was talking about so enthusiastically was unknown, he felt an urgent desire to discover its secrets. And the one with the light-colored eyes took on the task of instructing him and began to lay out the ABCs of "the ballgame." My lover listened, spellbound, staring at him and nodding, though I am sure that he understood nothing about pitchers, strikes, and home runs. To him runs, or *carreras,* continued to be the roads in Bogotá that run parallel to the hills, and nines, or *novenas,* the prayers you say in December to celebrate the coming of the Baby Jesus.

As much as I strained to listen in, I heard no comment about La Duse's premiere, scheduled for twenty-four hours later, nor, fortunately, about the murder in Chinatown.

Somebody tapped me on the shoulder with a fan and, on turning, I saw myself in front of the opulent Esperanza Iris. Contrary to what I thought, she remembered me perfectly and chided me, with her Aztec sweet-talk, for not having attended her performance at the Payret the night before. I made up an excuse and promised her that I would go see *The Girl Lupe* without fail. "I'll come looking for you if you don't keep your word," the *divette* threatened me. Fortunately Wen, tired of his baseball lesson, rescued me from her clutches.

La Gerbelasa fluttered from one place to the next, like a dragonfly or a fairy, wearing a pale rose Bengali silk dress and beaming with joy. She came up to us for a moment, said she appreciated that we had weathered the rain to come to her soirée, and then headed toward some other guests. "She seems more developed than the last time I saw her," Emilio whispered and, since we looked at him not knowing what he was talking about, he explained: "Her chest. It's more . . . evident. I bet she is taking Dr. Brum's Circassian pills they sell in the Sarrá Pharmacy. They say they work miracles." We nodded, trying not to laugh, and at that moment Wenceslao noticed Vázquez Garralaga, who was talking to his mother and some other ladies in a corner. We waved to him excitedly but, to our surprise, he pretended not to notice us.

"I wonder what crawled up his ass?" De la Cruz asked.

When we saw his group heading toward the chairs in front of the presidential table, we quickly found our seats. The program was beginning.

The first to address the audience was Olavito, who, after evoking the birth of José Martí and citing a few verses about white roses and thistles eaten by caterpillars, or something like that, went out of his way to praise the gentle writer who that afternoon was presenting to the world the memories of her youth. The panegyric concluded by asserting that *The Reliquary* marked a turning point in the belles lettres of the Island. Afterward, the critic Rafael U. González spoke and, after declaring with the utmost seriousness that the prose in the new book by La Gerbelasa resembled, on reading it, a gentle and mild stream that glided on the floor of a slopeless valley, through the wildflowers and under the immense blue pupil of the sky, predicted many clamorous triumphs for its creator. And lastly, it was the guest of honor's turn. She warned that, dazzled by so much unearned praise and not knowing what to say not to disappoint the select audience, she would rather read a fragment from the introduction of her *Reliquary*. She paused to allow the guests to honor her with applause and began her reading.

"Since my soul enjoys the vain lyricism of thinking myself dead, I wanted to make a blurry offering to my readers. Taking them for worms in the tomb that is the earth, I give you the perfumed cadaver of my infancy, put away in a printed reliquary. You can be sure that, if it doesn't invigorate you, it will not make you ill. So devour it with delight."

As the young woman read, I felt a growing and suffocating unease. Countless unpleasant feelings amassed inside me. How could the members of the audience remain unperturbed when the new author pretended that we were worms? The invitation to gobble up the corpse of her infancy brought the image of Mei Feng's head in pieces to mind, and I had to blink various times to chase it away.

"Pathetic," Wen pronounced when, once the speeches were over, the guests abandoned their seats, either to congratulate the speakers or to praise each other over cups full of liquor that the waiters offered. "I wouldn't read that book if they paid me."

Some minutes later, on noticing that Olavito and his mother were dodging some guests and trying to leave, we caught up to him before he left the hall.

"My friend!" Wen exclaimed, approaching him with his arms open for a cordial hug, but he froze when the poet, striking him down with a look said, "Save your effusions, Señor Hoyos."

"What's wrong, *viejo?*" De la Cruz interjected. "*Coño,* don't start with your crap!"

"Don't try to save your pals," Olavito replied, raising his chin. "I know from a good source that during Montes de la Oca's soireé, as I read from 'Madame Butterfly,' they both went out to the terrace to laugh at me," and looking at us enraged, he challenged us. "Dare to deny it! Someone saw you, a witness heard your laughs and had the decency to tell me all about it, from A to Z, so that I would know the type of people I was making friends with."

And dragging his mother, who nodded remorsefully, away by the arm, he left the premises. Before disappearing down the stairs, he returned and, with an expression of cultivated sadism, hurled the worst of threats:

"As far as La Duse is concerned, don't even think that I am going to intercede on your part, on the contrary! I will tell her that you two are the worst of the worst, the scum of the barrel."

Wenceslao looked at me, fuming.

"It was Graziella," he declared, without a shadow of a doubt. "She was the only one on the terrace that night."

"Are you sure?"

"So sure that I am going to expose her right now," he affirmed and, not giving me time to stop him, left in search of the gossip, who was chatting a few steps away, ignorant of the imbroglio and just being her charming self, with Enrique Uhthoff and the empress of the operetta. Very impertinently interrupting their conversation, Wenceslao stood in front of the young woman and glared at her eye-to-eye, with furrowed brow for a handful of seconds that seemed an eternity. Then he turned around and, without saying a word, returned to us.

To the surprise of her companions, La Gerbelasa followed a few steps behind.

"What's wrong?" she asked with a wounded voice when she reached him. "Why do you do such things to me?"

"Do you have to ask?" I intervened, pushing Wenceslao back to prevent a scandal. "You, gratuitously and perfidiously, have been the cause of our falling out with Vázquez Garralaga."

"Me?" Tears welled up in the eyes of the young woman. "You are mistaken . . ."

"Olavo told us what you told him, señorita, and what he said you told him, you never should have told him," Wen jumped in, and De la

Cruz couldn't help but to laugh at such gibberish. "And as far as *The Reliquary* is concerned, you should know: it stinks!"

The three of us made for the exit, but La Gerbelasa, not giving up, held me by the arm.

"I did it out of jealousy," she explained. "I wanted to be your friend, but Vázquez Garralaga, as always, took you from me and stole the show."

Convinced she was delirious, I tried to escape her grasp.

"You must understand that it was because of you," she exclaimed, out of patience, and looking into my eyes, with an audacity that would be unthinkable in a young lady from Bogotá, she added, "Do you believe in love at first sight, Señor Belalcázar?"

"No," I lied and, bidding her good night, ran to the door as the authoress furiously beat the marble floor with one of her heels and broke down weeping.

That night we looked through the evening editions of the papers to see if they said anything about the murder. But the leading news was about the capture of Aurelio Rodríguez Fontes, alias Negrótico, a known drug dealer, several times condemned and sent to prison before, whom the cops had been able to grab after following his tracks for almost a year. The reports said that in the moment of capture, in a house on Calle Picota, Negrótico had on him a cigar box full of morphine wrappers. Three neighbors who were there buying merchandise (five pesos for one-gram wrapper) had been detained as well. The reports on the murder on Calle Campanario were, on the other hand, very succinct, and none mentioned my uncle. They limited themselves to describing the state of Mei Feng's body, to ruling out robbery as a motive, and to guaranteeing that the detectives of the secret police would catch the murderer. When referring to the scene of the crime, they described it simply as "the house of a businessman whose present whereabouts are unknown."

Already in bed, we had an argument on account of Julio Antonio Mella and Eleonora Duse. Forgetting about the meeting we had scheduled the following morning with the leader of the university students, Wenceslao had invited Katherine Garnett to visit the gardens at La Tropical and later to lunch at the roof garden of the Seville-Biltmore.

When I told him that this seemed a low blow not worthy of him, he replied that the *affaire* with the Communist was a lost cause: a whim of mine, which I was stubbornly holding on to despite the fact that the chances of that guy even letting me put a finger on him were minimal, if not nil. On the other hand, the plans with the Englishwoman promised to yield much. One good word from her, at the right time and place, could be the magical key that opens the door to La Duse's chambers. Since Vázquez Garralaga wanted to impede Wen's access to La Duse (and Wen very much did believe him capable of fulfilling his threat after what the felonious Graziellita had told him!), he couldn't rest on his laurels. He had no other choice but to court, in the most sophisticated and painstaking manner, that lady who could so intercede in his favor.

Since I knew how stubborn he was I was able to arrange a compromise that would suit us both. We could go to the beach with Mella and return to the hotel early, and that way he would have time to lunch with La Garnett. But the offer didn't suit him and he refused to sacrifice the trip to the gardens, proposing that those bucolic surroundings, full of trees and flowers, could prove not only beneficial but decisive in his plan.

"You go off with Beauty, if that's what you want, and we'll meet here in the afternoon, to go to La Boston," he suggested.

"And what do I say if he starts talking to me about strikes and revolutions?" I protested, disappointed, taking off my clothes.

"Make it up, my darling," he replied sarcastically, freeing himself from the problem. "There is a reason why you are Baal and write for magazines. Squeeze those brains, like I did." I wanted to strangle him.

"I can't believe that you are so fickle."

"And you so gullible . . . not to mention stupid."

"All you think about is yourself; everybody else can go to hell!" I yelled. "Five years together and all of a sudden I don't even know you! How can you be so selfish?"

He assured me that to accuse him of selfishness was unjust, being that if we got the interview, I would be the principal beneficiary.

"You're a manipulator! I couldn't care less if we interview the old woman or not. Aren't you ashamed to be spying on her and reading her telegrams?"

"And you? Drooling over some boy. Hedonist!"

"Oh really, and you have suddenly become chaste."

"If knowing what one wants and never deviating from the course is a defect, then so be it," he considered, not losing his cool, which made me even angrier. So, to get at him, I screamed that I would rather drool over a magnificent dark-haired beauty, however inaccessible, a hundred times than follow around a neurotic, shabbily dressed, disheveled Italian woman.

He stared at me, frozen, and with a rudeness of which I would have never thought him capable, he responded by letting out a long, thunderous fart.

"You have just unmasked yourself, Wenceslao Hoyos!" I brayed, out of my wits. "You have finally shown your true colors!" And, overcome with anger, I turned my back to him.

We slept at opposite edges of the bed.

I'd rather not talk about Gabriele. But I'll do it nonetheless, I suppose. I always end up talking about him, whether I want to or not.

When I met him, he was already twice famous: as a poet and as a conqueror. His body wouldn't make anyone lose sleep: short, pale, thin, with sparse hair, bulging eyes, and almost no eyebrows or eyelashes . . . Why then so many lovers? How was he able to ignite such an overwhelming fascination in women? I can't speak for all of them, naturally. As for me, he seduced me with his words and his talent; whispering the right things in her ear conquers the most scornful lady, and Gabriele knew these things very well.

It all started when we were both in Venice and we made a pact: he would write great plays and I would perform in them. We would found an open-air theater, on the shores of Lake Albano, amid the olive and fig trees, a sort of temple that would reveal beauty to the multitudes. I was thirty-nine and was under the impression that I would never love again. Maybe that's why I lost my mind. I ceased to be who I was and I became his shadow, I allowed him to do with me as he pleased. I made him into something more than a lover: a son or a sort of quasi-deity. He loved it when I called him figlio mio, when I bathed him in the mornings and put him to bed at night. He purred like a cat. He was only five years younger than I, but when I realized how much this pleased him, I brought up our difference in age often.

Matilde Serao, who was capable of being shockingly honest (and, in general, was), tried to convince me to put an end to the relationship. Although she and Scarfoglio, her husband, were friends with Gabriele, she told me terrible things about him. He was an immoral libertine. He was selfish, incapable of loving anyone but himself; he would use me to augment his prestige and then toss me aside; I shouldn't be stupid and should see what he had done with all the others. She admitted that he was a brilliant writer, but she couldn't see me with him. She said that I was blind, that I was acting like a schoolgirl, like an idiot.

When she realized that her warnings were useless, that I had given myself body and soul to this irrational passion, she asked that I should at least not let D'Annunzio meddle in my career. She told me once and again that his plays were bad and wooden, pure blah blah blah with no action, and that I should stop performing in them. "The bedroom is one thing and the theater another, Nennella," she admonished. I responded that they weren't that bad, but different, and that, in art, whoever tries to break with tradition always has obstacles to overcome; but she didn't want to listen to my reasons. "If what you want is to give him money, then you should continue with your old repertoire," she said dryly. "Better to play in Odette or The Wife of Claudius than to make a fool of yourself. At this stage in your career, you can't afford that."

It was useless. I performed in his plays, in spite of the audiences' indifference and the poisonous reviews of the critics. Glory was a disaster that not even the names of Zacconni and Duse, appearing together for the first time, could save, and as for Francesca de Rímini, which almost ruined me, perhaps it's better not even to speak of it. I was able to prevail with La Gioconda after an unsuccessful opening night. But how could Gabriele write for me a role where the woman loses her arms when she falls on a statue made by her husband. He, who extolled the beauty of my hands!

Was I really convinced that this was the theater of the future, as I affirmed defiantly at each opportunity? The future I predicted then is here already, and D'Annunzio's plays still do not have many followers. Was it an illusion? Did love forbid me to see what to others was so evident? In any case, I am not one of the ones who give up easily, and La città morta is still in my repertoire, as an act of defiance. There it is, in spite of everything. Or is it an unconscious scheme to arouse the public's curiosity?

I did not know how to love Gabriele without suffering, without pain, without tears. Maybe he was expecting something else, something sweeter and gentler, from me. But there is some cruelty in every type of love. Why should mine be the exception? My soul's harmony, always precarious, was lost the moment I was not by his side. The whole world, and with it me, turned murky if I was not with Gabriele. But what could I do? I needed to go on those long tormenting tours to make money and then I had to work some magic, some real magic, so that so much anguish, so much sorrow, so much rancor, became art.

Some think that he wrote *Il fuoco* behind my back, that its publication was a merciless blow, an act of treason. It's not so. I knew the plot of the novel and encouraged him as he wrote it, convinced of his talent, that he was gestating a work of art, without caring that it told of the love of an old and shabby actress (me, obviously) and a young man, beautiful and full of life (him, a very idealized him, but him). Of course, I was shaken when the book appeared. Who wants her name on everybody's tongues? I became an object of mockery and pity. I allowed it without an argument. I was in love. In love with the man who once received a telegram addressed to "The Greatest Poet in Italy," and returned it unopened, convinced that he was the greatest poet in the world.

Soon he left me. But before doing so, he plunged in the last dagger, the coup de grâce. It wasn't a surprise. I had earlier proof of how cruel he could be. Didn't he allow Sarah to premiere *La città morta*, when, as he said, he had created that role for me? During rehearsals of *La figlia di Iorio* I became ill and Gabriele insisted that it was impossible to postpone opening night. He proposed that Irma Gramatica step in for me in the role of Mila and I, proud and wounded, agreed. Agreed, thinking that it would prove a lesson to him, that *La figlia di Iorio* would be a failure and Gabriele would regret his decision. But he had the luck that this play—precisely this play, the only one that I did not perform in—was his only success. Luck? The word "luck" is an invention of ours. It's the name we insist on giving to a law we do not understand. That's not from me; it's in the *Kybalión*.

Afterwards I found out that he had a new lover, a beautiful and distinguished woman. Young, of course. I suffered a lot, more than I thought myself capable. I humbled myself. "Don't take away from me the illusion that you need me," I begged him. I let him know that if he loved me, I was willing to wait for his little adventure to end. I wrote the woman a stupid letter, smeared by tears, asking her if she thought herself capable of loving him as I did. Finally I fled, I escaped from that hell, and, like it or not, capitulated. A more sensible creature would have retired D'Annunzio's plays from her repertoire, would have never performed them again. I kept them on and kept sending him his money. Because I was stubborn, I think. Because I didn't want my arms twisted.

Two years ago we saw each other in Milan. He had gone to give a speech and I asked him to see me at the Hotel Cavour, to talk about the possible revival of *La città morta*. I wanted his permission to make a few cuts. The commandant, that's what they called him since the war, agreed. I was afraid to see him again, and for him to see me after twenty years of separation. Would he recognize his Ghisola in this old woman? He gallantly pretended not to notice my wrinkles, my gray hair. He, too, was old, bald, and wizened, but just as arrogant and sure of himself.

He told me that he would speak to Mussolini so that the state would grant me a pension: someone like me deserved it after having given so much for the glory of Italy. I responded that Mussolini was busy enough trying to keep the peace in the country to be worried about such nonsense. There were other people more in need of his help. "An artist, never," I said to him. "An artist should work, and I can still work." He made a face, not very convinced. "Oh, how you loved me!" he blurted out later, just as he was about to leave. I lowered my eyes and nodded, with a grave expression, although inside I was dying of laughter. Gabriele, the commandant of the archangels, you'll never change. You are full of illusions! If I had really loved you as you think I did, I would have died when you abandoned me. But I was able to go on.

8

I was under the impression that Agustín Miraflores, alias Scissors, was feeling me up more than necessary as I tried on the suits we had ordered from La Boston.

"Oh, we have to take these pants in a bit," he said, pins clenched in his teeth, and he saw fit to give me a tap on the ass.

Since Wenceslao's clothes also needed slight modifications, we asked him if we could take any of the outfits to wear that night, at Eleonora Duse's premiere.

The negro looked at the four suits pensively, and then, choosing two, assured us that because it was us, in a couple of hours they would be brought to the hotel, ironed and ready to wear. The others would be ready the following day. We thanked him effusively, left the store, and walked silently through the neighboring streets. Since the argument of the night before, we had barely talked. I had gone down to breakfast, very early, leaving Wen in bed, with a pillow on top of his head, pretending he was asleep. I didn't return to the room to say good-bye and left with Mella when, as agreed, he came to meet me.

I felt an enormous desire to tell Wen about the events of the day and I am sure that he felt the same, but since neither of us wanted to give in, we stupidly insisted on acting offended and prolonging the effects of the fight. So, we wandered around Old Havana with our mouths closed, sticking our noses into whatever first-rate store we came upon: the umbrella shop Galatea, the jewelry store Palais Royal, the sports store Champion, the toy store El Bosque de Bolonia, the haberdashery Madame Sovillard, and two bookstores, the Wilson and the

Morlón, which didn't really impress us, compared to La Moderna Poesía.

"How did it go with the Englishwoman?" I asked finally, trying to tinge my words with a marked disinterest.

"Terrible," he declared and, after a pause, told me that during his visit to the gardens of the brewery, Miss Garnett had tried to kiss him under a palm tree. On noticing that, instead of becoming excited, the gentleman was recoiling in obvious confusion and, why not put it plainly, in annoyance, the lady blushed up to the roots of her hair, her eyes filled with tears, and she pronounced angrily, "I don't understand anything! I swear, I don't understand anything!" The incident ruined the outing and, even though Wenceslao tried to make it seem unimportant, the current of sympathy that until then had flowed between them was cut short. His exhortations that they should stroll through the groves, cross the tiny, picturesque Japanese bridges, and gaze at the rose bushes in flower, or sit and chat under the pergolas, all made little difference. Katherine couldn't hide her discomfort and insisted that they return to the hotel immediately, saying the pollen wasn't good for her. On the way back, she couldn't stop whispering to herself, "That's absurd!"

"You don't know how hard it was to get her to have lunch as we had planned. She made a thousand excuses and I think that if she finally came with me to the Seville-Biltmore, it was only because of the acute sense of duty that her people have. Nevertheless, she hardly tasted a thing and took any opportunity she had to let me know how upset she was by my actions. Or, to be more precise, my lack of actions. I swear, the crafty witch almost made me feel guilty. As soon as they had pulled the dessert plates, she insisted that we return to the Inglaterra without delay, saying La Signora became very sensitive before every premiere in a new place and that perhaps her presence was needed."

"So, did you happen to mention anything to her about the interview with La Duse?"

"I alluded to it," he revealed. "But she listened to me undaunted, without promising a thing. She only said, sarcastically, that my wish was excessively ambitious."

On seeing his expression of defeat, I let out a cruel little laugh.

"And what about you, did you have fun?" he asked with a sigh.

"More than expected," I said, and stealing a look at him, added, "You don't know what you missed out on!"

And then I described, in luxuriant detail, a visit to the beaches at Marianao, in which Mella and I played around in the crystalline waters and swam out to sea, and rubbed each other on the back with our towels and finished off by drying stretched out under the scorching sun, chatting, at first, about topics relating to politics and, later, about many others. When my lover wanted to know, wary, what other topics, I answered ambiguously, "Life in general." I told him also that, when we were about to leave, the revolutionary had not hesitated to go into the same changing shack as me and shed his bathing trunks in front of me, exposing all his goods. "Which are good, indeed!" I insinuated. I waited and, on seeing that there were none of the questions that, under other circumstances, would arise after a comment of such nature, I decided to spice up the story. "To say that something happened, well, nothing happened, but . . . am I mistaken or is that *chico* on the very edge of the precipice and all he is waiting for is a little charitable push to dive in head first?" Not being able to hold it in anymore, Wen asked disdainfully what made me think so. "Everything," I answered at once. "But especially the rascally and mischievous way that he looks at me, as if there were something implicit between us," I specified.

"Congratulations," he said, and wanted to know the next time we were seeing each other.

"Tomorrow, I think," I answered and immediately added, magnanimously but without conviction, "you can come, if you want."

"No, thank you," he replied. "I have a lot to do and, as you know, I never really cared much for him."

Oh, Judas, God will punish you, I thought and took on the task of shattering that armor of false indifference. The first thing I did was to begin a long-winded description of the student's body, praising him with as many adjectives as came to mind. I offered plenty of details about the contrast between his wide and hefty shoulders and the narrowness of his waist; about his olive cast and the perfect size of the nipples that crowned his pectorals; about his flat, hard stomach, similar to one of those wooden chopping boards that Toña uses to chop vegetables on, garnished with a string of soft hairs that began at his belly button and was lost under his shorts and, lastly, about his shapely, muscular calves, worthy of a sculpture of a god carved by Praxiteles.

Since Wen very stubbornly continued not to show the slightest interest, I went on with Mella's topography, seasoning it with more revealing details. I mentioned that the young man possessed an ass that made one want to fall on one's knees before him and thank God for taking such care when creating it. As far as the front instrument was concerned, I guaranteed him that it wasn't a fife, nor a piccolo, nor even a *flûte d'amour,* but instead a true transverse flute, cylindrical with a golden mouthpiece, three octaves long, and not a single accessory missing. Had Bach, Handel, and Lully had a flute at their disposal like the one the student had, they would have used it much more often in their compositions, and Frederick the Great, the Prussian monarch who was so enchanted by the instrument, would have forced Johann Joachim Quantz to play it for him day and night, and found great delight in such expanse of beauty. I wasn't exaggerating in the slightest, no: all you had to do is take one look at the prodigious tube to want to emulate the Pied Piper of Hamelin, to bring it to your mouth and play it without stopping.

Despite the liveliness of my descriptions, Wen remained unmoved. As it had happened in previous strolls through the city, we randomly ended in front of the Noble Habana fountain. That afternoon, for whatever reason, the dolphins weren't shooting out their spouts of water. The fountain was dry.

"Maybe they're cleaning it," Wenceslao remarked, abandoning his silence.

"Probably," I conceded.

We sat on a bench, under the shade of a fig tree, and watched the passersby. Before us paraded shoeshine boys, lottery salesmen, policemen on foot and on horse, priests, nuns, office workers, clerks, thugs, and beggars. An ill-smelling gypsy approached us, her hair loose and a string of bells in the hem of her skirt, determined to read our fortune, but I frightened her away with a wicked look.

The heat was suffocating. Quite the "winter"! Fortunately, it was almost five and perhaps it would cool off by nightfall.

"Scissor's suits have a flawless cut," I opined, to break the silence.

"Perfect," he agreed in a low voice.

"You look very lovely in the one they are fixing up for you for tonight," I flirted, feeling suddenly sad and destitute. "I'll have to hire a bodyguard so they don't steal you from me."

He gave me a smile.

"I'm dying to kiss you," I added.

"What?"

"I want to give you a kiss, my love."

"So what are you waiting for, you fool?" he challenged. "Give it to me then."

I moved toward him, pretending that I was going to kiss him in public, and at that moment, he moved back, letting out a huge laugh. The gypsy, who loitered nearby, looked at us, intrigued; it seemed that she was considering the possibility of approaching us again, but, thinking it over, went on her way. I took a deep breath: the spell (a curse, it couldn't be any other thing) that a heartless witch or some envious sorcerer had cast on us to upset us and raise a thorny hedge between us was shattered.

"It was all a lie," I confessed.

He said he knew that.

"We went to the beach," I told him, "but the idiot didn't even bring a bathing suit. I had to go by myself in the water and content myself with how he waved at me from the sand. Afterwards he wanted me to tell him about the situation with the banana workers and I had no idea what to say. Then he began to rant and rave about imperialism, to tell me about what the conference 'The Failure of the Political System' should impart to the workers enrolled at the Universidad Popular and, what was worse, to talk about Oliva and how in love he is with his girl. Then he dragged me to a streetcar and insisted that I go with him to the local syndicate, on the other side of the world, to visit a certain Alfredo López, an unbearable printer and pseudo-anarchist, with a face that looked constipated. We were there for half an hour, surrounded by red flags and effigies of Lenin, when Baliño appeared, a senile old man who has to ask one foot permission before he moves the other, also a Communist, whom Mella introduced very respectfully, explaining that he was one of the exiles who signed the documents of constitution of the Cuban Revolutionary Party created by Martí in Key West. I don't even know how it happened, it could be that during the visit I dozed off a little too long or I made some not-so-manly gesture, but I am almost sure that the two men realized that I belonged to the other club. They started to look at me suspiciously and ask me trick questions about the Bogotá group of Bolsheviks from Silvestre Savitski's laundry, and to talk about the pestilence of the bourgeoisie who lead a life of dissipation and vice, not caring about the suffering of the people. Sick and tired of that pair of simpletons, I told Mella that I had some urgent things to take care of and fled that nest of Bolsheviks. It was a frightening morning!"

"Let's go the hotel," he proposed. "You owe me something and I want to collect with interest."

We arrived at the Inglaterra at the moment that Eleonora Duse crossed the lobby and we could watch her at our pleasure, for on that occasion she wasn't wearing a veil. The color of her skin struck us: she was beyond white; the actress seemed to be made of wax, transparent. She had rings around her eyes, and her face was no longer smooth as in the oft-seen pictures of yesteryear in Wenceslao's scrapbook. That being said, if not for her rejection of any type of cosmetics, she could very well have knocked some years off herself. Just dabbing a little color on her lips and her cheeks, and dyeing, as is the custom of women her age, her gray and wavy hair would be enough. As for the rest, her figure, while thin, was harmonious, and that afternoon, as opposed to the day of her arrival in the *Tivives,* she walked erect, with the lightness and flexibility of a young woman. The dress she was wearing was black, and, truth be told, it fit her horribly: too long up front and too short in the back. A real scarecrow. Beside her were the company's manager, Guido Carreras, and the unavoidable Katherine Garnett who fixed her eyes on her shoes to save herself the trouble of having to say hello to Wen. Behind them were María and Désirée, and I noticed that the latter was looking at us out of the corner of her eye, very curious. When La Signora passed by us, Wen bowed courteously. The tragedienne, glancing at him, flashed him a brief smile.

We waited and saw how the entourage went out, crossing San Rafael Street and heading for the back entrance of the Teatro Nacional, the same one we had used to go to Pedrito Varela's office to buy our series tickets. No one who was walking in the street paused to watch the actress. If somehow they had heard about the visit of the great Duse, they would never think that that somewhat slovenly señora of guarded appearance could be her. What a difference from what happened thirty years before in St. Petersburg, when her admirers carpeted the road from her hotel to the theater with rose petals! Or in Vienna, during the same period, where even the coach drivers excitedly applauded her from their seats, upon seeing her in the streets! When the Italian and her retinue turned the corner of Consulado and disappeared, Wenceslao remarked, "Seeing that plan A failed, we must put plan B into action."

Deducing that the said plan A was to get the help of Miss Katherine Garnett, I was curious about what the other one was. "The Austrian secretary and the Italian maid," he murmured. "Chocolates for both." And, very sure of himself, he remarked that even if many people undervalued the secret power of such servants, he wasn't thinking of making the same mistake. The secretary, for example, was crucial. She had been with La Duse since before the war, sharing with the actress the years of glory and the years of poverty. One comment from her, a phrase uttered at just the right moment, could guarantee our success.

My lover ran to the Manzana de Gómez to personally choose the chocolates and I went up to our room. I threw my shoes in a corner and undid my tie and suddenly discovered an envelope on the bed. There was nothing written on it, and so I opened it, very intrigued. What I found inside made the blood beat at my temples and forced me to sit down on the mattress. Wenceslao found me in just that posture, dejected and unnerved, when he returned to the room an hour later, after delivering a bunch of roses to La Duse's dressing room and giving instructions to Regla on how she was to give, in a discreet manner, a box of bonbons to the secretary and the maid each.

"What is wrong with you?" he exclaimed and grabbed the envelope from my hands. He pulled out the yellowy parchment, looked at it once, and let it fall on the floor, as if touching it would burn him. "Where in the hell did you get that from, Lucho Belalcázar?" he confronted me.

I shrugged, got up, picked up the manuscript by de Casal that we had previously seen framed in my uncle's house, and I put it back in its envelope. When he discovered that I had found it on top of the bed, Wenceslao picked up the phone and demanded an explanation from the employees at the reception desk, but they assured him that they had sent up no correspondence. Not satisfied with this, he summoned Regla immediately to the room and put her through a rigorous interrogation. The chambermaid swore and swore again that she did not know anything about the mystery.

"They did not come in with my key. Maybe they used the manager's key," she ventured.

As the infuriated Wenceslao got in touch with the management, determined to solve the mystery, I went into the bathroom and, strangely enough, I found the mirror above the sink all fogged up, as if someone had left the hot water running.

Standing in front of the glass, I noticed with growing astonishment, how over the misty surface of the mirror there began to appear, drawn with grace and agility by an invisible index finger, a string of letters. It was a message and no doubt it was addressed to me. Completely terrified, I wailed for Wenceslao, but as soon as he burst into the bathroom the steam disappeared and with it the six words that read seconds before, "Your uncle needs to see you."

"What's wrong?" Wen asked, shaken by my scream.

"Nothing," I replied sotto voce, embarrassed. "I think that you should stop asking questions. Let's just leave things as they are, I don't want to get involved with the police again."

He looked at me suspiciously.

"All right," he said, and returning to the chambermaid, ordered her to forget the situation with the envelope.

A little later, they called up and said that the messenger from La Boston had a package for us. It was the suits, wrapped in tissue paper, ironed masterfully and accompanied by a note written by Scissors: "Enjoy."

Wenceslao said he was going to take a bath, and I checked my watch. It was six-thirty, and I calculated that scrubbing his whole body with soap, washing his hair, and shaving would take him at least half an hour. As soon as I heard the water running, I told him that I was going out for a little walk and headed at full speed for Chinatown.

On arriving at Águila Street and stopping, out of breath, in front of the building marked 187, I was dumbstruck. The store window full of Chinese artifacts and the musical door of El Crisantemo Dorado were not there. In the space where the store had been there was a run-down, darkened restaurant. Surprised (not only by the mishap, but by the fact that the replacement did not seem so strange to me), I went into the shabby eatery and approached a foursome of Asians who were seated around a table playing dominoes. I was hoping one of them was the owner of the establishment that we had visited two days before, but none of them was so ancient.

"Good afternoon," I called out and, getting right to the point, I asked if any of them knew of the place called El Crisantemo Dorado. They said that they didn't, not really paying me too much attention, and noisily moved the domino pieces on the wooden surface. Before they lost themselves in the game again, I mentioned the name Fan Ya Ling. Did they know who he was? Where I could find him? They said no again, evidently annoyed, and began to chatter among themselves to let me know that they did not want to be bothered with any more questions.

I turned around and, without saying good-bye, letting myself be dragged by another irrational impulse, I ran to the Teatro *Chino* on Zanja Street. Once there, I beat on the front door, still closed, till a pair of men (one of them Chinese, the other Cuban) came to the door to see what the matter was. I asked them for José Chiang, but neither of them seemed to know him. I described him as best as I could and added that he had been at the theater on Sunday, during the performance of *The Fate of a Flower.* The guys laughed and said that that night there had been hundreds of people at the performance. "My friend, you're pushing it," the Cuban said. Since I continued to insist, each time more vehemently, they shut the door in my face, noticeably irritated. I tried to kick it in, to the surprise of some passersby, till the Chinese and the Cuban threatened to call the police. Suddenly realizing how demented I was acting, I apologized and, wanting to be swallowed up by the earth, left them.

With great strides and walking on the pavement to avoid the crowds on the sidewalks, I headed back for the Inglaterra. I got back to the room just as Wenceslao came out of the bathroom, rosy and clean-smelling, ready to dress. Luckily, the bath had taken fifteen minutes longer than expected.

"Where did you go?" he asked. "You're all sweaty."

"I was looking at the statue of Martí," I lied. "Have you noticed that it has its back to the theater?"

"Yes," he said, not paying much attention to me. "But you have to hurry."

I obediently took off my clothes and stepped without delay into the bathtub. I let the water run over my entire body. From the door, as he dressed, Wenceslao watched me critically. Little did it help that I made a great effort to hide my belly.

"You've gotten fat," he pronounced with disapproval and, changing course suddenly, grumbled. "I don't how that damn paper ended up here, but I am sure of one thing: it was your uncle's doing."

I asked him why he would want us to have it.

"Perhaps he wants it in a safe place," he conjectured. "Or as a sign that he is alive, to get in touch with you."

I was about to tell him about the mirror and what I had found in Chinatown, but I held my tongue. It would only make him worry and ruin the night he had waited for with such anticipation.

At eight-thirty, radiant as two princes going to a ball at the palace, we crossed San Rafael and arrived at the entrance of the Teatro Nacional, where De la Cruz punctually awaited us. As much as the poor man had taken great pains to hussy himself up for the occasion, it had done little to improve his appearance. Seeing him, so puny and big-nosed, I remembered something my mother used to say: "You can dress a monkey in silk, but that won't change the monkey's ilk." If he had been there that night, Juan María Vengoechea would have sworn, without the slightest hesitation, that it was no accident that we allowed such an unattractive specimen in our company but, in fact, we used him to serve a specific purpose: to enhance our own good appearance. But of course, modesty aside, neither my charms, nor Wen's, which are obvious and indisputable, need to be underlined with tricks of the sort.

With our companion, and not without a certain intensity of feeling, we went into the theater. I am not exaggerating when I say that on stepping into the carpeted lobby, I had the impression that I had crossed a magic barrier and was entering not a theater in the Caribbean, but instead one of the most elegant salons in Vienna or Paris. A wide, marble staircase led to an exquisitely decorated foyer with white columns and abounding with numerous mirrors on the walls. I noticed, with great pleasure, that the ladies and gentlemen who surrounded us were all very refined. Compared with such lavishness, the Colón in Bogotá was a tiny, provincial theater. As I casually and approvingly observed myself in one of the mirrors, Fontana, the social chronicler whom we had met at the Montes de la Oca's party, came over to say hello and introduced us to the theater critic José Pérez Poldarás, who would write about the performance for *Diario de la Marina.*

"In truth, the review is already mostly written," Poldarás remarked. "I just have to drop by the editorial offices, after the show, to add a few finishing touches. It begins like this: 'La Duse, the immortal Eleonora, could say, like the victorious Corsican Austerlitz and Jena, like Napoleon Bonaparte: "Time and I are twin lions; but I am the first-born." ' "

At that moment, a person who had just come up the stairs walked over to De la Cruz and gave him a slap on the back. The men from the *Diario de la Marina* scattered as if they had seen Lucifer himself, and on noticing how upset we were by the whole thing, Emilio tried to calm us down: "They can't stand the sight of Genaro Corzo."

The newly arrived gentleman, also theatrical columnist, but for *El Heraldo,* offered a cordial hand.

"I don't know if I'll stay till the door closes," he said, alluding to the title of the play by Mario Praga that would be staged that night, adding, "since I want to stop by the Principal de la Comedia to see the last act at least of María Tubau's debut in *A campo traviesa.*"

Wenceslao's polite smile disappeared immediately and he warned the critic that it wasn't right to grant the same status to the fireflies as to the stars. De la Cruz and I burst out laughing to mitigate the rudeness and, somewhat in a huff, Genaro Corzo continued on his way into the theater.

We followed behind. A young usher led us, through a red-carpeted hallway, to our seats. An enormous chandelier hung from the ceiling like a luminous arachnid on a thread. The orchestra wasn't completely full, but the *grilles* and the box seats were. When I asked the usher the capacity of the theater, he said two thousand people. "And how many will be here today?" I wanted to know, but the young man shrugged and said that he didn't know.

Pedrito Varela hadn't lied to us: our seats were among the best. After settling in and pulling out his opera glasses for a quick look around, Emilito stated that the cream of the crop of Havana society was there. The leader of the republic, Dr. Alfredo Zayas, was there with the first lady, María Jaén. The Italian ambassador and his wife, a skeletal old woman, accompanied them. But other members of the diplomatic corps, all dressed to the nines, were also there to enjoy the genius's art: ambassadors from Germany, France, Spain, England, and China, each with their consorts. On seeing the Chinese ambassador, I couldn't help but jump up in my seat, because he looked unbelievably like the fat José Chiang. He had the same jowl, the same pug nose, the same mocking expression in his fleshy mouth. Could it be, in fact, the real diplomat, or was it an impostor? I almost excused myself to get nearer to him in order to study him up close and remove all doubt, but what I did instead was to grab the glasses from Wenceslao and focus them on him. After I studied him carefully, the similarities didn't seem so great and, thinking myself crazy, I rejected the outlandish idea.

Emilito elbowed me to let me know that Madame Buffin was waving at us with her fan from a box seat on the right side of the theater. Beside her was Habib Steffano, the professor from Damascus who was helping her put together the Ball of a Thousand and One Nights, and a beautiful woman with huge black eyes. "The Syrian's wife," Emilito said, adding, "From what they say, she will be Scheherezade at the ball."

"And the caliph, have they chosen him?" Wen wanted to know.

"Not yet, but there are various candidates that can stop traffic," our friend whispered and caught us up on the names of other distinguished persons who were present at the function. Some, like Teté Bances de Martí, the wife of the apostle's son, and Fernando Ortiz, we remembered from the Montes de la Oca's party or the presentation of *The Reliquary.* But also at the theater that night were José Raúl Capablanca, the Cuban chess champion, who soon would travel to New

York to defend his title against the Russian Alekhin and the Yankee Marshall, both of them kings of the learned game in their respective countries; Rita Montaner de Fernández, a light-skinned *mulata,* with a mole in the middle of her forehead, married to a lawyer who, days before, during a tribute to His Majesty King Alfonso XIII, had electrified the audience gathered at El Casino Español by playing various songs on the piano, peerlessly, and later singing like an angel; and, recently arrived in Cuba and surrounded by a cloud of suffragists, Mrs. Carrie Chapman Catt, the most famous *gringa* battler for the right of women to vote, whom the mayor of Havana, on behest of a group of ladies, had just declared honorary citizen.

Four countesses represented the blazons of Havana nobility: Buenavista, Rivero, Castillo, and Jaruco; while the abundant band of millionaire plebeians was headed by, among others, María Luisa Menocal de Arguelles, Antonio Rodríguez Feo, and Federico and Josefina Kohly. Not unnoticed by our eagle eyes was the presence of Mimí Aguglia, who wasn't performing that evening, and who, in Wen's opinion, had attended her countrywoman's premiere to see if she could learn something about the art of acting to put into effect the following day. We also did not miss Dulce María and Carlos Manuel Loynaz, accompanied this time by their sister Flor and another older family member. "The kid is a bonbon, that's for sure, but he can't match Enrique, the other boy in the family," Monkeyface made sure to point out, just as Generala Lachambre had done. And on remembering the old muse of the modernists, I looked for her everywhere in vain. Could she be seated, perhaps, in a box on the second floor?

Wen warned me, with a whisper, of the proximity of Olavo Vázquez Garralaga. His mother accompanied the rhymester, for a change, and he was in a box adjacent to the suffragists and had his back to us, in an ostensible show of rudeness. Next to them was a sensual, dark-haired beauty with prominent curves, whom De la Cruz identified as the bard's fiancée, a fact that bent us over with laughter.

Since the actors would be speaking in Italian, Wenceslao found it necessary to lay out the plot of *La porta chiusa* for us. Emilito and I listened to him silently. The young man Giulio Querceta (the role to be played by Memo Benassi) finds out, by chance and with understandable horror, that he is not the son of the man whose last name he bears and by whose side, unaware of the lie, he has grown up. In truth, his father is none other than Decio Piccardi, an old lover of his mother and now a close friend of the family. Upon discovering himself to be the fruit of adultery, he is overcome with terrible anxiety, and thousands of contradictory feelings begin to disturb him. Giulio would love to bring the truth to light, but finds it impossible because of social conventions. The love he has for his mother and the respect he has for the maker of his days make him accept the necessity to prevent a scandal. Yet, at the same time, he cannot stand the misery that is consuming him: he cannot go on living in the house of the one who is not his true father, enjoying all his goods, and because of this, in a fit of desperation, he decides to undertake a journey to Africa. Before fleeing, he confesses to Signora Querceta the state of his soul. The poor mother, overwhelmed by an inexpressible sorrow, desolately sees him off.

As if it were necessary, Wen made clear that Eleonora Duse would undertake the difficult role of Bianca Querceta, the virtuous mother, once-respected adulteress, and added that, according to the judgment of the *gringo* critics, it was impossible to express in a more impassioned manner the pain of a remorseful woman who had redeemed her sin with a virtuous life but whose error weighed like a slab of marble on her son's life. The other characters would be played by very accomplished actors: Leo Orlandi would give life to Piccardi and Gino Galvani to Ippolito Querceta, the false father unaware of the tragedy. María Morino would play Mariolina, the young woman, and Alfredo Robert, the abbot Ludovico. Finished with his detailed synopsis, Wenceslao turned to the curtain and ignored us, trying perhaps to guess what was going on behind the velvet cascade the color of old gold. His hands were sweating, and I understood that he was excited by the imminent fulfillment of one of his great wishes.

Just before the cannon fire at nine o'clock made us jump in our seats and the bells announced the beginning of the performance, the only box seat remaining empty on the first floor was occupied by María Cay, who sat in her seat, alone, erect and elegant. Without exchanging greetings with anyone, or looking around, she became engrossed in reading the program. Dressed in black, with fiery ruby earrings and brooch, the Cuban-Japanese lady was a paragon of class.

The house lights dimmed and, amid excited stares and last coughs from the audience, the curtain rose. The stage showed the living room of a bourgeois house in Italy at the turn of the century and various actors were already on stage, standing or seated on the furniture, as if they were in the middle of a conversation.

"It is her!" Wen blabbered, pinching me on the thigh, upon realizing that La Signora was already on stage. I imagine that the rest of the audience, used to the triumphant and dramatic entrances of leading ladies (orchestrated to provoke cheers and ovations) was a bit thrown off by that unusual and unimpressive appearance. But, on realizing that before them was La Duse, the famous Italian actress, the mythic rival of La Bernhardt, the audience broke into applause, at first timidly, but quickly with growing enthusiasm. Eleonora remained still, in a dress that to me was the same one in which we had seen her leave for the theater. Without even the slightest sign that she noticed it, she waited, with the rest of the cast, for the warm reception to end. Once silence had been restored, the performance began.

What can I say about that first time? After listening so often to all kinds of marvels about La Duse's art and reading in the silver and mother-of-pearl scrapbook dozens of opinions about her style of acting, finally I was watching the actress with my own eyes. Did she fulfill my expectations? For a few seconds I felt as if the world were spinning around me and I wouldn't be able to see what was happening on stage, but slowly I calmed down and, putting my hand on Wen's forearm, I was able to concentrate on the spectacle.

Almost without drawing a breath, I waited for the first minutes to pass, during which the actress moved about on stage, speaking indifferently, as any matron would within the four walls of her house, in the presence of family or friends. Not knowing it, I was under the impression that after that prologue Eleonora would begin *to act*. In spite of the fact that, on the last night of 1923, Aníbal de Montemar had warned us that the miracle of the actress was to be found precisely in that "acting as if you weren't acting" well into the first act, I continued to wait, stupid me, for La Duse to justify her fame as a tragedienne by fainting or with some other bombastic gesture or great expression of sorrow. Those grand words or actions never came, but gradually the magic of her simplicity seduced us. Forgetting about the arched eyebrows and stabbing hands that would have been offered by any other prima donna, we fell like flies into the thin invisible web that the actress, an old and shrewd spider, wove on stage. The lack of makeup on her face helped create the illusion of perfect naturalness and, without having to project it in an artificial manner, her voice reached every corner of the theater.

For half an hour I paid as keen attention to the great Eleonora as I remember ever paying to anyone. And I say "to the great Eleonora" because, even if I made sure to lose none of the details of the plot and to capture the meaning of the speeches spoken in Italian, it has to be said that the whole production revolved around her. The rest of the actors limited themselves to fulfilling, without much pretension, their duties, and it seemed as if the example of the leading lady served as a barrier to prevent them from any excessive histrionics. The scenes in which La Duse did not appear became periods of waiting, pauses in which the audience could take a deep breath. But as soon as La Signora returned, without her encouraging it or doing anything to achieve it, the audience would be hanging on the expressions that crossed her tired and pallid face, her slightest gesture, the inflections of her voice, and even to her stillnesses and her silences. La Duse managed to manifest any state of mind with great delicacy: sometimes, through the slow poetic movements of her long-fingered hands, which were still beautiful and suggestive; other times, it sufficed with a look, or with an almost imperceptible trembling of her lips.

The end of the first act provoked an emotional torrent of applause. The curtain rose several times so that, first the diva and then the rest of the actors, and then she alone, could step forward to receive, amid *bravos* and *bravíssimos,* the welcoming from the Havana public. When the ovations finally ended, Wenceslao let out a deep breath, as if he had just gone through a mystical experience, and, strange as it might seem, he, who so much liked to chat and flirt during the intermissions, said he would stay in the box.

"You go," he murmured. "Believe me when I say that I am exhausted."

Leaving him on his own, De la Cruz and I went down to the lobby to smoke, and there we ran into Bartolomé Valdivieso, who was jumping with joy, for before the start of the performance Fortune Gallo had told him that Thursday he would take him to La Signora's chambers, so he could give her the sonnet, "Eleonora the Sublime."

"An occasion on which I will say a word on your part," he promised before vanishing.

Since De la Cruz had gone off to say hello to some acquaintances, I went back up the stairs and for a while walked around by myself, first in the foyer, where there was barely any room, and then in the hallways, listening to countless praises for La Duse. I said hello to María Cay in her box. She shook my hand with a cool courtesy and, as if she were an entirely different person from the one who had made us dizzy with her stories in the Ideal Room, she hardly said a word to me. It caught my attention that she did not ask whether I had been able to make contact with my uncle. Or could it be that she was all too informed about everything and her coldness had something to do with our mentioning her name to the secret police? I said good-bye, feeling awkward, and went back to Wen to list for him all the adjectives that I had overheard during my walk: unprecedented, majestic, marvelous, chimerical, one of a kind. . . . They were all dazzled by the actress's genius.

"The best is yet to come," he replied scornfully. "They should save their praises for the next act, when Giulio tells his mother that he is leaving."

At that moment Corzo, the critic from *El Heraldo,* came into the box and asked us what we thought. To my surprise, he wrote down in a notebook whatever Wenceslao said and two or three silly remarks that I contributed, and then disappeared.

The performance continued and, true enough, the audience rabidly applauded the scene in which the son, at the feet of Bianca Querceta, tries to persuade her that to put an end to the anguish in his soul, he must leave the country. During the following intermission, we couldn't remove Wen from his seclusion and, leaving him in a state bordering on ecstasy, Monkeyface and I went to visit Mina López-Salmón de Buffin in her box. The millionairess received us effusively, leaving an old man with whom she had been engaged in a lively chat with the words caught in his mouth, her attention focused on us, or specifically me. She introduced us to Dr. Steffano and his wife, Adela, and, pointing to the lady, murmured mischievously: "Our seductive Scheherezade." Looking this way and that, as if half the theater didn't know it already, she warned, "But don't tell anyone, I beg you." We swore that we would mention "the secret" to no one, and immediately Madame Buffin proclaimed that the Ball of a Thousand and One Nights would be ruined if a certain two gentlemen from Bogotá whose names she did not want to mention did not attend (accepting her compliment with a smile, I wondered if the old woman had the slightest idea what our names were) and, finally, she gushed with flattery for La Duse, underlining the fact that the performance was incomparable.

As the gossip continued, I glanced toward our box and saw that now the theater critic from the *Diario de la Marina* was there, seated next to Wenceslao and taking down everything he said. "I gave him some ideas for his review," he confirmed seconds before the curtain rose for the third and final act. During this part of the performance, I noticed that Emilio De la Cruz was making a superhuman effort to keep his eyes open and was beginning to nod off. I felt for him: a bout of sleepiness during a play is horrible. The eyelids rebel, the eyes get crossed, the head wants to hang forward or backward, the neck turns to rubber and, what's worse, one knows he is playing the fool and everyone is watching.

But Monkeyface wasn't the only one who, exhausted by the length of the play, by boredom or the unintelligible chatter of the Italians, struggled against the onslaught of Morpheus. The same was happening to Carrie Chapman Catt, the Spanish ambassador, the editor of *El Figaro,* and La Montaner's husband, who every once in a while beat their chests with their chins and had to be awakened by their concerned and embarrassed companions. As far as the Countess Buenavista was concerned, her situation was dismal: the respectable matron, sprawled out in her seat, was peacefully snoring. I noticed also, that in the orchestra there were more empty seats than at the beginning. It seems that part of the refined and cultured audience had taken advantage of the last intermission to escape with the utmost discretion. I imagined that the following day, the fugitives would tell their friends about the unforgettable performance and chide them for not having attended.

The scene with which the play ended was, in my judgment, the culminating moment of La Signora's performance. The bitter smile with which she said good-bye to her son as he left for Africa, where it was possible to catch a glimpse of Bianca Querceta's secret anguish and mourning, made it clear that, in spite of the years and physical deterioration her art was still of the highest caliber. I tapped Wenceslao so that he could see how La Aguglia was weeping in her box, but he raised an eyebrow and scolded me harshly. "She's acting to catch the eye of fools like you. Keep your eye on the stage and forget about that one."

The entire audience (President Zayas and his wife Mariíta included) jumped to their feet to bestow on La Duse and her troops shouts of admiration and a final ovation that lasted ten minutes. Several flower arrangements (among them, the one sent by Wen) were placed at the foot of the old woman, who took a lily, kissed it calmly, and placed it on the stage as a sign of her gratitude.

Out in the foyer, we saw Bartolomé Valdivieso with a small group of ladies and gentlemen, among which were the Loynaz brothers. The *mulato* made a discreet signal for us to approach. An elegant and enthusiastic individual (under his breath, De la Cruz informed us he was Francisco Ichaso, a journalist from the *Diario de la Marina*) was responding to a señora who was not pleased with the diva's gray hair and lack of makeup.

"La Duse's art is based precisely on the simple decision to not wear makeup," Ichaso argued convincingly. "She doesn't paint her face and doesn't paint her spirit. The one and the other appear on stage with the same simplicity, plainness, and naturalness as in day-to-day life. The very act of smearing the face with rouge, lipstick, or white lead denotes a certain degree of insincerity."

"Then, according to you, all women are insincere," the lady protested.

"Don't misinterpret my words, I beg you. I am referring to the world of the stage, to actresses who don't dare show their faces as they are and cover them up with the lies of makeup."

"But the same thing happens in life," Dulce María Loynaz noted in a soft voice, leaning on her brother's arm, "and not only with women. From a moral point of view, we also smear our spirits, afraid to show them naked to others."

"Well, that pretense that you see in life becomes an invariable norm when we move from the farce of the world to the world of farce," the Italian's champion continued. "Convention, lies, and artistic hypocrisy are all predominant in the theater, and Eleonora Duse has fled from all three in her artistic life."

"From that," Wenceslao interjected, taking a step forward, "and from conformity in diction, in gesture, in stage dynamics, that are as malignant, if not more so, than makeup."

Ichaso looked at him, glad to have an ally, and continued his line of defense.

"That is why the actress appears on stage with her snowy head and her wrinkled face. The truth doesn't need makeup."

"But is it appropriate to talk about *truth* when referring to a stage production?" Flor Loynaz protested impatiently. "Señora Duse is marvelous, but her art does not disguise, after all, what it is: the theater!"

"A superior theater, my girl," Chacón y Calvo, a gentleman that we remembered from the presentation of *The Reliquary,* specified kindly.

"Agreed, good sir," the adolescent conceded respectfully, "but to say the theater, even when talking about a marvelous experience like tonight's, is to say artifice, simulacrum . . ."

"Lies?" Chacón y Calvo added with a touch of irony.

"Yes," the younger Loynaz deemed with a certain dose of arrogance. "Lies. Harsh as the word may seem."

"But . . . what kind of lie?" her brother Carlos Manuel interjected timidly. "St. Augustine distinguished eight types of lies and the fifth type was the lie to recreate."

The conversation then shifted to the nature of truth. Could what we had just seen be classified as such?

"What we saw and heard, what we perceived tonight, is not truth but an illusion," Dulce María opined, steeling herself with courage. "An illusion of reality."

"I would rather call it an artistic truth," Ichaso said.

"To my understanding," Chacón y Calvo interrupted, "the greatest aspiration of an actor is to persuade the audience that what he is presenting is real."

"Real, my good man, but not necessarily naturalistic," Alejo Carpentier, the baby-faced journalist from the magazine *Social,* who also had been at Gerbelasa's party and spoke dragging his *r*s, refuted. "In the theater, the eagerness to approach a semblance of reality could become a burden for the emotional part of the art."

"I think that sensation of truth that La Duse evokes emanates not only from external appearances but from an internal search for honesty," Wenceslao reflected.

"On that we agree, my friend," Ichaso expressed. "But could any common actress, with dentures and makeup, transmit that sincerity that emanates from deep within?"

"I must insist that to label her art as the truth is not only excessive but unnecessary," Flor explained, her cheeks flushed. "When art aspires to reproduce the truth, it is always an imitation, given that truth is not a tangible quality, but an abstraction, something nebulous that comes from the consciousness and experience of each person."

"You are all getting away from the subject!" Chacón y Calvo protested. "It is not about labeling things, but it is clear that in La Duse's performance there is a pursuit of realism."

"Yes, but in the end, what is reality?" Ichaso laughed. "Nobody knows for sure. Is reality a sort of personal dream that exists dependent on the human spirit, or does it exist whether we perceive it or not? Remember what Descartes said: 'Sometimes I dream . . . or am I always dreaming?' "

"I think that Señorita wants to make us see," I dared butt in, to see if I could put an end to this discussion that threatened to go on forever, "that La Duse is no servile copyist of reality, but instead someone who wants to move others, touch the spirit, to create and not simply to reproduce life with gleams of truth," and I searched for the younger Loynaz's approval. "Am I wrong?"

"Oh, no, you're not wrong," she answered, her eyes shining, "you have expressed it in a very clear and precise manner."

"Let us say then, dear friends, that tonight Eleonora Duse has shown us a lie," the journalist from *Diario de la Marina* said in a conciliatory manner, and then added mischievously, "That adorable lie that we call art." And we all laughed.

"But then, what is La Duse's secret?" the señora who wasn't in accord with the actress's disdain of cosmetics inquired.

Francisco Ichaso scratched an ear, an expression of dismay on his face, before he answered. "The secret? That's a difficult one! I don't think that there is a secret, since everything is on display. Her art consists, it seems to me, of having understood that the emotional energy of words is not in the emphasis with which they are enunciated but in the tone and nuance with which they are uttered."

"And in that, a subtle, suggestive gesture could be more expressive than a violent, sensational grimace," Wen added.

"Another thing that caught my attention was her pauses," Ichaso continued. "Did you notice that when she is silent in the middle of a dialogue, there is suspense, as we wait for the words to pour forth from her mouth? In Eleonora's art, the silence is as important as the word."

"Like in music," Carpentier corroborated.

Bartolomé Valdivieso, who, like De la Cruz and the person who accompanied the Loynazes, had not uttered a word, now took the opportunity to introduce us to his countrymen and tell them that we had traveled all the way from Bogotá to see La Duse.

"And was it worth it?" Carlos Manuel asked courteously.

"I would go to the end of the world to see her," Wen replied, looking him directly in the eye, and thinking that the absent Loynaz might be twenty-five thousand times more divine, but the one we had in front of us, rosy and long-limbed, with that pair of coffee-colored eyes, was a true delicacy.

"You will not have to go far," Dulce María observed, grabbing her brother as if she sensed he was exposing himself to great danger. "Next Saturday you will find her here again, transformed into Señora Alving."

"Ibsen and Duse! What a combination!" Chacón y Calvo pointed out. "Come prepared to see a torrent of moral beauty!"

"And all other sorts of beauty, I hope," Ichaso stressed.

The group broke up and everyone went their way. We were the last ones to leave the theater. When we got to Louvre Street, in front of the Inglaterra, with Emilio De la Cruz, he mentioned that having fed the spirit, it wouldn't be a bad idea to give some nourishment to the body. Wenceslao accepted gladly and, led by our tropical Virgil, we closed out the night sinking our teeth into some gargantuan pork sandwiches and sipping martinis and manhattans at the bar of the Plaza Hotel.

There are two types of dreams, those that you have when you are asleep and those that are born in the vigil.

To dream while asleep is like being a prisoner. You are tied down, unable to escape the world where you have arrived. You struggle, you try to escape, but you are stuck there. Sometimes I dream that I am a girl again, that I am with my parents in some town where we are performing. My mother bathes me, the ears especially; she combs my hair with care, dresses me in my finest clothes, Sunday shoes, and takes me by the hand to school. The teacher welcomes me with a look that wants to be kind and sits me not on a bench with the other kids, but on a chair near her desk. Then the class continues, and I try to catch every single one of her words, not to notice how the others look at me, whisper, and laugh. "The actors' daughter, the actors' daughter," they murmur and point at me. Why doesn't the teacher scold them? Why doesn't she get up and protect me? Why does she pretend not to notice? I want to disappear. Turn into smoke and escape through the open window, and dissolve in the country air. I want to run and hide in the dark, pestilent room where I live with my parents. But I can't, just as I can't escape this dream.

If I had the choice, I would only dream when I am awake. They are dreams born from a reason or an emotion, never by chance. Yet I do not agree with those who say that I am a hopeless dreamer. I have had some dreams, yes, like everyone. But not as many as they think. Some I fulfilled, others burst on the way. I dreamed of being a famous actress and, right before I nearly gave up, I achieved it. One fine day my name was atop the billboards, they began to talk about me, to publish articles, to write plays for me. I dreamed of lasting love and that dream, in contrast, never came true. I dreamed of a theater, an open-air amphitheater *where I could make art, not having to worry about ticket sales or having to please the ignorant and fickle public, and that one also did not come true.*

Some dreams end up as nightmares, like mine to create a refuge for actresses.

It happened before the war. In those years, while I was removed from the theater (forever, I thought then), it occurred to me to found and maintain a place where young actresses could stay during seasons when they were not working. A modest place, clean and pleasant, with many, many books. A respectable hostel, where they could rest for a few months, gather their strength, and nurture each other till the storms passed. The idea came to me while I was thinking of my own life, the many times that I wanted to say, "Enough! I need a little bit of time, a lull to decide where I want to go," and I couldn't do it, for who guarantees an actress a roof over her head and hot food while she decides the course of her career?

So, convinced that it was a laudable project and that it was worthwhile to put money and effort into it to make it real, I looked and I looked till I found an ideal place: a Roman villa in Piazza Caprera. I sent furniture from my house in Florence there, and several boxes full of books that I had collected in my years of travel, and I began to put together, with the help of Désirée, the Casa delle Attrici. That was the name I chose. Beautiful, no?

I invited certain people of distinction to sit on the executive committee, but, to my surprise (how naive I was, till just recently!), not even actresses were excited about the idea. Including the shameless Ema Gramatica, who dared tell the papers that she thought the house a tremendous foolishness. If her sister Irma thought the same thing, at least she had the decency not to say a word, perhaps remembering the years when I furthered her career by letting her play the role of Bianca María in the debut of *La città morta*. But the long-tongued Ema talked and talked, telling anyone who would listen that such a thing was a useless whim of mine, that I'd forgotten what it was like to be an actress in those times. In the end, so many outrageous things were published in the press, so much mockery and disdainful comments, that I became annoyed and took the criticisms as a challenge, and that made me go forward, alone, not listening to anyone.

I hired a librarian to organize the books, and a guard. The house was inaugurated with a ceremony. It was pretty, with five or six small, well-lit rooms, each with a bed with white sheets; a big kitchen; and many, many books. But, just as they had predicted, no one came there to seek refuge. Actresses, in fact, care about almost anything except a place to rest and read and refine their spirit. Some came, but only to ask for money.

I considered moving to live there with Désirée, but we never did. We were horrified of staying alone in an empty house, without electricity, in an out-of-the-way, dark neighborhood. We rented two rooms in the Eden Hotel, and there I finally convinced myself that this dream, too, like many others I had to abandon throughout the course my life, was not viable. With some honorable exceptions, actresses and books are not compatible. The majority of the actresses that I have known have only read the plays that they performed. And not completely, no, only their parts, to memorize them! Since then, I have stopped worrying about them. Not that I am indifferent, or that I don't try to help them: there are the Morinos, Jone and María, they are proof of that. I try to polish them, make them understand that during a performance the important thing is not to move fluently, nor to enunciate properly, nor to look beautiful, but to feel the gift. I watch them, I scold them, I congratulate them, but they are no longer in my dreams.

What was I talking about? Oh, yes, the Casa. I then

asked Désirée to send the books back to Florence, but I changed my mind straightaway and decided to donate them to a public library. The same with the furniture, it went to charity. That was the end of a dream that was short-lived and the beginning of a war that lasted too long.

9

The morning after the premiere we slept very late and sent up for breakfast in bed. As usual, Regla brought the telegrams that La Duse was sending to her daughter and various friends in New York, Paris, London, and several Italian cities, so that we could look at them. For the most part, they were messages of little importance, such as "I miss you" or "Thankfully, the weather is better."

"She's going to go broke sending so many telegrams," I said.

When the chambermaid would not leave, I asked her if she had anything to tell us, and she informed us that while La Duse's secretary had accepted Wen's chocolates gratefully, asking, in fact, who sent them, the reaction of the maid ("she's such a *pesaá*") had been very different. La Avogadro not only rejected the gift without opening it, but also threatened Regla, in broken Spanish, that she would complain to the management of the Inglaterra if it were to happen again.

"What do I do with the chocolates, sir?" a chastened Regla wanted to know.

"Eat them and enjoy them," Wen replied, not thinking much of the matter, and, sliding a bill into her apron, hurried her out.

Seated on the bed, we read the reviews of *La porta chiusa*. In *El Heraldo,* in a deplorable failure of the imagination, Genaro Corzo titled his article "Duse Debuts," while in the *Diario de la Marina,* in a similar vein, José Pérez Poldarás headed his with "Eleonora's Debut." Both writers used, without the slightest scruple, Wen's comments. Corzo wrote: "In the great tragedienne's glances, in her smile, in every single one of her actions there is an indescribable power of suggestion. Her voice, dulcet and sorrowful, remains pure and sonorous." And Poldarás went on: "In her irreproachable enunciation, where feelings palpitate, there is a loyal correspondence to the emotional state, to the sad gesture; but it is in her pauses, in silence, where La Duse proves that she is Eleonora, and that there are none like her."

Annoyed that the writer of *El Heraldo* had finished his review by labeling the actress "an exceptional comedienne," Wenceslao swore never again to "help" such a dolt again. He was a little happier with Poldarás, who finished up with an acknowledgment of his source. "The cultured and educated public last night made a brave show of their artistic refinement by paying La Duse a great tribute. *La porta chiusa* was not for the Havana audience, great fans of the eminent tragedienne, 'the closed door,' but instead an open door to glory."

That thirtieth of January, La Duse remained holed up in her room without receiving anyone. She didn't even allow her employees to open the door to Fortune Gallo when he came knocking, accompanied by Guido Carreras, insisting that they had important decisions to make. The producer had no choice other than to scream, in front of the *porta* unyieldingly *chiusa,* while on the other side the efficient Désirée wrote down the messages to give to Eleonora so that, later, she could respond by telephone. From our half-open door, we heard, first, Gallo's protests, and right after the words Carreras sought to calm him, explaining to him that after performance La Signora was a ball of nerves. No, please, it was nothing personal! He could swear on that. Eleonora was always like this, with all her producers. Even Schurmann, the Dutchman who wrote a biography of her and who, it was said, was able to put up with so much, because, aside from being a producer, he was also a psychiatrist and a diplomat.

Gallo's prime concern was the tour's program, since the four functions in Havana had been cut to three. Which of the announced plays would be canceled? To cancel *Spettri,* which was scheduled for Saturday, would be a slap in the face of the Havana public. He thought best to cancel either *La città morta* or *Cosi sia.* After further discussion, which we couldn't quite hear, Gallo concluded by mentioning the son of a senator, a poet, who wanted to give the actress a sonnet written in her honor. Could La Signora give him five minutes? The young man idolized her and he had *so* insisted.

Désirée promised to get back to him as soon as possible and said good-bye with an affectionate *au revoir, Monsieur Gallo.* The producer turned and, without waiting for the elevator, went, cursing, down the stairs, followed by the manager.

That Wednesday, Wenceslao continued his plans to soften the servants. Since, because of shyness or an acute sense of modesty, La Avogadro seemed allergic to strangers, he concentrated on Désirée. He ordered a dazzling orchid from El Clavel to be delivered that afternoon and put Regla in charge of getting it to the secretary. His objective, he said, was to be able to get a letter into the hands of La Signora.

"A letter so beautiful, so full of life and sincere, so clearly emanating from the depths of the soul, that La Duse will have no choice but to be moved, and, encouraged by Désirée, who will only have good things to say about us, she will agree to see us. And once with her, we will ask for our interview."

I nodded, so as not to seem a killjoy, and asked what the letter would say.

"I don't have the slightest idea," he replied ipso facto. "You are writing it, my dear, so make sure you squeeze the tears out of La Signora."

It would be easier to squeeze blood from a stone, I thought and said that I would begin to consider the content of the letter.

Another one of the informants recruited into Wenceslao's secret service, a young polyglot, thin and with a face full of pimples, who worked the morning shift at the telephones of the Inglaterra, got in touch with his *"jefe,"* to give him the latest news. Désirée had called Gallo to tell him that, as far as the cancellation of the play was concerned, La Signora preferred to dispense with *Cosi sia.* As far as the senator's son went, she would receive him, briefly, the following day, Thursday, *très tôt.*

"What luck!" Wenceslao murmured. "I hope that he keeps his word and says something about us."

After lunch we decided to take a walk. The night before we had heard of the annual exhibit of paintings in the gallery of fine arts, so we went to see it. Since the headquarters of the Association of Painters and Sculptors was a few blocks away, at 44 Prado, we walked.

The exhibition was good, especially a sculpture titled "The Eternal Kiss," by a certain Mateu, and the portrait of a woman who reminded us awfully of Juanma Vengoechea's mother.

On leaving the gallery, we ran into Rogelio and Armando Valdés, two brothers whom we had met during our visit to the university stadium. They were both heading to the Academy of Sciences, for one of their fellow students was singing a Puccini aria in a sort of gathering taking place there, and not knowing why, we allowed them to convince us to come along.

The auditorium was full of ladies of all ages and types: the gathering in question was a tribute for Mrs. Chapman Catt, the champion suffragist. The members of the male sex couldn't have numbered more than a dozen.

After the performance of two lively damsels who assaulted a Steinway piano with all their strength, our acquaintances' friend climbed up on stage to sing, backed by one of the bangers, *"Un bel di, vedremo,"* from the second act of *Madame Butterfly*. To my surprise, for nothing good was to be expected from the woman's timid manner and scrawny body, she had such a beautiful voice that she made us forget her horrific accompanist.

When they announced that the speeches would commence, we whispered to the Valdéses that we had to go, and tried to escape, but we soon noticed that several suffragists with the attitude and bodies of firemen stood in front of the exit, their arms crossed belligerently, determined not to allow anyone to escape, come what may. So, intimidated by their stern glares, we returned to our seats to listen to the speakers.

First to speak was Señora Morlón de Menéndez, president of the women's associations in Havana, who welcomed the *gringa* and announced that the visitor would be on the Island for a week to see for herself the state of local women's lives. Afterwards, a young woman recited a poem about the importance of giving women access to the voting booth, and lastly it was the eminent guest's turn. Amid warm applause, La Chapman and her translator rose to the podium. Lean, unpainted, and exasperatingly lively, the distinguished foreigner began by expressing her joy to be finally in one of the few civilized nations that she had never before visited, warning that her speech would be short, after which she spewed out a harangue of almost an hour's length about women's progress and the right to vote. Every so often, her diatribe was interrupted by applause. Since neither Wen nor I once moved our hands to clap, we noticed that the ladies around us were watching us sullenly and I feared that that horde of skirts would soon pounce on us, the representatives of the Enemy, to avenge their usurped rights. Luckily, Carrie Chapman's speech ended suddenly and we dashed out of there.

On the street, the Valdés brothers ran into some students who were coming back from the university who told them how well the election for the new rector had gone. I gave Wenceslao an obvious look, pleading with him to save us from such bores, especially on hearing one of the youngsters mention Mella's name, which made me want to hurry from there even more.

From what they said, my adored boy, my torment, had just caused quite a scandal. Minutes after the assembly had started, without anyone knowing the purpose of his visit, the president of the republic had appeared in the main lecture hall. On seeing him arrive, several students, led by Julio Antonio, left the room with the intent of breaking the quorum and boycotting the proceedings. The situation got tense: for it was a secret to no one that in the hall, mixed in with academics and students, there were various members of the secret police.

However, since they couldn't achieve their purpose, Mella and his followers returned to their seats, disturbing the proceedings with lively protests over Zayas's presence. The outgoing rector, who was running the assembly, asked the unruly ones if they were going to participate in the elections or not. Rising to his feet, Julio Antonio answered yes and added, "Mr. Rector, just as the people of France condemned and embarrassed the kings with their silence, we, the youth of Cuba, also hurl our damnation against the unjust rulers of this country by remaining silent."

His words electrified the audience. There arose, in fact, a tense silence and all eyes were directed toward Zayas, who squirmed in his seat and seemed on the point of rising, but thought better of it and stayed in his seat, pretending he had not understood what had transpired.

"The voting will commence," the rector announced, and the secretary of the assembly began to call out the delegates that professors, alumni, and students had chosen to vote. When Julio Antonio Mella's name was called and he rose to the stage to put his ballot in the box, he was given an ovation.

"And how did the sly thief react?" Rogelio asked, referring to the president.

"He made as if to pick some lint from his jacket," one of the tellers responded, "but even from far away you could tell he was boiling."

Once the votes were counted, Zayas congratulated the new rector, elected by a wide margin, and addressed the audience, assuring it that on witnessing the smooth workings of the university assembly he felt a satisfaction comparable to a father who stands over the triumphs of a son. That provoked many voices to rise in protest, reminding the leader that the assembly had not been created by him but by the struggle of the students.

With a strained smile, the president clarified that it wasn't his intention to claim the glory of reforms made possible by the students and, amidst thundering boos, disappeared, flanked by his bodyguards.

"I bet he's regretting the moment he decided to show up," one of the students said.

On the way to the hotel, free of the Valdeses, I felt an urgent need to see Mella and to find, with Wenceslao's help or not, some way to have a fling with him.

"Do what you want," my love exclaimed suddenly, guessing my thoughts, and a chill went up my spine. "But don't be surprised if he punches you in the face and you end up with a broken nose."

"I don't know what you are talking about," I said, feigning innocence.

"I hope I'm wrong," he replied suspiciously and receded into a reproachful silence.

Since I wasn't thrilled over the prospect of a new fight about the Beauty less than twenty-four hours after our reconciliation, as soon as we got to the Inglaterra I began to compose the draft of the letter to La Duse. But, wrack my brain as I might, I couldn't even come close to the passion and power of seduction demanded by Wen.

"Pretend you are asking for a date from your Bolshevik," he suggested caustically, on rejecting my first attempt. "Maybe then it will be a little more eloquent."

We soon found out that the orchid had reached Désirée without complications and that, when she went out to the stores, the secretary had it pinned to her chest, a clear sign of how much pleasure she took from receiving such attention. "That mango is ripe and ready to pick," Regla pointed out villainously, winking at her patron.

Ten minutes later, getting his nerve up, Wenceslao picked up the phone and asked to be connected to the Señorita Désirée Wertheimstein. He took a deep breath, like an actor about to walk on stage, and for a quarter of an hour chatted in German with her. It wasn't necessary to know Goethe's language to understand, from the inflexions of the voice, affected and suggestive, that he was subjecting the Austrian to a bombardment of flatteries. When he hung up, his face was radiant with satisfaction.

"Oh, this is going just as planned," he said.

"You said the same thing about La Garnett," I replied, and immediately regretted it.

Shooting me a hostile look, he begged me not to mention the Englishwoman again. The sweet and rather bored Désirée Wertheimstein was a bird of a different feather. A simple suggestion had been enough not only to make her offer to give our letter to La Duse, but also to be an advocate on the behalf of her South American admirers.

"Now everything depends on you," he challenged me. "We need the letter now, all right?"

I sat down at the desk with the intent of filling the blank page with persuasive words, but I couldn't concentrate. I tried to think of La Duse, but it was Mella who rose in my imagination. I shook my head, as if to ward off an insect, chase it away. Lying on the bed, Wen watched me closely, intuiting, perhaps, my inner suffering.

The unexpected appearance of Bartolomé Valdivieso put an end, at least for the moment, to my torment. The pharmacist came to tell us what we already knew, that his meeting with Eleonora Duse had been granted. Gallo had just told him the good news. We pretended to be happily surprised and had to hear him repeat a dozen times, in rehearsal, his famous sonnet, for his mind was set to recite it to the genius before giving her the parchment. If the poem was atrocious, I have to admit, for the love of truth, that on reciting it with his frightening Cuban accent, the author made it sound even worse.

"I don't know what I would have done without you," he finally said, with eternal gratitude. "I am *so* nervous."

We saw him off, advising him to go to bed early and making him swear that as soon as his visit was over to run over to our room to tell us all about it.

That night, we couldn't decide whether to go to the Payret, to finally see the empress of the operetta, or to the Principal de la Comedia, where María Tubau was performing. Intrigued by the praises that the papers heaped on the Spaniard, Wen was leaning toward her, thinking that we would have plenty of opportunity to see La Iris, whose run threatened to last forever.

La Tubau was young, pretty, and graceful; the play she performed, insignificant, and the price of tickets laughable, compared to what we paid to see La Duse. It didn't surprise us, then, that the Principal de la Comedia was overflowing with spectators and that they rabidly applauded the actress's hairdo, outfit, and grimaces.

After we left, we wandered around Parque Central until by chance we ran into the ears of Paco Pla. We invited him for a drink in one of the open-air cafés of the Prado.

"This place brings back good memories," the rower insinuated and smiled lasciviously, showing off his choppy teeth.

When we told him that we had gone to La Chapman's tribute with two friends of his, he told us the story of Rogelio and Armando. Their mother was Teresa Trebijo, a rich heiress who lost her heart to a married man, ran away with him, and changed her estimable last name to the common Valdés. "Then they are bastards?" Wen inquired. Señor Ears nodded and continued with his tale. The said Teresa gave birth to her two sons in Santiago de Cuba and there she lived, with them and her lover, until lack of funds forced her to return to Havana. They put the boys in a boarding school, and the guy tried to convince Teresa to claim the fortune that was rightfully hers. Because she refused wholeheartedly, he left with another woman, and she never saw him again. La Trebijo tried to support herself and pay for her kids' school by sewing on the side, but in the end she didn't have any choice but "to prostitute" herself.

"What about the inheritance?" Wenceslao asked, shocked.

"Her brother, José Ignacio Trebijo, got all the money. You met him at the Montes de la Oca party: a greasy fat man who thinks himself God's gift to mankind."

Teresa reached a compromise with her brother. If José Ignacio would see to the health and education of his nephews, she would renounce what was lawfully hers. Delighted with the settlement, Trebijo promised to give a monthly stipend to the bastards and pay for their schooling, but with the caveat that he would never recognize them as his flesh and blood, nor welcome them in his mansion.

"Everybody knows the story, although, because people take pity on the boys, who are not to blame, it is hardly ever told," Paco Pla explained.

"And what about the mother?" Wen pried.

"About a year after reaching the agreement with her brother, they found her stabbed in the rented apartment where she lived. At first it was thought that a lover who, wicked tongues say, treated her horribly, had murdered her in a fit of jealous passion. But since the secret police couldn't prove anything, the case was dropped. Rogelio and Armando stayed in the boarding school, not even leaving for Christmas vacation, and didn't find out about their mother's death till much later."

Since Wenceslao, fascinated with this Havana melodrama, insisted on asking for further details about its protagonists, I got up to urinate, not because I really needed to, but simply not to have to listen to it anymore.

On the way to the bathroom, someone stepped in my way.

"Well, well," he exclaimed and, even before I got a chance to see his face, I knew that it was one of the detectives from the secret police, the well-built Aquiles de la Osa. "Having some beers, Belalcázar?"

I nodded and, not knowing if I was doing right or wrong, I asked him point-blank how the investigation of the murder of the Oriental was going. He pointed to an out-of-the-way table and we sat down.

The detective was wearing a cigar-colored overcoat that fit him divinely, which he apparently was very well aware of, judging from his cocky demeanor.

"I shouldn't tell you anything, since you haven't wanted to tell me anything," he joked, pinching his mustache, after he had ordered two cold ones.

"I don't have anything to tell you," I protested.

"Oh, you don't?" he responded mysteriously. "Are you sure that you don't have anything to add to your statement?" he insisted, looking at me with a complicity that made me nervous.

"I am sure," I replied. At that moment they brought the two beers and, because of how quickly I drank mine, or because of how cold it was, or both, I was overcome with a coughing fit.

The detective tapped me on the back and waited, with an amused expression, till I recovered. Then, as if repeating a lesson to a slow child, he said, "My friend, we know everything, and if we don't know it, we make it up."

I told him that I didn't know what he was talking about and, with a resigned sigh, he gave in and answered my original question.

"We still have not found out the whereabouts of your uncle, but we have fished out the little frog that visited him."

"Who is he?"

"Apparently, he himself doesn't know who he is," de la Osa remarked. "The guy tells this novel-length tale we don't know whether to believe or not. He says he lost his memory in a shipwreck and that he doesn't remember anything about his life before a cargo ship picked him up and dropped him off at the port of Havana. One thing is certain: he's not riffraff, he's educated, has manners, and you can tell right away that he is used to giving orders."

I asked how the Frenchman had met my uncle.

"He is a gentleman and has not wanted to go into details about the matter," the detective answered mischievously. "I think that the French consul introduced them, who, between you and me and with the utmost discretion, is one of your uncle's best clients." I watched him, very curious, and he laughed. "Please, don't tell me that I have to explain to you the nature of your uncle's business."

Suddenly, I felt exasperated and made as if to get up.

"Wait, you haven't heard the best part," De la Osa said, holding me by the wrist with a chilly hand.

"Why do you assume that I would know what kind of business my uncle is involved in?" I blurted out, unable to hide my anger. "My family has not had any news from him for thirty years and he disappeared before I had a chance to ask him."

"It was a joke, Belalcázar," he placated me.

I wanted to say something back but before I could put the words together in my head, he added something that petrified me.

"Jean Bonhaire, that's the Frenchman's name, or that's what he says it is, was detained today thanks to a tip from an informant. We snuck into the hotel where he lives, and, among his things, we found a .45 with two bullets left in it." He looked me directly in the eye. "The bullets are identical to the ones that blew your uncle's 'secretary's' brains out."

At that moment, a boy passed in front of us, selling newspapers. The detective whistled for him and bought one. He placed in front of me the news that told of the arrest of the suspect, and I read it. While the detainee admitted knowing Mei Feng, he refused to admit guilt. However, all evidence showed that the murder of the Oriental had been his doing and, according to the article, only a miracle could save him from spending a long vacation in a cell at La Cabaña. I noticed that, as in previous reports, my uncle's name was once again kept from the readers. I didn't think it wise to ask the detective about this uncommon discretion.

Lastly, my attention focused on a photograph of the detainee. He was good-looking, well-dressed, and appeared to be about forty.

"On his person he had a watch, a chain, and a ring, all gold, which, according to Atanasia, the servant, had belonged to Misael Reyes, the same as some silver cufflinks that we found in the hotel. The Frenchman maintained that they were gifts from Monsieur Reyes, who liked him very much and wanted to help him overcome the difficult situation he found himself in, alone and without means in a foreign country. The servant corroborated his story, asserting that the last two times he had visited the house he was wearing the jewelry as well as a pair of boots that were also given to him by the good man."

I tried to give him back the paper.

"Keep it," Aquiles de la Osa said, "so you can show Señor Hoyos."

I got up and this time he didn't try to stop me.

"I hope that some day you come looking for me with something interesting," he stressed as I was taking my leave. "For example, if your uncle tries to get in touch with you by sending you papers and such."

I forced a smile and promised to keep him up to date in the unlikely case that something happened. We shook hands (how could his be so cold when I was sweating?) and I returned to Wenceslao and the rower, who were still chatting animatedly, although not about the stupid Trebijo's sons but about the upcoming Ball of a Thousand and One Nights, which Pla was thinking of attending as a *tuareg.* I found the choice ideal: underneath the turban, his ears wouldn't detract from his appearance. I was happy that, distracted by their talk, they had not noticed what I did during my absence. I preferred to keep my encounter with the detective to myself.

Suddenly, blondie let it be known that he would love to see our room at the Inglaterra and, to my surprise, Wenceslao invited him to come with us without consulting me.

At the hotel, after taking our clothes off, Señor Ears was slowly and carefully gagged. If his moans awoke our distinguished neighbor at such a late hour, the help of a hundred Désirées would not be enough to convince her to grant us an interview. The gag seemed to excite him, just as it did Wenceslao, who took it upon himself to bite, jostle, and overpower his complacent victim with a sadistic streak uncommon in him. The performance was long, consisting of numerous and various scenes, with a few encores; although it should be pointed out that my unimpressive participation lacked the slightest hint of initiative. Worried about the news I had heard from Aquiles de la Osa, I limited myself to obeying Wenceslao's directions to the letter. "Do this to him, do that to me, go over there, turn him over here." He was like Michel Fokine choreographing a dance at the Ballets Russes de Diaghilev, demanding the *coryphée* to twirl, leap, and move faster or slower. It didn't even occur to me, as it would have under different circumstances, to fantasize that the body in our bed belonged to Mella.

My will reasserted itself only when, the acrobatics and suckfest concluded, Paco Pla asked timidly if he could sleep over.

"I don't think so," I answered brusquely and, without letting Wen intercede on his behalf, I made him get dressed and go.

"Poor boy. Who knows what time he'll get home?" Wen said in a reproachful tone when we were alone.

I pretended to be asleep not to have to reply. But after a while, after repeatedly adjusting the pillow under my head, and after twisting and turning and tangling myself up in the sheets, I opened my eyes and told him about my encounter with the police all at once.

"Do you think he really knows that I got the poem or he is trying to entrap me?" I asked.

"He likely knows."

"All right, let's say he does know. How?"

"Maybe he is the one who put the poem on the bed," my friend ventured, sleepy-voiced, and begged me to forget the matter. Tomorrow would be another day, and I had to get up early to write my letter to La Duse.

I felt like revealing other things that I was keeping from him not quite knowing why—the six words written on the bathroom mirror, the disappearance of Fan Ya Ling's store—but his rhythmic breathing and snores, light at first but soon noisy, made me hold back.

As I tried to fall asleep, a voice began to dictate to me the letter I needed to write to Eleonora. A letter without equal, overwhelming, capable of shaking her up and making her agree to our petition. Who was whispering those words in my ear? I don't know why, but suddenly I was certain that it was the poet and composer Arrigo Boito, one of La Duse's old lovers, dead some years back, creator of the opera *Mephistopheles* and the libretto for Verdi's *Otello*. How did I know? I have no idea, because the voice spoke to me in Spanish (with a slight Colombian accent) and Boito was from Padua. Once in Bogotá, while drinking cups of hot sugar water to keep the cold at bay, Wenceslao had told me about the discreet relationship that La Signora and Boito maintained for many years. The fact that D'Annunzio was the great love of the actress's life was common knowledge, but Wen was inclined to think that Arrigo Boito had been her soul mate. Boito, or whoever it was, continued to dictate the letter to me, which was in the lyrical and slightly sentimental style that, I had a feeling, La Duse would find pleasing.

"Of course she'll like it," the voice asserted, interrupting the dictation with a confidence that allowed no room for doubt. "No one knows Lenor like I do."

I asked timidly if he was Boito, and he snorted yes.

"The first time that I saw her was in Milan, performing in the *Cavalleria rusticana.* She was a tiny, twenty-five-year-old woman, ambitious but unsure of her talent, and already the papers were writing about her often. The night the season ended there was a dinner in her honor at the restaurant Cova. They sat Negri, the mayor, on her left, and I was on her right. She seemed very intelligent, especially for an actress. I asked her for a picture, and in the months that followed we exchanged some letters. We were not intimate, however, until four years later, around the time that she left Cesare Rossi's company, where she had gained such acclaim, and decided to become her own producer," the ghost said.

As I listened to him, I asked myself if all the inhabitants of the other world were as loquacious as the ones that appeared to me. Finding a laconic phantom is a real exception; in general, the dead spoke out of every orifice when the opportunity presented itself, probably because they spent so much time in silence, as their situation dictated.

While I was searching for a justification for his verbal torrent, the deceased nonchalantly continued with his monologue. "Some time before the premier of *Otello,* Verdi and I went to see her in *Pamela nubile,* an old comedy by Goldoni that no one puts on anymore. In that play, as in others by the same author, Eleonora demonstrated that, aside from being a tragedienne, she is also a deliciously fine humorist. After all, wasn't her great-grandfather a comic? When we went to say hello to her after the performance, her fingers became intertwined with mine for some seconds that seemed eternal and I left very disturbed. Truth be told, it was Lenor who came looking for me, who resorted to friends we had in common to come nearer to me, until on the twentieth of February 1887, at nine in the evening, we became lovers," he said.

I tried to remember the day, month, year, and exact hour when Wenceslao and I had begun our romance and found it impossible. I

ANTONIO ORLANDO RODRÍGUEZ

have always had a terrible memory for dates. How did Boito remember the events with such precision? Is it possible that our memory improves when we arrive in the hereafter?

"Privately, I called her Bumba, Bimbuscola, or Zozzoletta, and she called me Bumbo, Bombi, Zozzi. . . . What fools, you say. But what is being in love if not a license to be ridiculous? She traveled all over the country, and I, too, was devoted to my work, so our get togethers were quick as lightning. Each of us got on a train and we met, for a while, in some small hotel of a town midway," Boito continued. Then suddenly, without warning, he resumed the interrupted dictation of the letter that Wen so desperately needed.

I told myself that I shouldn't put it off any longer: I had to get up, turn on the desk lamp, and write down the precious words before they vanished, before they dissolved in the breezy Havana night. But a sudden exhaustion kept me in bed. I knew, without wanting to, that it was impossible for me to move from there, so I resigned myself to wasting the invaluable help that the spirit of La Duse's lover was offering. Before falling asleep, I comforted myself with the thought that, with a little bit of luck, I would remember something on waking up.

We love to blame the ills we suffer on the wicked. We forget that it is our indifference or our fear that makes such things possible.

When the war started, I had not acted in five years. Free for the first time, I committed myself to enjoying my liberty. To look at the heavens like a sailor, to see if the winds were favorable or not for sailing.

If the press published some article about my retirement, I asked Désirée to write to them, clarifying that when and if La Signora Eleonora Duse decided to end her career, the press would be notified immediately. But why lie to ourselves? Although I didn't want to admit it, I was retired. I didn't feel the slightest desire to return to the stage. I was tired of dealing with producers, bored with contracts that always promised juicy profits and in the end produced only losses, weary of training stupid actors, sick of ships and trains and hotels and dressing rooms. Besides, I was fifty. ("Only fifty," Sarah would have said.)

My savings were in Germany, in a good bank, well invested and looked after, and the income that Robi Mendelssohn sent me each month from Berlin allowed me to live not in luxury but comfortably.

I traveled, traveled a lot, and invented projects for myself, like the unfortunate Casa delle Attrici. Did I tell you about that? It was also the period in which I was closest to Isadora Duncan, who went mad when her two children, Deirdre and Patrick, drowned in a stupid manner. I sent her a telegram urging her to stop roaming everywhere and come stay with me in my little house in Viareggio. She listened to me, and I tried to console her as best I could, in my own manner.

"Isadora," I said, looking her in the eye. "What has happened is not the end of your misery, it is merely the beginning.

Don't toy with fate. Happiness was not made for you. Forget about it. Resign yourself to live alone in your art."

But she didn't listen to me. She couldn't. Isadora had a mark on her forehead. A mark invisible to all others but I saw it on the day I met her. The sign of the wretched.

She rented an enormous, light-filled villa. There she, Hener Skene, and I got together. Skene played the piano: Chopin, Schubert, Beethoven. . . . One afternoon, he played the adagio from the *Pathétique* and suddenly, for the first time since the death of her children, Isadora danced. Watching her, I breathed a sigh of relief. She was saved.

But she never learned her lesson. I introduced her to a young sculptor who wanted to make a bust of her, and she pigheadedly set her mind to have a child with him. She did, but the child only lived a few hours. The worst thing about sad stories is how similar they always are.

And then, to make us understand that grief should be humble and discreet, the great tragedy was to come. In Sarajevo, they assassinated Archduke Ferdinand and war broke out. At first distant, but soon spreading all over Europe like the plague.

Italy, apparently, was neutral. But the confrontations between the neutrals and the allied parties were a sort of shadow war. On the twenty-third of May 1915 we entered the great contest. *Viva l'Italia! Viva l'italianità!* I tried my best to fulfill my patriotic duty by helping soldiers and refugees, first the Serbs, in Rome, and later ours, who invaded the streets of Florence after the catastrophe in Caporetto. Poor people, forced to abandon their homes, renounce everything, with the hope of saving the only thing that is truly indispensable: life.

During that time I thought a lot about my little boy. If he hadn't died, he would have been in the trenches. Or would he be one of those boys with shaved heads who returned from the front, with their chests full of crosses and medals, but without an arm or a leg. What idiocy! I also thought about Boito, each day more ill, till he died, leaving me very desolate. And about Gabriele.

I hadn't seen Gabriele in years, but knew everything about him. He had enlisted in the army at the start of the war as a lieutenant and commanded a squadron of valiant aviators. The archangel was finally showing the power of his wings. The papers wrote about his exploits, of the way he relentlessly harassed the Austrians, and I read those reports and became worried. I wrote to him and he replied that I shouldn't fear for his life. Nothing could happen to him, for in every mission he carried with him his talismans: his mother's wedding ring and two emeralds that I had given him.

One day they asked me to go to the front, with other artists, to entertain the troops with historical plays. I refused, on principle, to participate in such a sinister irony. Something, I don't know if it was modesty or anger, impeded me. I couldn't get into my head how someone who lives with the heat and blood of war, someone who is about to go into battle, needs to be entertained. To arrive there, perform, create an imaginary world and then addio! return to the city, fleeing from death and the truth. I couldn't do it!

I went to the war zone many times, not as an actress or a "tourist," but as an Italian citizen, to be of whatever use I could be. I visited the wounded and the sick, helped them write letters to their families, talked to them. I listened to them, tried to understand them, to comfort them just as their mothers would.

I had a blue dress made, because in black I looked dressed up as a priest and I wanted them to be happy to see me. I wanted them to forget, at least for a while, the blood-soaked bandages, so much burned flesh, so many ruined young men, to get out of their heads the discolored flags, the harsh roar of cannon fire, the Red Cross stretchers, the burials. No, I will not make the mistake of labeling war as bella, as Boito the poet did in a patriotic fit. Not even our war. Never!

One night, on returning to the small hotel in Udine, stooping with the pain of the bodies and the souls, I found my room destroyed by a bomb and I started to laugh. People looked at me as if I were mad. Was I? Am I still?

War is more than death, destruction, and politics, as they have made us want to believe to simplify its meaning. War is, above all, a matter of physical and moral horror.

The war (the one I came to know at the front; the one I followed, day after day, in the newspapers) was a butcher shop. Each country sent their young men to battle as if they were sending cattle to the slaughterhouse to be quartered. Italy, Italy alone, lost almost half a million men. Why? For what? In the name of whom?

Finally, the end came. Victory for some, for others a defeat on which rancor feeds. The jubilation of the winner and the humiliation of the defeated. And afterward? Forgetfulness. But do mothers who never see their sons again forget? In those days, my heart swollen with sorrow, I came to understand with a painful clarity that war is not a mishap, a whim, or an example of the temporary cruelty and idiocy of man, but a manifestation of an innate state (sometimes hidden or latent, sometimes unfortunately let loose) of the human soul.

10

"She's a witch," the pharmacist reported, bursting in like a gust of wind. "A harpy!" he insisted, and we knew that his meeting with La Signora had not gone well.

After we sat him down in the rocking chair and forced him to drink a glass of water, the author of "To Eleonora the Sublime" was in better condition to tell us what had happened.

Aware that among the many obsessions of the old woman one was punctuality, Bartolomé Valdivieso had arrived at the Inglaterra with plenty of time to spare. At fifteen minutes before eight, the time of his appointment, he was already by the door of the tragedienne's room. Well-dressed and perfumed, with his gift in one hand and a watch in the other, he waited until the hands indicated seven fifty-nine, and only then did he knock on the wood with his knuckles.

From within he could hear coughs, footsteps, and remarks in French. After a few seconds, Désirée Wertheimstein half-opened the door and Valdivieso told her, in his recently learned and stammering Italian, who he was and why he was there. The secretary made him come in to the receiving area, and, signaling toward the sofa, asked him to make himself comfortable. La Signora would be with him in a moment, she said before disappearing.

The pharmacist took the opportunity to examine the room. Next to a vase of flowers he saw three or four books. One of them, bound in leather, was open, and the young man couldn't resist the temptation to pick it up and see what work it was.

"*Macbeth,*" La Duse pointed out, passing through the door, and, because of the suddenness of her appearance, the visitor almost tangled his legs together trying to get up as quickly as possible. "Translated into the French," she specified, using that tongue. "My English is paltry." She shook the man's hand and signaled, with a gesture, for him to sit again. "During one of my first trips to New York I wanted to learn that language, and the producer became furious. He told me that if one day I did speak it, I would cease to be 'exotic' and that would be disastrous for ticket sales."

The woman then was silent, waiting for her visitor to open his mouth. On seeing that the senator's son was in a state of paralysis, she added, "Signor Gallo said that you wanted to give me something."

"Oh!" Valdivieso finally reacted, grabbing the crocodile leather case and not quite sure whether to speak in French or in his precarious Italian. "I am a fervent admirer of yours, Signora Duse," he said, opting for French. "And if I may be so bold, I hope you don't mind, I have written a sonnet in your honor."

"Grazie," the actress murmured, half closing her eyes, and tried to take the case, but the pharmacist reacted quickly and put the gift out of her reach.

"Before giving you the poem, I would like to read it to you," he clarified hastily.

La Duse nodded—resigned, I imagine—and sat back in the wicker chair. Resting her chin on the palm of one of her slender, expressive hands, she prepared to listen to the poem.

At that moment, as Valdivieso told us, he was overcome with an uncontrollable trembling, and gathering up all his courage, he opened the crocodile case and took out the parchment scripted with golden letters. He coughed to clear his throat and, under the benevolent glare of La Duse, recited his composition in the most emotional way possible.

"Grazie mille," the honored one whispered as soon as he had finished reading and, to put an end to the visit, she grabbed the parchment and case. She rolled up the paper, put it inside, and then looked with interest at the case. "What leather is this?" she asked, intrigued, caressing the buffed surface with her fingertips. "From what animal?"

When the pharmacist told her that the hide had covered the body of a caiman, an incredulous look settled on the old woman's face.

"Caimano?" she uttered. *"Cocodrilo?"* she insisted with a thin voice, and on seeing that Bartolomé was nodding with a fatuous smile, La Signora tensed up with dread. *"Per l'amor del cielo!"* She returned the case abruptly, as if it were alive, and getting up, very upset, asked the pharmacist to leave immediately. Since the disconcerted poet did not move, the old woman began to scream as if she were being strangled, calling for Désirée and La Avogadro, both of whom appeared immediately. Out of her mind, on the verge of tears, screaming like a vegetable vendor in a plaza, the actress scolded her employees in Italian, while she pointed with disgust at the gift. She spoke so fast that the pharmacist only understood certain words, *cubani* and *selvaggio,* repeated disdainfully several times. Finally, turning around and without looking at the troubled sonneteer, she left the room followed by her maid.

"I didn't do anything," Valdivieso said, in a shaky voice, to the secretary. "I don't understand what got into her."

"She hates lizards and all types of wild animals in general," the Austrian revealed severely. "I don't understand *you people,*" she added in a reproachful tone, taking the poet by the hand and leading him to the door. "To whom, in the civilized world, does it occur to give such a present to a lady?"

When reaching that point of the story, Bartolomé Valdivieso was overcome with a fit of anger, and began to jump on the crocodile case till it was ruined. Then, taking the parchment, he tore it in two, four, eight, and many more pieces and tossed it out the balcony. Standing by the railing, we saw the fragments of "To Eleonora the Sublime" flutter in the air for a moment before landing on cars and passersby on San Rafael Street below.

"She is dead!" the pharmacist screamed resentfully. "As far as I am concerned, that fucking *vieja* is dead and buried!" and he left the room, leaving behind a wake of insults.

Wenceslao closed the door and we looked at each other contritely.

"Poor Bartolomé," he sympathized.

"Well," I said, stretching, "if you look at the matter without letting your feelings get in the way, the truth is that La Duse is right: the crocodile is a disgusting beast."

He admitted that he really wasn't concerned with the ruckus over the gift, but about the fact that the pharmacist hadn't had a chance to mention our names during the turbulent encounter.

"I think that it was best he didn't get to say anything about us," I said. "After that incident, we, too, would be excommunicated."

My reasoning pleased him.

"Very true," he agreed, "if the idiot had mentioned us it would have been a mess."

I said that I was as hungry as a piranha. Should we order breakfast or go down to the restaurant? "Neither," he replied and led me to the desk. "Don't lift your butt from here until this letter is written," he exclaimed. When I asked him what the hurry was, he reminded me that, since he had the Italian ambassador on his side, Olavo Vázquez Garralaga could be received by La Signora at any moment now. And if that happened, and the rhymester took advantage of the reading of his play *A Victim of Her Sin* to slander us as he had threatened, then we could say good-bye to our audience with La Signora. "As you well know, there is no time to waste," he admonished. And holy inspiration, I don't know if it was the hunger or if I had been convinced by his logic, but the truth is that I began to write immediately. It is possible that some remnant of the words dictated to me by Boito were still floating around in my brain, for the letter to La Duse poured out of me with a frightening fluidity.

The letter (how I regret that neither of us had the forethought to make a copy or to keep, at least, that first draft!) began, don't ask me why, describing the steep green hills of Guadalupe and Monserrate, almost always seen by us in Bogotá through the persistent fog, but objects, nevertheless, of profound and everlasting veneration. After that poetic, and yes, I'll admit, confusing introduction, I went on to make an analogy. There are artists that, just like the distant mountains, insist on safeguarding their private lives and maintaining a prudent distance between their peaks and the mortals; she, the divine Duse, belonged to that race: hounded by the inexcusable and eternal curiosity of the masses, she was forced to guard her privacy. However, just like the mountains of Bogotá allowed themselves to be seen as they truly are, in a spectacular manner and with the consent of the sun, so do the great figures of art make exceptions and allow themselves to be unveiled before certain of those who venerate them, and who they feel are worthy of their confidence, of a part of their privacy.

After praising her style of performance and saying that, more than an actress, we saw in her a priestess of the theater, I went on to talk about Wenceslao's scrapbook, comparing it to a missal; about the extraordinary admiration that had propelled us to travel to Havana, defying an ocean, with the simple purpose of applauding her; of the indelible impression her interpretation of the character of Bianca Querceta in *La porta chiusa* had made on us, and of the anxiousness with which we awaited the upcoming performances.

I seem to remember that in the last paragraph the letter spoke of the pilgrims that each year travel to Mecca or trace the path of Santiago, praying and making all sorts of promises, with the hope that their longings will be fulfilled. So we, too, were pilgrims, devoted to her art, and through her and only through her could we be recompensed for all our efforts.

Summarized in this manner, the letter loses much of its impact, but it was *very moving.* After hearing it, Wen thought it perfect. Between the two of us we translated it into the French and he transcribed it, in blue ink and in his best script, on linen paper. As he copied the words very carefully, biting the tip of his tongue, he asserted that that very afternoon, when he took Désirée Wertheimstein to El Anón (the secretary had confessed on the telephone her addiction to ice cream), he would give it to her. He was so happy and optimistic that, in a fit of generosity, he promised me that if we were able to convince La Duse to grant us an interview (that she would receive us he took for granted), he would shake the earth and the sky to personally serve me the university leader on a tray.

The outing with the Austrian was a success. The lady laughed at all his jokes; very fond of sweets, she tasted the mango and *guanábana* sorbets, and listened attentively to him talk about his long journey from Colombia with a journalist friend with the objective of obtaining an interview with La Duse.

Of course she would give her the letter, but not right away. She, who had been with La Signora for some years now (she was careful not to say how many), knew her changing moods like no one. Yes, she would put it in her hands, but only at the right moment, when she saw that her mood was just right. And to make clear how much support she was willing to lend such a handsome and gallant young man, she revealed a secret.

Few people, except the tragedienne's very close friends, knew about her fascination with champagne. It was a pleasure that she indulged in gleefully any chance she could. Flowers, perfume, and jewelry didn't really interest her; books she welcomed, for they helped relieve her unquenchable thirst for knowledge; but drinking a glass of champagne made her rapturous, produced a kind of ecstasy.

In New Orleans, some weeks before leaving for Havana, the poet Amy Lowell, who knew about the diva's weakness, had surprised her by sending her a few bottles. Such a gift, right in the middle of Prohibition, had no equal. Désirée couldn't guarantee anything, but it was possible that if a sophisticated and cultured person gave her high-quality champagne, the actress, who was not wont to make new friends, could be predisposed to allow them entrance into her tightly knit circle of friends.

And of course, it went without saying, these breaches of confidence were to be mentioned to no one. If La Signora Eleonora found out that she was sharing intimacies of such a nature with a stranger, she was liable to leave her in Cuba without a return ticket.

By the time they had left El Anón and walked back to the hotel, they had come up with a plan. He would make sure that a chilled bottle of the finest champagne would be sent up to La Signora's room, anonymously. If Désirée noticed a favorable reaction from the old woman, she would give her the letter right away, explaining to her that it was from the gentleman who sent the champagne.

While Wenceslao conspired with the secretary, although I had told him that I would be in the room reading a novel, I was prowling around the neighborhood of Dragones Street, supposedly out for a stroll, but secretly harboring the hope that I would run into Mella. I didn't remember his address exactly but I knew it was near there. Unfortunately, it wasn't the Communist that I ran into, but Graziella Gerbelasa, who passed by in a taxi, with her aunt. On seeing me, the writer ordered the driver to hit the brakes, leaned half her body out the window, grabbed me by the arm, and warned me that I needed to go with them, for she had some very important things to tell me. I tried to free myself from those ten fingers that clutched my sleeve like hooks, but I soon found out that she was not willing to let me go.

Their pleading voices, the impertinent advice of passersby who watched the scene, and the horns from a line of other cars urging us to stop obstructing traffic forced me to get in the car.

The taxi took off right away and the driver, an old Negro, said jokingly. "The things you see these days! In my time, men chased women, now it's the other way around."

Graziella Gerbelasa ignored him and, looking at me tenderly, wanted to know if I was still angry at her.

Just as I was about to say yes, the young woman's aunt took over and told me that since the day of the presentation of *The Reliquary,* Graziellita had lost all her appetite and barely slept, all because of my coldness.

"No, señora," I replied, "it could be because her conscience is eating at her." The girl, who was neither emaciated nor sleepy-eyed, blushed. "Your niece behaved very badly with Wenceslao and me."

"And who is this Wenceslao?" the driver wanted to know.

"Another Colombian," Graziella said, so he would stop bothering us, and then told me she was very sorry for her behavior, it had been irrational and childish. "I tried to break up your friendship with Olavo out of jealousy," she reiterated. "If you want, we'll go to his house right now and I'll apologize to him also."

"Whose house do you want to go to now?" the driver asked.

"No one's, señor, and please stop butting into our business," I begged him.

The Negro clicked his tongue, stopped the car, and demanded, offended, that we get out right then, an order which I obeyed without protest, followed by the writer and her aunt.

"Lucho," Graziella exclaimed, animatedly planting herself in front of me, and I wondered how she had found out what my close friends call me, for I didn't remember telling her, "never play around with a woman's feelings, even less so if it is a woman in love."

"In love with whom?" I asked, not wanting to hear.

"I love you and I am not afraid to admit it," the girl replied. "I have been crazy about you from the moment I saw you."

I thought, in fact, that she was crazy, but long before she ever laid eyes on me. What was I doing at five in the afternoon on Reina and Amistad, on such a busy corner, playing out such a scene? I scooted behind the aunt to use her as a shield and protect myself against any charge by the exalted Graziella.

"Señora, can you please tell your niece to behave," I begged her.

"Lucho, don't you dare go. . . ." La Gerbelasa warned. "It is necessary that we settle things."

I didn't mind looking ridiculous as long as I escaped that grotesque nightmare. Ignoring her threats, I took off running. From the sidewalk across the street, I stopped and looked back and saw the poetess crying with rage and the aunt embracing her. I turned and got far away from there, asking myself, why me, why precisely me?

Some moments later, I heard some horns behind me. I hurried my step, convinced that La Gerbelasa had found another car and was following me, but a familiar voice made me stop. Behind me was Emilio De la Cruz, on the driver's seat of his shining Dodge Brothers. I jumped in and asked him to speed off.

"What happened?" Monkeyface asked, worried about the anguish evident on my face. "Were you robbed?"

"Worse."

"Tell me, *chico*."

"La Gerbelasa, she's infatuated with me and just put me through hell."

He laughed, but on seeing how I glared at him, put on a serious face and tried to calm me down.

"Take it easy," he advised. "All of us find ourselves in this situation at some point in our lives."

"I'll have to let her know that I don't feel any attraction for her or for any member of her gender," I remarked.

"It would be a waste of time. If she is obsessed, she is not going to leave you in peace. Women are stubborn and, on top of that, many suffer from what I call the redemptive pussy syndrome."

I asked him to please explain to me what he was talking about, and he took on an academic tone.

"A large number of women have trouble realizing the preferences of the members of our club. They go through life blindfolded and fall in love with those on the opposite side of the street with a frightening ease. And if one tries to enlighten them, so the blindfold can be loosened and they can see the truth, they tighten it once again. As the saying goes, 'There is nothing worse than a blind pussy.' Now, when the thing becomes so obvious that they can no longer ignore it, then they change strategies. They reluctantly accept that you have a problem, but, convinced that your sickness is neither incurable nor lethal, they take it upon themselves to save you, to *rescue* you. The idiots think that they have the panacea between their legs. They think that if you try their medicine, you will forget about your strange inclinations and take the right path. In a word, they are sure that pussy redeems. God save us!"

I nodded, thinking that there was something to his theory, and I asked him, "Have you ever seen a pussy, Emilio?"

"A pussy? In person? Never!" he replied, slightly offended. "Not even on the day my mother brought me into this world, for on passing through I took the precaution to close my eyes and didn't open them again till the midwife slapped me to let me know that the danger had passed."

I let out a sigh, still worried.

"Forget that little lady and tell me about something that matters," Monkeyface said, trying to cheer me up, so I told him the story of Bartolomé Valdivieso meeting with La Duse and about the advances in Operation Désirée.

"That old woman is something," he said. "I heard that Mina de Buffin sent her an invitation to preside over the Ball of a Thousand and One Nights, and she responded not to count on her. La Buffin, who is no wallflower, wrote her again, telling her that the ball would be in her honor. But the Italian said no again and, as a supposed show of respect, said that she would send two actresses from her company on her behalf! I don't imagine that Mina found this reply too amusing. Of course, with Duse or without her, this Monday will be quite the bash," and without a transition, supposing that Wen and I would definitely attend the *soirée,* asked me what we were thinking of going as.

I told him that I didn't have the slightest idea. "Truthfully, we haven't even decided if we are going," I clarified.

"Oh, no way!" Emilio jumped. "It's going to be the event of the year and you are not missing it for anything in the world."

He left me in front of the hotel, warning me he would be back in two hours, so that we could go to the Payret together to see the empress of the operetta.

"Why don't you park the car somewhere so you can have dinner with us," I proposed.

"Forget it, for the next two hours I am going to gorge myself on this delicious little thing I met last night," he replied mischievously, and blinking at me, was on his way.

In the room, I found Wenceslao in front of a mirror, finishing dressing up. He had just sent the bottle of champagne to The Sublime One and was waiting for news from his ally.

He was so happy that he didn't even ask where I had been. I kissed him and we went down to dinner. As we went at our main courses—stuffed rabbit for him, chicken breast with oysters and a blue cheese sauce for me—the waiter, who looked like a Russian prince and whom we thought we had seen before, came by to fill our glasses. He discreetly slid a piece of paper under Wen's napkin.

As soon as Prince Mishkin moved away, I looked inquisitively at the boss of the spies.

"The report," he said, still chewing.

He swallowed and, after looking in all directions to make sure that no one was watching him, he opened the message and read it.

"And?" I asked, because his expression betrayed nothing. "Did it work?" I urged him.

"Listen and draw your own conclusions," he said and proceeded to translate the message, which was written in German, in the mode of telegrams. "Gift received gratefully. I will now proceed to give her the message." He took a deep breath and looked me in the eyes. "The first battle is won."

"Don't count your chickens yet," I replied with caution. "We'd better wait to see how she reacts."

"I have blind faith in that letter," he insisted. "Let's toast."

To please him, I raised my glass and clinked it with his.

"Here's hoping you're right," I said.

We finished dinner hurriedly, fearing that De la Cruz would appear at any moment. He was, however, nowhere to be seen.

"Maybe dinner didn't go down well," Wenceslao, who was in a

great mood, joked, and asked me if I was really interested in seeing Esperanza Iris in *Benamor,* because, if I didn't mind, he would rather leave the *divette* and go celebrate at the Casino Nacional. I shrugged, wiped my lips with the napkin, and, standing up, told him that I would be by his side until the end of the world. We went up to the room to get some money and, while my friend put a bundle of bills in his pocket, we heard some discreet knocks on the adjacent wall.

Wenceslao put his index finger to his lips, begging me to be quiet, and put his ear to the wall. Eventually he, too, knocked. After a series of knockings that seemed to follow some secret code, he fell on the bed face up and sighed.

"What happened?" I said, fearing the worst. "Bad news?"

"No," he replied, "only that since it is late and she is tired, La Signora put off reading the letter till tomorrow."

"Oh well," I said, trying to assume a serenity that I was nowhere near feeling. I lay down beside him and caressed his ear. "Everything will come out all right."

"It has to come out all right," he insisted and sat up with a renewed optimism. "Let's go."

I don't know what time it was when the car of some young men that we had flirted with in the casino returned us to the Inglaterra, for I have to admit that I was drunk. However, I do remember that that night we lost quite a respectable amount at the tables and became very popular because of the good humor with which we faced our slights of fortune. "One less cow!" Wen exclaimed, guffawing, each time the roulette wheel fell on a number we hadn't chosen, and a chorus of laughter greeted his joke. "And now I have lost a young bull," he would say ipso facto, because bad luck continued to hound us all night. I wondered if Dr. Hoyos could be sleeping peacefully while his heir squandered the heads of cattle from the Chiquinquirá ranch.

I am not sure, either, at what time in the morning the phone rang, disrupting our sleep yet again. Wenceslao let out a curse and threw himself on the apparatus.

"Hello," he said with the voice of a cave dweller, but then immediately changed his tone. *"Meine liebe Freundin!"* I sat up to watch him, naked, outlined by the light that came in through the shutters. "It's

Désirée," he said, a hand over the speaker, and before hanging up, he exchanged a few other emotional words with the secretary.

He ran back to the bed and jumped on top of me, holding me to his chest, and gave me a long kiss. His mouth tasted horrible and I consoled myself with the fact that the same could probably be said about mine.

"She read the letter?" I asked, pushing him to the side so that he wouldn't suffocate me.

"Uh-huh."

"And?" I insisted impatiently.

"We will get a message from her inviting us to tea on Sunday afternoon," he said, as if it were nothing.

"Excellent," I sighed and, more than joy, I felt an enormous relief.

"Don't you think we should celebrate?" he suggested, and his feet caressed mine.

"What sort of a celebration?"

He whispered an obscenity in my ear.

Afterwards, recently bathed and smelling of cologne, De la Cruz stopped by for a visit, to apologize for standing us up the night before. "Due to circumstances beyond my control," he said slyly. On learning the good news, he congratulated us and wanted to know how we were thinking of convincing her to grant us an interview.

"In its own time," my mate replied. "The first thing was to get to see her, and that we have achieved."

Our chat was interrupted by a new phone call that Wen answered right away. He listened for a few seconds, without saying a word, to the information someone was supplying him. He went pale, and his face went blank.

"Did she cancel the tea?" Emilio asked when he had hung up.

"No, but she might," La Duse's devotee said in a funereal voice. "What I most feared has happened."

The telephone operator had just heard a conversation between La Signora and the Italian ambassador. The tragedienne had agreed to lunch on Sunday with Vázquez Garralaga so that he could talk to her about the play he had written for her. I felt as if the roof had come crashing down on us, and since De la Cruz didn't understand anything, we had to explain to him the implications of the news.

"If Garralaga follows through on his threat and says terrible things about us, it is probable that the old woman will cancel her invitation," Wen guessed.

"Maybe we are making too much out of this, no?" I asked and, looking at Emilio, I asked him what he thought. "Would he do such a thing?"

"An angry Olavito is capable of that and much more," he confirmed. "I don't mean to scare you, but things don't look good."

Wenceslao began to pace from one end of the room to the other, to curse the poet and lament how short-lived happiness is. I tried to calm him down, but it was the worst thing I could do, and he reacted like a cornered beast.

"Of course, what do you care? This means nothing to you. Your thoughts are in some other place," he admonished me, "with some other person."

Emilio tried to settle us down. Although, in his opinion, the situation was grave, there were solutions.

"The first is to seek a quick reconciliation. I could go to Olavo's house and convince him to smoke the peace pipe with you."

"And if that doesn't work?" Wen urged him.

"Then, in that case, you have to stop him from making the lunch," Monkeyface pondered and, realizing we didn't understand, was more explicit. "We'll pay some guy to detain him by force on Sunday and let him go after you have had your tea."

Wenceslao asked whom we could put in charge of the kidnapping.

"I know someone," De la Cruz said. "Off with those long faces, please, because at least we found out about it in time. Let's get some food in our bellies and we'll take care of this right away."

After a lunch, during which Wenceslao refused to eat at all, and I barely picked at my food, and Monkeyface stuffed himself, we took off in the Dodge Brothers toward the Cerro neighborhood, where Vázquez Garralaga lived.

"You stay here," Emilito ordered, getting out of the car. "If the reconciliation is on, I'll send someone out to get you," and with a resolute step he headed toward the front door of the mansion.

"I hope everything works out," I said.

"You'd better hope, because if it doesn't, I'd be willing to pay someone to kill that son of a bitch," he replied in a harsh tone, and I knew that he wasn't joking.

Monkeyface took longer than expected, and as soon as I saw him come out, I knew that his mediation had been unsuccessful.

"There's no way that he would listen to reason," he informed us, taking the driver's seat. "At first he was very warm, but all I did was mention you and he went into convulsions. I tried to get his mother on my side, but the señora just made things worse. She alleged that you were a pair of hypocrites and that such friends could only bring harm to Olavito. And it didn't help at all when I told them about how much you cared for him, how it had all been a misunderstanding, gossip made up by La Gerbelasa. And, at the mention of her name, who comes into the room, looking as if she couldn't harm a fly? None other than the authoress of *The Reliquary,* who was paying a visit. She told the owners of the house not to be fooled and confirmed that the two Colombians went around mocking Olavo's poems any chance they had."

"What a two-faced bitch," I whispered.

"I'd scratch her face off," Wenceslao asserted.

"The worst thing was that, in the middle of all this brown-nosing, the Italian ambassador calls. Olavo spoke with him and then announced to us, very smugly, that La Duse had invited him to lunch so that he could read her one of his shitty plays. And, egged on by the Reliquary, he said that he would not forget to mention to her what a pair of ruffians those two were."

"Well, he asked for it," Wen decided and, without getting worked up, asked Emilio to make the necessary arrangements so that Vázquez Garralaga could not make his appointment with La Signora.

"Scissors has a relative who would kill his grandmother for five pesos," Monkeyface revealed. "I once contracted him to beat up this guy who had stolen this *chiquito* from me, and I was very satisfied."

"Do what you want, as long as there is no violence," I interrupted, trying to ease my conscience.

"Would there be any danger of being blackmailed?" Wenceslao asked.

"*Coño,* don't be like that," Monkeyface replied. "Scissors can be trusted, he is good people. Well, I don't have to tell you, you know him better than I do."

We parked the car near La Boston and walked toward the tailor's shop. There, we told Agustín Miraflores everything he needed to know, leaving out the unnecessary details.

"A cousin of mine can take care of this, no problem," Scissors guaranteed.

"The same one who helped me last time?" Emilito said.

"No, another one. Do you want to go take care of it now?"

And since Wenceslao nodded, the tailor led us to a stinking tenement house on Jesús del Monte Street. We knocked on one of the doors, and a negro in an undershirt full of holes poked out his nose. On recognizing Scissors, he smiled from ear to ear and made us come in. The room was tiny, a rickety cot the only furniture. Emilio, Wen, and I sat on it and we told El Ecobio (that was the nickname that Agustín's cousin went by) the details of the case. Twenty pesos to grab the guy as he left his house on Sunday and hold him somewhere till that night. He would be given ten now and ten after it was done.

"That's it?" El Ecobio asked, incredulous. The task seemed too simple for such a substantial sum. "You don't want me to rough him up a little bit, a good kick in the ass?"

I knew that Wenceslao was tempted to say yes, but the look I shot him made him resist.

"It's not necessary. Detaining him will be sufficient," he said and, suddenly remembering that Vázquez Garralaga would have with him a manuscript of *The Victim of Her Sin,* he added, "Oh, and any papers that he has on him, make sure you burn them."

De la Cruz went on to provide a meticulous description of the prey and give the hired thug Vázquez Garralaga's address. Lastly, Wenceslao asked me for a ten-peso bill. I gave it to him instantly; he gave it to Scissors, who gave it to his cousin.

"Consider it done," the man guaranteed us before we left.

On the street, De la Cruz asked Wenceslao if he was feeling better. "Much," he confessed.

"My cousin is the best," the tailor assured us. "Although you may not believe it, he is not stupid. He knows his business and knows what he is doing. He has a very select clientele."

Back at La Boston we said good-bye to Agustín.

"You don't know what a great help this is," I remarked.

"I scratch your back today, you scratch mine tomorrow, Luchito," he replied, holding on to my hand and caressing it with a suggestive movement of his thumb. "Hopefully we'll see each other when we have more time on our hands, one of these nights."

De la Cruz tried to get us to go with him to Azuquita's brothel, but we excused ourselves. After such an intense day, we wanted to turn in early.

At the hotel reception desk, several messages awaited us.

The first was a note from Madame Buffin, inviting us to be part of the jury that would award the prizes at the Ball of a Thousand and One Nights. There was another one, from María Cay, complaining that we had forgotten her. "But she treated me like dirt at La Duse's premiere!" I protested. "Why do you insist on looking for a rational explanation for women's behavior?" was what Wen replied.

Another who lamented our disappearance and who asked to send him signs of life was García Benítez, the Colombian consul. Would we like to have lunch with him and the señor ambassador the following week? The fourth message was signed by Aquiles de la Osa. Unlike the others, it was addressed only to me. It had a phone number and an urgent request: "Call me!" Wenceslao watched me, intrigued, and I shrugged. There was also a message from Señor Ears, inviting us to a baseball game. A letter several sheets long, signed by Graziella Gerbelasa, I tore in pieces and tossed in the wastebasket without even bothering to read it.

The last message was from Mella, and in it he reminded us about the tribute to Lenin that would take place Sunday, at noon, in the Worker's Circle. He hoped he would have the pleasure of seeing us there. My heartbeat doubled.

"Do you want to go?" I asked Wenceslao with a calculated indifference.

"Tea is at five."

"We have time."

"Isn't it too much fuss for one day?"

"Truthfully, no."

"All right then, whatever you want."

"Not whatever I want," I insisted. "I asked you if you wanted to go."

"Fine," he consented coldly. "Why not? We'll go."

It's likely that as soon as I finish saying it, I'll be sorry I said it, so I'll just blurt it out all at once, without giving it a second thought, so I don't change my mind: I have seen mermen. Yes, you heard right. I saw them with these very eyes.

It was right before we reached Alexandria, after a blustery crossing. I left my cabin early, before dawn, and went on deck. There were still some stars left in the sky. It was cold, and the shawl I had draped over my shoulders was too thin. I heard laughter, the sort of merrymaking that you hear from children playing ball in a *piazza*, but there was no one around. So I approached the railing and I saw them, in the foam of the sea, only meters away, emerging out of the dark waters, enjoying themselves, unaware that I was watching. There were three, young and with healthy complexions, their bodies a spectral white. Their hair, wet and long, fell over their backs.

At first, I only saw their naked torsos and thought, stupid me, it could be some sailors taking a dip without telling their superiors. But, suddenly, two of them threw themselves on their companion and, in a joyful struggle, forced him to flip over. And at that moment I saw that the creature had no legs but a fish's tail, a powerful tail covered in purplish scales with a fin at its tip.

"Mermen," I whispered, I think, and looked over my shoulder, hoping that there was someone there to share such a wonder with. But I was still alone, alone in that sort of phantom ship. Amazed, I watched the mermen, no longer trying to hide from them. They went on with their games, not seeing me, or perhaps ignoring me.

After a while, when the horizon began to turn orange, two of them plunged down and never reappeared. The last one remained still and watched the fading moon. Then suddenly, he opened his mouth and let out a sort of wild song. It was like the braying of an old and sorrowful animal: a pitiful lament that poured forth, incongruously, out of that vigorous body.

Leaning on the railing, I heard him, and tears ran down my cheeks. The merman dropped his chin to his chest and, noticing my presence, he looked at me in disbelief before plummeting into the waters, which for the moment seemed strangely pasty, perhaps to join, in the deep, the other members of Poseidon's court?

Mermen . . . Those are stories for the uneducated, pure mythology, I would have been told had I told anyone on the ship about it. I kept my mouth closed and said nothing. Only afterward, on returning from Egypt and before leaving for Russia, did I dare tell Arrigo about it. He looked at me tenderly, as if I were a girl, and said that it must have been a dream.

Never, on any of my trips, did I see those creatures again. I went out to the deck, and go out still, at the most unusual hours, hoping to see them again, but in vain. I would be ready to admit it was a dream had I not heard that lament. That song, that sort of dirge, still resounds in my memory. About sirens and other creatures I don't know a thing, but mermen exist, they live at the bottom of the sea, hidden from us. They are strong and beautiful and they sing.

11

Señores, we can accuse the imperialist Yankees of anything, except of being cowards, because you have to have a lot of courage to ask us to tighten our commercial belt. Tighten how? How can we tighten when our tongues are already sticking out? The Platt Amendment is not enough for them, the base at Guantánamo, a large part of the sugar mills, half the banks, and all the commerce, or, that is, all of Cuba and her honor?" Mella began and I asked myself if he, too, would forget that the purpose of the meeting was to pay tribute to Lenin.

The first speaker, a lawyer named Pérez Escudero, dedicated most of his speech to the case he was defending, of a worker accused of poisoning beer and of insulting the rulers of the country. Professor José Miguel Pérez, who climbed the stage afterwards, talked for less than a minute about Lenin's character and more than half an hour about how easy it would be to guide the Cuban people toward revolution if there existed any workers' organizations capable of realizing their goals. Lastly, it was Mella's turn. We listened to him on our feet, in a hall at the Workers' Circle, located on the ground floor at 37 Zulueta. The place was packed: at the summons of the Communist group, the Workers' Federation of Havana—hundreds of people, mostly men—had attended. At the beginning of the function, the master of ceremonies had mentioned the collectives present: the Havana Electric Workers' Union, the Marble Mason's Syndicate, as well as the Carpenters' Syndicate, the Professional Association of Varnishers, the Bakers' Union, the Launderers and Dry Cleaners Syndicate, the Union of Cigar Rollers, and the Syndicate of Chorus Girls and

Prompters, among others, as well as a considerable number of university students. A photograph of Lenin, located at the back of the stage, presided over the event. It was decorated with garlands of wildflowers and two flags hanging beside it: on one side the Cuban flag and on the other one, a red one, the symbol of Communism.

Suddenly, a group of uniformed adolescents climbed on stage. A large woman, who, I imagined, was their teacher, led them. On noticing Wenceslao's surprise, I explained to him that the Rationalist School, supported by the Workers' Federation, was located on the upper floors.

"If people keep on coming in, this oven is going to explode" he protested.

The lack of air was intolerable. We were being steam-cooked in the middle of a dish of many different aromas. Like many of the others present, Wenceslao and I fanned ourselves with our hats. We no longer bothered to wipe our faces with our handkerchiefs, for we knew the thick copious drops of sweat would soon stream down again.

"I don't think I can take this much longer," Wen warned me, annoyed. "If this torture goes on, I'll melt. Why do they talk and talk about the same thing without the least bit of consideration? Can't they feel that the heat is unbearable," and exacerbated by the applause for Julio Antonio, he added, progressively raising his voice, "Why do they encourage him to keep on talking? What is this, a sort of mass suicide? Are they the followers of some cult and want to see us die of dehydration?"

Since some of the men were beginning to give us ugly looks, I fanned him with my hat so he would calm down.

"It should be over soon," I ventured without really believing it. "Let's try to hold on till it is over."

Although hot and sticky, the additional ration of air seemed to calm him down, and I could focus my attention on Julio Antonio. At that moment, shaking his closed fists, the young man roared out a diatribe against President Zayas, labeling him servile, a swindler, and a shame to his country. At this stage of his harangue, he had still not mentioned the name of the deceased Bolshevik, and I wondered if he ever would. He had to allude to him at some point, not doing it would be unforgivable. Wasn't the meeting in his honor? But what kind of a tribute was this, for God's sake? A tribute is an elegant and pretty affair, with music and maybe someone who can say a word or two, not this succession of boring speeches, this congregation of wretches who sweat, stink, and stir, stoically putting up with this unbearable heat.

"Is this señor all right?" a peroxide blonde, who I imagined belonged to the Syndicate of Chorus Girls, said, pointing at Wenceslao. "He is very pale."

"He is not used to the heat," I explained.

The woman nodded, opened her bag, and pulled out a small flask with a blackish liquid.

"Coffee," she said, unscrewing the top and offering it to Wenceslao. "Have a little sip, it will revive you. If it's any consolation, we are in the middle of winter, imagine the heat in July and August."

To my surprise, Wen raised the flask to his lips without protesting and handed it back to the woman, thanking her. The liquid, in fact, did seem to revive him, but just in case, I continued to fan him.

"As things stand today, no politician can be trusted," Mella went on tirelessly. The heat, instead of weakening the young man, seemed to lend him a growing strength. "They are all scoundrels who sell off our land in the name of sovereignty and morality. They are all made from the same stuff, political mud."

With great effort and concentration, I tried to shut out what Julio Antonio was saying and limit myself to watching him. But even though I put all my efforts into silencing him, isolated phrases of his speech, like flashes, reached my brain. "The citizens' revolution will rise against the dollar!" "Tomorrow we can negotiate, today we must struggle," "Lenin's titanic effort heralded a new era for mankind . . ." I sighed, relieved that he had finally mentioned the Bolshevik. In passing, but he mentioned him. Could it be true that social revolution was a fatal and historic act that not even countries on this side of the world could escape?

"I need air," Wenceslao murmured, once again at the point of fainting. I shook my hat more fervently over his face, begging him for just a bit more patience and not taking my eyes off Mella. I had the impression that the student's gaze fell on me for a second, and, despite the infernal heat, a chill ran up my spine.

Why did he have this miraculous power over me? Just seeing him would make me fall into a trance. Oh, what would it be like to have that *papazote* in my arms? "The time has come for the struggle, the arduous struggle." Arduous is what I am for you, you bad boy, bad boy, burning like Joan of Arc in the bonfire of his look. "Some think that Cuban history ended with Marti's death, that the glorious epic poems are all finished." Glorious is your ass, how I would love to sink my teeth into it! Child, has no one told you that your beauty is lethal? An overdose can wipe out anyone? "Cuba is an orchard where the few eat the food produced by the many." And I would eat you right now if you let me. I would swallow you whole, clothes and all, and spit out the buttons afterwards. "The people, unaware of their rights, are slaves." Enslave me, *mi cielo.* "The anti-imperialist cause is the national cause." And you will be the cause of my death, at this moment I die, I dissolve, I soften, I melt, I fall to pieces and not from the heat but from a fever. "The victory over corrupt leaders will only be possible if the proletariat comes together as a powerful and spirited body." Or, in other words, a body like yours. What did your mother, the Irish-woman, feed you? What an anatomy! God bless it! But what good is a body, such a marvelous body, if not to caress it, to rub it against an-other body, perhaps one not quite so marvelous, and with that friction produce the spark of pleasure? Don't speak, Julio Antonio, don't move, don't breathe. I don't care about you, that is, your self; all I want is to be near that body, that fascinating wrapper that holds you to-gether, that sustains you. That sensitive shell, that enormous poppy petal that probably contracts if you graze it with the tips of your fin-gers. "The struggle for the social revolution in the Americas is not a utopia of madmen and fanatics." I tell the same thing to Wenceslao when he says that I have lost my mind, that I am seeking the impossi-ble, because you will never get in a bed with another man, much less let anyone play with your ass. I, however, believe in ideals. Didn't Lenin prove that, if there is a will, the impossible becomes possible? "Rivers do not overflow because of the will of man; rather a river leaves its bed when the water becomes too great to be contained in it." Oh, don't complicate and muddle things; don't make a big drama about something that is so simple and easy. Stop thinking, please, abandon reason. Forget about your prejudices and let our bodies find each other, let them communicate their secrets in silence. That visceral, tactile language can only be understood through the body. "Cuba has never been independent." But the body is, the body is independent, independent like the country that belongs to the Soviets. Don't subjugate it, I beg you. "The proletariat will be the new liberators." Your body is free, my love: let it be its own king and slave, let it be sovereign and enjoy anything that it longs for. "We are not rebels, but revolutionaries." Whatever you say, my heaven. "We are not seeking to install new tyrannies, but to put an end to them." I am almost at my wits' end. "We want everyone to eat according to his hunger, so that each one will be fully satisfied." Satisfy my hunger, give me a little nibble to eat, don't be cruel. "The transformation, for it to be real and just, will have to begin with the destruction of the economic system." You are destroying me, without the slightest bit of mercy. Oh, how embarrassing, Lucho Belalcázar, hide that bulge in between your legs, do something to cool your blood, do it now or you will leave this meeting-tribute with a stain on your pants, and if that happens, what would the Communists say? How are you going to look the union leaders Carlos Baliño and Alfredo López in the eye? And the teacher and the students from the Rationalist School, what will they think? Don't move, don't blink, don't breathe, do something before it is too late and your seminal vesicles burst: count backwards from forty to one, think about La Generala, about the ugly sisters, say a prayer to the Blessed Child so that he cools your gonads.

Suddenly, as if someone had listened to my prayers, a rotten egg flew across the hall over the audience and burst on Lenin's effigy.

"To hell with the Communists," a loud voice said, and a group of saboteurs started to boo and hurl more eggs, and vegetables, and stones, and other such projectiles.

"Friends, let's not let ourselves be provoked," Mella roared and had to duck to get out of the way of a bottle that passed over his head with great speed and shattered against the back wall. "Calm down, shit, calm down!" he screamed, and at that moment several gunshots were heard.

What followed was pandemonium. Everyone was shoving and punching each other and trying to make it to the exit. Chairs flew and blood flowed abundantly from wounded heads.

"Congratulations," Wenceslao said sarcastically, "what a great idea to come to this inferno."

I dragged him by the arm and we barely made our way through the howling, kicking, striking mob, and found refuge in the back of the stage. Hidden behind the Cuban flag, we watched the chaos that, far from being settled, was growing worse.

"This proves how much the Communist ideas have taken root," Carlos Baliño pondered out loud, as he hid a few paces away, behind the red flag, accompanied by the chorus girl with the coffee. "If the government sends their agents to disrupt a meeting, it is because it feels threatened."

Mella was still at the pulpit and persisted with his efforts to calm the proletarians. At the top of his lungs, and dodging tomatoes and radishes, he blamed everything on Zaya's corrupt government. But on realizing that no one was listening to him and that the tribute to the deceased had turned into a sort of Roman circus where dozens of gladiators tested their strength, he abandoned his sermon, let out a long and terrifying war cry and, leaping from the stage, fell on one of the saboteurs and assaulted him with blows.

"And now what do we do, Lucho Belalcázar?" Wen exclaimed, exasperated.

"Find a way out of here."

It wasn't easy. The only door available was blocked, and it was at that spot that the vortex of the hurricane was located. Just as we were about to head there, to get out at whatever cost, police whistles were heard. I don't know how, but several uniformed men were able to make their way into the site and, committed to putting an end to the melee, whacked with clubs anyone who got in their way. Ten minutes later, the situation was under control, and in small groups, in an organized manner, we left the hall.

Outside, beneath a torrid sun, a diverse crowd watched the protagonists of the disorder. We were ready to get away from there as quickly as possible, but a friendly and smiling Mella, his face bathed in blood from a cut on the eyebrow, detained us.

"My Colombian pals! So good that you came," he said, slapping us on the shoulders. "What did you think of the meeting?"

"Very moving," Wen deemed.

"Although Zayas pretends to be permissive, today he showed his claws," Mella explained. "Now you have a story for when you go back to your country," he joked and said good-bye.

Although I had not been wounded, there was an enormous blood-stain on my suit. At some point, without noticing, I must have bumped into someone who was bleeding. We hurried the five blocks to the hotel, trying to ignore the stares of other pedestrians, and as soon as we got there jumped in the shower.

"Don't be upset," I asked Wenceslao as I washed his back. "It could have been worse."

"Yes," he replied. "They could have cracked our heads or broken our ribs, and then how would we show ourselves to La Duse?"

All of a sudden, he seemed to remember something and, naked as he was, he stepped out of the tub and ran toward the phone, wetting the rug. He returned beaming, before I had finished rinsing off, and told me that they had just confirmed that Vázquez Garralaga had stood up The Sublime One and the Italian ambassador. After waiting for him for a long time, they had called him at home to investigate his tardiness. And finally, since he still didn't show up, they had no other choice but to have lunch without him. Signora Duse did not seem too pleased with this lack of decorum.

"I wonder where they are keeping him," I said.

"I don't know, and I don't care," Wen stressed. "The important thing is that he is not our problem anymore."

We had a light lunch, set the alarm for four and lay down for a little siesta. As soon as he lay his head on the pillow, Wenceslao was asleep; I was still under the effects of the meeting and couldn't sleep.

As if I were watching an absurd movie, full of ups and downs, backwards, I recalled the most recent events.

The morning before, Saturday, we had received a note, written by La Duse herself, in which she thanked us for the champagne and in-vited us to her room for tea. *"Quelque chose de très simple, samedi à cinq heures, pour avoir le plaisir de les connaître."* I answered it im-mediately, letting her know how honored we were by her invitation and, since I already had pen and paper in hand, I took the opportunity to reply to the other messages. To Madame Buffin, that it would be an honor to serve on her distinguished jury. To the consul, that we would love to have lunch with him and with the señor ambassador. Where and when? To Paco, that it would be impossible to go with him to the stadium: why, instead, not go with us that night, to the Nacional, for the production of *Ghosts*? (The prospect of being charred in the sun while watching some guys try to hit a little ball with a stick did not seem seductive at all.) A messenger from the hotel promised to deliver the letters before noon.

Because Wenceslao insisted, I tried to get in touch with Aquiles de la Osa, but an ogre voice told me that he was out. Since I never called him again, we never found out why he so urgently needed to talk to me.

Wenceslao wanted to go shopping, so we went to El Encanto. They sat us on some high stools, in front of a counter in the men's section, and two employees started bringing us what we asked for: Holeproof socks, Arrow shirts, Omega and Longines watches, Panama hats. . . . Wen bought a box of handkerchiefs that were embroidered with a *W* with many arabesques, and a gold-plated Gillette shaver with a box, also gold-plated, for the blades, and insisted on buying me a pair of brilliantly colored silk ties, very pretty, I'll admit, but I could never wear them in Bogotá. The only thing that I really wanted was a box of La-Mar slimming soaps, imported from Ohio. According to the clerks taking care of us, they were amazing: after only a week of washing with them the belly and jowl would noticeably begin to shrink. I wasn't, nor am I now, fat, but what is it that they say about an ounce of prevention?

Before leaving, we chose a perfume in the ladies' department to send to Désirée. If the meeting with La Duse were going to come true, it would be in large part her doing and she did deserve some reward.

Afterward, we went with De la Cruz to see El Vedado for the first time. When we got there and we wanted to get down and walk, Monkeyface said that it was ridiculous to walk in this heat and insisted that we tour the neighborhood in his "machine." We said absolutely not and explained that what we wanted was a peaceful stroll on the streets near the sea, a walk under the shade of the almond trees and these other leafy trees with very red flowers, which the Islanders called framboyanes, to admire the luxury and comfort of the big houses and find out who lived where. Relenting and calling us eccentrics, the chauffeur agreed to let go of his Dodge Brothers for a little bit. When we passed in front of the mansion of the Loynaz family, we stopped to admire, through a tall grille, a wild garden, full of chapels, small fountains, begonias, honeysuckle, and underbrush. With the exception of a cockatoo, there was no one there that Saturday, and we missed out on catching a glance of the much-heralded Enrique, the oldest of the sons.

That Saturday night, at fifteen minutes before nine, we arrived at our box in the Nacional to watch *Ghosts*. Emilito could not come with us, saying his uncle needed him for an urgent matter, but Paco Pla took his place.

"What a game you missed!" he exclaimed on seeing us. "Caribe, the team from the university, against the Police. Not one boring moment!"

The theater was not as crowded as on the night of the premiere. In the series tickets' booth we found the same faces. Mina de Buffin with her inseparable Arab professor. The three Loynazes and their relative. Olavo Vázquez Garralaga, unaware of the kidnapping we had arranged for him the following day. And if President Zayas was conspicuously absent, Mariíta, the first lady, was there with the daughters from her first marriage, Herminia and Rita María. As it seemed to be her custom, Cay arrived at her box two minutes before the beginning of the performance. She was with a very spruced-up older gentleman.

"What an enormous chandelier," Paco Pla said, dazed, and our eyes were directed toward the ceiling. "If it falls one day, God forbid, there won't be a fool left standing."

At that moment, three bells were heard and the house lights began to dim. I realized that Wenceslao hadn't told us the plot of the play. Would we be able to understand it? I decided that it would be wise to concentrate. I knew *A Doll's House* and *The Wild Duck,* but I didn't have the slightest idea what the story was in *Ghosts*. For the moment, the stage set was rather explicit: it was the spacious living room of a house in the Norwegian countryside, near the shores of a giant fjord. Two characters were already on stage, an elderly man, with one leg shorter than the other one, and a girl wearing a bodice and a maid's apron. They began a lengthy conversation, and I seemed to understand that the girl was the man's daughter. He was trying to convince her to go with him someplace, but she refused scornfully. Finally, the lame man left and was replaced by another man, wearing the collar of Protestant pastors. But nothing much else happened. The servant and the pastor talked and talked, while the audience waited for *something* to happen. Finally, the girl left and the pastor remained alone, pacing in the living room in a pensive mood. I glanced at Wenceslao, who watched the performance in a trance, apparently understanding all the Italian perfectly, and then at Paco Pla, who did nothing but snort and fidget in his seat. At the moment I looked back at the stage, La Duse was making her entrance.

Wenceslao took advantage of the welcoming ovation to give us, in a low voice, some details of the plot.

"Elena Alving is the widow of a chamberlain considered by everyone to be an upright person, but who in reality was a rake and a womanizer. To prevent a scandal, she put up with her husband's vices, suffering quietly, and now she is building an asylum in his memory."

Paco Pla and I nodded, grateful for the information, and fixed our eyes on La Signora, with the hope that with her arrival the story would become understandable. The actress took a seat and began an endless conversation with the pastor.

"What are they talking about?" I asked Wenceslao, not being able to contain myself.

"About Regina, the servant," he explained in a whisper. "Her father wants to take her to work for him in a hostel for sailors and Señora Alving, whom she has worked for since she was a child, doesn't like the idea at all."

Memo Benassi appeared at that moment. He was wearing a thick coat and smoked a meerschaum pipe. He approached the other two actors, shook hands with the pastor, and kissed La Duse on the forehead.

"Is it her husband?" Paco Pla ventured.

"Didn't you listen when I said that she was a widow?" Wenceslao said impatiently. "It's her son, Oswaldo, who has just arrived from Paris. His mother sent him away to study when he was seven, so he would not find out about the licentious life of the chamberlain."

The three characters talked for a while, without moving from their seats, and then Benassi left and so allowed Señora Alving and the pastor to continue their conversation alone. I erased the set, erased the actor who shared the stage with her, and my attention centered on Eleonora Duse, trying to capture the essence of her art. Did it consist, perhaps, in talking and moving as if no one were watching her?

"She is telling him what she went through, years before, the day she found the chamberlain in the greenhouse kissing one of the servants, and explaining to him why, in spite of all the terrible things that her husband did, she is going to open an asylum that bears his name."

"Why?"

"To squelch rumors in town and protect the honor of the Alvings."

Oswaldo reappeared and, on his heels, the maiden Regina, who announced that dinner was ready. The two headed for the dining room and you could hear them laugh and joke with each other from there. Then suddenly, Regina's voice was stifled, as she asked Oswaldo to let her go and asked him if he had gone mad.

Señora Alving fixed her eyes on the half opened door that led to the dining room and what she managed to see made her recoil in shock. The pastor, incensed with the frolicking of the two, asked the widow what all this was about.

"*Spettri! Spettri!*" La Duse answered, her voice hoarse, not knowing where to look, taking some unsure steps toward the dining room, and the curtain fell at once, leaving the audience on the edge of their seats. Not heeding the warm applause, The Sublime One did not come out for a bow, which disappointed the audience a little bit.

"There's nobody like her," Wen declared and we went out to the main foyer to smoke. As we went down the marble staircases, I asked him to continue telling us what happens in the following two acts, which he did immediately. "Now Oswald confesses to his mother that he is very ill," he began.

"How about that, he looks very healthy," Señor Ears interrupted.

"His illness is not physical, but spiritual, moral," Wenceslao clarified. "It's an inheritance from the dissolute life led by the chamberlain."

"But he grew up far from home!" I protested.

"Oswald announces that he wants to marry Regina, and poor Señora Alving becomes very upset."

"Don't tell me it's his sister," the rower slipped in.

"Yes, as a matter of fact, the fruit of some fling that the chamberlain had with one of the servants," Wen revealed.

"*Coño,* just like in *Cecilia Valdés,*" Blondie asserted. "Do you know that novel? Cecilia and Leonardo get together and have a daughter and everything, not knowing that they are half siblings. Of course things there are worse, because Cecilia is a *mulata.* Here, at least they are both white."

"Do you want me to go on?" Wenceslao said coldly and, after a pause, continued. "When Señora Alving decides to reveal the secret to the two young people and is about to tell them that they share the same blood, something unexpected happens . . ."

"The asylum burns down?" Ears guessed.

"You've read the play, Paco Pla," my mate thundered.

The rower swore that he hadn't and attributed his accuracy to the fact that all those stories were very similar, lovers who happen to be siblings, houses that burn down, people who commit suicide . . .

"Does anyone commit suicide?" I asked.

"More or less," Wen answered. "When Señora Alving lets out her secret, after the fire, Regina leaves and Oswaldo asks his mother for a fatal dose of morphine to escape the hell he lives in."

"Some people just like to suffer," Señor Ears surmised. "They are rich, they don't have to do manual labor, they have a nice house, with servants and all the amenities, and since they don't have any problems, they invent them."

On the way back to the box, we went to pay our respects to Madame Buffin, who that night was wearing a Nile-green crepe suit and was suffering like Job to keep her neck straight, because of the weight of her gold earrings. With the help of Dr. Habib Steffano, the millionairess told us the latest news about the Ball of a Thousand and One Nights. Since La Duse declined, because of health problems, the honor of presiding over the jury, the president of the republic's wife would take over the task. "We wanted it to be Alfredo," La Buffin said to us in confidence. "But you know how he always has a thousand obligations. And for what, at the end of the day? This country is damned and no one can fix it!" Another bit of fresh news was that the role of the caliph of Baghdad had been assigned, after very complex deliberations, to the young Adolfo Altuzarra, who, aside from belonging to one of the families of the best lineage in the capital, had the physical qualities required in abundance. "He's around somewhere," Mina said in passing, pointing to the orchestra with a vague gesture. "He came with his fiancée." Scheherezade, as all of Havana already knew, was going to be played by Professor Steffano's wife in a sumptuous dress and genuine Arab jewels. The organizing committee had released a statement to be published in the major newspapers, reminding people that to attend the ball it wasn't necessary to wear costumes. What was required, for gentlemen, was tails or smoking jackets.

"Tickets cost five pesos and you can buy them anywhere," Mina de Buffin said. "I hope that we can raise quite a bit for the *crèche,* because it so needs it."

"I've seen that Altuzarra before," Paco Pla maintained on the way back to the box. "He's quite a catch," and letting us know he was about to piss his pants, he ran in search of a bathroom.

Wenceslao and I took the opportunity to say hello to María Cay, who was wearing a salmon silk bengaline dress, with the same pearl necklace that she had worn to the Ideal Room, and she held her ever-present fan in one hand. On seeing us arrive, she offered us a pleased smile and introduced the old man next to her.

"Don Aniceto Vadivia, Count Kostia," she said. Addressing the old geezer, who still had not paid any attention to us, she whispered in his ear, *"Ils sont les colombiens."*

On getting this information, the count deigned to look at us and scrutinized us curiously.

"You're handsome," he admitted on finishing his examination, pointing at me. "But your uncle was even more so."

"Perhaps he wasn't as handsome as he was ... defenseless," the *China* offered. "I've always thought that was what made Casal lose it."

"You mean what made Casal win it," the old codger corrected her sarcastically and, letting out an unpleasant, cascading guffaw, looked at Wenceslao and added, "Being that, in matters of love, it is impossible to tell with certainty when one loses and when one wins."

"It is a pleasure to meet you. Ever since we set foot in this city all we have heard talk about is the famous Count Kostia," Wen lied shamelessly. "You are a true legend."

"Oh no, just a survivor from the time Havana was an elegant place," he gabbled, blushing with pleasure. "Who knows what Generala Lachambre has told you about me! In any case, I warn you not to believe a thing she says. *Marie est une exagérée.*"

For a few more minutes, we spoke more nonsense. The count remembered his years as a diplomat in Europe, and Wenceslao brought up Bernhardt. Had he by chance seen her act? The old man clucked and nodded several times.

"Of course I saw her. First, in the Comédie, and then in her own theater, the Renaissance. From the very beginning she was a red-haired demon, a volcano on the verge of erupting, and *le tout Paris* gave in to her charms. Neither Réjane nor Bartet could compare with her. *Elle était la plus grande.* Now there was someone who knew how to act, *mes amis!*" he added, making a mocking gesture toward the stage. "Sarah spiced up any role."

"But some critics have written that her style was a bit unnatural," Wenceslao replied.

"What critics?" the count said contemptuously. "Francisque Sarcey, that long-haired traitorous pig? Shaw and the rest of the English? They all hated her and discredited her when they were willing to praise even a broom that is put on stage," he snorted. "Natural? If I want to see something natural, I wouldn't bother to put on a smoking jacket, I'd stay in my house and watch my cook pluck a chicken!" he laughed. "Theater, young man, is exaggeration, magic, carnival, never faces without color and insipid prattle."

All of a sudden, María Cay stood up, busily fanning herself, and asked Wenceslao to come with her for a little walk and, without waiting for his approval, took him by the arm and forced him to exit the box. Obviously it was a stratagem to leave me alone with Count Kostia.

"Your uncle is very disappointed with you," the old man blurted out.

"With me?" I repeated like an idiot. "Why?"

"He sent you a message, or should I say, two messages, and you have not made any effort to contact him."

"And what am I, a psychic, that I should know where he is hiding?" I protested. "Why doesn't he call me so we can arrange a meeting?"

The count took a deep breath, gathering his patience, before going on.

"He is *très déprimé,*" he assured me. "The detention of the Frenchman has wrecked him, believe me, he is falling apart over it. I am afraid that he is capable of doing anything to get him out of jail."

"And was it, after all, the Frenchman who murdered the Oriental?" I asked.

"I don't see how that is of the slightest bit of importance *now!*" he continued, not trying to hide his exasperation. "Misael has to leave the country for a little while, exile himself in the United States or Mexico, and return only when things have cooled down. You are the one who has to convince him."

I was about to ask what influence I could have over an uncle I hadn't seen since I was a child, but at that moment the bells rang, announcing the continuation of the performance and, grabbing my hands, before La Cay and Wenceslao returned, the count gave me the address of his house and made me promise to be there at nine the following morning.

"Can I bring my friend?" I was able to ask, and he replied in the affirmative.

When I told Wenceslao about the conversation, he confined himself to saying that we would have a busy Sunday: early on, a visit to the count; at noon, the Communist meeting, and to round out the afternoon, tea with La Duse.

What I am going to say right now fills me with shame. But if up to now I have related events without straying from the truth, it wouldn't be wise to distort the truth for the sake of saving face. At the beginning of the second act, as soon as Señora Alving and the pastor reappeared, I fell asleep. Deeply and completely asleep, as if during our trip to El Vedado a tsetse fly had flown out'of the Loynaz garden and bitten me.

Since I had my right elbow on the balustrade of the box, and my chin resting on the open palm of that hand, I think that neither Wenceslao nor Paco Pla realized my treason against La Duse. I woke up at intermission, but I didn't want to go out to the foyer and mingle. I did, however, run to the bathroom, to wash my face and see if I could wake myself up. On returning, I noticed that La Cay and her guest were no longer in their box. Wenceslao and Paco Pla came back after a while, very excited, saying they had seen the caliph. "The choice was perfect," Wen pointed out with the authority of an expert.

Although I was determined to stay awake for the third act of *Ghosts,* as soon as the performance resumed, I plunged into a deep slumber that I came out of only with the final ovations. A disgrace, I know, especially when dealing with such a superb artist, but I couldn't help it.

"Is it true that you fell asleep for the last part?" Wenceslao asked as we crossed San Rafael, after we had said good-bye to the rower.

"Yes," I admitted embarrassedly. "I am very tired," and I yawned exaggeratedly.

"Don't tell me you missed the ending, when the son, sprawled on the sofa, asks Señora Alving to hand him the little morphine box and she, in all that desperation, is not quite sure whether to give it to him or not!"

"Oh no, please! That, I saw, of course," I lied, not to upset him. "I only slept a little bit. Eleonora was brilliant."

"And tomorrow we will have tea with her," Wenceslao said. "And we will convince her to grant us an interview," he added emphatically.

We left the hotel at eight-thirty in the morning on Sunday, in a taxi, heading for the home of Aniceto Valdivia. The count himself greeted us, dressed in a red velvet *robe de chambre,* a bit worn at the sleeves, and sporting on his chest the Great Cross of St. Olaf, which he had been awarded by the Norwegian monarch. He made us walk into a room full of books—French literature, for the most part—and at his insistence we accepted a couple of glasses of port. He had a martini. A servant brought the beverages and, at the old geezer's signal, left the room, but not before looking at us insistently, as if she wanted to warn us about something.

Since on arriving we had told the count that we didn't have much time, we thought that he would go right into the matter of my uncle. But it wasn't to be. Without getting to the point, the geezer began to criticize the *gringos* for wearing silk collars with their smoking jackets, when it was very well known that, although silk was more comfortable, the proper thing to do was to wear a hard, straight, doubled-over collar, spiky or sailor-style, well starched whatever the case.

"But who cares what is right or wrong today? All you have to do is notice some of the shirts that some wear with their smoking jackets. Someone who wants to be elegant chooses one with a hard, straight front or, if he wants, a soft one, with a wide pleat, but never, never, should he wear one of those horrible ones with thin pleats, which look like towels."

Wenceslao and I looked at each other not knowing what to do, while the dissertation about the rules of elegant dressing continued. With the smoking jackets, the shoes had to be thin-soled, or flats with no toecaps, with heels made of cloth and patent leather, or with heels made of matted leather. To wear anything else would be to introduce into the ensemble a note of bad taste. In summer, straw hat or Panama; in winter felt or black derby. And the cane, light in summer, matching the hat, and black or a crosier in winter, the only thing that was irreplaceable, he concluded, rapturous, was the tie, which should always, always, no excuses, be black and silk.

"And well, to tell you the truth, I don't really like the smoking jacket that much, what I really love is tails," he confessed. "That is the true sovereign of formal dress!"

For a moment we thought that he was about to break into a second diatribe, but instead, he stared us down, as if he had just noticed we were there, and asked us out of nowhere what the purpose of our visit was.

"You asked us to come at nine," I dared answer.

"*I* asked you?" he said. "Are you sure?"

"At the Nacional, yesterday, during Eleonora Duse's performance," I insisted, trying to refresh his memory. "You asked me for help in convincing my uncle, Misael Reyes, to leave the country for some time."

"Oh, yes, of course," he remembered, or pretended to remember. "I asked you to come see me. I remember."

There was an irritating silence that Wen took care to break.

"Where is Señor Misael?" he asked.

"He went out early," the old man sighed, holding his medal in one hand and cleaning, with the thumbnail of the other one, the metal cross. "I couldn't keep him," he added, very focused on his task. "He went to the police."

"Why?" I asked, amazed.

"To turn himself in, why else?" the old geezer replied and, when his servant reappeared, he said he had to go, his midmorning meal was ready and he was very hungry.

"He's crazy," Wenceslao said, as we hurried out on our way to the headquarters of the Workers' Federation, on Zulueta Street, from which, through a miracle, we had barely escaped with our lives, a short while earlier.

Havana is a huge insane asylum, and one becomes infected and loses one's mind the minute one sets foot in it, was the conclusion I reached on finishing my review of the events of the day before and of that Monday morning, and I was able to sleep for a little bit until the alarm notified us that it was time to get ready for the tea.

Finally, when it was a quarter to five, with a huge bouquet of Perla de Cuba roses and a box of chocolates from Bruselas, we knocked on the door of Eleonora Duse's room. I mentioned nervously that it was as if we were suitors. María Avogadro let us in, took our hats and, before going to look for La Signora, indicated that we should have a seat. But we were both so nervous that neither of us did. We remained standing, looking around the place. Unlike Bernhardt, who on her tours brought along her favorite furniture, tapestries, and carpets, as well as oils, mirrors, porcelain figurines, and her dogs, cats, squirrels, monkeys, canaries, toucans, and macaws, La Duse liked to travel with as little impediment as possible.

Some minutes later, following an expressionless Désirée, the actress appeared, in a simple gray dress and glasses. With a light smile, she took the flowers that Wenceslao handed her, as well as my chocolates.

"Come with me to the studio," she said in a barely audible voice. "It will be quieter there."

Thinking that the fact that she was taking us into another room was a good sign, since she had attended to the pharmacist right there in the vestibule, I followed behind Wen. The studio was also spartan: just as much furniture as necessary, a few books, some photographs in picture frames. I looked at one of them closely. On it was an old woman next to a young woman and two children.

"It's my daughter and my grandchildren, Hugh and Eleonora," she explained on noticing my interest. "They live in Cambridge. Enrichetta's husband teaches there."

Poor old woman! Imagine what she would say if she found out one day that all the messages that she had sent Enrichetta had passed through our hands before reaching the telegraph office. She settled into one of the armchairs and asked us to do the same. I began to feel cold, and I knew that it was from emotion. We were alone with the renowned actress, who watched us indulgently. What now? The following step, according to the determined course, was to charm her, seduce her with our sparkling and pleasant conversation, get her to become fascinated with us. Once that was accomplished, and not before, we would ask her for the interview. To chat, yes, it was imperative to initiate a dialogue as soon as possible, but chat about what? Toward which topic should we steer the conversation? When outlining our plan of action, Wenceslao had been merciless: any topic but the theater! It was a given that the Italian was sick and tired of hearing praises about her art. We felt that, after so many years of listening to compliments, she yearned to be treated as a simple and common mortal, which, of course, she wasn't. Our strategy, admittedly a risky one, was to conquer her by talking about other things, but what? My mind was blank and for a moment I thought that so was Wenceslao's. What if La Duse got bored with having these two idiots who wouldn't say a word in front of her, stare at her as if she were a museum piece, not even blinking? It was Eleonora who remedied what was sure to be a disaster, by speaking first of the beauty of the city we were visiting and then of the peculiar fashion with which its inhabitants moved. She said that she had spent an entire morning watching people go by under her balcony and, not shy about it, did a delightful imitation of the way Cubans gesture. "They speak with their hands!" she exclaimed, amused. When we asked her if the same thing applied to Italians, she laughed and replied, "No, in Italy we scream with our hands." But not everywhere: a Roman or a Neopolitan did not gesture in the same manner as a Paduan or a Florentine. From then on, the chat flowed very naturally and animatedly, without our having to make an effort to keep her interest or to charm her. She praised the sophistication of the Cuban capital. "I didn't think that there would be so much luxury, so much culture here," she confessed. Her accent, muted at first, slowly came to life, and her pale face became rosy. Was it true that she could blush at will if the scene she was playing required it? The conversation took, I don't remember why, another path: movies. She loved the films of Charlie Chaplin. That little man is a genius! And from Chaplin we hopped to books recently read. I asked her if she knew Valle-Inclán. No, she didn't know if there were translations in Italian or French. She confessed that in the last few years she almost never read new writers, she preferred to reread work she already knew. "The book is the same, the reader is not," she suggested. These days, she was immersed in Shakespeare, the great William: Lady Macbeth was a small role but juicy, she would have loved to play it. The problem was where to find a good Macbeth. Oh, these actors, all shameless and ignorant. Could there be more of a sacrilege than putting an ass on stage and asking him to bray Shakespeare? No, it was too late for Lady Macbeth. Also for King Lear, whom she had been tempted to play by shearing her hair. At least there was the consolation that she had played, at the right moment, Juliet and Cleopatra. I thought that we would end up talking about the theater, whether we wanted to or not, but an unexpected turn took us from Cleopatra to the discovery of Tutankhamen's tomb. She listened, not being able to conceal her envy, the news that our best friend was going to Luxor to see the young pharaoh and she said that she was mysteriously attracted to everything related to Egypt. Oh, she so much, so much regretted that she had not ridden a camel the two times that she had been in Cairo.

We went from one topic to the next until the arrival of La Avogadro with the tea interrupted the chat for a moment. La Duse dismissed the maid with a movement of her eyebrow and took care of serving the infusion herself. There were pastries and sponge cakes of all kinds. We ate and drank, talking of our favorite foods. She ate little and was not very demanding when it came to food. Anything was fine, except for bland English food. And Colombian food, how was it? What did we eat there? *La Colombie,* that enormous country, with jungles and snowcapped peaks. Were the Indians dangerous? Did they still use poisonous arrows? Or devour the Jesuit missionaries? And, changing the topic, did we know of a fizzy drink that she had discovered by chance on arriving on the Island? It was a delight we could not miss out on: it was called Ironbeer. Coca-Cola tasted, in her opinion, like *scarafaggio.* To think that the *gringos* were addicted to such garbage! Could we believe that during one of her first trips to the United States, some dentist tried to sign her up for a publicity ad about false teeth? *Capisce?*

La Avogrado, who had already returned to interrupt the chat to take the dishes and cups, appeared a third time and handed a note to the old woman. She read the paper and nodded uneasily. The servant vanished immediately.

"María and Désirée take good care of me," the actress said. "Sometimes I would rather they didn't protect me so much. . . ."

I glanced at my watch and realized, amazed, that it was past seven. We stood up, embarrassed.

"I am afraid that our visit has been too long," Wenceslao apologized. "You must have a lot of important things to do."

"Not really," she replied. "Only to receive some quack, who is coming to examine my lungs and who will prescribe mountains of pills that I will later refuse to take. Anyway! I am sure that my health is not going to 'bloom again,' as the silly Marguerite Gautier would say."

She accompanied us to the door. In the vestibule there was the Austrian and a fat man with a doctor's bag. If my nose didn't deceive me, Désirée was wearing the perfume from El Encanto.

"I would love to see you again," La Duse muttered, reaching out to us with her famous hands. I looked at Wenceslao, as if asking him if it was proper to bring up the interview, but he paid me no mind.

"Thank you for a marvelous afternoon," was all he said.

"Maybe we can go out on a stroll together," I dared to suggest.

"Può darsi . . ." La Signora said, without betraying much enthusiasm.

Anyone who has worked half of the time I've worked would be rich. And if not rich (because I have never met anyone who truly considers themselves rich, it always seems that they can have more), if not rich, I repeat, then the beneficiary of a reassuring income. Anyone but me. At this stage in my life, I can say it freely, I am a glory, but not in business.

I value and don't value money, depending on the circumstances. When it is lacking, it becomes important. Some people say, with disdain, that money doesn't guarantee happiness. Which is true, but you have to admit that it does shorten the journey there.

I had to return to the theater to keep a roof over my head. When I thought that I would be secure in my old age, that I would never have to set foot on a stage again, the war came and I lost everything. Fortunately, audiences still come to see me. With a curiosity that is sometimes malicious, I think, but in the end . . . they come, and that's the important part.

Ever since I was a child I have wanted to be a success. But the definition of success hasn't always been the same. At first, it was just to have a full theater. Children learn fundamental things without their having to be explained. In that case, the maxim was very simple: "Full theater, full belly; paltry audience, paltry food."

Later, during my youth, success became something else. At that time, success was applause, praise, recognition. If, at the end of a performance, the ovation wasn't as enthusiastic as I expected, I was overcome with anguish, felt something comparable to guilt, a sort of remorse. I would lock myself up in my room to go over each one of my movements during the performance, each one of my words, trying to find out where the mistake had been, where I had failed.

Later, everything changed. I started to worry less about others and their reactions and began to search for something within me. It was a painful search and I came to the conclusion that success is viscous and slippery. The papers could print excessive paeans, the audience could bring down the house with their ovations, but what good was all this if I myself wasn't satisfied, if in spite of the favorable reviews I knew that I hadn't found *the gift?* What good is an ovation if you are unhappy? At one point I began to hate the old French dramas, my biggest successes! I detested them because I was forced to turn to them to please Schurmann and fill the houses, because they offered a sort of success that no longer satisfied me. I had perfected my performances to the point where I could lie easily to others, but not to myself, never to myself.

Recently, the notion of success has been simplified substantially. Success is making it to the last act. That my strength holds up to the final curtain: there is the greatest success. What would the spectators do if they ever saw me gasping, hooked to an oxygen tank, in between scenes? Would they take pity? Would they feel deceived? Would they mock me? Years before, success could have meant many things, but now it is only that: to pull oneself together, to hold on. To finish the performance.

12

That morning winter decided to make itself known. The sky was cloudy, the temperature cold, and Désirée forced La Signora to cover her neck with a shawl as we crossed the bay, in a barge, toward Casablanca. With the exception of the pilot of the craft and of two or three sleepy lads who were seated near the motor, we were the only five on board.

"Now it is empty, but on the way back we're not going to fit," De la Cruz warned.

La Duse nodded, withdrawn, and at first watched the blackish and choppy waters, and afterwards the rows of phantasmagoric houses that you could see on the other side of the bay, one perched on top of the other and dotted with palms. When the boat docked at the pier, she was the first to get off, helped by the pilot.

The idea for the outing had been hers.

The day before, barely an hour after our visit to her room, Désirée phoned us to tell us that La Signora wanted to take a little excursion with us. That we should choose a place to go, something picturesque, but not too far away, and free of crowds. They would bring a basket with provisions. Dumbfounded by the surprise, Wen said yes to everything and promised the secretary to return her call in a few minutes to give her the details. It was hard for me to believe the news.

"The problem is, where do we take her?" I reasoned.

"Try to get in touch with Emilio!" Wen implored. "We have to get his advice."

Luckily, De la Cruz was at his uncle's house. He had nothing to do Monday morning, so, if we thought it appropriate, he could come with us. The best thing, according to him, would be to go to Casablanca, the small fishing town on the other side of the bay. There we could have a snack and, when we got back to the city, he would take us to some interesting places in the Dodge Brothers. Lastly, Monkeyface said that we should be ready at eight in the morning and hurriedly said goodbye. Wen called Désirée so that she could tell La Duse about the plan, but the old woman insisted on talking to him without the Austrian as an intermediary. She seemed to love the idea of going to Casablanca, *une ville de pêcheurs,* and did not raise a single objection to the outing. No, no, there were truly no inconveniences: the time was perfect; she could be ready earlier if necessary. Getting up early wasn't a problem for her; she awoke before dawn ever since she was a girl.

We met her in the lobby of the hotel. De la Cruz greeted La Duse and her secretary as if he had known them all his life and took us in his car to the port and gave us a little tour around it. An enormous ship, flying an English flag, had just arrived, and the San Francisco breakwater looked like an anthill; the pier where boats left for Regla was also very crowded with travelers. The one to Casablanca, however, was deserted. "A lot of the faithful go to Regla to ask the Virgin for favors," De la Cruz explained. "In Casablanca, on the other hand, there is no one to plead to and nothing to do." I imagined my companions were all asking themselves the same thing I was, why in the hell were we going then? On seeing the precarious barge, which looked like an old shoe, in which we were to make the crossing, my expression darkened.

"Don't be afraid, Lucho," Monkeyface said, trying to ease me. "These things were born old, but not once have they ever shipwrecked."

We, in fact, survived the crossing, and went everywhere in Casablanca, from one end to the other. Although no one said it out loud, we agreed with our guide that there was nothing interesting to see there, with the exception of the building where the observatory was based, from which meteorologists announced their forecasts, and the high and unsettling walls of La Cabaña. Our Cuban guide insisted that we climb atop a steep hill, where some scrawny goats grazed, and not knowing the reason, we obeyed him. From there we had the privilege to see an exceptional sight: on the other side of the bay, half hidden by a fog that the sun was beginning to dissipate, Havana arose, docile and golden, showing us all her magnificence. The top of the hill was an incomparable vantage point, and we thanked De la Cruz for leading us there.

Under the shade of some trees, after laying down a blanket on the still-dewy grass, we had our morning snack, which was rather frugal, it should be said. It seemed that Eleonora was convinced that the rest of the world ate as little as she did, because the menu consisted of a tiny, more or less bland, sandwich and a minuscule glass of orange juice for each traveler.

"The things that happen in this country you don't see anywhere else," De la Cruz said as he devoured his portion of the victuals.

"Oh, the different countries," La Duse said softly. "In each one impossible things happen."

"But what happens on this tiny island you can't compare with anything else," Monkeyface replied forcefully, and we were silent, waiting for him to offer proof for his argument. "Some years ago, when the current president of the republic was director of the lottery, in the drawing that Christmas the big prize was won by the ticket number 4444. And where do you think that pile of money ended up? A mystery! Who was the beneficiary of such a godlike fortune? It was never known. And time passed, and birds migrated . . . But in one of those twists of fate, it has just been revealed that soon after that drawing, Alfredo Zayas, better known as Tití, invested in bonds, through an American bank, exactly the same amount paid to the winner of the lottery. What a coincidence, eh?" Emilito said ironically. "The number 4444 had happened to be in the hands of the director of the lottery!"

El Heraldo just published an article about the whole scam on its front page, with well-documented proofs that the rumors were true.

"Who would have thought it," Wenceslao remarked. "The president seems so European."

"And you think that Europeans don't steal," our *cicerone* concluded. "Keep on living in your fantasy world, you fool."

The barge, which was about to set sail when we got back to the pier, was named *Margarita* as was written in blurred red letters near the prow, and it was almost full. But still, De la Cruz thought we should get on. Since the trip was short, he thought it was better to be a little uncomfortable than to wait the half hour for the next boat. We settled into some empty spots on the rustic benches and, while we waited for the crossing to begin, we watched the other passengers— children, the young and the old, for the most part white or *mestizo.* They were, by all appearances, the families of fishermen or country folk. Simple people, dressed in humble but clean clothes. Some had hens, ducks, and rabbits with them, probably to sell in some market. They also looked at us curiously, wondering, I imagine, what people of our standing were doing in Casablanca: who the old woman was, white as a candle and attended to devotedly by the younger woman; who the short, ugly man was, and who the pair of distinguished and handsome gentlemen were, a bit annoyed, it seemed, with all the bustle.

On hearing that we spoke a language different from theirs, the children, curious, came closer to see us better. What sounds were those, whose meaning they could not decipher? All of a sudden, when we were halfway through the crossing, an old man who had come on board with a piglet under his arm, stumbled, and the animal escaped.

The uproar that ensued was indescribable: the pig began to run from one end of the raft to the other, looking in vain for a way out, squealing like a demon; several people followed him, trying to grab him; rabbits, ducks, and hens added their cries to the concert, and the pilot had to warn us in a thunderous voice that if we didn't put an end to the brouhaha we would end up in the bottom of the bay. Trying to save itself, the pig found refuge behind the legs of Emilio De la Cruz, who let out a howl that was more hair-raising than the noise of all the animals put together. When the fugitive was finally captured, to applause and laughter, the crisis finally overcome, the passengers got ready to disembark, realizing that we would be docking soon. We let them get out first and followed behind.

"What an amusing crossing," Wen joked.

"Goldoni would have loved such a scene," Eleonora assured us.

De la Cruz paid some coins to the boy who had been left in charge of not letting any hoodlum get near the Dodge Brothers and, taking the driver's seat, took us around to see several places in the city. For the most part, Wenceslao and I were already familiar with them, but for the ladies, all the time holed up at the Inglaterra or the theater, to see the fortresses, the cathedral, the Palace of the Captain Generals and the monument with Antonio Maceo on a horse was quite an event.

"Now I am taking you to Guanabacoa," the chauffeur announced and stepped on the gas.

Guanabacoa, which long ago had been an independent city, had become one of Havana's most populous suburbs with the growth of the capital. He parked wherever he could and we followed him through a labyrinth of streets. The sun was becoming stronger, and La Duse took off her shawl and handed it to Désirée. On passing by a house, we saw through the open windows a girl practicing scales on a piano.

"There are many artists here," Emilio commented. "It's as if in the village of Pepe Antonio folks are born knowing how to sing, play some instrument, act, or dance."

I was going to ask who this Pepe Antonio was, when someone crossed our path. I must have gone pale on seeing the negro that we had hired to kidnap Vázquez Garralaga, and immediately I remembered that we still owed him ten pesos. Was he upset over our delay in paying him? It didn't seem so from the friendly way that he was smiling.

"Were you satisfied with the way the little job was handled?" he said as a way of greeting us.

Wenceslao and I nodded like *Guignol* dolls, wishing the earth would swallow us. How could we explain to La Duse our ties with El Ecobio? Even though the delinquent looked a little better that Monday than when we had met him in his room at Jesus del Monte, you wouldn't have to be too clever to know what his kind did. I let out a relieved sigh on noticing that behind him there came, very elegant as always, his cousin.

"What are you guys doing around here?" Agustín Miraflores exclaimed joyfully and was ready to give us a hug when he noticed the two ladies with us and immediately assumed a more formal attitude.

Taking charge of the uncomfortable situation, Emilito explained to his countrymen "of color" that we were showing Guanabacoa to La Signora Duse and her secretary. On hearing the tragedienne's name, Scissors looked at the old woman with surprise and leaned toward her.

"I am one of your many admirers in Cuba," he let her know.

I translated the phrase for the actress, who nodded, reserved.

"Señor Miraflores is one of the best tailors in town," Wen made sure to inform her. "If we dress somewhat elegantly, we owe it to him," he added, trying to make clear our relation to the negro. As far as El Ecobio went, he preferred to forget who he was or how we knew him.

The Italian informed the tailor that the quality of our clothes was very striking and congratulated him on his abilities. To her, who couldn't even sew on a button, anyone who could transform pieces of cloth into beautiful outfits was a sort of magician. Agustín swelled up with satisfaction and said that he and his cousin (La Duse looked at El Ecobio and lowered her chin to greet him) were going to a family party. There would be food and drums, singing and dancing. Would the ladies like to come? The invitation, of course, did not exclude the gentlemen. I was going to speak up, and say that we appreciated the invitation but we were in a hurry, but La Duse beat me to it, leaving all of us, including Désirée, with our jaws dropped, when she said that she would love to go, but only if they were sure that her presence would not be an intrusion.

Mina López-Salmón de Buffin never found out about it, but ten minutes later, Eleonora Duse, the same one who had refused to go to the Ball of a Thousand and One Nights that would be celebrated that very night in her honor, was attending a feast thrown by negroes, holding a plate of yucca with garlic sauce in one of her beautiful hands and bringing a slice of fried pork to her mouth with a silver fork. Scissors explained to us that the celebration, which took place in a rear courtyard, was in gratitude to Babalú for having saved the life of a nephew of his, who weeks ago had been very ill. The boy in question, a *negrito* who was about eight years old, dressed in white pants and a shirt of the same color with blue stripes, moved nimbly among the guests, serving sweets and drinks, without showing the slightest trace of sickness. "Several doctors said that he would not survive, and he became thin as a skeleton and ash-colored, but St. Lazarus y Babalú

Ayé, with his power and goodness, gave him back his health," the tailor explained to La Duse, and she, signaling to me with a gesture that it was unnecessary for me to translate into French, for she got the meaning of the words, nodded gravely.

"Neither my sister nor her husband, who is a lawyer, cared much about the saints, but, despairing, they had no choice but to turn to them. The *iyalocha* Ludonia La Rosa said that a hellish curse had been placed on the child, quite a *mayombero* hex, and explained to them what they needed to do to save him," Scissors continued. "The first thing was to put on the little angel, who ended up being the child of Babalú Ayé, the necklace of his saint, made of black beads, and then to bathe him in an infusion made from seventeen herbs. Seventeen, yes, not one more or less," Agustín nodded, on noticing that La Duse was listening to his story with a growing curiosity. "You can't imagine the effort it took to find all of them. We had to clean the child with bitter broom and toasted corn, pass a hen's egg all over his body, to gather up all evil, and crack it right afterward on the road, saying, 'Babalú Ayé, eat the flesh and leave the bone, save Ramoncito!' The same thing for a whole week."

The remedy had been infallible: on waking up on the morning of the eighth day and going to the sickbed, the mother watched, horrified, as a small scorpion came out of her son's belly button, ran down his bony leg, dragged itself down the sheets wet with sweat, and finally, very quickly, snuck into a hole in the wall. That filthy thing had been gnawing at her child's entrails until St. Lazarus, through his powers, had forced him to come out of there. That morning, Ramoncito awoke cured. No one realized, until the *iyalocha* respectfully pointed it out, that it was the seventeenth of December, St. Lazarus Day.

Those at the party, who at first watched the strange guests with Scissors with much curiosity, soon forgot about our presence. Almost all of them were very dark negroes or mestizos, although there were a few Caucasians here and there.

The boy's mother, a tall, good-looking *negra* named Gardenia, who gracefully wore a purple dress, whispered something in Agustín Miraflores's ear, glancing at us, and the tailor let us know that his sister wanted to show us the altar. We followed the owner of the house into one of the rooms inside and came to a gigantic statue of St. Lazarus, on top of a table covered with a rustic cloth. The plaster statue showed the leper on his feet, dressed in rags and held up by crutches, and with a pair of scrawny white dogs licking his wounds. Around the saint there were dozens of lit candles, rag dolls shaped like dogs, small amulets, black feathers, and several plain casserole dishes and pumpkins cut in half and full of offerings: grains, smoked fish and strips of red meat, toasted corn ears, green coconuts, slices of burnt bread, and strings of garlic and onions.

La Duse took Ramoncito's mother's hands in hers and, pressing them affectionately, told her something that I couldn't hear. *La negra* got carried away and hugged the Italian. The two women stayed pressed together for some moments, under our disconcerted stares, and then came apart laughing, as if mocking their sentimental outburst, but with tears in their eyes.

The sound of drums made us return to the courtyard. Several musicians assembled on wooden benches, under a lemon tree, and were beating fervently on the skin of three drums of different sizes, all varicolored and adorned with bells and seeds. An obese young negro came out of the house, his flesh jiggling, and went to the musicians. He took a deep breath, closed his eyes, and began to sing a hymn in an African language. The conversations stopped, almost all of the guests made the sign of the cross, and some joined the corpulent soloist repeating certain phrases of the chant.

I noticed that Désirée was trying to convince La Signora to take a few steps back and move away from the first file of spectators. The old woman escaped from her grasp, slapping her on the hand, never taking her eyes from the performers of that primitive and bewitching music. When the fat man began another song, something unexpected happened. El Ecobio, who up to now had remained between Emilio and Scissors' brother-in-law, drinking the bitter-orange concoction that had been offered by the hosts, suddenly leapt into the air like an acrobat, and fell flat on the ground, a few steps from the drums, at first rigid, but very soon overcome by savage convulsions. Incredibly, the singer and drummers went on with their music, unperturbed.

"He is a horse for Babalú Ayé," the tailor whispered in my ear, while El Ecobio snorted and furiously beat his head on the ground. "The saint rarely comes down, but when he does he likes to ride him with gusto."

I searched, suspicious, for Wenceslao's eyes, but he either didn't notice or didn't want to pay attention to me: the same with La Duse, who watched El Ecobio with a hypnotic stare. With his eyes bulging and his back twisted, the negro made an effort to get up, and then, teetering, because of his numb legs and arms, he began to dance. I realized that for the guests of the feast, Agustín Miraflores's relative had ceased to be who he was and had become St. Lazarus himself. What were we watching? Was it a true possession or a farce in which we were all complicit? Continuing to move to the beat of the drums, the "horse" began to clap noisily above his head, as if a cloud of insects were descending on him. He spoke in a clogged-up voice, and a greenish secretion began running out of his nostrils. The courtyard became filled with flies and mosquitoes, and a sudden gust of wind blew dry leaves over our heads. El Ecobio came toward us dancing, brought his face almost right up to Désirée Wertheimstein's and, staring at the secretary with a teasing expression, said: *"Alacuattá!"* Then the possessed limped off towards a very old *negra,* seated in a wicker chair, and knelt down by her feet respectfully. "That is Ludonia La Rosa," Scissors explained as his cousin lifted the *iyalocha's* skirt up to her knees, letting us see the bloody bandage that she had tied to her calf. In one motion, El Ecobio pulled off the rag, a horrible pustule was exposed for everyone to see and, not giving us the chance to close our eyes or turn away our faces, he began to lick over and over, with great relish, the pus-filled wound.

"This is too much," I think I whispered, and with the utmost discretion, went into the house. Standing up by a corner of the altar, Ramoncito was improvising a fight between two of the rag-doll dogs. When he heard me enter, he fixed his eyes on me and smiled sympathetically. With a movement of his head, he bid me to come closer. I obeyed and put a hand on his shoulder.

"What are you doing here alone?" I asked, just to say something.

"Better to be alone than in bad company," he answered in a voice that was absolutely unsuitable to him, in a demonic, booming voice that could in no way be his, and it terrified me. On noticing that I was growing cold as an icicle, the boy let out a gross and coarse guffaw and threw his head back.

The laugh was interrupted by Gardenia Miraflores's entrance.

"What were you talking about?" the tailor's sister asked, coming toward us.

"Just silly stuff," Ramoncito answered, regaining his child's voice, and he ran out to the courtyard.

"You'll have to forgive him, he's been a little ill-behaved since after the illness," the woman said, and then informed me that the younger of the two ladies that had come with us wasn't feeling well and wanted to go.

When I returned to the courtyard, my companions were already leaving. The Austrian had lost all semblance of color and walked precariously, held up by Wenceslao and La Duse. The drums continued with even more insistence. Seated atop a stool, his head drooping, El Ecobio seemed to have come out of his trance and was sweating profusely.

I shook Ramoncito's father's hand and slid some bills in Scissors' jacket pocket, explaining to him they were for his cousin.

"May the boy stay well," I said to Gardenia on saying good-bye, and, turning around, headed toward the others. I paused when I heard someone hissing, trying to get my attention. It was Ludonia La Rosa, who was still seated in the same wicker chair, and wanted to see me. I retraced my steps and squatted beside her. An adolescent girl who was bandaging her sick leg anew, pretended not to hear us.

"*Oye, mi'jo,*" the *iyalocha* began, "listen to them as if your life depended on it." I asked her what she was talking about and she looked at me cunningly. "You don't have to pretend with me."

"I swear that I don't know what you are talking about, señora," I maintained.

"You can't deny that you are Oyá's child. You are all the same! Suspicious like owls," she pondered. "I am talking to you about the dead, *carajo*. What they want you to do," she clarified, taking out the cigar that she had put away in a pocket of her skirt. The girl lit a match, and reached it up to the *iyalocha* who sucked on the cigar. "Remember that they know everything, *everything*," she went on, exhaling smoke and coughing. "If they sometimes say confusing things, it's just to fuck with you."

I remembered about Arrigo Boito. Aside from the Italian, I thought back, no other spirit had communicated with me in the two weeks that we had been on the Island. Unless she was counting the recent pointed remarks by Ramoncito as an attempt at communication. Only Boito, that's it, but La Duse's old lover had not asked me for anything.

"But they will ask!" Ludonia guaranteed in an irritated voice, reading my mind, and then added, "How can you be such an unbeliever? What you need is a good cleansing. Come see me in my house one of these days. Tell Agustincito to bring you."

I tried to clear my mind completely so that the old woman wouldn't continue stealing my thoughts.

"What are they going to ask me for?" I asked.

"That, I don't know," the *iyalocha* confessed. "What I can tell you is that a hell of a storm is brewing up there," and she pointed to the heavens. "And there's horrible things headed our way. A great curse, something very ugly."

"But what do they want with me?" I persisted.

"Go on, go, they are waiting for you," Ludonia La Rosa pressed me. "And don't forget what I've told you!"

The fresh air that came in through the car windows revived Désirée. As if the five of us had made a silent pact, no one alluded to the shocking scene we had witnessed at the feast of St. Lazarus. La Duse limited herself to saying that the world of the negroes was as mysterious as it was dazzling. De la Cruz preferred to qualify it as hair-raising and said that, for our trip to have a happy ending, he would take us to the Almendares River, and so he did.

If the sight of the crystalline current didn't quite make us forget the grotesque images of El Ecobio's dance, it brought forth at least a stroke of harmony into our spirits. The sun had gone back in hiding and several children played near the banks. Wenceslao threw a coin into the waters, bidding them to go search for it, and they all plunged in yelling and screaming.

"I am tired," La Duse announced, her eyes heavy. "I think I would like to return to the hotel."

We nodded and made our way back toward the car. Wenceslao and La Signora straggled behind, and I thought that at that moment he would ask her for the interview. I turned around to watch them. My friend spoke animatedly and La Duse listened to him with a circumspect smile. Every two or three steps she would shake her head slowly.

The look of dejection on Wenceslao's face when we were all in the Dodge Brothers left no doubt in my mind what the reply had been to his request. La Duse rejected the petition in a pleasant but decisive manner. *Impossibile!* Afterwards, I found out what her exact words had been. "At first, in my youth, I granted several interviews, but soon I came to understand that to allow the public to know things about me made no sense. Now that time has passed, and that my private life lacks any vestige of the romantic interest that it could have once provoked, I want even more so to remain loyal to my customs."

Little did it help that, on the way to the Inglaterra, Wenceslao boldly persisted, putting to use arguments of different natures that we had prepared days before. La Duse remained firm in her denial. *"Impossibile, impossibile!"* she reiterated and put an end to the discussion by saying, with unexpected severity, to ask anything of her, except the one thing she would never grant him: an interview.

Out of the corner of my eye, I watched the actress, who looked out at the passing landscape with a harsh expression, and I understood how Wen and I saw her entirely differently. To him, she was the greatest living tragedienne, an indelible name in the history of the theater, the protagonist of his scrapbook; to me, on the other hand, she was an older woman, whose savings had vanished during the war with the ups and downs of the market, who went back to the stage reluctantly, in spite of her bad health, because she knew no other way to make a living.

On arriving at the hotel, we saw that San Rafael Street had been closed off to cars. During our absence, they had constructed a sort of tunnel, adorned with flowers, that joined the front door of the Teatro Nacional with the restaurant of the Inglaterra.

Eleonora thanked Monkeyface for the unforgettable outing and, with the Austrian on her tail, headed for the elevator. We had to run to catch up with them. As we rose to the fourth floor, La Duse remained with her eyes stubbornly on the floor. Désirée looked at the contrite Wenceslao and then at me, raising her eyebrows impotently. The farewell was short; courteous but cold.

"I need a drink," Wenceslao declared as I was about to put a key to the lock in our room, and I suggested that we order two whiskies. "No," he said. "I'd rather go down to the bar," and to specify that he wanted to be alone, he added, "You stay here, I'll be right back." Without waiting for a reply, he turned and headed for the stairs.

"Nothing is going to be resolved by being like this," I protested, but he didn't even bother to answer, so I went into the room.

In the shadows, seated on a chair, with Julián del Casal's manuscript on his lap, Detective Aquiles de la Osa awaited me.

"What are you doing here?" I managed to ask. "Who let you in?"

He replied, without getting upset, that after working twenty years with the secret police he had learned things that were a lot more difficult than sneaking into someone's room.

"If Mohammed doesn't come to the mountain . . ." he said as a way of explanation and, taking the newspaper that was atop my bed, handed it to me. "I suppose you don't know that your uncle turned himself in."

I took the newspaper and, at the same time, took back de Casal's sonnet.

"Yes, I did know," I answered, sitting on the rocking chair, and devoured the article dealing with the matter. Señor Misael Reyes, a Colombian national and resident of this country for many years, had shown up at the headquarters of the secret police, asking to be received by Inspector Donato Cubas. When Cubas came, Reyes confessed to the murder of the Chinese Mei Feng, adding, in passing, that he had left the murder weapon in the hotel room of Señor Jean Bonhaire in an attempt to incriminate him. The decision to turn himself in was precipitated by a remorseful conscience: he did not want to bear the burden, aside from the murder, of letting another man be condemned in his place.

The detective waited for me to finish reading and then said, "If you ask me, that fairy tale seems a little suspicious. But that afternoon, the judge gave the orders that since we had a confessed murderer on our hands, we should release the suspect. So the Frenchie is free."

"So you think that my uncle confessed to get the other one out of jail?"

"I am not asking you to believe it, Belalcázar, I have only suggested it," he clarified, getting to his feet and walking toward the balcony. "In truth, to say believe, really believe, then I only believe in God," he confessed. *"Sometimes,"* he specified with a note of cynicism, after a pause, and, pointing to the pergola covered in flowers that crossed San Rafael, he asked me if I was going to the Ball of a Thousand and One Nights.

"Yes, why?"

"No reason. Just curious. I imagine that you will be among friends."

I walked toward him and looked out at the street closed off to cars. Several men were putting the finishing touches, across the way, on a replica of an Ottoman pavilion.

"Wenceslao and I are part of the jury that will award the prizes," I commented.

"Would you like to see your uncle?"

"In prison?"

"He is not in prison," Aquiles de la Osa explained. "He is detained."

"Who killed the *Chino?*" I asked without equivocation.

"The Frenchman," he answered instantly.

"But will they condemn my uncle?" I said.

"If that's how he wants it. It is difficult to convince a judge that a fellow who is accusing himself of murder is lying."

We agreed that I would be at the secret police headquarters at eight in the morning.

"Don't say anything to my uncle," I begged.

"Don't worry about it," he said. "I love surprises, too."

He took his hat from the bed and, pushing it down to his ears, advised me to keep de Casal's manuscript somewhere safe.

"Today it is not worth a thing," he admitted. "But who knows what a collector may pay for that piece of paper one day?" On noticing my surprise, he let out a guffaw. "Does it seem strange that a policeman knows the old poets? If you weren't so busy, I would take you to the cemetery, to see de Casal's grave. This is some country! Years and years of taking up collections and we still haven't put a plaque on the house in which he was born. Take care of that manuscript, Belalcázar," he insisted. "And it is a family memento as well," he added mischievously. "Say hello to Señor Hoyos," he said before he left.

I fell on the bed, completely exhausted. I lifted the paper and reread the article. The ringing of the phone startled me. It was La Cay.

"You don't know how sorry I am about all this," she declared, not wasting time with prefaces. "The count told me that Misael Reyes was up to something, but I thought that it was just his own suspicions."

"The count is demented," I replied in an even voice. "And you . . ." I left the phrase unfinished, not sure whether I should say out loud what I thought of her.

"And I?" she challenged me to go on.

Knowing how insulting I was about to be, I hung up the phone. And as if shot up by a spring, I went to the desk and, at great speed, wrote a letter. It was addressed to Eleonora Duse and in it I said that, with her denial, she was causing Wenceslao a damage that she could not begin to imagine. For me, whether to interview her or not was of no matter, but for him it was much more important than he cared to admit. I concluded by appealing to the largesse of her feelings and begging her to reconsider and help prevent a great disappointment in such a pure soul. Didn't it seem to La Signora that there was enough suffering in the world? Why add to it? I folded the paper, put it in an envelope, and went to slip it under La Duse's door.

I had just entered the shower when I heard Wen return. He came into the bathroom, took off his clothes, and kept me company under the warm water. I embraced him and he put his head on my chest.

"Easy," I said, and I told him what I had just done.

"I doubt she'll change her mind," he murmured, not even thinking about soaping up.

"He who perseveres, triumphs."

"Not always."

He was right. Not always. The best example was my interest in Mella. What good had it done to persevere, listen to his diatribes, go with him to the greasy syndicate and attend the meeting-tribute, putting my life, and Wen's, in danger? None at all. It had all come to nothing. That body would never be mine. Changing the topic, I told him about my conversation with Aquiles de la Osa but he didn't say a word about the detective's impertinence in breaking into our room. We remained like that, embracing, till our fingers got wrinkly from the water.

"Are you hungry?" he asked then.

"Very much so," I confessed.

"Let's go down and have dinner then. The ball starts at eleven and who knows when it will be over."

Gossip is a deep-seated pleasure, a vice that we label as a weakness, but in which all of us, or almost all of us, participate.

Why the obsessive need to bring to light what has been kept shut, what others want to keep hidden? Why is it that we love to spread secrets? Sometimes, after committing an indiscretion, whether involuntarily or consciously, I ask myself what was it that made me say what I shouldn't have. Usually, the answers are different: sometimes it is a need to expose some obvious fact about the matter; other times it is tricky, you say something to hear some other thing in return; and sometimes you want to help or you want to hurt; but almost always you speak more than you should with the simple desire to stir the fires . . .

On a certain afternoon, when the papers were beginning to praise me, two people whom I trusted, whom I was meeting, came rowdily into my room. They found me seated on a chair, by an open window, with a dish on my lap. The gentlemen (for they were men: two young, promising writers) seemed ill at ease, thinking that they had surprised me in the prosaic act of feeding myself before the performance, and asked if they should return later.

I said no, and this made them even more intrigued. First, because they noticed that the plate that I had before me was empty and, furthermore, because they saw that I was drowning in tears.

I wasn't eating. I was crying. And the purpose of the plate before me was to gather the thick tears that fell abundantly from my nose and cheeks!

"Are you sick?" my visitors asked, alarmed. "Should we call a doctor?"

I said no and tried to ease them with a smile.

"I am going to tell you something," I said. "But promise me that you will never repeat it."

They both swore, gulping, consumed by curiosity.

I then told them about the fourth act in Odette, *the play by Sardou that I was going to play in that night; it so moved me that tears flowed unstoppable from my eyes. A lover of moderation and subtlety, I was afraid that my tears would seem excessive. I was, that is, facing a dilemma. Not to cry at all during the performance would be unthinkable; crying too much, without control, would be . . . embarrassing. I could, I know, not do the play, toss it out and replace it with some other . . . but you don't often find a play that audiences love so!*

So then I found the solution to finding the proper balance: a sort of trick to cry enough but not so much as to wet the folks in the first row. Every time I did Odette, *I summoned the scenes in the fourth act before leaving for the theater, I wept for a while beforehand, and, in this manner, used up a large part of my tears. The method, though uncommon, was infallible and, thanks to it, my weeping was controlled during the performance.*

The two gentlemen laughed and said that, had they not been witness to the incident, they would never have believed such a story. I reminded them that it was a secret and that I had their word that they would not tell anyone. They repeated their promises of discretion and we moved on to another topic.

A week later I traveled to a distant city and, on arriving at the theater where I was performing, someone asked me out of nowhere if it was true that I cried before my performances to be able to control my tears. I became upset in vain: the story was already on everybody's tongue.

I never knew for sure which one of the two señors had been disloyal (or had they both been?), but I learned my lesson. Whoever reveals a secret must know for certain that sooner or later what has been revealed, important or not, will become public knowledge. It is a plain fact: discretion, if it ever existed, is today an extinct virtue or very soon to vanish from the face of the earth. We human beings feel a particular pleasure, a sickening delight, in revealing other's intimacies. It's as if, once we are in the possession of a secret, it burns our tongue and we have to tell others right away, anyone, to be rid of it as soon as possible.

With this I want to make clear that I don't have any illusions about your circumspection or reserve. Whatever I have said up to now, I know, will be repeated by you, by those who hear it from your mouths, by those who hear it thirdhand from them, and continually, in growing circles, each time wider. On sharing them, the words that I have said, the stories I have told you, have been condemned to lose, if they ever had it, their status of secrets. In the end, it really doesn't matter much anymore. Why should I be interested in taking so many secrets with me? They are a heavy burden, a hindering weight that takes up too much space. Two or three is enough. It is well known that they do not make coffins as wide as they used to.

13

That one is Mella," I assured Wenceslao and pointed to a strapping young man in a red mask, lilac silk pants, and a dark vest accented with a string of beads who stood out in a group that passed by us.

"I think you see that boy everywhere," he replied disdainfully. "Come back down to earth, Lucho Belalcázar! How can you even think that one of the champions of the revolution is going to come to the Ball of a Thousand and One Nights?"

To myself, I admitted that it didn't make any sense, but I said that if it wasn't Julio Antonio, then it certainly looked like him.

The theater in which we had applauded La Duse the night before had been transformed into a gigantic bazaar of many colors. From the balconies there hung authentic Persian rugs, serving as tapestry, and a *draperie* in orange and blue hid the vault of the ceiling and the mouth of the stage. The reflectors created marvelous combinations of lights, in many colors, heightening the fantastic aspect of the set: sometimes the hall seemed to have the radiant clarity of the moon; other times the shadows of nightfall. The orchestra, carpeted and raised to the level of the stage, had become a great dance floor.

At midnight exactly, the curtain rose and everyone broke into rabid applause. The set on the stage, which brought to mind a palace in Damascus or Baghdad, was magnificent, and Habib Steffano had scrutinized every detail for its authenticity. The throne of the great caliph was located in the center, and all around it there were soft cushions, embroidered with jewels, and several coconut and betel palms from the Garden of the Phoenix. Five enormous oil lamps surrounded the set.

Trumpeters announced the entrance of the powerful Harun ar-Rashid, who came out from behind the set, surrounded by several dignitaries from his court. Scheherezade then arrived and threw herself at the feet of the sultan.

After this prologue, Mina Pérez-Salmón de Buffin made her entrance, on the arm of Habib Steffano, dressed as a night fairy. The outfit, silver *lamé,* embroidered with pearls and pastel jewels, was beautiful, but the most striking part was her enormous headdress: a rose *lamé minaret,* finished with very long blue and green feathers, which the millionairess had trouble balancing on her head. Madame Buffin offered a word of welcome and thanked everyone present for their help to the *crèche* and the asylum that bears her family name. She explained that for reasons beyond her power, the ineffable Eleonora Duse, to whom the *kermesse* was paying tribute, could not make it. However, the tragedienne had sent two actresses from her company on her behalf: the talented and beautiful Señoritas Maria and Jone Morino. A spotlight shone on the box where they were seated (Maria, whom we had seen play Mariolina in *La porta chiusa* and Jone, Regina in *Spettri*), next to Fortune Gallo and Memo Benassi. The organizer of the soirée then let Dr. Habib Steffano, who was dressed in the same outfit that he wore in ceremonies of the court of Faisal I, have a word. He began by reciting an Arab poem, in which he praised the delights of the Syrian colony. Then he said a few words about Oriental culture and urged the guests to enjoy the memorable evening, the product of the tenacity of the altruistic and kind-hearted Madame Buffin.

The heart and soul of the ball left the stage, and Señorita Lyla Schap Labrousse performed a dance around the caliph and Scheherezade. Afterwards, different groups filed past the throne: the houris, the Arabian princesses, the ladies of the harem, Ali Baba and his forty thieves (who were all men), and others. The costume of the houris, designed by Dalmau, was unimpressive, compared with the others. At the moment that the next-to-last group—the little princesses Deryabar—began their number, I whispered to Wen that I would be right back and slipped away to the bathrooms. I was in one of the stalls when I heard some footsteps and voices. I seemed to recognize one of them, so I pricked up my ears to see if I could hear what they were saying.

"When they give out the prizes," one of the men said.

"And what if he doesn't give them out?"

"It doesn't matter if it's Zayas who gives them out or your damn grandmother: when they give out the prizes all hell will break loose," the voice I seemed to recognize stated.

I could have been mistaken the first time, but not again. I half opened the door to the stall carefully, so that they would not see me, and confirmed what was already beyond suspicion: the one in the red mask (could it more obvious? red!) was none other than Julio Antonio Mella.

"Who has the flyers?" one of his companions asked.

"I do," replied another one, opening his jacket, and I was able to see not the papers that they were referring to, but the butt of a pistol.

At that moment, one of the men told the others to be quiet and signaled suspiciously toward the stalls. Had I involuntarily made some movement that betrayed me? The conspirators looked at each other, suddenly serious, and were about to start coming toward me when several Syrians came into the bathroom speaking in loud voices. The revolutionaries made as if they were drying their hands and hurried out.

Suddenly, my legs began to tremble and I pulled the chain and got out of the stall. Ignoring Habib Steffano's countrymen, I splashed my face with water. What were these madmen planning? To cause a ruckus in the middle of the masquerade? Terrorize *la crème* and ruin their great night? I ran back to Wen. The last group, the Mameluke sultans, was still performing.

"Come back down to earth, huh?" I said in a vengeful tone and told him about my little adventure.

"We have to tell Mina," was the only thing he could say.

"Are you crazy?" I replied rashly, and noticing that other members of the jury turned to look at us, I went on in an almost inaudible voice. "That would be a betrayal."

"And if we allow them to set off a bomb, what would that be?" he argued.

I told him that no one had said anything about bombs and convinced him not to say a word. What was going to happen was going to happen, but we shouldn't go looking for problems. This was probably related to the scandal with the lottery that De la Cruz had told us about. The most likely thing was that they were going to air Zayas's dirty laundry in front of all the distinguished families of the capital.

When the people began to get bored with all the groups filing past, Harun ar-Rashid walked out, followed by Scheherezade and her vassals, and they were replaced by two popular orchestras on each end of the stage, the one from Casino Nacional and the one from Country Club, both of which were donating their services as a special favor to Madame Buffin. The one from Casino Nacional took over first and, breaking into the most modern foxtrot in their repertoire, shook up a good part of the audience. Bending down so that the feathers of her night-fairy headdress wouldn't brush against the ceiling, Mina came into the presidential box to give directions to the qualifying jury. On arriving at the Nacional we had learned that, for strategic reasons, two presidents would lead the tribunal: the first lady of the republic and the countess of Buena Vista. Also in the jury were the countess of Rivero, Cartolica Zaldo de Mendoza, and Ángela Fabra de Mariátegui, wife of the Spanish ambassador. The Señores Héctor Altunaga and Ricardo de Saavedra, two journalists—Fontana and Uhthoff—and Wenceslao and I completed the select group. At the last moment, one more judge was added, the Countess Pears, the former Duchess of Mignano, a distinguished representative of Italian nobility who, placing her artistic devotion before the conventions of the aristocracy, was also a singer and went by the name of Donna Ortensia. With the illustrious old woman who had just arrived from New York, Primo de Rivera's ambassador, and two Colombians, the jury had a certain international chic.

"The prizes will be announced after the parade of candidates, which will be at two in the morning," the organizer said. Half an hour before, we would get together to choose who would be in the running for the prizes. Until then, we were free to roam about as we pleased, watching the guests, making note of their costumes, which, through their luxury or singularity, captured our attention. "I hope that Alfredo shows up at the last minute!" La Buffin said, taking the hand of the president's wife. "Oh, my dear, I wouldn't hold my breath, if I told you how many days it has been since I've seen him . . ." María Jaén de Zayas replied as they left the box, and added in a wounded tone: "The country is going to bleed that man dry." "If he doesn't bleed the country dry first," the countess of Buena Vista whispered in the ear of her counterpart of Rivero.

"Have you seen *The Girl Lupe* yet?" Fontana asked us, and when we said we hadn't, he urged us to do so as soon as we could. "The work is a dream! And La Iris is better than ever. Isn't it true, Enrique?" he added, looking for Uhthoff's support.

"Although I shouldn't say it, since it is not fair to judge something that I am part of, I have to admit that you are right," the author of the libretto for the operetta exclaimed. "Esperancita has not held a thing back. When she decides to do something, she goes all the way. As soon as it begins, one is transported to Mexico during the Maximillian Empire."

"That's why she is who she is, *chico,*" Fontana concluded. "Because, gentlemen, if I may be blunt: La Duse, despite her fame as a tragedienne and those stories about her beautiful hands, has not been able to fill this theater. On the other hand, Iris has been packing them in at the Payret for over a month."

"These comparisons are odious," I interjected, to prevent a certain enraged *cachaco* from uttering three or four obscenities at the social chronicler from the *Diario de la Marina,* "and even more so when dealing with such obviously different artists."

"I agree with you," Uhthoff stated.

They both left to join the *divette* after making us promise that we would meet up with them in the grotto set up by Magno Vermouth in a corner of the lobby to sell glasses of punch. A promise that, of course, we did not mean to keep. We went down, yes, but to the main hall, which was more crowded than it looked from above in the boxes. Viziers and odalisques, sultans and princesses, houris and afreets, Turkish slaves and Ali Baba's thieves, all danced joyfully to the music of the Country Club orchestra. But not all costumes were related, as I had thought, to the world of a Thousand and One Nights. The theater was full of gypsies, Pierrots, sylphs, Trojans, Spanish cigarette girls, mandarins, Cleopatras, musketeers, geishas, Napoleons, and countless other characters. Maria and Jone, La Duse's representatives, had charmed the young men of the capital with the wild fashion in which they danced the foxtrot and now were trying, between giggles and flirtations, to learn the Cuban dances. Near the cloakroom, surrounded by admirers, Memo Benassi was signing autographs on napkins. Dressed as a vestal virgin and with a glass in her hand, Mrs. Chapman Catt, the champion of the suffragists, proselytized to a chorus of señoras.

A shabby-looking man in a djellaba and an Indo-Chinese-style cap, who planted himself right in front of us, turned out to be none other than Emilio De la Cruz.

"This is unprecedented," he said very excitedly. "It took me two long, painful hours to get here! There are hundreds of cars outside and a wall of latecomers," and *sotto voce* he told us some gossip that he had just heard: María Garralaga de Vázquez was very upset because her one and only had not been asked to be part of the jury.

A wave of newcomers burst in, separating us: Monkeyface and Wenceslao ending up in one place and me in another. When I was able to get to them again, I found them a bit upset: they had just recognized, in spite of the costumes, several detectives from the secret police, among them Pompilio Ramos, the assistant inspector, who was dressed as a pirate, with a patch over one eye.

"I don't know what they are doing here," Monkeyface explained. "What are they afraid of, that someone will be killed?"

"You never know," Wen replied, looking at me.

I felt my stomach jump and looked around in all directions, trying to make out, in that whirlwind of colors, a red mask. I saw not one, but many, because all the Arab princesses wore these. I was suddenly seized by an irrational fear. I needed to find Mella, tell him that the place was crawling with policemen, that the outcome of the ball could prove fatal.

"I would tell the organizers," Wen insisted.

"I already told you, it's not even an option!" I exploded.

"What's wrong with you two?" Monkeyface intervened. "Let's hear it, please." And Wenceslao told him about the bathroom incident. *"Coño!"* Emilito said, biting on a nail. "We're in for some shit here."

"Were you talking about me?" Fontana said, as a joke, and, as he laughed, his hips swayed. Begging my friends' pardon and swearing that he would return me safe and sound, he dragged me toward the grotto of Magno Vermouth. "There is someone who is dying to see you, my darling," he said roguishly.

That someone was sporting a rose-silk costume with white pompons and a hat sprinkled with different kinds of beads, and spoke with a Mexican accent, immediately scolding me for not having been at the opening night of *The Girl Lupe.*

"And you swore!" Esperanza Iris said. "Such a little liar!"

Uhthoff, who was next to her, assured her that, if she found it fitting, he would bind me and take me to see the very next performance of her operetta.

"I am *very* jealous," the *divette* confirmed, clinging with an annoying familiarity to one of my arms. "A little bird told me that you have been to every one of La Duse's performances."

I tried to come up with an excuse but none came to my bloated brain.

"Let's dance," the empress of the operetta decided, and she was able to take only one step in the direction of the orchestra, because, with an energetic, not to say brusque, movement, a woman coming from who knows where, and draped from head to toe in a dark veil, broke us apart.

"Forgive me," the stranger said, disguising her voice. "But Señor Belalcázar promised me this dance." And, taking me by the hand, she led me to the dance floor.

As I examined her, we began to dance. And suddenly I froze. A light went off in my head and I realized that it was Graziella Gerbelasa.

"I warned you that I never wanted to see you again," I said, stepping back from her.

"And I told you that it wouldn't be so easy to get rid of me," the young woman rebutted, and through the veil I could see the fire in her eyes.

We probably would have argued for a while, but at that moment I got a glimpse of a pair of lilac-colored pants and, not listening to the poetess's protests, I ran after them, hoping that they belonged to Mella. And, in fact, they did. I caught up to him and grabbed him by the arm, separating him from his entourage.

"What are you doing here?" was the first thing that came out of my mouth.

"Having fun," he said, not showing surprise at all. "Why else would you come to a dance?"

I warned him, in his ear, that the theater was full of policemen in disguise. He smiled and limited himself to pinching my chin affectionately and saying: "They are everywhere, my friend." Then, dodging the growing number of guests, he slipped away to where his comrades awaited him. I got up on my tiptoes and stretched my neck to see where they were going, but someone tugged at my arm, calling my attention.

"What did you think of Scheherezade's dress?" Habib Steffano asked, pointing to the splendid outfit worn by his wife at his side. "Don't you think it deserves the prize?" he said shamelessly. The lady lowered her face, modestly, and made a small Damascene curtsy.

Attributing the seriousness on my face to his comment, the Syrian blushed and said that it wasn't his intention to influence one of the members of the distinguished jury. As he begged a hundred pardons, I noticed that Graziella Gerbelasa was coming toward me, and I escaped through the dancing couples.

Amidst the music and the noise of conversations, I heard a chorus of voices calling out my name. I looked around and saw, near the extreme left-hand side of the stage, where the orchestra from the Casino Nacional played, Wenceslao and Monkeyface signaling for me to come rejoin them. Paco Pla was with them, dressed like a toy soldier, as well as Bartolomé Valdivieso, who wore sapphire-blue pantaloons and a felt fez hat characteristic of the Ottomans. I made my way towards them as best I could and, when I reached them, proposed that we go out to the portico of the theater to get some fresh air. The *mulato* and Ears were engaged in a discussion over the sum raised by the ball. The former was sure that it was twenty-five thousand pesos, and the latter insisted that he should add ten thousand to that amount. In any case, they agreed, it was an outrageous amount, an unprecedented success. Changing the topic, De la Cruz commented on how terrible Olavo Vázquez Garralaga looked, despite the striking genie costume he was wearing.

"Haven't you heard?" the *mulato* tattled incredulously. "They abducted him yesterday, when he was leaving his house. They locked him up in the latrine of a tenement house and ripped up the manuscript of a tragedy that he was going to give to La Duse."

"Poor man," Wenceslao sympathized, with a sorrow that seemed almost genuine.

The entrance to the Nacional and San Rafael Street were extensions of the ball. Two more orchestras, of lesser quality, of course, thundered into the night, and hundreds of pairs whirled to their beat. A cordon of guards kept an eye out so that no one who had not paid could enter the party. Dozens of people passed through the improvised tunnel that joined the Inglaterra with the theater, in search of food, which, according to what had been announced, would be served all night at the restaurant. I looked at La Duse's balcony and I imagined that she had not been able to sleep. And on the eve of her last performance! Had she read my letter?

A while later, we were back in the box of honor with the rest of the members of the jury. La Buffin said that we should put together a list of candidates for the prizes. The favorites would be called up to the stage so that the public could appreciate the quality and beauty of their attires. Then, the musicians would play a couple of numbers while we made our final decision, and right after that, we would announce the winners. If Alfredo arrived (she looked at Mariíta de Zayas with the expression of a victim), he would hand out the trophies; if not, then the two presidents of the jury would do it. Then, Mina proceeded to read us the list of possible candidates that she and the ladies of the organizing committee had drawn up, to see if we found it fitting. The choices were all welcomed, but Donna Ortensia, the countess of Rivero, and Uhthoff made clear their wishes to add some names, which Madame Buffin wrote down reticently, furrowing her brow. When the matter seemed over and done with, the social chronicler from the *Diario de la Marina* remarked:

"I think that we are committing a grave injustice and if I don't say what it is, I am going to burst."

"Speak, Fontana, to see if the matter can be fixed!" the first lady challenged him.

"If there is someone that deserves a prize for her costume, it is

Mina de Buffin," the fat man assured us and we all agreed, for, to be truthful, he was not exaggerating.

The millionairess brought her hands to her heart and argued that her name on the list of candidates might be misinterpreted by some. Her greatest and most yearned-for prize she had already received with the unquestionable success of the party, she assured us with tears in her eyes. And, after squeezing the fat man's hand as a sign of gratitude, she went off to give the list to Habib Steffano, who would be in charge of rounding up the candidates. A moment later, the president of Cuba came into the box, greeted everyone, and apologized for his tardiness, which he attributed to annoying government obligations. His presence, noticed immediately by the guests at the ball, was welcomed with courteous applause. If they knew about the rumors of the scandal, they preferred to pretend that they didn't. After all, many probably thought, the thing with the lottery had happened so long ago. Was it fair to make a man suffer for a peccadillo from his past? Because, señores, let him who is without sin . . .

The Country Club orchestra finished the number they were playing, and its conductor announced a break to watch the parade of the most noteworthy costumes. The president from the National Academy of Damascus, flanked by two trumpeters from the court, who took turns sounding their fanfares, began to call out the names of the candidates. As they heard their names, ten ladies and five gentlemen got up on stage and received moderate or thunderous applause, according to how the guests felt about their costumes.

It wouldn't be easy to pick the winners. Big money had been invested in those varied, but all splendid, costumes. I made a mental note of my favorites with the aim of standing up for them tooth and nail during the final debate. I loved, for example, the Sittukhan princess costume of Rosita Sardiñas de Mazorra, which was made up of garnet pants, a little green skirt, stiff and sparkling, and a headdress made of flowers, fruits, and emeralds. I also thought that the costume of Lindaraxa, the bride of Alhamar, the builder of Granada, was worthy of a prize: it was made of silk pussy-willows on satin, with pearl appliqué, and Conchita Martínez Pedro de Menocal wore it gracefully. The outfit worn by María Luisa Gómez de Cagiga, of a

Byzantine goddess, took one's breath away, and Fontana pointed out that when she wore it a few months before, for a party at the Paris Opera, she had left the French green with envy; they couldn't believe that a piece of clothing made in the Antilles could be so dazzling. As for the men, my trophies had already been decided: they were for the clubman Emilio Obregón, dressed as Prince Farid, in a golden satin tunic with black and scarlet appliqué, taffeta pants, wide down to the knees and then very tight-fitting, and a white turban with a blue cabochon; and to Adolfo Altuzarra, Harun ar-Rashid of Baghdad, not so much for the clothes, but because of the young man himself, who was good enough to eat and deserved not only the prize, but was fit to be given away himself as the night's biggest award.

Dr. Steffano's wife, with her Scheherazade costume, accented by thick, sparkling, gold bracelets, closed out the parade of candidates.

The trumpeters were set on making everyone in the room deaf with their final set piece, when Mina de Buffin walked hurriedly on stage, causing the feathers in her *minaret* to oscillate dangerously from one side to the other. She went up to Dr. Steffano and told him something, shaking a paper in front of him. The Syrian looked upset. However, at the insistence of the ball's organizer, he had no choice but to explain to the audience, that, as in fairy tales, a mysterious stranger had just arrived late and asked for the favor of being presented to the court.

"Our dear Madame Buffin assured me that her costume was so sublime that it would be a sin to deny you the privilege of seeing it," the master of ceremonies said and, on his signal, one of the musicians played his trumpet. "Titania, the queen of the fairies!" he called out.

The crowd made way, in respectful silence, for a woman who moved toward the stage, very erect and sure of herself. La Buffin's decision was more than justified. Titania seemed indeed to have escaped from a midsummer's night dream, in her attire of green-and-silver brocade, with topaz arabesques, turquoise, and multicolored bugles, and her long tulle cape embroidered with tiny pearls. An artful tiara and a mask of daring simplicity, black with no decoration, finished off the outfit. Recovered from the surprise, the audience broke into cheers.

A fanfare from both trumpets indicated to the guests that they could dance again while the jury deliberated. In the presidential box, the members of the tribunal looked at each other not knowing how to proceed. But La Buffin, flushed from so much running around, came in ready to help us. After letting Zayas know how happy she was to have him at the ball and reminding him of his promise to hand out the prizes, she spoke to the jury. With the greatest respect and in the interest of making our jobs easier, the organizing commission had prepared a list of the winners and, still out of breath, submitted it for our consideration. After we read it, she wanted to know what we thought. Were we happy with it? We looked at each other uncomfortably, understanding that we were meant to say yes, and that, in fact, was what we said, although to give the prize to Catalina Lasa de Pedro seemed to me a mistake, no matter how expensive the getup that they had put together for her at the Casa Callot.

"In agreement, but with a caveat," Wenceslao specified.

"And what would that be?" Mina asked, intrigued.

"It is necessary for us to create a special prize, or something to that effect, for Titania, the queen of the fairies," my lover declared and, looking for the support of others, added, "There is no doubt that her costume has no equal."

Mina, in conciliatory fashion, declared that she agreed. She herself, dazzled by the sublimity of the attire, had thought twice about changing the rules of the game so that, in spite of her lateness in arriving at the ball, Titania could go up on stage. And that was fine, but to give her a prize wouldn't be wise. It could prove disastrous. The rest of the candidates were persons of high standing, of very prominent lineage, while the identity of the queen of the fairies was a mystery.

With a tenacity that must have seemed abominable to the millionairess, Wenceslao stood his ground, reasoning that to leave without a prize the candidate who was most applauded could result in a revolution by the audience. The word "revolution" made the hair on the back of my neck erect: with so many feathers and fake jewels I had forgotten about the Mella affair.

"There is another problem," Madame Buffin asserted, upset with the uncomfortable situation, "all the prizes have already been spoken for: the Oriental shawl, the soup tureen from the Quintana house, the peacock-feather fans, the bas-relief of Mateu . . . There is nothing left to give Titania!"

"This argument is ridiculous," the countess of Buena Vista interjected, pointing out several persons who, from adjacent boxes, delightfully eavesdropped on our debate.

"Yes, please, enough," Donna Ortensia agreed and, taking off a diamond brooch, gave it to Mina. "Give this to Titania as a prize!"

"All right, you win," the organizer conceded reluctantly. "God willing, we won't be disappointed when she takes off her mask."

"Don't worry about that, my dear Mina," Zayas said, getting up to go with her. "A woman in such an outfit can't be just anyone."

"Of course, honey," Cartolica Zaldo de Mendoza comforted her. "Go, go and give out the prizes so that this can be over with."

The candidates, Habib Steffano, and the trumpeters appeared on stage again and were joined by the quartet of Alfredo Zayas, La Buffin, and María and Jone Morino. Many of the spectators were shouting themselves hoarse, fervently calling out the names of their favorite contenders. The master of ceremonies asked for silence so that we could listen to the honorable president of the Republic.

"Good evening," the leader began. "Or should I say, good morning?" he jested. At that moment, a bang from one of the boxes in the second balcony made the audience scream, and all heads turned there. "It seems that someone brought champagne and is celebrating the victory of his candidate," Zayas joked without losing his composure, looking to steal the attention of the audience from the struggle and screaming from up above. "My friends, we have to learn to control our feelings," he went on, trying to make the audience believe that the motive for the incident was the masquerade contest.

I sprung up and left the box just in time to see two of the young men that I had seen in the bathroom running toward the door of the foyer. With Wenceslao right behind me, I ran to the stairs leading to the floor above and climbed them rapidly.

"Are you crazy? Come back!" he yelled from behind me. "You haven't lost anything up there, damn it."

We stopped on the final step. The attempt at disruption had been stifled quickly. Several policemen in costumes had Mella and three other young men handcuffed, and pushed them from behind, forcing them to move toward the stairs where we were. From the entrances to the boxes, numerous people were incredulously watching the scene.

On passing by us, the Beauty winked at us.

"If you see Oliva, tell her that I won't be home tonight," he requested with the hint of a smile.

Unable to move, we watched as the policemen and the revolutionaries descended the stairs. As soon as they disappeared, the inquisitive stopped watching and everything returned to normal. Pompilio Ramos came out of the box where the incident had taken place and, taking off his eyepatch, approached us slowly, carrying his pirate's hat in one hand and in the other a package of pamphlets that the revolutionaries were going to rain down on the guests at the ball. With a blank face, he asked us to take one of the pamphlets and we obeyed without saying a word. It was a broadside against Zayas, denouncing him as corrupt. He waited, scrutinizing us, for us to finish reading and then said, "What inappropriate friends you have!"

"Mella is not a friend," Wenceslao specified, handing him back the pamphlet, "he is only an acquaintance."

"Tell me who you are with, and I'll tell you who you are," the assistant inspector insisted.

"Appearances can be deceiving," my partner retorted.

"Where there is smoke, there is fire."

"Innocent till proven guilty."

Tired of the tense exchanges, I pulled Wenceslao by his shirt sleeve and, coldly saying good-bye to the policeman, we returned to the jury box at the moment that the president of the republic, assisted by La Duse's actresses, gave the prize for the best pair to Sissy Durland de Giberga, who was Aida, and her husband, dressed as Othello. Truthfully, a good part of the contestants (if not all) received some kind of prize, as well as the group of ladies of the harem, the houris, and Ali Baba and his forty thieves. Even Mina de Buffin got a small gift: a toy sultan dressed in red and gold and seated on a velvet cushion, who had in one hand an ebony cup and in the other a hookah. Thanks to an ingenious internal device, the toy could bring the cup to its lips and blow out smoke through its nose.

When the Syrian announced, to conclude, that the jury was awarding a special prize to Titania, the crowd went mad with enthusiasm. The queen of the fairies made her way to the center of the stage and with a small bow showed her appreciation for our display of sympathy. "The mask! The mask!" the people screamed, wanting to see the face of their favorite contestant. The request, accompanied by a chorus of clapping, ended up becoming a sort of conga.

The mask! The mask!
Take off the mask!

The woman turned toward Steffano, surprised, and he urged her to do as the audience asked. Then, with a majestic gesture, the queen of the fairies ripped off her mask, threw it into the screaming crowd, and the face of Esmeralda Gallego was revealed.

Not believing what we were seeing, Wenceslao and I ran toward the stage, wanting to embrace La Gallego and find out what in the hell she was doing in Cuba, but it was impossible. She was surrounded by a human wall, dozens of Habaneros wanted to congratulate her on her triple triumph for her elegance, her beauty, and her distinction. When the music started again and an army of couples began to dance around us, we finally got to the leader of the fairies to say hello.

La Gallego laughed, very pleased that her joke had succeeded, and told us how a few hours after arriving in New York, she decided to postpone her trip to Luxor. The one at fault was someone very special, with whom she was currently involved in a torrid affair. Tutankhamen could wait.

"My dear, come meet my friends," she asked in a loud voice, and a man dressed as a boxer, with boxing gloves, who was standing a few paces away, came forward and grabbed her by the waist.

Could it be that it was Luis Vicentini himself? Theirs had been love at first sight, Esmeralda said as she planted a kiss on the Chilean. They were in Havana since Sunday morning, staying at the Almendares Hotel. But we would have time to chat more peacefully, in a quieter place. It was impossible here. The journalist Carpentier, dressed as a scarecrow, and the photographer from *Social* magazine were calling up to her so that she could be immortalized in her rendition of Titania. She kissed us and, escorted by the boxer, moved away with the gait of a queen.

I asked Wenceslao if he wanted to stay at the ball any longer, since our duties were done. He said no without moving his lips. From the other end of the hall, De la Cruz screamed at us and we waved good-bye to him.

"I don't want to go to bed yet," Wenceslao said after we were able to leave the pandemonium behind and were on the sidewalk of the Louvre, in front of the hotel.

I proposed that we walk toward the sea by way of the tree-lined Prado, and we ended up at the *malecón:* him seated and me on my back, watching the sky, which was clear and replete with stars. The breeze threatened to mess up our hair, and the waves crashed deafeningly on the coastal reefs. I asked him if he felt betrayed by La Gallego. After all, she knew better than anyone his obsession with Vicentini.

"Betrayed? Why?" he said disdainfully. "I couldn't care less one way or the other. Let her enjoy him as much as she can. Besides, in person, he doesn't look that great."

I don't know if it was from exhaustion, or the punch, or thinking of Mella and my uncle Misael in a jail cell, but I felt depressed.

"You know what?" I said after a while. "I've been thinking that the thing with Julio Antonio is impossible."

Wenceslao let out an "about time you admitted it" sigh.

"I think that he is one of those creatures that God sends to the earth every once in a while to punish those of our club," I continued. "Even in the hypothetical case that one were to have something with him, it wouldn't work. I am sure that at the most heated moment he would begin talking about Lenin or imperialism. That boy is not right in the head."

"This clarity needs to be celebrated!" Wenceslao exclaimed, jumping up to walk. "Come," he hurried, "let's go into the first bar we find."

Although it was four in the morning, on the little streets that flowed into the Prado some seedy places were still open. We went, as Wen had said, into the first place we ran into: a dark tavern, narrow and not very full, with a bar and four tables placed right next to each other. At the first table, two overly made-up whores surveyed the scene in the hopes of making a few pesos before morning; at the next table, a very young *mulata,* a mere girl, was trying to convince some sleepy-headed guy, burly and with an enormous mustache, to go to bed with her; the third table was taken by a negro troubadour wearing a guayabera, who monotonously caressed the strings of his guitar; and at the last table, several men played cards. We went up to the bar and asked the man there for two whiskies. As we drank them, a handsome, corpulent Spaniard, a *gallego,* came out of the bathroom, settled himself right next to us, and poured himself a drink from an almost empty bottle of *aguardiente.* He gulped down his drink and examined us out of the corner of his eyes. This itch needs a scratching, I thought.

One of the whores came up to us, to see if she could wheedle something out of us. She had blue eyes and that sort of delicate white skin that quickly deteriorates in the tropical heat. She said that she would do anything and anywhere, but we frightened her away with a grunt. The witch picked up her bag and walked out to the street banging her heels and complaining at the top of her voice about how difficult it was becoming to make a simple living. The bartender asked us if we wanted anything else, and when we told him not for the moment, he went over to sit with the card players.

From outside we could hear the hotheaded voices of a man and a woman and then the noise of a bottle exploding on the cobblestones. As if this were his cue, the musician began to sing in a melodious voice, "In the mysterious language of your eyes . . ."

The little *mulata* helped her companion get up, apparently having reached some satisfactory agreement with him, and said good-bye to the buxom prostitute with the peroxide hair, who was smoking distractedly at the first table. She left the tavern holding up her prey, who stumbled, his chin pressed to his chest.

"Havana might be a den of crooks and pencil-pushers," the *gallego* exclaimed, his words all twisted, enveloping us in a penetrating stench of alcohol, "but once in a while it is good to come here." And without eliciting a response, raising his voice so that he couldn't be drowned out by the negro's song, he told us that he lived in Oriente, where he owned some fincas. He had been in the capital three days, resolving a very complicated matter, "paperwork, you know," and since he grew bored at night with nothing to do, he always ended up in this bar. You only live once and if you don't have fun you are an idiot. That night he had already fucked two bitches and he was just waiting for his *cojones* to fill up with milk again to put it in somewhere else, the first one that came in his path. He was a rooster and he needed many hens, to pluck them all, he assured us, rubbing his package. On any other occasion, we would have done something to free ourselves from this drunk, but who's to say if it was because of apathy or just to punish ourselves, we continued listening to his drivel. When he was a nobody, back in his native Galicia, he became a soldier so that he could leave behind the hunger of his village; soon afterward, they put him on a ship and sent him to Cuba to kill the insurrectionists. What he saw of the Island he liked. Someday the guns would be put away and those lands would be waiting for someone to become rich off them. That someone could just as well be him. After the war, the *galleguito* returned to the Iberian Peninsula with the definitive idea of going back to Cuba as soon as he could. And, in fact, as soon as he could, he made the ocean crossing again, without a cent in his pocket. He was an animal when it came to work and he got together with the Americans who were building sugar mills. There were many forests to cut down, many sugar cane fields to plant. He began by himself, but it wasn't long before he hired a couple of fools to work for him. He got work for the group and then took a big cut. Peso upon peso, he bought his first *finquita.* And then another one and another one and all the rest. If God granted him health, he was going to buy the whole province, and later—why not?—the whole shitty country. Who said that the whole Island couldn't be a great finca? He would fill its four corners with sugar cane, sell sugar to the gringos, and he would leave everything, land and money, to his children. The ones he already had and the ones he was thinking of creating. As long as his rod worked, he would keep on fucking. "And I have rod to spare here," he concluded, pressing the bulge in between his legs and letting out a loud laugh.

The *gallego* got up from his stool and stumbled toward the urinals. Wenceslao waited a few seconds and, without saying anything, followed behind him. I drank what was left of my whiskey and waited a few minutes before I went to join them. The troubadour began another song, with renewed brio. "Here come the golden rays of a new, rosy morning . . ." I suddenly realized that the last of the prostitutes was seated on my left. Her eyes were rolled up in her head, and a string of foamy saliva dripped out of her mouth.

"Kill him!" she ordered in a soft voice and, when I looked at her, befuddled, she insisted. "Kill him, Belalcázar!" I then realized that though the whore was moving her mouth, it was Anatilde de Bastos who spoke with that voice of such unmistakable cadence. "You're going to kill him, aren't you?" she asked adamantly.

I asked her, disparagingly, what the hell she was talking about. "Of getting rid of the *gallego,* my prince, what else can I be talking about?" she replied teasingly and slid the palm of one hand over the polished surface of the bar. She held it beside me and, when she slid it back, I saw an open blade, small and sharp. "Slice his neck, open his belly, plunge it in his heart. Do whatever you have to, but finish him off, cut him up like a pig, sever the thread of his life."

I returned the blade by sliding it back on the wood.

"The man is not evil," Anatilde de Bastos wheezed. "Not any more evil than the others," she rectified. "But he is foolish and domineering. You have to kill him to save this place from a century of misery."

"I had taken you for a wise soul," I grumbled.

"I am, my prince, I still am," she assured me, letting out a little hollow laugh that made the whore drool even more. "You have to rub out that stud so he doesn't engender the damnation of this Island. He is an instrument of Beelzebub, who is going to make use of his seed and plant pain, misery, desperation, and rage, and so much fear that you cannot begin to imagine. Cut him up like a pig, my prince! Kill him to kill the son that he is destined to procreate, to prevent, in two years, six months, and eight days, the birth of The Unnamable. Kill him so he doesn't go on fucking, so that the abominable monster never sees the light of day."

Getting closer to my face, the woman looked at me with her dead eyes. "It was that seed and none other that St. Paul referred to in his Letter to the Thessalonians." And taking a biblical tone, she recited, " 'And the man of sin will appear, who should perish miserably, and who, setting himself against God, will rise above all the things that refer to God, till he sits in the very temple of God, passing himself off as God.' " She pushed the blade toward me again, as she tried to persuade me. "Kill him before the son ensnares the people with false miracles and marvels, before he establishes new tablets of law and sinks the Island into dark poverty!"

I again slid back the sharp blade.

"You can exorcise the curse, my prince. If you want, you can save the people from their executioner," the seer howled, in a fit of anger, this time placing the blade in front of me with such a loud thud that she made the negro slip out of tune and froze, for a moment, the customers' game at the last table.

"Stop insisting, Anatilde," I replied coldly. "How dare you ask me such a thing? You have the wrong person," and I returned the weapon for the third time.

She took the blade, closed it, and resignedly put it away in her bosom.

"Maybe you are right," she said, "maybe you are not the one. Or perhaps each people receive as much horror as they deserve and it is not worth it to try to change it. Let him be born, if there is no other choice, the poisoned one, the one who will be loyal only to his perverse designs."

The whore's head fell on the counter and it sounded like a dried coconut. Knowing that Anatilde was done with her peculiar communication, I went to the bathroom, which was a dank and stinking hole. Wenceslao and the *gallego,* one beside the other, were standing in front of the only urinal. Each handled his erect member while closely watching the manipulations of the other.

Seeing them like that, their backs to me and concentrating on their handiwork, I realized how easy it would have been to do what the *Portuguesa* demanded. One quick swipe at the throat, and that towering man would have fallen without ever realizing what had happened. I cleared my throat to get the idea out of my head and let them know I was there. They looked at me but neither of them seemed too perturbed by my presence.

"It's late," I said, repulsed, and made a gesture for Wen to follow me without delay.

"What an idiot!" he remarked, when we were out on the street. "We already had our cocks out and still he kept on talking about his stupid hens," he said very animatedly, with a naiveté that I found touching.

We hurried to make it to the Inglaterra before dawn. I had told Aquiles de la Osa that I would be at the headquarters of the secret police at eight o'clock and I wanted very much to be on time.

For many years now the public has not stopped feeling a curiosity that is sometimes candid, sometimes morbid, for the least interesting of my characters: me. For years, with a persistence suited for better causes, they have spread without mercy, from mouth to mouth or through writing, all kinds of anecdotes, gossip, and slander about my personal life; they have asked me for photographs and autographs; they have attributed to me countless lovers; they have pointed at me on the streets, in hotels, in train stations, they have watched without the slightest scruple, just as if I were the bearded lady at the circus.

Only someone who has suffered through it knows what an agony it is to live in a fish bowl, surrounded by people who assume the right to pry into your personal life, swimming in front of hundreds of eyes on the lookout for what you do and say.

Welcome ladies and gentlemen! Here before you, Eleonora the goldfish. See her gills, her fins, her tail. Her scales are a little bit deteriorated, that's what the years do, but remember that the famous D'Annunzio, lover of thousands, once fell before her charms! See with what elegance and discretion Eleonora the goldfish eats. Watch the gracefulness with which she swims among the water plants and the little stones. If you are patient, continue watching her and you will see how she sleeps. And some of you, any one of these days, will watch her go still, very still, no longer breathing, and die.

14

When Aquiles de la Osa asked me if I wanted to take a look at him, I said very squarely that I didn't. What good would it do me to see the body of Misael Reyes?

My uncle had committed suicide early that morning. The policeman who was on shift was going to bring his breakfast and found him seated on his cot, leaning against the wall, with his head fallen to one side and his eyes open. In one of his hands he had a little flask of poison.

"A fitting end for such a bizarre story," was the only thing that I could think of saying. Wenceslao took care of saying good-bye to the detective and took me outside.

We walked on the avenue of the port, silent, and turned on O'Reilly Street.

"I am very sorry," Wen said as we passed by the Plaza de Armas.

"Yes, it's a shame," I answered him softly. "But what sense does it make to feel sorrow over the death of someone I hardly knew?" I continued, trying to be as Cartesian as possible.

Since we had had a light breakfast, we decided that some hot chocolate with *churros* would be nice, and went into a café. Although it was busy, we found an empty table and sat down. A young man took our order.

"Do you know that I really admired him? He was a lion," I said suddenly. "But he lived as he wanted and died when he wanted. In his own way, he was a hero."

The waiter brought the cups of hot chocolate and plate of fried *churros,* and we started eating. A shoeshine boy approached the table.

"Those shoes are filthy, sir," he said, pointing at them.

I had to admit that he was right. He made me put my foot on top of a wooden box and went at his task. We watched in silence as he brushed, polished, brushed again, and lastly buffed my shoe with a blackish cloth. "Done," he said on finishing, tapping me on the toe with the brush. I paid him generously.

"You as well?" the shoeshine boy asked Wenceslao and since Wen said no, he quickly put away his instruments in the wooden box and went off in search of new clients. A little while later, before leaving the place like an arrow and disappearing among the passersby, the boy gave me a sealed envelope. We saw, surprised, that it had my name written on it.

"What are you waiting for? Open it," Wen said.

It was a letter that began "Dear Nephew." I turned to the last page anxiously, looking for the signature: "Your uncle Misael." My hands were beginning to shake and Wenceslao, impatient, grabbed it from me.

"Let me read it," he proposed.

And so the letter said:

Havana, February 5, 1924
Dear Nephew,

It is possible that this letter will seem like a bad joke to you. You have just been told that I have passed away and, moments later, very unexpectedly, you get news from me. Perhaps you are thinking, he never wanted to talk to me when he was alive and now he decides to do so after he has died. I suppose that in some ways you are right. But you know that I have always been thought of as the eccentric one in the Reyes family.

I wonder if you have seen the rigid body that till a few hours ago held my spirit. I hope that you haven't. I wouldn't want to leave a shocking image like that for you to remember me by. Or did you see it? Whatever the case, those things are no longer important.

I would have loved to have given you a hug, but circumstances made it impossible. The day that I saw you for the first time, when you went to El Crisantemo Dorado, I felt very proud of you. Ever since you were a child, it was said that you would be beautiful, and you fulfilled those predictions easily: I was surprised by such good looks. I should say, so that Wenceslao doesn't get jealous, that he, too, is very handsome. But in you, Lucho, I saw gestures, expressions, and ways of looking at others that had been mine in the past. Seeing you has been like looking into a mirror of the image I was. They didn't exaggerate when they said that you were a living portrait of me.

I owe you some explanations. Why I didn't make it to the appointment we had in my house the night that Mei Feng died, for example. I was far from there, trying to convince someone that the ties that bound me to the *Chino* were only affectionate and not carnal. Perhaps, if my words had been more convincing, Mei Feng would be alive today and this story would have another ending. It wasn't like that.

The wretched Mei Feng came into my service when he was seventeen. He had just gotten off the boat from Liverpool. He was thin and flexible as a reed, he had skin like a peach, and in bed could be ardent or tender. How could I, someone who had learned to love the exoticism of the Orient through the teachings of Julián del Casal, resist his charms? For almost fifteen years, Mei Feng and I were inseparable. I don't exaggerate when I say that what he felt for me was something close to idolatry; something that, whatever we call it, I was far from deserving of and could not reciprocate. Time passed, and what had begun as, at least on my part, quiet affection, ended up becoming a habit, a sort of loving custom.

It is likely that things would have continued like that, *per secula seculorum,* if the *Dixmude* had not exploded on its way to Africa. Not all the soldiers of the French army who were traveling in the blimp perished, as it was reported erroneously in the press. One of them, the least suitable perhaps, was saved by an unexplainable miracle (are there any that aren't?) and tumultuously walked into our lives. I am referring to Saint-Amand, the commander. Some fishermen picked him up in the high seas and took him to their village. Once there, he had no strength to face the shame of having survived and not died with his troops. He made up a new identity and told everyone that he was the only survivor of a shipwreck. He fled Europe on the first ship that sailed for this side of the world and one afternoon got off in Havana, with a change of clothes and a pair of shoes full of holes, with no other hope than to erase the past.

We found each other, because it was written that we should, and Jean Bonhaire became my reason for living. I went to bed thinking about him and woke up with a painful need to see him. I didn't know if this feeling was as powerful or more than the one that brought me together with Casal; what I was sure of was that I was thirty years older.

At first, Mei Feng didn't pay much attention to the intruder, but, little by little, he became aware of the threat that Jean posed to him. However, he took care not to show in front of me the antipathy, if not the hatred, that he felt for Jean Bonhaire. On the contrary, he was very deferential and an improper word never passed his lips.

The first thing I asked myself after I found out about the tragedy was why Mei Feng, always so intuitive and shrewd, didn't go away in time. He should have admitted that he had lost, and vanished. God forgive me, but I think he got what was coming to him.

Rémond de Saint-Amand took Mei Feng's life, yes, but it wasn't a premeditated crime. I am sure that he lost control in a jealous fit. That *Chino* had a stiletto for a tongue, he could drive a saint to sin. He could utter the greatest atrocities without raising his voice or losing his composure. He could say "I despise and curse your mother for bringing you into the world!" as if he were offering a cup of Ceylon tea.

Who knows what he told Bonhaire that night to make him react the way he did? He must have really pushed him, for afterwards the Frenchman was remorseful. He swore, broken up, that it hadn't been his intention to blow out *Chino*'s brains, that he was carrying a pistol by coincidence. I believed him. Believe him now. I am capable of believing anything he tells me.

When the secret police detained him, I thought about planting a bomb in the building where he was being held, to get him out of there. I couldn't stand thinking of him locked up in jail for who knows how many years. I also couldn't see myself waiting for him, I am too old for that. I was ready to get him back any way I could, but the old man Fan Ya Ling, who for many years has been my advisor, a sort of higher conscience by which I let myself be guided blindly, appealed to my good judgment and warned me to be guided by my intelligence and not my passion. He had a plan and wanted to tell me about it. If we played it out, Bonhaire and I could go off together to wherever we wanted and no one would bother us about the murder again.

Perhaps a less desperate person would have made some alterations to his proposition, but I agreed to do everything he said.

The first thing I had to do was go to the secret police, turn myself in, and make sure to tell them that I was responsible for Mei Feng's murder. Once they locked me up and set Bonhaire free, Fan Ya Ling would move into action. He would figure out how to smuggle some poison into the prison that I was to drink without delay at a determined hour.

Do you know the Taoist tale that tells of how the soul of Li Tie Kouai ends up in the body of a lame beggar? I am afraid you do, because Pepe Chiang loves it and he tells it to anyone he can. In case you haven't heard it, it is about a person who decides to make a journey only with his soul; but when it returns, a few days later, he can't find the body he used to live in anywhere near where he left it and he ends up finding refuge in the body of a beggar who has just died. So, Fan Ya Ling's proposal involved repeating Li Tie Kouai's feat. If I followed his instructions to the letter, I had nothing to fear.

The body that remained in the cell, rigid and cold, and that I don't know if you ever saw or not, is only the wrapping that

provided shelter to my spirit for many years. The plan was followed through with the precision characteristic of Orientals.
According to Fan Ya Ling's calculations, the poison would take
a few minutes before it took effect. Following his directions, I
drank it at exactly five in the morning. At that same hour, he
and Bonhaire manacled a sailor who was stumbling around
half-drunk in the port, not being able to find the pier where
his ship was docked, and took his life. It was something that
happened quickly and was easier than I imagined: I left one
body and entered another one. I can't say that it didn't feel
strange at first, as if I had put on clothes that weren't mine,
but that feeling quickly disappeared.

Given that the circumstances didn't allow me to be too
fussy, I was allowed to ask Fan Ya Ling for only two things:
first, to find a body that was young, robust, and as pleasant as
possible to look at, and second, not to kill him with a bullet or
a sharp instrument, but to suffocate him. This way, the body
would be in a perfect state, without holes or cuts, when I
moved into it. I have to admit that my new "suit" has exceeded
all expectations. I have made real the fantasy of fusing the experience of a long life with the energy of an appealing and
vigorous body.

So, now my soul looks at the world from behind other eyes,
inhales through another set of nasal cavities, and speaks from
another mouth. However, behind this different appearance,
I am still the same. My thoughts, my emotions, have not
changed a bit.

In the past few days I have been very close to you and your
friend on several occasions. I have watched you, confused, in
the crowd, I have spied on you with a mixture of shame and
delight. Now, as I finish writing this letter, I see how you dip
your *churros* into the hot chocolate and bring them to your
mouth. Easy, Wenceslao, or you'll burn your tongue. I imagine
that when you come to these lines you will look around curiously, trying to find me in the faces of one of the guests. Don't
waste your time, it is futile. I am not going to reveal myself. If
by chance one of you comes up to the table where I am sitting

and speaks to me, I would look you up and down and tell you to leave me alone. How can you think that I am Misael Reyes? That gentleman died a few hours ago in a cell of the secret police. His corpse should be in the morgue already, frozen and rigid. About my remains, don't worry. I left directions to be cremated. Fan Ya Ling will make sure my wishes are fulfilled.

Tonight I will be leaving the country, Lucho. Forever, I think. I am going to miss this hallucinatory city. I never felt that she was all mine, even though she welcomed me whole-heartedly and in her I was fortunate enough to have two great loves. Whoever asks for more is an ingrate. I am leaving, though I won't tell you where, with Rémond de Saint-Amand. Don't judge him too harshly. These things happen. He loves my new body and, from the way he looks at it, I know that he is impatient to come to know it intimately. That excites me. From now on I will be, in a certain way, the younger one. Being the younger one in a couple has certain pleasures, it allows you certain privileges.

Before turning myself in to the police, I wrote a statement that a notary friend of the count authenticated. In that docu-ment, I give all my goods to my godson José Chiang: the capital that my siblings owe me in Bogotá and the sum from the sale of my house and furniture, the porcelain pieces and other valuable objects. No, I haven't gone crazy. Chiang, whose god-father I am, is someone whom I trust entirely and will be use-ful as a figurehead. You can be certain that the money will reach my hands with little difficulty. Manolo, Melitón, and your señora mother are going to be furious when they find out that a *mestizo* from a *Chino* and a *negra* is the beneficiary of part of the Reyes fortune. But, you know what, I don't really care.

As for you, my dear nephew, I ask you insistently to keep the sonnet "Supplication." Read it once in a while and think about who inspired it, your poor uncle. That piece of paper was, before I met Bonhaire, my most valued possession and I would never have given it to anyone. It continues to be very important, but I can't start a new life dragging such a heavy burden. I would prefer to leave it in good hands: yours.

I have to end this letter and I don't know quite how to do it.

Let the family think that my death was from a painful illness.

You two, love each other always and abundantly. It's how I would have liked to have loved Julián and how I intend to love Rémond de Saint-Armand.

Au revoir, and good luck.

Your uncle,
Misael

Wenceslao was perplexed when he finished reading and asked me what I thought. I shrugged. At that moment, a guest passed by our table, on the way to the door of the café, and I noticed that he was watching us furtively. He was a man of medium height, and strong constitution, with blue eyes and the bronze skin of someone who has spent a lot of time in the sun. Could it be Misael Reyes? How could we prove it? Like my uncle said in the letter, any investigation into the matter would not only prove unproductive, but would make us seem ridiculous. I turned in my chair to look at the man again before he went out into the street and I said that, in the hypothetical case that that was my uncle, Frenchie was going to have a banquet.

I folded the letter and swore to Wenceslao that, as soon as we returned to our room and put away the letter in the same envelope with de Casal's manuscript, I would forget about the whole thing.

"The chapter on Misael Reyes is closed," I added, feeling a curious relief.

And that's how it was.

We didn't have to look for Esmeralda at the Almendares Hotel, for she appeared unexpectedly at ours, dragging the Chilean gladiator. Although she was wearing almost no makeup that morning and was dressed discreetly—a patterned chiffon dress that wasn't much, and a simple little hat à la Lillian Gish—her arrival caused a great commotion among the employees of the Inglaterra, because someone identified her as Titania, the winner at the Ball of a Thousand and One

Nights, and news traveled mouth to mouth. During the time we were in the hall, neither Vicentini nor we were allowed to utter anything other than sporadic interjections. La Gallego talked the whole time, bringing us up to date on what had happened in her life during the last few weeks. She told us about incidents on the trip from Bogotá to Barranquilla in the plane *Bolívar,* piloted by Camilo Daza, and the fright that she went through when he got it in his mind to do stunts called "falling leaf" and "loop-de-loop"; the journey from the Port of Colombia to New York in the French ocean liner and the chance encounter with the boxer in the offices of some Jewish lawyers in Brooklyn.

"Seeing each other and falling into each other's arms was one and the same thing," she summarized. "Perhaps there is no need to tell you that we were locked up in my hotel room for three days. I don't know how we survived!"

It was during that lusty seclusion that Esmeralda decided to make a lightning-quick trip to Havana with only one purpose in mind, to surprise her best friends. And, as a matter of fact, how were the performances of Eleonora Duse, the talking mummy? Had we managed our interview?

Wenceslao's face darkened and I quickly interrupted Esmeralda, asking her if she and Vicentini would like to come to the racetrack at Oriental Park, in Marianao. We hadn't been there yet, but everyone said that it was a great place and that the lunches they served in the gardens were stupendous. While we walked to the taxi, La Gallego hooked onto my arm and asked me, in a whisper, if she had put her foot in her mouth.

"All the way in, my dear," I answered and quickly caught her up on the outcome of the Duse case. "Everything seemed to be going smoothly and then . . . nothing!" I complained. "She didn't even bother to answer a letter I wrote her."

Wenceslao wanted Esmeralda to meet Emilio De la Cruz and asked Monkeyface, by phone, to join us at the racetrack. After betting with atrocious luck on all the losing horses, we went to have lunch in the terrace and we talked about *The Strong Man,* Harold Lloyd's last movie, which they were showing at the Capitolio; about the next visit to Havana by the very famous Ukrainian choir, considered to be the only human symphonic orchestra, and of the possibility of making a journey by train to Matanzas, to see its three rivers: the Yumurí, the Canímar, and the San Juan. In what other place in the world could there be a city called Matanzas? I thought, "The Killings," and concluded that only in Cuba, the kingdom of absurdity. I asked De la Cruz the reason for such a chilling name and he shrugged. "I think it is because of all the Indians that the Spanish slaughtered there," he responded and, after some moments of reflection, added. "Or maybe not, because in that case they would have called the whole island Matanzas." While we talked like parrots, Vicentini was very much engrossed in himself. I watched him closely and I noticed that he could barely hide his yawns. The Chilean was as bored as an oyster. It was obvious that he didn't understand any of our chat, which moved recklessly from the picturesque locale to the universally sophisticated. Who the hell was Margarita Xirgu, who, according to Monkeyface, should just be disembarking around that time at the San Francisco pier and who would premiere on Wednesday at the Nacional playing in *L'Aigrette* by Darío Nicodemi? What did he care that the *gringos,* those scoundrels, wanted to strip the genius Finlay of his merits as the discoverer of the vaccine for yellow fever, and that Joaquín Blez, the photographer of the fashionable crowd, would be trying for the first time, in his studio on Neptuno Street, a new system of mercury vapor lamps that flawlessly lit his creations? We had to get our photograph done by him, without fail. But don't even think about showing up without an appointment, he would be furious. He was an artist. Overcome with a fit of mercy, I was about to get out of the conversation and ask Vicentini about his upcoming fights, but I suddenly held back. Whose fault was it that he was so rude? Let him suffer and learn how to behave. Life is more than just throwing punches.

Halfway through the meal, the Chilean couldn't stand it anymore and threw in the towel. He made up something that he needed to wire his manager, said he regretted having to leave in the middle of such a delicious lunch and, after assuring his lover that he would see her in the hotel, fled.

"I am so sick of him," Esmeralda confessed, when he had vanished. "He is so unrefined it is frightening."

"Sometimes that can be its own charm," the Cuban said in a conciliatory tone, chewing on a crispy *chicharrita.*

"In small doses it may, my good Emilio," the painter replied. "But after five days, it can become hell."

Not caring about the boxer's flight, Wenceslao brought up his concerns about La Duse's last performance. Would the employees at the Nacional have the theater ready by eight? The task wasn't simple: they had to remove the *draperie* and the decorative carpets and put all the seats in the orchestra back in their places.

"Of course they'll do it, *chico,*" De la Cruz assured him. "The same thing happened with the Feast of the Second Empire. The following day, I don't know who was performing, and they had it ready on time. They know what they are doing." And, changing the topic, or should I say, pursuing a variation on the topic of La Duse, he started talking about a peculiarity of that night's performance.

Mimí Aguglia, Esperanza Iris, and María Tubau had announced to the press their intentions of coming to the Nacional to applaud the dean of the tragediennes in *La città morta.* The producer Gallo wanted, as a publicity stunt, to put them all in the same box of honor. If, to the list of those three famous ones the names of Donna Ortensia and Margarita Xirgu (it would be inconceivable that the Countess Pears and the first lady of the Spanish theater would miss such a grand event) were added, then a constellation of stars would shine over the audience.

"All applauding the biggest star," Wenceslao added.

When De la Cruz took us back to the Inglaterra after leaving La Gallego at her hotel, the young man at the reception desk handed me a letter. *Monsieur Belalcázar* was written on the front. It was, without doubt, the tragedienne's reply. I opened it right there, in the lobby, and right away I noticed that it was very short. All of four lines. "Impossible—I must reiterate that, sadly, it is impossible," the first line said. And below: "My friend: to think that we can stipulate sorrow or happiness is an absurdity. We are only instruments of those things called divine will, destiny, or fate."

I handed the paper to Wenceslao, who, when he finished reading it, crunched it up into a ball and tossed it into the spittoon by the elevator. His reaction upset me: although it was a denial, that handwritten note was an item of great value for his scrapbook.

"We did what we could," he said with a sigh.

"I've been thinking of trying through La Garnett," I said. "Who says I won't have better luck than you?"

"Forget it," he refuted dryly. "The thing about the interview was childish. You don't have to keep on trying."

"I could write her again," I insisted.

He looked at me angrily and I knew he didn't want to talk about it anymore. Was he really giving up? I found it hard to believe. That the interview was a whim, I knew: but I also knew that there were very few people in this world who were as persevering as he was. As soon as we got to the room, my lover threw himself on the bed without taking off his shoes, and I fell into the rocking chair. The phone rang and, since Wenceslao did not show the slightest intention of moving, I answered it. It was one of the spies at his service, who, confusing me with him, notified me that at two in the afternoon La Duse had received in her room the Italian ambassador and the poet Vázquez Garralaga. The visit lasted ten minutes, and the diplomat and the bard left the hotel furious. Another piece of news was that Margarita Xirgu had just been added to the list of guests at the hotel. Would the gentleman also like to receive information about her? I said no. Not about her and not about La Signora Duse. No more reports, understood? No more. After thanking him for his services, I hung up and told Wen the latest news.

"At least there is the solace that it didn't go well for Olavo, either," he said with satisfaction, not even opening his eyes.

I waited patiently till he fell asleep. Then I went out in the hall and knocked at La Duse's door.

"*Qui est?*" María Avogadro asked without opening.

I said that I needed to speak with *Fräulein* Wertheimstein, and the maid answered in a neutral voice that she wasn't there. I cursed under my breath and went down to the lobby convinced that I had been shamelessly lied to. But that wasn't the case, however, as I found out when, on coming out to the street, I saw La Signora's secretary hurriedly crossing El Prado in the company of Katherine Garnett. It was drizzling, and they each carried an umbrella. Désirée stopped when she saw me and, after a moment's hesitation, said something to the Englishwoman and came toward me.

"She is sad, very sad," she said, getting right to the point. "La Signora Duse feels betrayed. She thinks that you don't care for her, that you only got close so that you could get your interview. That is very painful for her."

"But it's not true!" I protested, drying the drops of water that fell on my face. "Or I should say it is not *exactly* true."

The secretary shrugged with a disheartened smile and looked at her companion who awaited her, impatiently, a few steps away.

"I should go," she said. "We only came out for a moment, to buy her some medicine. She is not feeling well and tonight she has to play *La città morta,* which is an exhausting play."

She turned around and rejoined La Garnett, then they took off toward the Inglaterra. The rain suddenly worsened and I, who didn't have anything to do, also ran, but in the other direction. Soaking from head to toe, I sought refuge under the colonnades of the Plaza Hotel. A thick curtain of rain separated me from the outside world and I tried to clear my mind. Was there the possibility of being granted an interview or should we just forget about this annoying topic? In the end, Wenceslao couldn't complain, a good part of his wishes had come true. We had seen The Sublime One on stage. We were able to climb over the walls of her isolation, have tea with her, and chat intimately. We had even spent a day wandering around with her in Casablanca, and Guanabacoa, and the rest of the city. No one in Havana could boast of such conquests. Not even Mina de Buffin, with all her millions, had been able to pull her out of her rat hole and show her off at the ball. Wenceslao was very stubborn if he didn't accept that this was more valuable than a dozen interviews. Maybe the lady had her reasons for saying no. Private and painful reasons that we should respect. Why harass her and put her in an uncomfortable position? That he didn't want the interview anymore? No, señor, that dog won't hunt! He can say what he wants, but he was still obsessed. He was suffering because of what he considered, childishly, a failure.

Tired of waiting for the rain to ease up, I took off my vest and threw it over my head, and trotted under the shower back to the hotel.

A car passed by and splashed me with water from the puddles near the sidewalk.

When I got back to the room, Wenceslao was already awake and he scolded me for getting so wet. He rubbed me with a towel and forced me to take a hot bath. He didn't mention the interview, and I, of course, didn't bring it up, either. Some hours later, we were at the Nacional.

There was not a trace from the *kermesse* of the night before in the theater. The Damascene tapestries had disappeared, as well as all the cloth that hung from the ceiling. Polished marble and stainless carpets, shiny mirrors, fresh flowers in their jars. All perfect for the farewell to her eminence.

The audience, though still a select one, had shrunk considerably. However, the faithful were there, dug into their trenches like soldiers, those who loved art and were willing to make any sacrifice to witness it. Madame Buffin, who, after the last page had been turned on the Ball of a Thousand and One Nights found it unnecessary to keep dragging Habib Steffano along, went up the stairs leaning on the arm of a friend. When she saw us, she smiled with a martyr's expression.

"My kidneys are killing me," she cried. "But how can I miss Eleonora's farewell?"

Since neither the president nor his wife would be attending the performance that evening, Mimí Aguglia, Esperanza Iris, and María Tubau shared the presidential box with apparent cordiality. La Aguglia, on the left, was dressed in vermilion, La Iris, in the middle, in turquoise blue, while La Tubau, seated on the right, was in white. Co-incidence or not, their dresses were the color of the Cuban flag and that fact became the joke around the theater. The three actresses con-tinually blew kisses and waved their fans in all directions to thank their followers for their show of support. In the hallways it was said that the gifts that La Iris's fans were giving to her at the next tribute had cost a fortune.

It was whispered, also, that at first Gallo had thought that the trio would be a foursome, but Donna Ortensia ruined his plan by refusing to see the play in the company of the others. Yes, they were all artists, in tragedy and comedy, or in song, but she was also a countess and, before becoming that, had relinquished the title of duchess. Next to the presidential box, dry as a piece of *bacalao* and stately, the aristocrat of bel canto smiled lightly, almost indulgently, at those who called out to her.

Suddenly, letting go of her distinguished severity, Donna Ortensia tried to get our attention by waving a gloved hand full of rings at us and inviting us over. Since I was sure that if I obeyed her, her neighbor, *la divette,* would take advantage of the occasion to chastise me for not having gone to see her at the Payret, I let the Countess Pears, the former Duchess Mignano, know through signals that we would visit her later.

We figured out that the woman with cavernous ears and dark hair pinned up at the back of her neck, who gave rise to so much curiosity, was the renowned Margarita Xirgu. Whether Gallo had tried to incorporate her into the group in the presidential box or not, no one knew for sure, but in any case the Catalan had a separate seat, far away from the rest of the artists. There she was, in black, in one of the rear boxes, surrounded by reporters and devotees.

Generala Lachambre had not yet arrived, which wasn't unusual. She would most likely appear at the last bell, right before the beginning of the performance. Some who were there though, punctual as ever, were the countess of Rivero, Josefina Embil de Kohly, and Angelita Fabra de Mariátegui, the Spanish ambassador. Vázquez Garralaga and his mother ignored us and we did the same to them.

In the orchestra, we made out Bartolomé Valdivieso and Agustín Miraflores. Had the pharmacist gotten over the incident with the sonnet? His smile made it seem that he had. We also saw, below, the critics from the *Diario de la Marina* and *El Heraldo.*

"Soon, they will both come so that you can help them with their reviews," I guessed.

"Poldarás, with all my love. The other one, Genaro Corzo, not even from the grave."

We weren't very surprised when we saw Esmeralda arrive alone. She looked splendid, in a long, sable coat, a fuchsia dress, and her often-used, but always impressive, decorative comb of rubies. As soon as she arrived, we became the center of attention for hundreds of eyes. La Gallego kissed us affectionately, sat in the first row and, without saying a word about the Chilean's absence, asked about De la

Cruz. When we told her that he would arrive by the third act, she nodded and dedicated herself to watching the audience through her opera glasses.

Wenceslao winked at me mischievously and leaned toward her.

"Where is the champion?" he said sarcastically.

"He left this afternoon for New York," she informed us. "I would be lying if I said that our good-bye wasn't sad, but I have to say I feel an enormous relief." On seeing that we nodded understandingly, she added cheekily: "He has powerful fists, but his love muscle doesn't last many rounds." And putting an end to the topic, she asked about the plot of the play we were about to watch.

Wenceslao summarized it promptly. That night La Duse would become Anna, a blind woman with an exquisite and clairvoyant soul, married to a poet. It took place in Greece, near Mycenae, and it was rather morbid.

"The blind woman's husband is a friend of Leonardo, a young archeologist, who lives in a small palace with his sister, Bianca María, and has his heart set on finding the treasure of Atreus. The wretched Anna soon sees (with the eyes of her spirit, of course) that her sweet, but not so innocent, little neighbor has begun a torrid affair. Alessandro, her husband, has lost his mind over her! And that's not all. Leonardo as well. What a scandal! A brother is prey to a secret and incestuous passion for his sister."

"And what happens in the end?" I wanted to know. "Does the girl go for the brother or for the blind woman's husband?"

Wenceslao refused to reveal the ending and said that we would find out in the fifth act.

"Five acts!" La Gallego protested, raising an eyebrow. "Why so *many*? Don't plays now have three acts?"

"That's D'Annunzio for you," Wen concluded just as the curtain began to rise.

There were whispers of approval about the stage set: the flight of stairs in the shape of a truncated pyramid; two tall Doric columns that held up the architrave; the large room, wide and well lit, that opened onto a balustraded gallery and, beyond, a fair sky and the burned, reddish scape of the lands where Atreus had his palaces: everything was reproduced with great verisimilitude. Seated on the highest step, with her head leaning on the shaft of a column, we saw La Duse, dressed in a harmonious white tunic, looking off into the distance. Also on the stairway, but on a lower step, in a still pose and dressed in dark clothes, was the wet nurse. The beautiful Bianca María (right away we recognized Jone Morino) was standing, holding an open book in her hand as she read, in a slow and viscous voice, fragments, which, according to Wenceslao, were from Sophocles's *Antigone.*

For half an hour that seemed more like a century and half, the actresses spoke to each other emotionally without changing their positions. I figured out that they were philosophizing and talking about their dreams, about life, about love, and other such silliness. They asked each other, concerned, why Leonardo was so quiet and taciturn. Was he ill?

The one who did begin to shift her position, at more frequent intervals, was Esmeralda Gallego. Not happy with acting out her uneasiness through her restless wriggling and jiggling, she made sure also to clear her throat, cough, roll up her program and even sip, discreetly, from the little silver flask full of cognac that she always had in her bag.

The first act ended without anything happening and I didn't understand what, according to Désirée, was so tiring about *La città morta* for La Duse. It's true that she was on stage the whole time, but leaning against a column, without taking a single step. Despite the boredom, the audience applauded warmly and, knowing, as we did, that the story was full of adultery and incest, resigned themselves to wait for the next act, to see if things would pick up.

Wenceslao and Esmeralda went out to the foyer and I, on seeing that Esperanza Iris wasn't at the presidential box, took a chance to visit Donna Ortensia. I found her disturbed. Eleonora had moved her very much, very, very much, with her performance. It had been twenty years since she had last seen her on stage, since before her affair with D'Annunzio, but that first act was enough to prove that her art was now of a subtlety that was incomparable.

"In spite of the play being detestable and soporific, she is amazing," she said and, after confirming that no one could hear us, added. "What I don't understand is why she keeps the play in her repertoire.

That she would perform it when they were having their affair, all right, that makes sense, but that she keeps on doing it after the scandal of *Il fuoco* and after the insults that bastard lavished on her, is incomprehensible. If a man does to me half of what he did to her, I would sink a knife into his heart," she said with her eyes sparkling, and I didn't have the slightest doubt that she was serious.

She told me that that afternoon she had talked to La Duse, who had been very excited about seeing her again. They would have lunch together the following day. In either her room or La Duse's. It didn't matter, since both of them were staying at the Inglaterra and shared a phobia of restaurants . . .

Without even thinking if I was being proper or not, I asked her if she wanted to help Wenceslao and me. With a few words, I told her about the tragedienne's denial to grant us an interview.

Donna Ortensia moved her head benevolently.

"We all have our obsessions, my boy," she remarked and promised she'd do what she could to convince her. "It could be that if I appeal to our old friendship I could get a yes from her."

I was about to give her a hug, but I reined in the impulse and limited myself to taking her hand and kissing the lilac glove various times as a sign of my appreciation.

"My friend and I are also at the Inglaterra," I told her and, on hearing the shrill laugh of Esperanza Iris, who was returning to the adjacent box, I said good-bye to the countess quickly, telling her that we were putting our fate in her hands.

Wenceslao and La Gallego returned as the second act was beginning. I wanted to tell them about my conversation with Donna Ortensia, but they asked me to be quiet without even looking at me. The new set showed the interior of the palace of Leonardo and Bianca María. The latter was alone, embroidering by a frame, when Alessandro, the husband of the blind woman, appeared. As much as they tried to conceal it, it was obvious that the fire of desire consumed them both. After a while, Anna entered, accompanied by her wet nurse, who served as her guide. Ten minutes of chatter later, the young archeologist, Leonardo, came on stage, played by Memo Benassi. Although he wasn't my type, it couldn't be denied that the leading actor was a fine specimen. Could it be true about the film with Pola Negri? Who knew!

The press, such a lover of gossip, was always inventing contracts in Hollywood for everybody. On Benassi's entrance, the three women exited circumspectly, and the men began a monotonous exchange. I looked in the program for the name of the actor who was playing the blind woman's husband. I didn't remember seeing him in either *La porta chiusa* or in *Spettri.* Wenceslao, without taking his eyes off the stage, pointed to his name with his index finger: Gino Fantoni. Now it was Leonardo's turn, and he made us suffer with an interminable monologue. As he spoke his lines with his Mediterranean ardor, I decided to watch my neighbors in the presidential box. The three actresses were showing an interest that, by its very intensity, seemed suspect. That Mimí Aguglia would be less bored than her companions was understandable, since, Italian as she was, she could understand the lines by D'Annunzio; but La Iris and La Tubau brought their fans to their mouths every once in a while to hide their yawns. María Cay's seat was still empty.

As soon as the second act was over, the critic from *El Heraldo* came into our box to ask Wenceslao his thoughts on the performance. Since he was responding in monosyllables, it was Esmeralda who began to blurt out her opinion so that the writer could scribble it down in his notebook.

I went by myself to the foyer, lit a cigarette, and sought refuge in a peaceful corner. Alejo Carpentier passed by me with a face that said "La Duse, what a marvel." And I made one that said "Incomparable." Scissors and the pharmacist saw me and climbed the stairs to say hello.

"I thought that you wanted nothing else to do with the Italian," I said to the *mulato* jokingly.

"Courtesy trumps vengefulness," he replied. "I found this one on the way," he said, pointing to the tailor, "and I had a hard time dragging him here. When Eleonora Duse is acting in Havana, not to see her is a sacrilege."

"Why? You can't understand shit," Scissors protested.

Before separating from them, I had to swear to Valdivieso that during the next intermission I would introduce him to Titania. On returning to the box, I found neither Wenceslao nor the queen of the fairies. But Emilio De la Cruz was there.

"I thought you wouldn't be coming," I told him.

"I didn't really want to," he confessed, "but duty is duty. This place is half empty," he said, looking around the theater. "How is the play?"

"Unbearable, but please don't tell anyone."

The absent ones returned from the refreshment stand and said hello to Monkeyface effusively. Wenceslao put a chocolate in my mouth and revealed that Esmeralda had to sign autographs.

The third act took place on the same set as the first one and began with the blind woman and her nurse on stage. Anna talked and talked with her eyes on the clouds, and the servant just listened to her and nodded and inserted, during a pause of The Sublime One, a word or two. After a while, the wet nurse exited, leaving La Duse alone, but it wasn't long before Memo Benassi appeared. If his monologue at the end of the last act had been extremely long, the one he now spit out at Anna was nothing to be ashamed of, either. As I shifted in my seat, trying to find a position that would make that verbal diarrhea bearable, I wished with all my heart that instead of making her blind, D'Annunzio had made her deaf. The only thing interesting in the whole act was that, unexpectedly, Anna had alerted the archeologist to the passion that her husband felt for Bianca María, which the girl knew about. It would be necessary for Leonardo to abandon his excavations, to forget about Atreus's ramparts and treasures, and leave with her, take her as far away as possible, the sooner the better, to save her virtue! There wasn't any doubt, given the affection that the brother felt for his little sister, that he would follow his neighbor's advice to the letter.

When the curtain fell, we laid out for Monkeyface, who was completely lost, a summary of what had happened so far.

"This is very graphic," he said, when learning the nature of Leonardo's feelings. "So what happens now?"

"Wenceslao doesn't want to tell us," La Gallego complained.

The four of us left the box. Esmeralda wanted to freshen up, so we went with her to the bathrooms on the first floor. When he saw us, Bartolomé Valdivieso came toward us and, while Monkeyface and Wenceslao took care of introducing Titania, I went over to say hello to Flor and Carlos Manuel Loynaz, who were at the refreshment stand and had looked at me in a friendly manner. I asked them about Dulce María.

"She stayed up there, thankfully," the girl said. "She is insufferable tonight." And she wanted to know my thoughts about the play.

"I am not sure that it is truly theater," I replied, trying to seem intelligent, "more like literature with hints of philosophy. A lyrical display with no real action."

"We think exactly the same," the young man said.

"*La città morta* deserves to be destroyed," the young lady pointed out cunningly. "Twenty Duses couldn't prevent us from dying of boredom!"

The three of us let out a laugh and, to say something, I asked them if they were going to buy season tickets for La Xirgu's performances.

"No," Carlos Manuel declared. "Truthfully, it is rare that we come to the theater. This was a whim on Dulce María's part."

"You should come visit us," Flor suggested suddenly, and I noticed a naughty gleam in her eyes. "If you come, maybe Carlos Manuel will play the piano for you," she went on. Was it me or was she being mischievous? Was she saying every word to be taken as a double entendre or was this just an impression of my warped mind? "He is shy, but I think that for you, he will play it," she insisted.

Just as though I were a cornered boxer, the bell saved me from the uncomfortable situation. Carlos Manuel and I were both blushing, and you didn't have to be a genius to see that the youngest Loynaz was enjoying it all very much. I assured them that it would be my pleasure to visit them, told them to say hello to their sister for me, and rejoined Esmeralda, Wenceslao, and Monkeyface, who were already on their way back to the box. Behind me I heard Flor's laugh and the serious voice of her brother, reprimanding her, but I did not look at them again. Their renown as *enfants terribles* was not unfounded.

The same steps and columns as the first and third acts framed the fourth act. The opening scene was taken care of by Leonardo and Bianca María: the girl asked him to take her far away from there and promised to consecrate herself to him, in the future, and forget Alessandro. Afterwards, the blind woman arrived and stayed alone with the young woman. She said something about the relationship with her husband, because Bianca María replied that nothing had happened between Alessandro and her and swore that she was still pure.

What happened after that, I can't tell you, because I became involved in a serious battle with my eyes, which were stubbornly trying to close, and I am afraid that I slept for a little while. An opportune elbow by Wenceslao brought me back to reality so that I could be witness to the most important scene of the play: the one where the husband reveals to Anna that Leonardo secretly loves Bianca María and not particularly with the love that a brother is wont to feel for his *sorella,* but as a man desires a woman!

I didn't want to go out during intermission. I had a headache and the chills. Wrapped up in Esmeralda's fur coat, I settled myself into one of the seats in the back so that no one would think of signaling to me or coming into the box to talk to me. Was I getting a cold? After the rain that afternoon, I didn't doubt it. Poldarás, from the *Diario de la Marina,* poked in his nose looking for Wenceslao. He needed his help urgently, the deadline was coming and the typesetting staff was waiting for his review. To get rid of him, I dictated a few stupidities to him. Not very pleased, he wrote down the words and hurried out to put them in his article.

The best thing about the fifth act was its brevity. It took place neither in the house of the blind woman nor of the incestuous archeologist, but in a spot in the woods, late at night. When the audience made out, in the middle of the leaf storm, the body of Bianca María, rigid and wet, it couldn't hold back some ejaculations of grief. On either side of the girl were Alessandro and Leonardo. The latter made sure to tell us that he had murdered his sister, drowning her in the river to save her honor. What an animal! Why didn't he drown himself, since he was the only impure one? Why then, since if we were to believe the words of the deceased in the last act, the blind woman's husband had been adulterous only in his mind? While Benassi tormented us with his third monologue of the night, I began to count the times that Monkeyface nodded off. After ten, Leonardo finished his soliloquy, and in the distance, Anna's voice was heard.

Although the fire on my brow left no doubt that I had a fever, I moved to the edge of my seat, not to miss anything. Yes, defying all logic, the blind woman emerged from behind a rock, alone, staggering through the woods. Where was the wet nurse who had been with her in all the previous acts? How could she let her go out like this, making her vulnerable to any accident? D'Annunzio might be a great writer, but his tragedy lacked common sense.

"Bianca María! Bianca María!" La Duse cried, teetering, her arms extended in front of her, groping her way not to run into a tree and scratch her face. I have to admit that the image of her was startling: skinny, vulnerable, of ghostly pallor. The hair rose on the back of my neck. Anxious and prey to a growing desperation, the blind woman continued advancing, watched by the two petrified men. Suddenly, she stopped. Her hands, her beautiful hands, drew something in the air, as if they were cleaning a glass, and she said: "Alessandro! Leonardo!" The two men continued to watch her drag her feet over the dried leaves and come nearer to where the unfortunate Bianca María lay, both incapable of lifting a finger or saying a word. When the blind woman was just about to touch the body with the end of a foot, her husband ordered her to stop.

But it was too late. La Duse had already felt the nearness of the still body. She bent down and began to pat the girl and smooth her wet hair into place. All of a sudden, like a wounded animal, she let out a shrill lamentation that made Esmeralda Gallego bring her hands to her chest, and awoke, with a startle, Monkeyface De la Cruz. All of her soul was in that cry, all the suffering of a lifetime. "Oh!" she uttered as the curtain began to fall. *"Vedo! Vedo!"*

The held-back emotions of the audience were released into applause and a roar of admiring shouts. I thought that for so few we made a lot of noise. Should the blind woman's horrifying final *"Vedo! Vedo!"* be taken literally or metaphorically? That is, did her words mean that she clearly saw the consequences of that passionate drama or that, due to the very emotional circumstances, she had recovered her sight? When I put this question to Wenceslao, he assured me that D'Annunzio's intention had been purely symbolic. I didn't want to argue, but truthfully, it could as easily have been one thing as another. Weren't there blind people who, through a stroke of fortune, recovered their sight?

The audience gave La Duse five ovations and five more times, alone, sad and exhausted, she came out to bow. She looked sick and I wondered if the medicine had had any effect. Maybe she had the flu, like I did? Or maybe something else, the flu was impossible, not with that voice with which she had just touched us. As in the previous performances, she didn't respond to the audience with either blown kisses or smiles. She remained serious and still, and only before leaving did she bow slightly.

On the way out we heard all sorts of comments. Francisco Ichaso told Fontana that the glorious one had reserved for her last night the deepest secrets of her multifaceted and inexhaustible genius. Josefina Embil de Kohly remarked to the countess of Buena Vista that, had she known the plot beforehand, she wouldn't have brought her fifteen-year-old niece. "Well, I think that you did the right thing, *chica,*" the aristocrat replied. "It's better that she learns early on what men are like, so she is ready." Pedrito Varela told whoever listened to him that Fortune Gallo had made a mistake when deciding the order of the plays. Had he begun the series with *La città morta,* the rest of the performances would have sold out. But he insisted on opening with *La porta chiusa* and following with ghosts, two plays that were far inferior to D'Annunzio's—screwups by a producer, who ignored the taste of the public. An unknown gentleman complained that Havana was the authentic dead city: lethargic, depraved, softened Havana that forgot about her heroes, looked at her flag without fearing losing it, and let herself be governed by audacity and concupiscence. Havana was dead and buried within itself like the ruins of ancient Peloponnesus that D'Annunzio's archeologist was looking for, drowning in the wave of its rulers' immorality. Esperanza Iris, whom I had avoided all night like the very devil, trapped me at the last moment and insisted that I give her my word as a gentleman that I would come to her tribute on the seventh. I swore that I would be there and made a sign to Donna Ortensia, whom I could see at a distance, to remind her of her promise. The old woman nodded and smiled complicity. I was glad that I hadn't said anything to Wenceslao. If she were successful, it would be a surprise, if not, I would have saved him from false hope.

When we got out to the street and I heard De la Cruz making plans for us to go partying, I told them that I couldn't come with them because I was sick. I tried to convince Wenceslao to go with them, but he refused outright. Leave me in the state I was in? Let Esmeralda and

Emilito go out partying if they wanted. He would stay by my side, end of argument.

"Do you want me to call a doctor?" he asked when I got into bed.

"What?" I was able to reply. "It's just the flu, nothing more."

My throat hurt a little bit, but I was sure that it would go away, with the fever, after I took a couple of aspirins. My limbs were overcome with a frightening heaviness. Wenceslao wrapped me in one blanket, and then two, and grabbing a book, lay beside me, set to look after me. After a little while he was snoring peacefully, rolled up into a ball near the edge of the bed.

Each person thinks of death in a different way. Or is it that death is different and unique for each person? Some see it as a gaunt cadaver, decomposing, dressed in a dark habit, with a scythe in hand. To others, it is a shadow, a strange beast, or a pale and beautiful woman, with long, dark hair and something grim about her stare.

In my dreams, a child of seven or eight frequently appears, a graceful, blond thing, nude, with rosy skin and freckles. At first I didn't know who it was, but one morning, when I woke, I realized that it was death. Since then, I have taken to watching him very closely. He smells like violets, very clean, and he goes everywhere, always with this innocent and cruel gaze, brandishing a pair of scissors, making them clatter rhythmically, like a rattlesnake. With it he cuts, whenever he wants, the threads. The threads that hold, that bind us to life.

Do you know that once, a long time ago, I staged a farce done in verse, by Giacosa, which was titled The Thread? It was fun. The actors move on stage as if we were marionettes, and from above, a puppet master guided us. But it wasn't very successful and we never performed it again.

Sometimes I dream that the boy visits me, that he comes to my bedside in the darkness of night. Although I don't see him, I hear the unmistakable click-clack of his scissors. He stands by me and whispers, "So che soffre. Ma non é lei l'unica a soffrire. Tutti soffriamo." I could turn my head, look at him, and beg, but I don't want to. Am I so stupidly arrogant? One should, in cases like this, forget about one's pride and beg. I don't know. I shut my eyes stubbornly and wait to see if the thread will be cut.

But the morning light comes, and I find, almost not believing it, that I am still alive. So many have died, yet my heart beats obstinately, although there is no clear reason why it should persist in its habit. Dawn is the bitterest hour. Oh, how mornings hurt, how this feeling of infinite solitude hurts. I sit in bed and it feels as if my feet were sinking in mud. Maybe I'll lie down a little bit longer, it's early yet, maybe I can fall asleep again. Dream that the curtain falls, dream that my life disintegrates like a dry, tumbling leaf. The child appears again and shows me an irresistible smile. I should hurry, run toward him before he changes his mind, and ask him to take me with him. He's gone, he abandoned me again. No, my little one, don't mock Eleonora, open and shut your scissors at once, *il filo, il filo, taglialo, ragazzino, taglialo, caro mio,* don't make me go back, it is enough, I don't want to go on, *non posso.*

15

The night was torture.

I would wake up, startled and with a terrible thirst, drink some gulps of water and return to the edge of sleep. The contact of the bedsheets, sticky from all the sweat, exasperated me, but at the same time I didn't want to throw them off: wrapped in that cloth and covered by the blankets, I felt as if I were inside a niche, or a capsule, in the golden sarcophagus of Tutankhamen, safe from all catastrophes. It was a half-sleep in which my mind didn't cease to function for one moment, projecting images in front of me at great speed, so that at times I didn't know if I was dreaming or if I was dreaming that I thought I was dreaming.

Wenceslao and I walked the streets of Havana admiring the abundant flowers and trees; the prominence of its mansions and small palaces; the appetizing aromas that gushed forth from kitchens; the piano music, light and bubbly. And unexpectedly, that brilliant world, full of colors and pleasant, becomes in my feverish brain an inferno, a landscape of ruins and charred vegetation; of rats that wrestle in the gutters; of war hymns sung by famished bodies, by the wretched multitude succumbed to fear and an appalling rancor.

On that stage set there goes, ambling blindly, not understanding a thing, not a thing at all, Mina de Buffin and the detectives from the secret police, Count Kostia and Scissors, the sons of General Loynaz and those of Teresa Trebijo, Emilio De la Cruz and Regla the maid, María Cervantes and Raúl Capablanca, all confused and bewildered, frightened by the fact that they are all suddenly, inexplicably, in the same place, in exactly the same circumstances, in a Havana that has ceased to be theirs and become a repellent, dirty, and common world. And they retreat, they recoil, assailed by a baleful mob of scum that stone them with absurd and patriotic howls. And at the vortex of the *mare magnum,* up on a pedestal so that no one will doubt his role as the protagonist, so the whole world knows that the catastrophe is his doing, a horse of a man gesticulates and whinnies with grandiloquence.

Although I still cannot see his face (thankfully! for it is the face of despair, abjection, and death), I know he is the son of the *gallego* that spoke to us at the bar. Oh, if he ever knew that he owed me his life! Don't be fooled: he is not a mere clown or madman: he is the Antichrist. (Can't you see that he has two faces, like the most powerful demons? One bearded, on his head, the other one up his ass.)

Where are the ice creams of El Anón, the famous sweets of Rafaela in El Lirio del Prado, the grocery stores with their stalls full of seafood, the pulpy *mameyes,* the *chicharrones* and *churros,* the linen pants with flawless creases, the Manila shawls draped over the boxes at the Nacional, the clean smell of vetiver and lavender, the shady gardens of Vedado, the joy of the people, the crisp, fine air one breathes in with regret, almost afraid to harm it, the transparent waters of the Almendares, the light that reveals colors never seen before, the elegant Havana of Julián el Casal? And, my God, where did so many other things go, like the cobblestones in the avenues and parks, to be replaced, perfidiously, by that blackish stuff that jiggles and melts in the sun, just like the soft brains and sanity of the people? And why are there holes and more holes wherever you walk, and ditches—hundreds, thousands, millions of ditches—boring through the floor of the island, putting it in danger of sinking, of being submerged in the Caribbean like a new Atlantis, and weapons and soldiers that predict the certain imminence of a most crucial battle, a war very often forecast and eternally postponed?

Ludonia La Rosa walks on the Malecón, holding on tightly to Ramoncito with one hand and to me with the other, and she screams at me for not having done what I should have done in the moment when I should have done it, everything has its time and it cannot be done either before or after, but when it should be done. Oh, great Virgin of Cobre, how easy it could have been, something that would have required so little skill, something that would have cost me nothing and saved so much tears and blood, so much suffering to this country that, although it is not mine, has treated me well. I listen to her with my eyes downcast, ashamed at not having slaughtered the *gallego,* and Ramoncito laughs like a fiend. Tired of accusations and ridicule, on the verge of tears, I tear myself away from the *iyalocha* and run. Run, leaving everyone behind, not heeding the cries of anguish, run, and as I get farther away, I see a group of soldiers fire on some young men who are trying to escape the Island swimming. Run, run from the nightmare, from the bloody corpses, the sharks that begin their great banquet; run till, out of breath, I trip and fall on the reefs, scraping my hands and knees, and find a dried, stinking starfish by my face. Dried and stinking like Havana, like the miserable phantom into which they have transformed the once-radiant capital.

And then suddenly, I am not in Cuba anymore, I have left behind the immense prison of zombies, of the living dead and the twice dead. I am no longer there, I can feel it, even though I have my eyes closed. I have returned to Bogotá, I have returned to the city surrounded by hillocks, to my native South American Athens. If I open my eyes, will I see my fellow countrymen dressed in peplos, walking in sandals down Real Street, singing to the sound of lyres? Oh, Bogotá, the birthplace of elegance and class, here to learn proper grammar or syntax it is not necessary to go to the classroom: all you have to do is sit at a table, in the intimacy of your own home, and listen to your distinguished family. Here I am safe. Or so I think before I open my eyes and see a woman pulling on the reins of a horse as a cart advances down an avenue littered with the dead. From high above, I don't know how, I move away from the capital. With my arms spread, reminiscent of the wings of Camilo Daza's plane, I fly over a looted Bogotá, its buildings and streetcars on fire. I see how the people, enraged, break into stores and houses, turn over cars, shatter the statues with hammers. The Mercado Plaza is a heap of smoky ruins, so is the Jesuit hospice. What has happened here, where nothing ever happens? The people jump, howl, fire their weapons, and duck from stray bullets, and all the while the woman keeps on driving her cart, like a sleepwalker, taking to her house a body wrapped in newspapers and bloody sheets. She is a young, elegant woman, and she is thinking about how stubborn men can be. She had told her husband the day before: "They are going to kill you, the Conservatives are going to kill you, and the people are going to go mad." And while she ruminates over her anger and sorrow, I go from roof to roof. I fly over the rivers of blood. I soar over Bolívar Plaza and the parvis of the cathedral, almost suffocating in the dense, foul smoke that covers the sky of the city, and I guess (don't ask me how: it is one of those things that can't be explained) that someplace in the city, maybe in a room in a cheap hotel, the *gallego*'s son is watching, with his nose pressed to a window and his heart palpitating, the chaos that has been let loose in Bogotá, changing it, darkening it, transforming it, suddenly and forever, into something different from what it was. What sinister designs have brought him to this place? Why has the Evil One chosen here? Is it he, whether he knows it or not, who is the cause of such chaos? With the help of some men, the widow takes the dead man from the cart and into the house. I close my wings a bit to descend and somehow find a way into the house, flying from room to room, near the ceiling. From one of the walls there hangs an oil painting where someone thought to portray a group of military men, with a strange insignia on their helmets, leading the Son of God to the cross. They have laid the body on a bed and are peeling off the cloths and newspapers that cover him. From outside can still be heard, now muted, the bellowing and gunshots. Suddenly, a gunshot, louder than the others, bursts my eardrums and, heavily, not being able to help it, I fall with a clamor to the floor, like a bundle. Blood gushes from my chest, but no one there, busy with tending to the corpse, seems to notice. I want to get up, but I can't. I try to scream, but I can't do that, either. I don't know why, at that moment, I hear in my head the "bat poems" that, as children, my cousins and I had chanted in the mansion at La Candelaria, and for the first time, I understand their meaning.

> *They stab you and cut you open,*
> *Beat you, hammer you, shear you,*
> *They harass you, taunt you,*
> *Divide you, pierce you, and slice you,*
> *Dismember you, part you, behead you,*
> *They cleave you, flay you,*

Squeeze you, bruise you, ruin you,
Undo you, confuse you, pummel you . . .

Am I dying? I don't want to look at me. I turn my face so as not to see myself in such a state. I cover my head with my pillow, insistent on not witnessing my death, and I shake in the bed and wail, till Wenceslao wakes up, shakes me again and again and, like a savior prince, gives me back my life.

"What's wrong?" he asks, worried.

"A nightmare," I am able to respond. "A horrible nightmare."

That Wednesday, I stayed in bed, with no strength to even get up. I convinced Wenceslao to take Esmeralda on a trip to El Sitio de Liborio, an ingenious miniature sugar mill that was twenty-five minutes out of the city. While he was gone, I studied some tiny water stains on the ceiling and thought about the meaning of life, about my uncle's transfiguration, about the years that my father had been sequestered in his room in La Candelaria like a vegetable, about whether, with the passing of the years, I would regret not having fathered a child, and about other such imbecilities. I asked myself if the cause of my illness was that I was sick and tired of Havana and La Duse. Wenceslao had not said anything about our date of departure, and that was starting to worry me. What if he asked me to follow the Italian on the second part of her *tournée* through Gringolandia? I didn't think him up to it, but you never knew with him. He is a Pisces: two little fish that swim in opposite directions. Sense and nonsense.

The call from Donna Ortensia in the middle of the afternoon didn't help my mood. Very sorry, but she told me that Eleonora not only reiterated her refusal to grant an interview but she had begged the ex-duchess never to mention the topic again. She so, *so very much* regretted not being able to help! But that Duse, she was so hardheaded!

Regla came in with clean linen and told me that next door they were packing their suitcases.

"The other gentleman told me he didn't want me to bring him any more news," she remarked. "And you as well?"

"Me as well," I confirmed, and I got out of the bed so she could change the sheets.

At night, I felt better and wanted to dine in the restaurant. Wenceslao ordered, at the suggestion of the *maître,* lamb. I ordered only a "substantial" soup and left half of it in the bowl. The after-dinner conversation was longer than foreseen. Apparently, my lover felt like talking.

"De la Cruz insists that we stay for the carnival," he mentioned. "It goes on for four Sundays: the old woman's, the piñata's, the dancer's, and the sardine's. Sounds like fun, no?"

I nodded without much conviction.

"However, Esmeralda thinks that two weeks in this city is long enough," he went on. "She is set on having us go with her, to see the pharaoh. Personally, I don't hate the idea. Anyway, we're in no hurry to get back to Bogotá. What do you think?"

I shrugged.

"We could offer her a compromise," he continued. "Stay till the carnival begins, to see if it's as good as Emilito says, and then go with her to Luxor."

I told him that I would like to think about it and asked him to join me for a walk. We went on San Rafael toward Galiano. The temperature was pleasant but there weren't too many people on the streets. After a few blocks, I got bored and said we should go back.

"Hey! The Colombians!" Mella suddenly exclaimed from behind us, and we turned around to look at him.

Dressed in white, smiling and divine, he came toward us. On seeing that he was about to give me one of his bear hugs, I put out my hand to keep him at bay. Wen did the same. If he noticed our coolness, he pretended not to.

"How did your little adventure with the police end the other night?" I wanted to know.

He told us that they had locked him up in a filthy cell till noon the next day and that, after preaching to him and fining him for disrupting the peace in a public place, the judge had let him out.

"McDonald, the English prime minister, declared that the government of his country is ready to recognize Russia," he revealed as he went on, happy with the news. "Of course, we have to wait for parliament's reaction."

"We don't care about Russia, nor the Bolsheviks," Wenceslao replied icily, staring at him with great effrontery. "The only political meeting that we have ever gone to in our whole lives was the tribute to Lenin. And you can be sure that we will never go to another one again," he continued, unstoppable. "We find politics hateful and boring, and we couldn't care one way or the other about the abuses of imperialism."

"But I thought . . ." Mella stammered, stupefied, searching my eyes in the hope that this was a bad joke. "I thought we shared the same ideas!"

"Wrong," my lover stressed haughtily, and I was afraid that the revolutionary's blood would rise and he would pummel him to pieces right there. "My ideas and those of Señor Belalcázar are drastically different from yours. And now, if you don't mind, we have to go. Good night."

I gave a half-hearted smile as good-bye and turned to go with Wenceslao. The student remained in the middle of the sidewalk, looking helpless, blocking the way. I imagine that night, on returning home, he would tell his wife that we were a pair of lunatics.

It was past eleven when we returned to the hotel. Three young women waited for the elevator to go to the upper floors, and a few steps away from them, to our surprise, we saw Eleonora Duse. Although she was wearing (at night! what eccentricity!) a hat with a veil, we recognized her right away. What was The Sublime One doing awake at this hour? Where had she gone so dressed up? It was the first decent *toilette* (or I should say, worthy of a person of her standing) that we had seen her in since she arrived in the Cuban capital. Katherine Garnett was with her. We approached her and exchanged greetings. La Signora, it was obvious, was not happy with the chance encounter. She fixed her eyes on the elevator door and nodded energetically when the Englishwoman muttered something in her ear.

The other women chatted very loudly, roaring with laughter, not realizing that right beside them was the ultrafamous Eleonora Duse. The elevator finally arrived and we all went in. We let the attendant know our floor—the chatterboxes to the third, the rest to the fourth—and the thing began its ascent with a droning buzz. It stopped on the second floor to pick up a *gringo* who wanted to go to the lobby, and then continued on its way. La Duse had placed herself as far away from us as possible, and Katherine Garnett continued whispering to her who knows what.

"Third floor," the attendant announced and opened the gate.

As they were getting out, one of the young women grabbed the other one's purse and ran out to the hallway, laughing at her prank. "Margarita, you are mad!" the victim protested and, as the elevator rose toward the floor above, those words began to tumble in my head like an authentic *totum revolutum: Margarita, you are mad. You are, Margarita, mad. Mad you are, Margarita. Mad, Margarita, you are. You're mad, Margarita. Margarita, mad you are* . . . Not knowing why, though rather obvious, at that moment I remembered the image of Margarita, the madwoman from Bogotá, wandering the streets, always in mourning. I saw her pass by our first-class coach again, at the slow pace of the train, on the day that we left for Barranquilla. I heard again the words that she said to us that afternoon: "Tell her that Lauro, her little son, sent you."

I felt an electric current go through me and I was sure that those words, which weeks before had seemed the delirium of an ill mind, was now the "Open Sesame" that would convince the Italian to grant us an interview. La Signora and her companion were already out of the elevator, walking toward their room, and I was still inside the metal box, paralyzed.

Wenceslao grabbed my arm to pull me out, but I pushed him aside brusquely and ran after the ladies. I stopped beside Eleonora just as María Avogadro opened the door. Katherine Garnett positioned herself in front of Her Eminence, ready to protect her in case I should get aggressive, and shot me her most threatening and aristocratic look.

"What do you want?" the Englishwoman asked, as if she were talking to a cockroach. "The lady does not wish to speak with you."

However, to the surprise of everyone—of María Avogadro, who watched from the half-open door, not knowing what was going on outside; of La Garnett, who was staring me down irascibly, with little red dots on her unpainted cheeks; of Wenceslao, who had reached me and was holding on to my arm, afraid that I would do who knows what; of the attendant, who had abandoned his post and watched the scene from the end of the hallway; of the *gringo* guest, who was peeking out of the elevator, trying to figure what the Latin Americans were quibbling about—and even to my surprise, the actress lightly pushed the Englishwoman aside, lifted her veil, and looked me in the eye.

"What would you like to say to me, young man?" she asked, serious and upright.

"We were sent by Lauro, your little son," I whispered so that only she could hear me. Although she tried not to betray any emotions, the words stirred in her an undeniable commotion. "Lauro, your little son," I repeated.

Her eyes seemed to abandon their orbits, and a muscle in her cheek began to tremble uncontrollably. I thought that she was going to faint, but I don't know where she found the strength to remain on her feet and answer.

"Fine," she relented in an almost inaudible voice. "I will see you." And addressing Wenceslao as well, she asked us to give her ten minutes.

Followed by La Garnett, who couldn't believe what had just happened, she went into the room and the door closed behind her softly.

Wenceslao looked at me and asked for an explanation. Truthfully, there was not much I could tell him. I didn't even know what my words meant. I had said them on a hunch. He nodded and leaned against the wall, as if he were dizzy.

The attendant asked if we needed anything, and with an exasperated gesture I told him to leave us alone.

"We are just about there," I told Wen with a sigh.

"Yes, I think so," he agreed, making an effort to contain his excitement. "It's strange. Has it ever happened to you that you wanted a thing so much and when you are just about to get it, you get nervous and you ask yourself what you can possibly do with it?" He looked at me tenderly and added, "I imagine this is sort of like a proof of your love, no?"

"Take it any way you want," I replied, not in the mood for weighty conversations on the stroke of midnight.

After a while we were sitting in front of La Duse, who seemed more pale and feeble than usual, in the same room where we had our tea days before. All the pictures and personal items had been removed and I was able to see, in the adjoining room, an open trunk. The Englishwoman was nowhere to be seen. Apparently, she had been banished to her chambers, which were adjoining The Sublime One's.

This time, María Avogadro brought not tea but a bottle of champagne. We waited in an uncomfortable silence as she filled the glasses. The champagne was cold, but not icy.

"Very few people know that I had a son," La Duse began slowly, choosing her words with the utmost care, "and only my closest friend, who accompanied me during those difficult days, knew the name I chose for him. Why did you allude to Lauro?" she asked, with a wince, as if pronouncing those five letters did her harm.

I told her the anecdote of the train and the impulse that had made me repeat the words of mad Margarita, not even knowing what they meant.

"But that is all she said? Nothing else?"

"No, nothing else," Wenceslao said with difficulty.

"Everything is so strange," The Sublime One whispered. "It's like a message that I can't quite make out, and that agonizes me, it drives me crazy. . . . Why are there so many things that I don't understand, that I will never understand? Why?" she added, becoming agitated.

I tried to calm her down.

"Maybe your son wanted you to meet us . . . or for us to get to know you better."

She thought about this for a moment, and then shook her head dejectedly. "It is unbelievable how many ghosts are all around us," she said with a smile, trying to play down the drama of the conversation. "They take us from one place to the other, they thrash us whenever they want, they force us to obey their designs."

Then she declared that since it seemed that we were apparently very interested in the interview, she would make an exception and grant it to us. But it had to be that very night. The following day, early in the morning, she was sailing on a return trip to New Orleans. The rest of the company would follow on Friday.

She did have, however, some conditions. First: we weren't to write her words down. That made her very inhibited; she would go mute when someone started to write down something that she said. Second: we would ask no questions. She'd rather speak freely. "About anything, or about nothing at all," she explained. We would listen. Like in the theater. As if we were in a box, listening to the soliloquy of an actress. Afterwards, we could make a summary of what seemed most relevant and publish it, if we liked, but only after her death. How did that suit us? I looked at Wenceslao and he nodded.

"Are you comfortable?" the artist asked. "I warn you, it is going to be a long night," she added sarcastically.

She refilled the glasses and raised hers in a toast.

"To all the actresses who should have retired a long time ago, to persistent gentlemen, and to ghosts who figure out a way to find us wherever we hide!" she said.

She took a sip, which seemed to animate her.

She got up, walked to the balcony, and opened the doors. The noise of the street (words, horns, music) reached us, muted, wrapped in cotton. I had the feeling that one of the angels with enormous marble wings that, from atop the little towers watched over the roof of the Nacional, had turned to look at us.

"Havana is more than a city with soul, it is an essence, a way of being and existing," she assured us, from out of nowhere, and continued talking. "Wretched is he who was raised here and abandoned it. He will never come to terms with losing that part of his spirit."

She returned to the armchair, settled in, wet her lips with the champagne, and began a monologue that lasted several hours, till roosters began to crow in the distance and we realized it was morning.

"Look at me. Watch me closely. Don't be embarrassed. I am used to it," she began in a lukewarm, strangely distant voice. "Make sure that I am woman made of flesh and blood. And if that is the case, please let me know, for sometimes I fear that I am nothing but a phantom, just another wandering soul . . ."

Epilogue

Lord and master, heed my cries,
Great is my woe, Lord.
The spirits I summoned—
I can't get rid of them!

J.W. von Goethe

Eleonora Duse continued her performances in the United States on the nineteenth of February of 1924, in Los Angeles. After playing in various cities, she arrived with her company in Pittsburgh on the first day of April. On the afternoon of the fifth of April, although it was raining very hard, she insisted on going by foot from the Schenley Hotel, where she was staying, to the Syria Mosque Theater. All the doors to the theater were closed, and the employees took a long time to find the keys that opened the main door. La Duse got to her dressing room soaked and shaking from the cold. She performed in *La porta chiusa* not feeling well at all and, after the third act, had to take ten curtain calls. That night she fell into bed, ill with pneumonia, and she never got up again. She died on the twenty-first of April.

The body was embalmed, and a wake was held the following day at the Samson Funeral Home; afterwards, there was a funeral service. But even though she was dead, her pilgrimage went on. Tipped off by D'Annunzio, Benito Mussolini gave directions to the Italian ambassador in the United States to transfer the body of Her Eminence, by train, to New York. There, it was placed in the chapel of St. Vincent Ferrer Church, on Lexington, where over three thousand people (some of them Fascists in black shirts) came to pay her tribute. On the first of May, a second funeral took place, officiated by Dominican priests. The Italian flag covered the casket, and a chorus of seventy-five children sang a requiem. Once in Naples, after a long crossing aboard the ocean liner *Diulio,* the body went on to Rome, where there was a third funeral. La Duse's last tour ended in Padua, where her mortal remains were buried, finally, in the cemetery of Sant' Anna.

Luis Belalcázar and Wenceslao Hoyos stayed in Havana till the twenty-fifth of February of 1924, when they sailed to New York with Esmeralda Gallego. From there they went to Luxor. During their lives, they went abroad together seven other times: six to Europe and once to Baghdad. They never returned to the Pearl of the Antilles. In the thirties, they inherited their respective fortunes, which made them significantly wealthier.

Just as the seer Anatilde de Bastos had foretold from the world hereafter, the two young men from Bogotá loved each other for the rest of their lives, although these weren't very long. On the ninth of April of 1948, when Bogotá became an inferno and people took to the streets to burn streetcars, rob stores, and break into mansions, in reaction to the assassination of the presidential candidate of the Liberal Party, a stray bullet killed Belalcázar. Hoyos outlived him by six months. According to the doctors, his death was caused by a heart attack, but those close to the couple didn't have the slightest doubt that it had been a fatal grief. On the day of his death, Lucho was fifty-eight years old, and Wenceslao, on his day, two years younger.

Inconsolable because of the death of her two best friends and horrified by the acts of violence that her countrymen had shown themselves capable of during the Bogotazo, Esmeralda Gallego sold all her property in Colombia and went to live in Stromboli, where she bought a villa. She died old, in her mid-seventies, and her money ended up with an organization that sheltered animals. In her last years, La Gallego feverishly painted hundreds of watercolors, seized by the imperious need to leave her mark in the art world.

Julio Antonio Mella made the struggle for social revolution the raison d'être of his brief and impressive existence. In 1925 he founded, with Carlos Baliño, the first Communist party in Cuba. At the beginning of the following year, he was forced to flee to Honduras and later into exile in Mexico, where he continued his tenacious struggle against imperialism. There, his wife Oliva joined him and gave birth to a girl. The young woman returned to the Island in 1927, and Julio

Antonio began an affair with a Communist photographer, the Italian Tina Modotti.

On the night of the tenth of January of 1929, when Mella was walking home with his lover, two men (from what they say, sent by the Cuban president Gerardo Machado) shot him point-blank. He died at two in the morning, in the Cruz Roja Hospital. Apparently, his last words were: "I die for the Revolution."

Luis Vicentini never became the lightweight champion of the world.

The *gallego* was not assassinated.

Bogotá, January 1999
Miami, March 2001

Author's Note

The author would like to thank the Luis Ángel Arango Library in Bogotá, and the Cuban Heritage Collection, of the University of Miami library, for the facilities offered to consult various newspapers and magazines.

Thanks to Sergio, for his confidence and patience, and for dedicating a portion of one of his vacations to document in the Jose Martí National Library, in Havana, Eleonora Duse's stay in that city.

Thank you, equally, to Chely and Alberto, to Daína, Iliana, and Nancy, and to Yolanda, Irene, and La Titi, for their observations during the months of writing. To Esperanza Vallejo for the stories she gave me. Also Lourdes, for translating *Der Zauberlehrling* and helping me with the sonnet. And to Marina. Thanks to Ernesto Mestre-Reed, for his translation and enthusiasm, and to Elaine Colchie, for her meticulous review of the manuscript. And to Thomas Colchie, my agent, because he always chooses the best roads.

I find it necessary to clarify that in 1924 a journey by train from Bogotá to Barranquilla, such as the protagonists take, was impossible; I altered the truth to make their way quicker and more comfortable and less boring for the reader and for me. I should also point out that the walk of the Prado in Havana did not take on the described characteristics until two years after the events of this novel. However, since I thought it awful that Wenceslao and Lucho couldn't experience the Prado with its bronze lions and streetlamps, I decided to push ahead the alterations of the tree-lined avenue a little bit.

In the monologues of Eleonora Duse, there are certain lines by

463

Sardou, Dumas *fils,* Ibsen, Gorki, Goldoni, and D'Annunzio, from characters that she played during her long career, as well as various remarks and ideas expressed by the actress herself.

For certain characters, the author was inspired by traits of different people that lived during the time the novel takes place, but did not try to portray anyone particularly. They should only be seen as what they are: fictional entities. The words and actions attributed to historical characters in the plot are, almost always, pure and simple fabrications.